THE
VIOLET
CROW

THE VIOLET CROW

A BRUNO X PSYCHIC DETECTIVE MYSTERY

MICHAEL SHELDON

LIBERTY ISLAND

NEW YORK, NY

Copyright © 2015 by Michael Sheldon

ISBN: 978-1-5040-1411-3

Liberty Island Media Group
New York, NY
www.LibertyIslandMag.com

Distributed by Open Road Distribution
345 Hudson Street
New York, NY 10014
www.openroadmedia.com

For Ellie—*always*

THE
VIOLET
CROW

They will get it straight one day at the Sorbonne.
We shall return at twilight from the lecture
Pleased that the irrational is rational . . .

Wallace Stevens

CHAPTER 1

WHOEVER WROTE THE SCRIPT for the weather that year must've been a Hollywood hack. Winter's brutally cold followed by a glorious spring. Then—*wham!*—this mass of cold air from Canada sneaks down across the Adirondacks and over the Catskills like the psycho in a cheesy thriller, waiting for the heroine to put on her nightie before he bursts in for the final assault.

High over New Jersey, the cold front crept forward and collided with a mass of moist air from the Carolinas, dumping six inches of snow on the area surrounding Exit 4 on the Turnpike.

The snow was a surprise and a temptation for eight-year-old Mimi Cohen-McRae. Spiked with energy like her dark, wavy hair, Mimi desperately wanted to play in the snow. *This is my chance*, she told herself. *By the time meeting's over, it'll all be gone.*

Mimi risked a quick surveillance of the situation. She was in the middle of a pack of 50 or 60 Gardenfield Friends School kids. They were on their way to the historic Quaker meeting house, which was tucked away behind a stand of trees, a five-minute walk from the school building.

Normally, the children would have walked two-by-two in silent contemplation. They knew they were supposed to be getting ready to talk with God. As the youngest kids attending, the third-graders each had a sixth-grade partner to help them maintain proper decorum on the way to and during the weekly meeting for worship.

Today, however, Mimi and her classmates had to tramp through the snow as best they could. Mr. DeKalb, the school janitor, hadn't made it in to shovel the sidewalks. Everyplace, with the exception of where the students were walking, was covered with a uniform white and pristine blanket of snow.

Mimi eyed the perfect drift that ran parallel to the long, exposed, plain-brick wall of the meeting house. A tempting target. Unfortunately, her meeting partner, Janet Wooten, was precisely positioned to block her assault. Typical. Janet was oafish and humorless. In Mimi's opinion, she was the meanest kid in the sixth grade.

Mimi saw that her best hope lay in the other direction. The Quaker cemetery looked especially inviting, with its ancient trees and stone monuments draped in white. She eyed the gate that Mr. DeKalb used when he needed to mow the cemetery lawn with his tractor. Once Teacher Grace entered the meeting house, Mimi figured she could somehow nip through and roll down the snowy hillside.

The double line of students advanced steadily toward the meeting house and Mimi got ready to make her move. But then her spirits plummeted. Somehow Teacher Grace had appeared out of nowhere and was now standing at the entrance to the cemetery. She nodded and mouthed the words, "Good morning, Mimi," without actually saying them out loud.

"Freaky," Mimi said to herself. "It was like she read my mind and stood there on purpose." Mimi had no choice but to follow her schoolmates in through the tall double doors with Janet trailing right behind her.

The long wooden benches were covered with thin olive drab cushions running the entire length. Mimi chose a spot with approximately two empty places separating her from the person on her right; Janet positioned herself the same distance away on her left. Then the silent worship began.

Inside Mimi's head it was anything but silent. She thought about her close call with Teacher Grace and the inexorably melting snow: *How long did meeting actually last?* Mimi wasn't sure. It ended when the elders, also seated at safe intervals along the facing benches, would lean over and shake hands and wish each other "good morning." That was the sign. The children would do the same: "Good morning, Janet." "Good morning, Mimi." Other than that, they had to maintain silence while still in the meeting house. But once they crossed the threshold it was officially recess. The building would seem to explode as children poured out, laughing and shouting as they raced toward the playground.

Still distracted, Mimi let her attention drift with the motes of dust visible in the sunshine pouring in through the large windows. She could hear kids shifting in their seats. Coughing and sneezing. Nose blowing. It was frustrating. She wanted everyone to be quiet. She wanted to listen for the sound of snow melting from the roof and splashing against the pavement. Then one of the elders stood up to speak.

It was a white-haired man in a blue suit named Mr. Landis, who was partial to The Book of Job. "*How often is it that the lamp of the wicked is put out? That their calamity comes upon them?*" he droned and wheezed.

This could go on forever, Mimi knew. The meetings never had a leader or music or any kind of planned service. Instead, the participants "held silence" and, if anyone experienced "the light within," they were free to stand up and speak about it. Mostly it was the elders who did this, much to the children's amazement, for these talks were interminable and quite impossible to follow. Mr. Landis' affinity for Job was grounded in his belief that children needed to learn about the unfairness of it all at the earliest age possible.

"*God stores up their iniquity for their sons*," the old man raved. But Mimi couldn't take any more of it. She turned to her right to avoid Janet's gaze, curious to see who was sitting on the other side. Strange. She hadn't noticed before. The girl was still wearing a coat, hat and scarf. And she wasn't sitting with a partner. Was one of her classmates absent this morning? Mimi went down the list, but got distracted.

"*One dies in full prosperity, being wholly at ease and secure*," Mr.

Landis continued, his voice rising. *"His body full of fat and the marrow of his bones moist. Another dies in bitterness of soul, never having tasted of good . . ."*

Mimi shut him out and studied the girl. Whoever she was, she appeared to have drifted off to sleep. She was slumped to one side, with her head leaning against the corner of the bench at an awkward angle. Mimi decided she'd better wake her before she got in trouble. She stole a glance at Janet, who scowled at Mimi and gestured for her to sit still. Mr. Landis was blinking furiously as he spoke. Mimi felt this was a sign. She had to act right away.

Mimi reached out, but the moment her hand touched the girl's shoulder she knew something was wrong. Instead of warm, soft flesh, she encountered a hard surface, lifeless and rigid. The awful knowledge struck Mimi like an electric current, as the body tipped clumsily in her direction.

No one ever got to hear the conclusion of Mr. Landis' recitation that morning. Nor did anyone stop to shake hands or wish a neighborly "good morning."

Mimi's scream pierced the silence and pandemonium broke loose. Everyone rushed for the double doors as if their lives depended on it. The teachers tried to stem the flow of shrieking children, but the situation was out of control.

Only Mr. Landis remained immune to the panic. He waited until the exodus was complete, before concluding: *"They lie down alike in the dust, and the worms cover them."*

CHAPTER 2

MAYOR HARRY DOVE had called Police Chief Bud Black to his office to talk business. The investigation was not going well and the lead editorial in today's South Jersey *Post* read, "Dim Bulbs Spark Race Divide."

The Mayor was furious; the Chief seemed to be taking it in stride. Everybody knew that the *Pest*, as the locals called it, was a muckraking wad of bum fodder. The Mayor knew it too. Though the editorial was unsigned, it was clearly the work of P.C. Cromwell, an ambitious, unprincipled scandalmonger, who still went by her childhood nickname, "Peaches."

"Look at this," he shouted. "Dim bulbs need to amp up. Who d'ya think she's talking about?"

"I wouldn't take that too seriously," said the Chief. "She says we're groping in the dark. But amping up would just blow the bulb or the breaker. She should have said we need more wattage."

The Mayor stared in disbelief. "Nobody in Gardenfield understands how electricity works. She called us dim bulbs. And somehow that makes us racist?"

The Chief was unfazed. "And she got the facts all wrong. Listen to this." He picked up the paper and read part of the op-ed aloud:

"Two weeks have passed since the commission of this heinous crime and we're having trouble deciding which is worse: the crime itself or the hapless nature of the investigation.

"The body was found during the Quaker meeting in early April. All of the children at Gardenfield Friends School were present. The victim was a girl, 10 or 11 years old, who has not been identified; Camden County Medical Examiner, Dr. Morris J. Cronkite, is calling her Ginnie Doe. According to Dr. Cronkite, the cause of death was a broken neck. The medical jargon fails to tell you that the perpetrator, in all likelihood, was a hit man trained in silent assassination techniques.

"The discovery practically sparked a riot on the spot. And the victim's tender age has created a nightmare scenario—not just in the Friends School, but also throughout the school system. Children are experiencing ongoing psychological trauma. If this goes on, South Jersey will rank with 'Newtown' and 'Columbine' as a synonym for school violence."

"What's inaccurate about that?" asked the Mayor.

Chief Black raised his hand and started ticking off points on his fingers. He was a strongly built man in his late 50s. His red-blond hair had dimmed down to a blondish-white hue, but he still had a full head of it. His robust constitution and keen blue-eyed gaze remained unimpaired. "First of all, you can't really call it a riot. The kids were scared and they ran out screaming, but that's not a riot. A riot is when people get mad and start firing guns or breaking windows. You have to at least break a few windows for it to be a riot . . ."

"OK, so it was a panic, not a riot."

"It wasn't a mass murder and it wasn't a shooting," continued the Chief, "so comparing us to Columbine is a complete distortion." He was now pointing toward his ring finger, saying, "And the killer wasn't a classmate. Peaches herself admits as much."

"Parents keep calling and writing to the paper saying their kids don't want to go to school anymore," Mayor Dove barked.

"Parents? You mean Bill McRae? Is he still threatening to sue?"

The Mayor scratched his head. "He's still pretty upset. Claims his daughter's personality has changed completely. Not necessarily a bad thing, if you want my opinion."

By coincidence, Mimi's father, Bill McRae, worked as the Gardenfield city attorney. The Mayor had firsthand experience of Mimi when, one day when she was about six, she'd visited her father at work and managed to deface the walls of the Municipal Building with globs of orange Day-Glo Silly String.

"Bill told me she's diagnosed with PTSD." The Chief looked genuinely concerned.

"Yeah, I know. But I'm guessing that's just legal posturing. The thing is, who's he going to sue? The Quakers? The Borough? That'd be like suing himself." The Mayor seemed pleased to have uncovered this paradox.

The Chief refused to allow him to change the subject. "I feel bad for McRae's daughter. You can see why she'd be shook up. Anyone would be. But things are getting better." He folded the paper neatly and started to hand it back to Mayor Dove. "Except for the *Pest*, all of the other media have backed off this story. At least we don't have TV crews getting underfoot like we did at first."

"So you think everything's going to turn out OK? That P.C.'s wrong and we can just ignore her? What about these charges of racism?" Harry Dove ripped the paper from Chief Black's hands. "Just listen to this:

"After two weeks with no leads, the County Task Force had no choice but to walk away. 'It's up to Gardenfield now,' our confidential source told us. 'We've got bigger fish to fry—and more of them—in Camden.'"

Mayor Dove swiveled angrily to face the Chief. "It's almost like she thinks we should have more murders here, just to even things out."

"Politics," said Chief Black. "Camden wants the suburbs to supply more of their funding. In our meetings, that's all they talk about. They'll say anything . . ."

"But Peaches doesn't have to print it. Here's the capper . . ." He picked up the paper and resumed reading:

"Although we've always supported Mayor Dove's administration in the past, the Quaker Killing is causing us to rethink our position. Something's going to have to change, and we have a few suggestions. **Get harder.** Be more diverse and hire people with experience with modern urban crime. **Get smarter.** Bring in the latest technology— DNA sampling, surveillance drones, and Big Data. Or **get creative.** A psychic was instrumental in apprehending the infamous Main-line Monster. Shouldn't we bring a psychic here to help us find the Quaker Killer and bring him to justice?"

Chief Black was finally provoked. "This is ridiculous. We have plenty of diversity on the force. We've got Michelle Coxe and Nancy O'Keefe who are female . . . and then there's Gary . . . Officer Malone, who is . . . you know. But that's not why I hired them."

"I know. I know," sighed the Mayor, who had been through this speech from Chief Black countless times. "Forget diversity. Drones, DNA testing, data mining? I don't know what they're smoking over there. What do you propose to do about this?"

The Chief wasn't sure if "this" meant solving the crime or responding to the criticism in the editorial. "It has never made sense to hire a full-time detective in Gardenfield. The truth is, we're not staffed properly for this type of violent crime. I'm the only one who has experience running a murder investigation."

Mayor Dove pulled at his fleshy right earlobe; his normally slack expression now showed signs of extreme effort. He was in a tight spot, he realized, but with clarity of thought and a little ingenuity, things could work to his advantage. "I want you to hire that psychic detective."

The Chief looked startled. "You're kidding."

"No. Why would I joke about something like that?"

"A psychic's a waste of time and money. I was hoping you'd agree to hiring a detective, because . . ."

The Mayor cut him off. "We don't need a detective. You said you've got experience. If we hire the psychic we'll have both, a regular detective and a psychic one, for the same price."

The Mayor swiveled in his chair so Chief Black couldn't see him beaming. "Old P.C. gave us an out. All we have to do is follow her recommendation; we'll give a press conference saying we're responsive to the community so we're hiring the psychic. Will it really work? I doubt it. But it'll buy us time. We can distract P.C. with updates on the psychic's progress. She just wants good copy. We'll give her as much access to the psychic as she wants. That'll give you the breathing room you need to solve this crime as quickly as possible. And you better get it done . . . as quickly as possible. Do I make myself clear?"

The Chief was too surprised to counter effectively. "So you want me to hire this psychic, but then ignore what he or she says and just investigate in the normal way?"

The Mayor swiveled around to face the Chief. "I think we understand each other."

CHAPTER 3

THE BOROUGH OF GARDENFIELD is home to some 35,000 peaceful souls nestled in the friendly confines marked by Tiny's Package Store to the north, the J. Kilmer Pub to the east, Lillian's Tavern to the south, and the Tiki Lounge to the west. A Philadelphia suburb, it is a prosperous community with colonial roots and a variety of pretensions, including a prohibition on the sale of alcoholic beverages within Gardenfield proper. In fact, thirsty Gardenfielders simply have to drive past the town limits on any of the major roads, in order to enjoy a beer or a cocktail.

Buddy Black was not a drinking man by habit. Nor was he averse to dropping by a tavern from time to time, to see what the locals were up to and let off some steam after work. Tonight he made a beeline for Lillian's. It had been a while. Lillian greeted him at the door. Rail thin and dyed blond, she appeared to be in her 60s and to subsist on nothing but whisky, cigarettes, and conversation. She welcomed Buddy with a hug. "Hi, hon. Nice to see you again. She's expecting you."

"How could she be expecting me? I only decided to come here 10 minutes ago."

"We read the papers, too, y'know."

"I'm that predictable . . . ?" The Chief freed himself from Lil's embrace and headed for the bar. "Daisy, did you really know I'd come here tonight?"

The woman behind the bar was dressed in tight jeans and a low-cut flower-print top. She was busy polishing a wine glass, and didn't look up until she'd finished her task. Then she flashed a smile that was warmer than Lil's rather spectral hug. "Buddy! I haven't seen you since—what?—Bay of Pigs. It's about time you came to see me." Without asking she opened a bottle of Rolling Rock and set it down in front of the Chief.

Daisy Fuentes was a second-generation Cuban. Her parents fled the island when Fidel took over, and she grew up in Miami as part of the exile community that lived for the death of the dictator. A busted marriage left Daisy stranded in South Jersey, but it didn't seem to get her down. A tropical personality and a generous figure meant there were always men who wanted to be her friend. At one time, she and Bud Black had dated rather seriously. But Daisy finally decided he was one of those men who might be on the rebound from his divorce—permanently—and had tried to let him down as gently as possible.

Buddy took a short swig of his Rolling Rock. "Bay of Pigs is ancient history. I really came to tell you that you look fabulous as always."

Daisy ignored the flattery and got straight to the point. "How's your love life, Buddy? You got any good prospects?"

The Chief blushed, but only for a moment. "Funny you should mention it. That's why I came here tonight. I have a proposal for you."

"You wanna get married all of a sudden? I thought you were waiting for your ex-wife to realize the error of her ways."

"She's strictly pre-revolution, Batista-era goods, I'm happy to say." He took another sip. "I've got something else in mind. I want you to come to work for me."

Without missing a beat, Daisy called out across the room, "Hey Lil, he's offering me a job!"

Lil made a dismissive gesture, like someone swatting a fly. "Tell him to go lock himself in jail."

"What would I do at the police station? I couldn't arrest nobody. I can't type . . ." Daisy proudly displayed her inch-long nails, painted

15

bougainvillea in contrast with her rich brown skin. "I have to say it'd be fun hanging around all day with you, Buddy. And that guy, Harry, who works for you, he's a load of laughs with his computers. The other one. What's his name, with all the muscles?"

"Corporal Herman Henderson, mostly known as Biff."

"Biff's a hunk, you know, but his conversation is . . . limited. So my top choices are Gary and Randy. Both are very charming. But Randy I think is in love with his cars. So I choose Gary. He's the only one who's not white. You should be proud of him . . ."

The Chief took this in stride. He knew his role was to be the straight man. "I am proud of Gary. I'm also proud of our women officers, Michelle and Nancy, and Debbie, our dispatcher. You didn't say anything about them."

Daisy giggled and turned to polish an imaginary spot on the bar.

The Chief refused to let Daisy off the hook. "The women? You have an opinion, I want to hear it."

"Yeah, OK," she pouted. "I'm not going to stand here and pretend I like women as much as I do men. Why should I?" She gestured around the bar. There were guys drinking and talking. Playing bar shuffleboard, watching TV. The women there were with dates who would've been there by themselves if they hadn't tagged along. "Counting up boys and girls is your problem, not mine." She put the wine glass away, rather too vigorously, and grabbed another. "You were right, Lil," she called across the bar. "He's here because of what that Cromwell lady said in the paper." She turned back to the Chief. "So you think maybe a hot Latina like Daisy Fuentes could add some salsa to the mix?"

"You're reading my mind."

"I'm a little bit insulted," Daisy said.

The Chief shrugged.

"I want to be hired for my talent, not my skin," she continued. "I work hard and don't want any handouts."

"That's why I'm offering you a job."

For the first time Daisy realized maybe he was serious. "Buddy, I couldn't do that. Not after what we . . ."

"I just want you to think about it . . ."

She put down the wine glass and moved closer. "Boy, they really got to you this time, huh?" She took his hand. "You're no racist. I know that. Everyone who knows you has a lot of respect."

The Chief leaned forward and lowered his voice. "It's this murder. People's nerves are starting to fray. Mayor Dove laid it on pretty thick."

"He's a pol-i-ti-cian." She let go of his hand and waved a finger, like a reed blowing in the wind. "I know this town, Buddy. Your job isn't as easy as it looks. It's not dangerous like Miami, but we got the high-speed train that brings in all the filth from Philly and Camden. Then there's the racetrack, the casinos down the shore, drunks, divorcees and everybody else. I talk to 'em every day."

The Chief felt he was making headway. "The tough part is dealing with all these prosperous people who are used to giving orders. They're bossy and obnoxious. It requires quick thinking, diplomacy and tact to successfully keep the peace in this town. You don't worry about getting shot so much as stabbed in the back."

Daisy straightened up and poured a scotch and water for another customer. "You're right," she said. "Working for you doesn't sound like very much fun." She came around to the Chief's side of the bar and gave him a playful hug.

He hugged her back, but it was not at all playful. "Want to get together later? What time do you get off work?"

She tried to push away, but he held her around the waist, as if they were dancing. "Poor boy, you feelin' sad tonight? Think maybe Daisy can cheer you up?"

The Chief released her immediately. He already regretted asking.

Daisy let him off the hook. "I can't tonight, Buddy. I got a big job offer I gotta think about."

It was half past six when Chief Black drove back through town. As he passed the police station, he spotted a barefoot teenager across the street, about to enter the Lenape King. Here was the town in a nutshell. The kid's friends called him Icky and he came from a well-to-do family; his father was a surgeon with a lousy temper, but his mother made up for it with a sweet, understanding nature. Despite these "advantages," Icky'd become involved in the acquisition, use and occasional redistribution of methamphetamine. He'd never finished high school and was lucky to have a menial job doing custodial work and after-hours security at the Lenape King, the colonial tavern that was the town's prized architectural monument.

Coincidentally, Icky and several of his friends all had red hair and appeared to be trying to set up a meth lab. Chief Black called them "The Red Headed League." He felt it was downright considerate of the little crank heads to make it so easy to keep tabs on them. Biff and Gary had the League under surveillance, waiting for an opportunity to catch them red-handed.

It was time-consuming work, and the Chief felt his resources were overtaxed already. Now he had a problematic murder to solve. And, worse, the Mayor expected him to babysit some psychic and keep the parasites at the *Pest* at bay while he did it. "Daisy's right," he muttered. "Being a cop in Gardenfield isn't easy and it certainly isn't fun."

CHAPTER 4

THE PSYCHIC WASN'T WHAT THE CHIEF EXPECTED.

He was dressed in a black Vestimenta suit and white shirt with no tie. Classy Italian duds, but about 10 years old and showing obvious signs of wear. He was less than average height and slightly overweight—typical for a guy in his late 30s or early 40s who didn't do much manual work. With thick dark hair, brown eyes and glasses with metal frames, he had the look of one of those orthodox Jews from Brooklyn, except he didn't have a beard and he wasn't wearing a hat.

Chief Black greeted him personally and began to show him to a room they'd prepared for him. He tried a mild pleasantry to break the ice. "We hope we got the *feng shui* right for your purposes . . ." The room was dark with a comfortable chair, incense holders, and other new-age paraphernalia.

"*Feng shui, shmeng fui,*" the psychic scoffed. "You should know, I can't tolerate incense. And who wants to sit in the dark? Let's go in your office. You can test me there."

"Test you?"

"Sure. Don't you want to find out if I really have psychic powers?"

The Chief said something lame about trusting the people who recommended him, then hated himself for saying it.

The psychic nodded and pointed toward the Chief's office. "OK. I get the picture. Shut the door please. Thank you. So you don't want to test my powers . . . ? You say you believe me . . . ? That's baloney! You don't care. You think I'm a *shnorrer*, a con man, a fake . . . But it was the newspaper lady's idea—what's her name, Cromwell, the one with the cute little *tuchus*?—to use a psychic, and you think I'm gonna do something that'll make her look stupid. Am I right?"

He gazed with disconcerting directness; he was right in the Chief's face. It was as if he had eavesdropped on the conversation with the Mayor. The Chief met his challenging look, but without saying anything.

"But what are you forgetting?" the psychic continued. "C'mon, Chief. You're forgetting something. Don't let me down; use your noodle. This Cromwell dame, you think she's gonna play fair with you?" Here he dropped the immigrant *shtick* and switched to a corporate persona. "You think she'll be *accountable* and take *responsibility* . . . ?"

"But it's in print," the chief protested. "She's on the record."

"Print, *shmint*! A week ago. Two weeks. Who's gonna remembra? Who's gonna care? If I don't produce, you'll be the one who hired me. You'll be the one who's payin' me. You're the one who's wasting the taxpayers' *furshlugginer* money. You'll be the one who's *accountable* and *responsible*."

"So what are we going to do?" The Chief didn't even notice that he was saying "we" rather than "you."

"We're gonna solve da moidra."

"But we don't have any clues. We don't even know who the victim is . . ."

"Of course. That's why you need me."

The Chief looked like he needed to curl up in the fetal position and crawl back into the nearest womb.

"So we got a deal?" The Chief glared, holding out to see if the psychic would retract his offered handshake. He didn't. They shook perfunctorily. Then the psychic put his business card on the desk and turned to leave, quickly, as if he wanted to get out before the Chief could change his mind.

Chief Black picked up the card gingerly by the edges and examined it carefully. There was a crude drawing of a flashlight emitting rays of light, with the detective's name and a phone number.

"Bruno X?" The Chief read the information aloud in a voice dripping with self-pity. "That's your name, Bruno X? And no address, just a phone number?"

"That's correct," said Bruno. "This is a dangerous business. The less people know about me, the better. I charge five hundred a day plus expenses. Call me when you're ready to get started."

CHAPTER 5

FOR CHIEF BLACK, the empty meeting house was devoid of emotion. Plain walls. Plain benches. No pictures. No symbols. No musical instruments, fancy costumes or other religious equipment. Only emptiness—and silence.

It was different for Bruno. He was in his element. Meditation, visualization were things he understood. But there was something puzzling about the place. He'd never been inside a Quaker meeting house before. After he got used to the initial starkness, he started to tune into an undercurrent of emotion that seemed to flow in layers. It was good not to have too many external distractions. He looked about with anticipation.

"You found no clues here?" he asked the Chief.

"Just the body—nothing else came in from outside. Nothing is out of place."

"Show me where you found her."

The Chief paced off a certain number of rows. He pointed to a spot at the far end of the row. Bruno frowned. There was no crime scene tape to protect the spot.

"Any sign of how they got it in?"

"No. There was an hour between the time the building was unlocked for school to start and when the classes came in for the monthly meeting."

"Pretty risky, breaking in in broad daylight," Bruno mused out loud.

Chief Black nodded in agreement. "Except there was no sign of a break-in. No picked locks. No broken windows. No footprints in the snow, tire tracks, or anything like that."

Bruno shuffled over to the spot where the body was found. He stood behind it, leaning forward with both hands on the back of the wooden bench.

"Everything you know about physical evidence is also true for psychic evidence. If the crime scene is disturbed I can't do my job." Bruno sat down in the spot where the victim was found. He slumped over, attempting to imitate the girl's posture. He sat that way in silence for several minutes. "Nothing here," he said finally, without moving or opening his eyes. "Normally there are powerful emotions associated with a violent crime. Both from the victim and the perpetrator. They leave behind residues of those emotions on things they're in contact with during the event. Just like fingerprints. Blood. Fibers. Candy wrappers. I can pick up traces of fear, pain, panic, anger, or lust. The intensity of emotion leaves psychic clues that I can retrieve . . ." He stood up abruptly and walked toward the Chief, "But not when the crime scene's been trampled on like this one has."

"I never worked with a psychic before," Chief Black stammered. "We thought we were finished here."

Bruno patted him on the shoulder. "No way you could have known. Just explaining for future reference." He shoved his hands deep into his jacket pockets and swiveled around to survey the room. "Boy, it's cold in here. When do you think this place was built?"

"Colonial times, I guess. Sign says the school was founded in the 1760s or something like that."

"They sure didn't know much about heating a building in those days, did they?"

"Maybe the Quakers didn't believe in it."

"Like it's a form of vanity to be warm? Hard to get in touch with

God when you've got a frozen *tush*." Bruno shifted to a different topic. "So, Chief, how do you think the body got here? What's your theory?"

"We don't have a very good one, I'm afraid. You'd have to suspect an inside job because there's no sign of a break-in. But none of the people with access to the building are very likely suspects. First of all, they're all Quakers. Most of the teachers are older women. Hard to imagine them breaking necks and hauling a dead body around. Master Quentin, the head of the school? He's famous for being a conscientious objector."

"What about the maintenance guy? The older guy who let us in this morning?"

"Bennett DeKalb. He's worked at the school for I don't know how long. Ever since Master Quentin got here. Sometime back he stole the school truck. We tracked him down. He apologized. Returned the truck in good condition. The school declined to press charges. And they let him keep his job. No problems since then."

"So he's the most likely suspect. Did you talk to him?"

"Absolutely. He has an airtight alibi."

"Really. Airtight?"

"Yeah. He plays darts at a bar over in Audubon. They were having a tournament that night, which he won by the way. At least a dozen people saw him."

"That's some alibi. What about Quentin?"

"Like I told you. He got drafted, refused to serve so they put him in some kind of medical unit . . ."

"I meant today. You say he's not around . . ."

"Not till this afternoon."

OK. Let's go see the girl. We can pop back in and see Quentin after lunch. Do you think the morgue'll be this cold?"

The Chief drove toward Camden, then headed north on Route 130—a dismal parade of bankrupt businesses, empty apartments, fast food, gas stations and a cemetery or two. Then he swung around into a residential neighborhood. Bruno wondered why they would put the morgue in the middle of a residential neighborhood. The Chief kept turning and Bruno grew more disoriented by the second. Finally they arrived at a housing project with a chain link fence at the end of its parking lot. Somehow the Chief found an opening and they drove up to a squat blue building that looked like a bunker. At the back was a loading dock with three bays, presumably for ambulance deliveries.

"I couldn't find my way back here in a million years," Bruno mumbled, half- dizzy, as he hauled himself out of the cruiser.

"Just as well," yawned the Chief. "It's not a place you want to visit, even under your own power." The parking lot was almost empty and there weren't any medic trucks in the back. A good sign. He looked closely at Bruno. "Are you ready to meet the victim?"

CHAPTER 6

THE BODY WAS SMALL AND DELICATE. She must have been about 10 years old. Dark hair. No marks, scars, tattoos. No fillings. No braces. No signs of sexual abuse.

Why would someone kill a 10-year-old girl? They must've walked up behind her, put her in some kind of headlock, and then given a single violent twist.

"The mob?" Bruno asked the Chief.

—"That's what the newspaper said, but it's not what *I* said." Dr. Cronkite was about Bruno's height, but thicker. He had a barrel chest and muscular hands with flashy, expensive-looking rings on several fingers. His dark brown hair was close-cropped, and his eyes, also dark brown, had a world-weary quality that only partially masked a mulishly focused sensibility. "*I* did not call it a 'gangland slaying,'" said the doctor. "I merely observed that the cause and manner of death were *painfully* obvious." He turned to address Chief Black. "Did you know we were the violent-crime capital of the U.S., two years running? Of course you did. Everyone around here knows that . . ." Now he seemed to be addressing Bruno, though he wasn't actually looking at him. "But they don't think through all of the implications: Since Camden's the crime capital, that makes me the number-one medical examiner in the country."

Bruno didn't know how to respond. Fortunately, Dr. Cronkite switched to a different topic. "Say, you look familiar. Your family from Camden?"

"My mother grew up in Parkside."

"No kidding. Mine did too. Never mind, it's all changed now. Look at this poor kid." He lowered his voice a notch. "*I* didn't name her Ginnie Doe. To me she was always 'the faceless girl.' It was the *Pest* that started calling her Ginnie Doe. And they were the ones who jumped to conclusions about mob involvement. I try to stick to the facts."

The Chief saw his opening. "I agree. The mob wouldn't do this kind of thing—to a kid. My staff says this doesn't square with mob 'family values.' In fact, the people we talked to were pretty upset when they heard about it. They said they'd never do something like this to a child."

"Yeah, they've sure got principles." Dr. Cronkite was distracted by an electronic beep coming from the front room. He looked toward it anxiously, then forced his attention back to the business at hand. "I didn't think you had much wise-guy action over in Gardenfield."

"Some of them live there, but they make it a point not to bring business home with them."

An awkward pause ensued as Dr. Cronkite started to move away, his attention obviously fading. Then a thought struck him. "I've been meaning to talk to you, Chief." He seemed more substantial, suddenly, as he turned to face them. "Ginnie Doe, here, is practically a cold case already. Why the sudden interest?"

Chief Black explained, "My associate, here, is a psychic. He wants to examine the girl for . . . evidence."

Dr. Cronkite shrugged. "You stay in this business long enough, you see everything." He tossed Bruno a pair of latex gloves.

Bruno put them aside. "I can't use these. I have to make direct contact."

"It's your life," said Cronkite. And he left the room.

Bruno turned away from Chief Black and placed his hands carefully above the dead girl's heart. He shut his eyes. He breathed deeply with palpable emotion.

"She didn't see it coming," he announced.

"No? How do you know?" asked the Chief.

"No fear. In fact, there's not much of anything."

"What're you telling me?" The Chief's voice was rising in frustration.

"This is unusual," said Bruno, opening his eyes.

"No kidding," said the Chief. "Usually when there's a dead kid, the parents are freaking out. Calling every 10 minutes. As if the next time they call maybe I'll tell them it isn't true. This time there's nobody looking for her. No missing persons reports. We don't know who she is. No one knows. No one cares."

Bruno looked carefully at the Chief during this outburst, but didn't respond directly. "I need to take a lock of hair. Is that OK?"

"OK with me," said the Chief, feeling deflated. "But you have to check it out with the Doc."

The Chief led Bruno to the front office, where they found Doctor Cronkite sitting at his desk, his dark eyes fixed on the computer screen. The Chief gave Bruno a nudge to get his attention and then moved a couple steps closer to Dr. Cronkite. "Hey, Doc," he shouted. "My friend here wants to take home a souvenir. OK with you?"

Doctor Cronkite ignored the question.

"You should see these numbers," replied Cronkite. "St. Louis is catching up. And we can't forget about Detroit. New Orleans. D.C. Don't forget, Chief, I'm counting on your help."

"Let's go," the Chief said to Bruno. They returned to the lab, where they found a pair of surgical scissors on a tray of instruments. Bruno snipped a lock of hair and placed it carefully in a Ziploc bag. He lingered a few moments, studying the body until the Chief pulled him away.

Out in the parking lot, Bruno seemed to revive. "Did you get what you needed in there?" the Chief asked.

"I won't know until I examine this at home."

"We could use a breakthrough. Soon. I mean, when's the psychic stuff going to start happening?"

"*Hoo hah*! Already you're starting to *kvetch*? You want psychic stuff, you'll get psychic stuff. I guarantee it. But maybe you should be a little bit careful what you wish for."

CHAPTER 7

THEY WERE ON THEIR WAY back to the school when a metallic blue Volvo sedan pulled around the corner at a high rate of speed and squealed to a halt. Out popped a woman in her early 40s. She was dressed fashionably in an odd combination of battle garb and ultra-feminine frou-frou—a black tactical jacket, black stretch pants, black leather driving gloves with open knuckles, set off by an ivory-colored ruffled silk blouse. Wraparound sunglasses pushed up on her head and some sort of highly volatile lavender fragrance completed the package.

Chief Black put on a phony smile as he approached her. "I could give you a ticket for speeding in a school zone."

The woman ignored his remark. "I heard you hired a psychic. Is that him?"

"We decided to take your advice," said the Chief. "P.C. Cromwell, crime reporter and editorial writer for the *South Jersey Post*, say hello to Bruno X."

"Bruno X?" echoed Cromwell. "You've got to be kidding."

"I understand you have another name too," Bruno interjected. "*Peaches.* Surely you understand why a *nom de plume* can be useful.

29

So is a *nom de guerre*. Though I have to say, I think Peaches is a lovely name. Very *heimishe*—down-home and comfy."

Peaches looked startled for a second, then quickly shrugged it off. "How's the investigation coming?"

"Off the record?" asked the Chief, who was used to playing this game with the reporter.

"Whatever."

Chief Black nodded to Bruno, giving him the go-ahead to talk. The Chief knew it didn't really make any difference. If Peaches wanted to print something, she'd find an excuse. In any case, the Mayor would be pleased to see he was following orders.

"I just started on the case today. We visited the site where the body was found and the morgue. Now we're on our way to talk to Master Quentin."

"Any leads? Insights?"

"As a matter of fact I have. But first I need to ask, did you ever used to go to any of those nice places in the Catskills? Grossinger's? The Concord? Even Nevele? I mean with your parents when you was a little *feygele* like Shirley Temple?"

Peaches shook her head. "No?" Bruno continued. "I could swear I saw you there. Did you ever hear Shecky Green tell his famous story about how he got kicked off the Sullivan show? No, huh? So where did your parents take you on vacation? The Poconos? Vegas?"

"Atlantic City. But I don't see what this has to do with the investigation."

"Atlantic City! The Jersey Shore! That's just fabulous. What great parents! What a lucky kid! Salt water taffy. The Steel Pier high-diving horse. Jitneys. And . . . what a *shmo* I am . . . of course the beach. You must have had a fabulous tan . . . "

—"Mr. X . . . Bruno . . ." Peaches interjected.

"That's right. That's right. Just call me Bruno. Bruno's fine."

—"OK, Bruno," said Peaches in a commanding tone. "There are a couple of things I need to know about you. Just on background. To start with, what kind of psychic are you? Do you do astral projection, distant reading, ESP?"

30

"Well, Peaches, those things are all good in their way," said Bruno. "But mainly I use Kabbalah."

"Kabbalah?" Obviously impressed. "You mean like . . ."

"Yeah. Movie stars, rock stars. Right now Kabbalah's hot."

"Can you tell me some of the basics? How you use it?"

"Funny you should ask that. Do you do any yoga?"

"Yes," responded Peaches, her interest growing by the moment.

"I thought as much. Do a headstand and I'll explain it to you."

"What?" she sputtered.

"There's a famous story," said Bruno, trying to unruffle her feathers a bit, "about Rabbi Hillel. To insult him, a non-Jew asked him to teach him the Torah while he stood on one foot. Instead of dismissing him as an impudent *shlepper*, as he had a right to do, Rabbi Hillel agreed to teach him. Do you know what he said to him?"

Peaches didn't.

"I don't remember either," Bruno deadpanned. "But it doesn't matter. I'm just trying to tell you that the Kabbalah is very complicated. All you really need to know is it works good when you're trying to catch bad guys. And that's all I've got to say today, off the record, on background. Hope it helps."

CHAPTER 8

MASTER QUENTIN'S OFFICE WAS PLAIN. He had no computer, but he did have a phone. And a pencil.

He seemed agitated. He was a black man in his late 50s. A thinner, shorter version of Duke Ellington with heavy circles under his eyes and graying, thinning hair combed straight back. He was also dressed immaculately in a plain sort of way. "I was afraid you might bring that reporter in with you," he sighed.

"Peaches is a piece of work," the Chief agreed.

"This Quaker Killer label she's come up with is offensive. She seems convinced that our pacifism is just a veneer covering sordid emotions and criminal behavior."

—"She called me a dim bulb," said the Chief. "I didn't appreciate that either."

"I don't think she's Jewish," added Bruno.

Master Quentin burst out laughing. "You two are funny. Quite a pair." Then he fell silent. The Chief started to ask another question, but Master Quentin gestured for him to wait. A full minute passed before he spoke. "Did you feel that?" he asked in a low voice.

Bruno and the Chief looked at each other and shook their heads. They hadn't felt anything.

Master Quentin looked slightly disappointed. "That's all right. You helped restore my composure. Anytime I can add a minute of quiet to my day . . . I'm sorry if it disconcerted you."

"Don't give it a second thought; glad you're feeling better," said Bruno. "Let's get down to business. So you don't know anything about the faceless girl?"

"You're speaking of the poor creature who was found in our meeting house?"

"Correct."

"As I've told Chief Black, she is not one of our students. I don't know her. None of our teachers know who she is."

"How do you think she ended up in the meeting house?"

"I have no idea. I'm sorry about what happened to her. And I'm sorry our meeting is involved. None of this is very pleasant."

"The Chief tells me the meeting house dates from colonial times," said Bruno, switching tacks.

"He did?" Quentin feigned surprise. "Maybe he is a bit 'dim' as our friend says. The original Friends Meeting in Gardenfield was built in the late 1680s, but on a different site. It was located where the Acme market is today—the brick one, which actually looks like a Quaker meeting house. Ever notice that? This was well after the Burlington Meeting, which was the first meeting house in the state. And New Jersey was earlier than Pennsylvania. A lot of people don't know that. But the original meeting house burned down, unfortunately. The building you see here today was built to replace it, just prior to the Civil War."

"It seems very solidly built. How could anybody get in without leaving signs of a break-in?"

"I'm afraid that's not my area of expertise. Don't criminals know how to pick locks?"

"Yeah, but it leaves marks," said the Chief. "Bruno, we've already been through this with Master Quentin."

"As I told the Chief, none of my staff are likely suspects. They are all gentle, non-violent people."

"Quakers may be pacifists," Bruno agreed, "but like Jews, they have the reputation of doing well in business. Competition can breed conflict. Any problems in your congregation?"

"We call it a meeting," said Master Quentin. "We're all equals. No one is in charge."

"OK. Sorry. Any conflicts amongst the Friends?"

"Not that I know of." He thought for a moment, then added, "I should mention that Dr. Fischer offered to provide security guards from his company . . . to help watch the school. Keep the children safe. I turned down his offer." He seemed to grow agitated again at the thought.

"What kind of company does this Dr. Fischer run?"

"It's a biotech. They do genetic engineering, I think. Located just north of Gardenfield in Maplewood."

"What kind of security issues do they have?"

"I never discussed it with him. It's not a very Friendly enterprise, tampering with the work of God. Because they grow genetically engineered crops, I would guess they have to control a perimeter to keep them isolated . . . and the protesters away. You'll have to ask him for details."

"That's it exactly," said the Chief. "We've helped them deal with political protests from time to time. More of a nuisance than anything else. But it's very important that you let me know if you decide to accept their offer. If I'm going to have a professional security team running around in my backyard, I want to know about it."

"I'll keep that in mind." Quentin looked nervously at his watch. "I will be needing to return to my duties. Do you have any more questions?"

"Just one more thing," said the Chief. "How's the little girl doing? The one who found the body?"

"As you know," said Quentin with increasing agitation, "her family is determined to protect her privacy. They gave me instructions not to discuss her with anyone."

"Take it easy. I'm not asking as part of the investigation. Just as a concerned friend and neighbor."

Master Quentin maintained his silence.

This time the Chief didn't let it linger. "Quentin, please. Just two words: 'She's OK,' or 'Not OK . . . '"

Master Quentin bowed his head. "I am sick of all this. Sick at heart about the poor girl who was murdered. And sick of answering questions. Why don't you just ask her father?"

"Two reasons," said the Chief. "Kids can be very different when they're away from home. And Bill McRae, as you might guess, is not exactly objective."

Bruno blanched. "It was his daughter Mimi? Mimi Cohen-McRae?"

Master Quentin didn't respond.

On the way back to the car, the Chief was in good spirits. "I liked the way you handled that. A lot of people would have backed off a guy like Quentin because of his religion. But you used that Jewish angle and it got him to talk about those security guards."

Then he noticed that Bruno looked less than enthusiastic. "No, I mean it. That's useful information."

"Glad to be of help," Bruno said. "But I'm very upset to hear that the daughter of Bill McRae is involved in this."

"Friend of yours?" asked the Chief.

"No. *Mishpokhe*—a relative, and a close one. Mimi Cohen-McRae is my niece."

CHAPTER 9

ICKY AND ALISON LIKED TO SAY that they were doing more than their fair share to keep Gardenfield's historical traditions alive and well. When Alison came back on the train from the University of Pennsylvania, she'd walk up Old King's Road to the Lenape King Tavern where Icky worked the night shift. The place had a revolutionary pedigree. Built in 1750, the tavern still looked the way it did when the Assembly met there, in '77, to declare that New Jersey would no longer be a British colony. British and Continental soldiers used the building in turn as they skirmished throughout the area, while the original Quaker meeting house, just two blocks distant, served as a hospital.

Yet today Gardenfield was a dry town and its former leading tavern was a boring museum. Alison and Icky were restoring some of the place's faded glory by shooting up speed in the basement. At least Icky did. Alison stuck to hash, mostly.

Supposedly, Dolley Madison had spent the night there when she was a teenager. She had the reputation of a hot number, before she married James. So Alison and Icky had tried to make it on her bed one night. It was up on the second floor, cordoned off with velvet ropes. It wasn't hard getting past those. The fancy bed frame and canopy made the spot look enticing, but Dolley's mattress was really a sack filled with straw. Lumpy, scratchy, and distracting. The horsehair-filled cover was not much better.

Now Alison and Icky confined their sexual activities to the basement. This, too, was a heroic act or a revolutionary statement, in their view, because the basement's traditions were also sadly neglected. Longstanding rumors held that the basement of the Lenape King had been a way station in the Underground Railroad. This was a system operated in large part by anti-slavery Quakers in the decades before the Civil War to help smuggle runaways out of the South and into the free states in the North. For years, historians had tried to debunk those rumors. They claimed that the underground labyrinth of brick-lined rooms and passageways was just storage space for kegs of beer. Now the entire basement was off-limits. Apparently, the mortar holding the bricks together was crumbling to powder at a rate that the state's building inspectors deemed to be unsafe. No one, not even the chief caretaker, was supposed to go down there. So the mystery persisted.

Alison and Icky had found some interesting nooks and crannies, and they'd set up one as their private quarters for the times when they needed a romantic escape. It was fitted out with a double mattress, bedding, Icky's works, Alison's bong—and little else.

That evening, Icky and Alison were entwined on the mattress, trying to have sex. Unfortunately, Icky's speed habit was undermining his performance. Alison had already had quite a bit of experience with this phenomenon.

"It's like trying to pry open a padlock with a wet noodle," she told him.

—"Or trying to put a condom on a rotten banana." That one was inspired by high school sex ed.

—"It's like trying to shoot pool with a lariat . . ." She'd heard that one in a cowboy bar.

And finally, "Icky, is that your . . . daffodil?"

Alison rolled over and pushed him back. She was bored and hungry. Icky was too high to care. "Let's go get something to eat. I'm starving."

"We'll have to wait until break-time," Icky whined. "And besides I'm not really hungry." The speed was destroying his appetite, too. "We'll have to be careful. I know the cops are watching me."

"Why do you say that?" Alison asked.

"I see them practically everywhere I go, for one thing. And now they're bringing in a psychic. I read about it in the paper."

"That could make things interesting."

"Interesting for you maybe. But I still live here. All this is too close to home for me. You told me it would all be over with by now."

"That's what I thought. Apparently I made the mistake of overestimating the intelligence of the police force. I guess I've been watching too much TV. Don't worry. You'll be OK. Psychics are fakes. You say something, and they expand on it. Hey, maybe we can hire him to work on your little *thingie . . .*"

Icky pretended to pout, so Alison would give him a hug. She did, but she couldn't resist teasing at the same time. "Just be yourself. If he tries to read your mind, it'll drive him crazy."

"I love you too," said Icky glumly, breaking free. "What are we going to do?"

"Well, I still have my paper to write. To do that, I have to figure out how to finish up this project. I want to make sure I get extra credit for this course. It'd be good if we could figure out a way to help the police without them knowing it's us. Or maybe I should just ask the professor for an extension."

"I vote for the extension. No way I'm getting mixed up with the cops."

Alison gave Icky a warm kiss, followed by a short, painful squeeze of the testicles—and a parting shot: "You're the one who needs the extension—lover boy."

CHAPTER 10

BRUNO LIVED IN A TRAILER out in the pines. It was set in a small clearing off a dirt road with no name. There was no house number and no mail service (he maintained a post office box in nearby Tabernacle). Propane heat. Well water. Septic system. Electricity from the county backed up by a Honda generator. And, of course, satellite TV, a hot tub, and cell phone service. A redneck Shangri-La.

This was his fortress against the welter of people's thoughts and emotions. The bereaved relatives, beleaguered cops, and the skeptical press. It was a dangerous business. When bad guys find out the cops are getting clues from a psychic, they tend to come after the psychic. No reason to make it easy for the bad guys to find him.

Bruno lived with Maggie, a beautiful two-year-old German Shepherd cross with an intelligent face. She had a thick coat and an impressive tail that she carried aloft like a sail. Bruno liked to talk to her and watch her changing facial expressions as she listened. She'd furrow her brow and cock her ears, clearly working hard to make out what he was saying: an admirable—and unusual—characteristic, in his view. Maggie would respond with a remarkable vocabulary of her own consisting of barks, whines, grunts, growls, licks, and pokes with her snout.

He carefully hung up his business suit and dressed for work. Boxer shorts and a tattered old Princeton sweatshirt. "Ah yes. Good old Princeton," Bruno hummed to himself.

Maggie whined in response and Bruno stopped humming.

Things seemed to be going OK, he reflected. Chief Black seemed like a good guy. The borscht belt *shtick* seemed to be working when he needed it. But now there was this dead girl with no name, and his ex-wife's sister's kid, Mimi, had been the one who found the body.

"Maggie, you know I sure hope we can solve this thing without talking to her. Because I really don't want to see Judy Cohen or her husband, Bill McRae—that *shmuck*—again."

Maggie's whines grew more persistent, and Bruno let her run outside. "Just stay away from that Carmine," he joked, referring to the neighbor's Australian Cattle Dog and Shepherd cross. Carmine's owners, the Terranovas, lived on the other side of the bog. Bruno didn't know them well, but they seemed to be authentic Pineys, judging from the light blue rusted-out 1974 Cadillac with official "classic car" license plates that was always parked in their driveway.

He heard Maggie barking excitedly. Had she run into that raccoon again? Then it stopped. Must've scared it off.

Now he was ready. He darkened the room and sat in his special chair. Not the one where he ate, read, and watched TV, but the other one, which was reserved for work. He opened the plastic evidence bag and took out a few strands of the girl's hair. He cradled them in the palm of his hand. He could barely sense that they were even there. With his other hand, he touched the hair with his fingertips, cleared his mind and waited.

Nothing came to him.

He shifted his position to imitate the posture he'd assumed in the meeting house, slumped over to the right. He pictured her soulless expression as he'd seen it at the morgue.

But all he felt was cold. Emptiness. Nothing.

"Like Adam," Bruno thought. It wasn't a vision, but a memory of something he'd read. He got up and turned on the light. On his bookshelf was a copy of *Kabbalah for the Complete Shmegegge* that he'd just picked up at the used bookstore. He sat in his all-purpose chair and looked for the chapter he'd been reading the other night. There it was. The Golem. Nothing like the one in Tolkien. The Golem was actually a figure from the Middle Ages. Made from clay by the Rabbi of Prague to protect the Jews from anti-Semites in Europe. The Rabbi traced the Hebrew word for truth, EMET, on his forehead to bring the Golem to life. When the anti-Semites tried to start a pogrom, the giant Golem routed them with ease. That scared the Emperor and he begged the Rabbi to deactivate the Golem. The Rabbi graciously complied by crossing out the first letter, leaving MET, which means death. That was a good story.

Reading further, Bruno spotted a passage that described how Adam was a Golem before God breathed life into him. That was it. That was the feeling he got from the girl. He couldn't explain it, because she was dead. Plain and simple. Just like any other corpse. Nobody could breathe life into her again, ever. What did he expect?

The difference was nobody knew who she was. Nobody claimed her. Where were her parents? Could they have killed her? What kind of parents, what kind of people, would do something like that?

He quickly picked up the hair between his thumb and forefinger and rolled it lightly. He felt grit, like grains of sand mixed with hair. He squeezed hard. Vague images entered his consciousness, building on events of the day. The old brick meeting house. The Lenape King Tavern. He saw a group of figures, a man and a woman and a third figure prostrate with exhaustion. They were fugitives hiding in subterranean tunnels, waiting to proceed to the next stage on their journey. Nothing relevant.

Frustrated, he put the hair in a separate envelope and went to get a Rolling Rock from the fridge. He switched on the TV. The Big 5 sports channel. Beach volleyball, Penn against Temple. That was different. Where'd they find a beach this time of night in Philly? Lots of diving in the sand. Tattoos. Sunscreen. Bruno grabbed another beer at the start of the third match, but fell asleep before it ended.

Then he had a dream. The statue of William Penn came to life. He climbed down from City Hall and walked to a dark field where he captured an owl by the wings. It is a life or death struggle. The owl keeps saying, "Who, Who, Who?" while William Penn sings in a funny sing-song chant, "What's the score? What's the score? What's the score?" And the owl replies, "50-3-2-60 . . ." over and over again.

At last, he wakes up to find that it's not an owl, but Big Bird singing. And it's not William Penn, but Peaches Cromwell sitting on his bed, holding a steaming hot grande Starbucks latte in the vicinity of his head.

CHAPTER 11

"WHERE'S MAGGIE?" ASKED BRUNO, STARTLED.

"Eating breakfast."

"I didn't know you could cook."

"It's actually a preparation similar to steak tartare, but without the sauce. I wasn't sure that'd be good for her," Peaches explained.

"I'm impressed." Bruno tried to get up.

Peaches prevented him by planting a forearm in his chest. "Where do you think you're going?"

"To get my notepad. I need to write down my dream before I forget it."

Peaches waved the latte near Bruno's cheek, threatening to spill it.

"OK. I guess I'll just commit it to memory."

Peaches eased her elbow away from his sternum, but didn't back off with the latte.

"I didn't know you were so domestic," Bruno quipped. "Next you'll probably be telling me about how you used to be a cheerleader in high school?"

"Now I'm impressed," Peaches returned with smooth sarcasm. "You're pretty good. You must be psychic. I did some research on you too." She paused for effect. "Joey. Kaplan. Kicked out of Princeton for cheating . . ."

Her knowledge of Bruno's real name was supposed to unsettle him, but he took it in stride. "Couldn't be helped. All the right answers seemed to pop into my head during exams. I didn't realize I was 'listening in' on Robert Darling, the star student."

"Then you went to New York and took a job in advertising. Same thing. A client accused you of falsifying focus group research."

"That's not exactly true," Bruno protested. "I 'interviewed' nearly a hundred people—who happened to be taking the day off on a beach near the city. They all seemed to be having fantasies about the Marlboro Man. I thought the brand was golden. But then we found out the population in general saw things quite differently . . ."

"Then your marriage to Sharon Cohen broke up the same way. You caught her cheating on a trip to California—without ever leaving New York."

"It was awful. One moment I was looking at her photograph. Next thing I knew, I was seeing *every*thing, just like I was there," Bruno recalled ruefully. "Say, you trying to steam clean the upholstery or you going to let me drink that coffee?"

Peaches ignored him. "Then you drifted around the West, got kicked out of Vegas and even the rinky-dink tribal casinos."

"That's where I perfected my Yiddish. You run into a lot of members of the lost tribe in those out-of-the-way casinos."

Peaches raised her eyebrows. "Drink the coffee. You're going to need it."

"What do you mean? And what are you doing here anyway?"

"I followed you."

"When?"

"Last night."

"What did you do? Lurk around in the bushes all night? That's why Maggie was barking." He called Maggie and she came running. She ignored Bruno and ran right to Peaches, sniffing at her oversized handbag.

"Nice doggie." Peaches patted the dog uncomfortably. "As you can see, she's quite fond of my steak tartare recipe."

"Maggie, off. Get away from her," commanded Bruno. Then, to Peaches, "You just got lucky. It's dangerous out here. A trigger-happy Piney might have found you . . ."

"I went home and came back this morning."

"You've been wasting a lot of gas. And hamburger. What I want to know is why are you doing this? If you wanted to talk to me, why not just call me on the phone? I gave the Chief my number. I've gone to a lot of trouble to keep my name and address private. Getting beat up or killed by bad guys is no fun."

"Well, I need something to write about," Peaches said, moving closer again. "You weren't exactly cooperative the other day. Interviewing people off the record is a waste of my time. On the other hand . . ." she acted like she was flirting, placing a hand on his knee and moving it along his thigh, ". . . exposing your 'credentials' would make good copy."

"You were the one who recommended that the Chief hire a psychic."

"I didn't suggest he hire a fake and a loser."

"I'm not a fake," Bruno retorted.

"Well then prove it . . . loser. Give me something I can write about instead."

CHAPTER 12

NEXT DAY, the following story appeared in the *Pest* under P.C. Cromwell's byline:

SEX AND KABBALAH AND ROCK 'N' ROLL
Cutting-edge technique casts doubt on police theory, psychic says

TABERNACLE, NJ—Somewhere in this warren of back roads, blueberry bogs, and scrub pine, a mobile home sits in a clearing. It is a nondescript place; a run-down doublewide with a woodstove and a satellite dish. You'd expect to find a local Piney or, for those given to flights of the imagination, some incipient sociopath or fugitive from justice—as opposed to a jet-setting law enforcement specialist who is connected to rock superstar and sex symbol Magdalena.

Yet that is what this reporter discovered after braving slippery roads, freezing temperatures, and an arduous all-night stakeout. Thanks to our careful investigative work, the South Jersey Post has discovered the base of operations for Bruno X, the psychic detective recently hired by the Gardenfield Police Department to assist in the investigation of the recent Quaker killing.

In an exclusive interview, this Bruno X—he uses this nom de guerre to protect himself from perpetrators who may attempt to disrupt his investigations through physical intimidation—revealed that he believes that the body found in the Friends Meeting House in Gardenfield last month may not have been the victim of a fellow Quaker. Quakers are known for deploring violence of any kind. Therefore it was paradoxical to find a murder victim in a Quaker meeting house.

Bruno X points out, "In the Middle Ages, goyim" (a colorful Yiddish word employed by the speaker to identify the dominant Christian populations in Eastern Europe) would dump murdered bodies in the synagogue in order to provoke outrage against Jews. It was part of something called the 'blood libel.'" The so-called "blood libel" refers to the mytho-historical, quasi-legendary practice where Christians accuse Jews of killing Christian children so they would have blood to make Passover matzoh. Bruno X believes it is possible someone may have moved the body to the meeting house to discredit the Quakers.

Who might have such a sinister objective? Mr. X declined to speculate.

When asked to explain the basis for this deduction, Bruno X revealed that he uses the Kabbalah to process the evidence he receives from psychic sources. Readers will recognize the Kabbalah as the mystical form of Judaism that has become high-profile since it was adopted by sex symbol Magdalena. Magdalena performed most recently in London on behalf of the starving millions in Africa. She also has authored a children's book that reflects her experience of the Kabbalah

The next 10 inches of the article were about Magdalena, female sexuality, and children's literature, except for the concluding paragraph, which stated:

Bruno X claims that in addition to physical clues, a crime scene contains psychic clues as well. Strong emotions leave a residue that can be detected by those who know what to look for. Psychic evidence needs to be evaluated scientifically just like other forensic evidence and the Kabbalah is the "technology" that he uses.

Bruno X adds that he did not study at the Kabbalah Co-op in L.A. and he does not know Magdalena personally. Or Tiffany Pupik. We commend Chief Black for his prompt action in bringing in such well-qualified outside resources. The investigation is already moving again and we look forward to a speedy resolution.

The reaction to Peaches' article in the *Pest* was swift and fateful.

Fully 66.6% of the families enrolled in Gardenfield Friends called Master Quentin's office to ask him what he was planning to do about security.

Against his better judgment, Master Quentin called Chief Black and asked him what security resources might be available from the town, as he still preferred not to entertain the offer from NewGarden Biosciences.

Chief Black hadn't read the story when Master Quentin called. As soon he got off the phone, he read the article and then angrily called Bruno to demand a meeting.

While Chief Black was on the phone, he missed receiving an angry phone call from Rabbi Nachman, of Philadelphia's oldest Orthodox congregation, Temple Emmanuel. The Rabbi was upset about the mischaracterization of the Kabbalah and was frustrated because he couldn't get anyone to take his call at the *Pest*.

Finally, Icky called Alison. He thought she'd be amused by all the Magdalena references. Instead, Alison became even more worked up than she'd been the day before regarding her term paper. She slammed down the phone and called her professor, Nathaniel Littlejohn, to make an appointment later in the week.

CHAPTER 13

"DAT PEACHES, she's some piece a woik," said Bruno, squirming under Chief Black's angry glare.

"Yes, I know," said the Chief, not willing to let him off the hook.

"She tracked me down, like a . . . like a . . ." Bruno couldn't think of an analogy.

"Like a scared rabbit?" the Chief suggested.

Bruno looked hurt. "Like a pickle in a barrel. She cornered me in my trailer. She defeated my security system. I was vulnerable. She threatened me. I had to think fast. It was the only way out."

"So you fed her this story to get her out of your hair . . ."

"That's right," said Bruno, thinking he was off the hook. "I fed her alla dis *bubbe-meise*—old wives' tales—about da blood libel. Actually that's not so bad, if I do say so myself. Pretty quick thinking. Anyway, she hears Kabbalah, right away she's thinking Magdalena. So we got pretty good exposure, right? She says we're on the right track."

The Chief glowered.

"OK. That business about 'casts doubt on police theory' wasn't so good. But I didn't write that. I didn't say it. The headline writer made it up. You know that's not what I think."

Chief Black laid down the hammer. "I know you didn't write the article. But you knew that Peaches did. Yet all you cared about was the fact that you handled Peaches all right with your quick thinking and your *bouillabaisse*."

Bruno opened his mouth to interrupt, but the Chief plowed ahead. "You thought you did fine, but you forgot about everybody else. Most important, you forgot about me. Dealing with the press is a war, not a battle. It's never over."

Bruno looked at his shoes. "What was I supposed to do?"

"Take one for the team. It's obvious. Peaches is going to write whatever she feels like writing. There's nothing you can do about it. Except call me. Right away. I needed to know what you told Peaches. Had I known, I would have been able to look at the paper first thing. And I wouldn't have been broadsided by a situation that I didn't even know existed. I was bombarded by phone calls; I was unprepared, and it made me look . . . like a *shlemiel*."

That was an act of kindness on the part of the Chief, leaving an opening for the psychic. "I think you mean *shlimazl*, Chief. In this case, I'm the *shlemiel*, da no-goodnik dat causes da trouble, and you're da *shlimazl*, da one with egg on his face . . . I'm truly . . ."

—The Chief cut him off before he could say "sorry." "Now you know what I expect. Now get your briefcase, we're going out."

Chief Black drove past the Little League fields and pulled into the parking lot for Tano's Deli, right across from the liquor store on the east side of town.

Inside was a brightly lit room dominated by deli cases and glass-fronted refrigerators stocked with cold drinks. On the walls hung cloth patches with embroidered insignia from police departments all across the U.S. Tano's was crowded with people waiting for takeout orders. Behind the counter, two heavily muscled and tattooed men were busy preparing cheesesteaks and hoagies and joking with the customers.

"Yo! Chief. How's it hangin'?" boomed the larger of the two.

The Chief's arm shot up in a friendly salute. "Chris. Ray."

"There's room for you in back," said Chris. "You gonna stick around or you want it to go?"

"Two of the usual for here," replied the Chief. "This is my friend Bruno . . ."

Chris got excited when he heard the name. "Bruno Sammartino! The world champion wrestler. The living legend."

Ray looked up from chopping lettuce. He squinted at Bruno, an unlit cigarette dangling from his lip, but didn't say anything.

Bruno just grinned and let the Chief lead him through a dusty curtain to the back room. It was tiny, crammed full of supplies and barely enough space for an old kitchen table with a scarred Formica top and aluminum legs, and two matching chairs with turquoise plastic seats. On the walls hung an old movie poster showing the eruption of Mt. Vesuvius and the Pirelli tire calendar from 1999 featuring a sepia-toned photo of a nude woman with an old-fashioned hairstyle.

"Chris' mom?" Bruno wisecracked.

"Don't let him hear you say that," warned the Chief. "Talk to me."

"The most unusual thing about this case," Bruno began, "is the lack of emotion. The girl was attacked from the back. She didn't see it coming, but still I'd expect a sense of shock and fear—or something—at the moment of impact. Here, there's nothing. I've never experienced anything like it before."

"Any theories?"

Bruno thought carefully before replying. "What if she's, you know, a vegetable? Brain damaged. Something like that. Family gets tired of taking care of her. Can't afford it. Ashamed to own up publicly. Frustrated. So they decide to . . . end it."

"Then they dump her at the Quaker meeting house? Why? It's not exactly your anti-Quaker blood libel scenario."

"Shows you can't believe everything you read in the papers," Bruno said.

"Suppose this is just a normal family. They have no experience disposing of a dead body. They watch a bunch of TV and figure the ground must be frozen because of the snow. If they don't bury her deep enough, some animal will dig up the grave. If they put her in the river, she'll wash up."

"So they use the meeting house, thinking it will confuse people . . . as it has. But they still need a way to get in. And they managed to do it without leaving clues. That takes a lot of skill."

"Or access to the meeting house. What if Quentin had an illegitimate daughter? Because of his role at the school, he might have wanted to keep it secret."

"That's what I'd call a tortured scenario," the Chief observed. "To make it work you need an illegitimate kid who's seriously handicapped. A guiltily obsessive father who won't even put her in a nursing home. Otherwise, she would've been reported missing."

Bruno picked up the thread. "Right. She'd have to be living at home somewhere. Probably with the mother, never going out. The only other person who'd know she existed would be her doctor."

The Chief shook his head. "It doesn't add up. The motive for killing her is to get rid of the burden? I can't see Quentin doing that."

"Maybe the mother did it, and Quentin's protecting her."

The Chief grabbed his phone to make a call. "That's a lot of 'ifs,' but right now it's all we've got. We'll check into it, but it'll take some time. There are a lot of doctors in the area."

Bruno hesitated. "What I just told you: There's logic to it. But it doesn't feel right. It all comes back to the girl. Why didn't she feel anything? There are powerful emotions at work here. There must be. But I can't find any trace of them. It's hard to imagine anybody, let alone parents, who could do something like that—without emotion."

"I know," said the Chief. This was the same brick wall he'd been running into since the investigation began.

Just then Ray rambled in with a couple of enormous cheesesteak hoagies wrapped in white paper. The smell of fried onions filled the room. Ray placed them on the table without comment and went back to work, leaving the velour curtain partly open.

"Dig in," said the Chief. Consuming a Tano's cheesesteak hoagie with everything on it requires both hands and considerable concentration to keep the contents of the sub from sliding out onto your lap. Both Bruno and the Chief worked in silence for about seven and a half minutes.

Then Bruno spoke. "I had this dream. About William Penn."

"William Penn?"

"The statue of William Penn on top of city hall in Philly. It . . . he was walking around."

"Things like that happen in dreams." The Chief continued eating.

Then Icky and a couple of friends entered the shop. The Chief could see him joking with Chris and hear him laughing out of proportion to anything that might have been said.

"Do the numbers 50-3-2-60 mean anything to you?"

"Sounds like a basketball score. College. 53-60."

"It's not basketball season. I was watching a volleyball game last night on TV."

"And?" The Chief was still keeping an eye, and half his attention, on Icky.

"And I think it was four different numbers. 50-3-2-60, not 53 to 60. Usually the high number goes first."

"True. True. Maybe it's the combination to a gym locker? Or a safe?"

"You know in Hebrew, the numbers are actually letters of the alphabet. So you can translate numbers into words and vice versa. I tried that, and it came out 'SBGN.' That mean anything to you?"

"SBGN?" the Chief echoed dully. "I dunno. Sonny Boy Good Night?"

"I couldn't make anything of it either," Bruno admitted. "Then I realized: There's more than one kind of Quaker . . ."

"There is? You mean like low church and high church, that sort of thing?"

"No. I was watching them play on TV last night."

"Right, the Quakers. University of Pennsylvania. Big 5 basketball. Crosstown rivalries. Great stuff. You don't think basketball fans did this? I mean it's basketball, not soccer."

"Well it was volleyball, but that's not the point. Are you paying attention?"

"Oh, right," the Chief said. "I guess I am distracted. See that kid in there with the bright red hair?"

Bruno turned around discreetly.

"Just go ahead and stare at him. There's no secret. He knows that we know that he's the town's biggest drug problem."

"OK."

"Can you read his mind?"

"Just like this? In a room crowded with all these people? Too many distractions."

"Go ahead. Give it a try anyway."

Bruno shut his eyes and tried to concentrate. Within seconds he was shaking his head, as if trying to ward off a hungry mosquito. "*Feh.* That's one messed up kid in there."

"What's he thinking?"

"I couldn't tell."

"But you said something . . ."

"Yeah, it's *chazerai*—a big mess. But that's just a general impression. A sense."

"Like an aura. Could you see his aura?"

"Not exactly. I don't do auras."

"C'mon," scoffed the Chief. "What'd you see?"

"Things don't look too good for that kid. I think he might be in big trouble."

"That makes sense. He's a drug addict. Do you have anything more specific?"

"No."

"Hmpf." The Chief seemed to be sulking.

"Anyway, I want to go right away and track down my lead about the Quakers."

"You call that a lead?"

"Most definitely."

"And how are you planning to follow up?"

"I'm heading over to the campus. Do some research in the library and then just . . . check things out."

"Check things out?"

"Yeah. Walk around. See what's going on over there."

"Well you can't."

"I can't? Why not?"

"We have an appointment. Tell you what I'll do, though. I'll have Harry—Sergeant Abraham—call the campus cops and do a sweep of the message boards. He's our best technology resource; maybe he'll

come up with something for you. And I'm going to have Michelle—
Officer Coxe—check the hospitals and clinics. I really think those are
our best shots right now."

The Chief started laughing.

"Wha's funny?" complained Bruno, failing to guess that Chief
Black had already moved on to another topic.

"I don't know how I could have forgotten. This Rabbi called. Name's
Nachman. Ever heard of him?"

"Not really. Name sounds familiar, but I can't place it."

"If you knew him I don't think you'd forget. He's a bit flamboyant.
Lit a fire under the Mayor. Asked a lot of weird questions about you.
Wanted to know how old you are. Whether you're married. Where did
you study? Whatdya think? Is he looking for a date?"

"Not my type. Must be an Orthodox Rabbi."

"Any idea what he's up to?"

"According to the Orthodox, nobody's supposed to mess around
with the Kabbalah . . . except themselves. They say if you're not at least
40, married, and haven't mastered the Talmud and all the other sacred
books, then using the Kabbalah will create a lot of trouble."

"What kind of trouble?"

"The evil eye. Avenging angels. False messiahs. Wrath of God. That
kind of stuff."

"Sounds bad. That's what happens when you talk to Peaches. Stay
away from her from now on."

"As if I can control that, now she knows where I live."

"Yeah, that's too bad." The Chief feigned sympathy. "But you can
handle it. Do you have a weapon?"

Bruno points to his temple.

"Right," crowed the Chief. "You're Bruno X, the psychic detective.
Living by your wits and the awesome power of your brain."

"You sound like my mother."

The Chief hit him on the shoulder to buck him up. "Don't get down.
It's just the cheesesteak talking. You'll be fine again in a coupla days."

CHAPTER 14

NEWGARDEN BIOSCIENCES was located to the north of Gardenfield, in Maplewood. To get there, Chief Black drove along Old King's Road, past Lenape Woods and through the security checkpoint.

Bruno noted that the grounds were mostly bare fields, which soon would be planted with corn. Off to one side was a cluster of abandoned military buildings from the 1960s. The property had been a Navy tracking station up until the defense cuts in the early 1990s. Then NewGarden took over and added a brand-new corporate complex consisting of research and administrative facilities, as well as greenhouses. The buildings were an impressive contrast of round and rectangular shapes—a gleaming statement in glass, alloyed metals and stone. And, for anyone who didn't get the message just by looking, it was spelled out in foot-high polished chromium letters on the wall next to the entrance: NewGarden Biosciences—*Transforming the way we feed and care for ourselves.*

The receptionist was a conspicuously beautiful woman in her mid-30s, dressed in a smart tweed suit with a surprising display of gold accessories. As if in counterpoint, there were also two armed guards, dressed in dark green paramilitary uniforms that were stiff and understated. They stood stoically in opposite corners, like potted plants, while the receptionist was all gracious gentility as she greeted the Chief and Bruno from behind an elaborate hardwood desk. A polished aluminum nameplate identified her as Rhonda Vick.

Rhonda emerged from the confines of the desk and shook hands with exceptional warmth. "Dr. Fischer and Dr. Jurevicius are expecting you and will be down in a mo*w*ment," she drawled, displaying a textbook South Jersey accent in her tightly formed, slightly nasal *o*'s. Bruno fell in love with her the moment he heard it.

Rhonda showed them to a conference room, offering coffee, water, or a soft drink. Bruno requested a Dr Pepper. And he practically melted in his chair when she said, "No pro*w*blem."

When she left, the Chief leaned over to Bruno and said in muted tones, "Dr. Fischer—he's the CEO here—and Master Quentin go back a long ways. They're both Quakers. I think that's why the company's offering to provide security for the school. But Quentin doesn't seem to want to have anything to do with Dr. Fischer."

It took Bruno a moment to get his mind off Rhonda and onto what the Chief was saying. "That makes sense," he stammered. "I mean, maybe he feels they're keeping an eye on him and doesn't like it. On the other hand, I can see why he wouldn't want to have goons dressed up like commandos guarding the entrance to the Friends School. I'd be afraid to go in, too."

"We could have them work plainclothes, if that's the only issue. There's something funny between Quentin and Fischer I'd like to know more about."

"Why don't you just ask him?"

Before Chief Black could reply, Rhonda reappeared with Bruno's Dr Pepper. "The da*w*gkters will be with you in just a few mo*w*ments." She smiled and disappeared.

The Chief had to yank on Bruno's sleeve to get his attention. "If there is something wrong between the two of them, Dr. Fischer might not want to talk about it. That's why I brought you along. To see what you can find out without putting him on the defensive."

"So you want me to . . . ?"

"Read his mind, at least check out his aura . . ."

Bruno started to sputter, "I am not an eavesdropper . . . and I don't do *furshlugginer* auras."

The Chief cut him off. "Calm down. They're coming in."

"Good to see you again, Buddy," said Dr. Fischer, vigorously grabbing the Chief's outstretched hand. He was a large man, at least six-two and overweight. He appeared to be in his 60s judging by his gray, thinning hair and the heavy creases worn into his face. He looked more like a rancher than a scientist, except he was dressed in a Brooks Brothers jacket, a button-down shirt that was too small at the neck, and a purple tie with tiny double helixes all over it.

"This is my associate, Serge Jurevicius," said Fischer. "Dr. Jurevicius is our Chief Operating Officer and head of the Agricultural Division."

Jurevicius stepped forward to shake hands. He was slim, in his late 40s, with dark hair combed back from his face and a carefully trimmed goatee. He wore charcoal gray pants and a black cashmere mock turtleneck.

"And this is Bruno X," said the Chief. "He's consulting with us on this difficult and troubling case."

The men shook hands all around as Dr. Fischer boomed, "He's not going to read our minds, is he?" His tone was jocular, but accompanied by a sharp look at Bruno.

"Nah. For that you need an appointment," Bruno deadpanned. "But if you want, I been teaching the Chief here to read auras, and he can do it for you free of charge."

The joke fell flat; everyone pretended to ignore it.

"We're here to talk about security," said the Chief, without missing a beat. "You gentlemen have generously offered to provide guards for the school . . ."

"That's right," replied Jurevicius briskly. "We can spare two members of our security team during school hours, with the exception of the week of our annual meeting. That's coming up late in May . . ."

"Which, unfortunately, is just before school lets out," Fischer said. "And we were counting on your help, Bud, during the annual meeting, as in years past."

Bruno was confused. "What happens at your annual meetings that you need police help?"

"NewGarden Biosciences is a biotechnology company," Fischer explained. "We genetically engineer plants that are healthy to eat, easy to grow, and good for the environment. We also do some work with plants and animals to biofacture medicines. Some people call it *pharming*, with a "ph." Cute, huh?"

"So you're worried about espionage? Protecting your intellectual property?"

Fischer gave the Chief a quizzical look, then turned to the psychic. "You must not read magazines or watch TV. You haven't heard of 'Frankenfoods?' That's the f-word in our industry. And what else do they say about us, Serge?"

Jurevicius supplied the quote easily, "We're devils disguised as entrepreneurs and engineers . . . presenting people with a Faustian bargain."

"People think we're creating renegade genes that are going to get loose and devastate the planet," Fischer continued.

"Like those *cockamamie* dinosaurs in Jurassic Park?"

"Exactly," huffed Fischer. "With just as little scientific justification. People create scenarios about what might happen and get themselves worked up that the world's about to end. Their idea of a solution is to try to disrupt our meetings. Consequently, we need to protect ourselves. But we're getting off the subject . . ."

The Chief consulted his notebook. "The school had some queries. They wanted to know more about the personnel. Who they are? What kind of training they have? That sort of thing."

Fischer laughed, "So Quentin has *queries*? That's a very Quaker word, you know."

"No, I didn't . . ." the Chief stammered.

". . . Very Quaker, indeed. When you see Quentin, tell him you want to 'speak to his condition.' Be sure to use these exact words. Say to him, 'Emmanuel Fischer wants to *speak to thy condition*, Friend.' Can you do that?"

"Yeah, but then what do I say?"

"Tell him the children are his responsibility. It's not a time to sit in silence. He has to act."

Silence filled the room as the challenge of the words registered. Dr.

Fischer rose to leave. Bruno interrupted him with a question. "Isn't this a strange business for a Quaker?" he asked.

Fischer tilted his head to bring the proper part of his bifocals into play. "If you weren't here with my friend, Chief Black, I'd say that's none of your business," he snapped. "Since you are here, and supposedly trying to help . . . I'm going to help you." He turned to Jurevicius. "Serge, I have another meeting. Could you please show these gentlemen the museum and provide them with anything else they might need?"

He shot another look at Bruno. "Maybe a little education will be useful to you. People assume there's a contradiction between religion and business. Quakers have never said that and I've always felt the opposite is true. I think my craft and my God-given talent enable me to raise up a lot of good, if I can help to feed more people or cure their diseases."

"But aren't you tampering with God's creation?" Bruno shot back.

Fischer went red in the face and turned to leave. "We'll discuss it some other time . . . when you actually have some notion of what you're talking about."

CHAPTER 15

THE MUSEUM WAS IN A HIGH-CEILINGED ROOM overlooking the NewGarden greenhouses. The interior walls were covered with oversized colored illustrations and grainy black-and-white photographs. In the center of the room stood a series of display pedestals dramatically lit by overhead spotlights.

"This room serves a public relations function," explained Jurevicius. The emotional scene with Dr. Fischer did not seem to have affected him. "We use it to explain the science of what we do. Don't feel bad, very few people know much about biotechnology and those who do are full of misinformation. We'll skip the technical section about how we splice genes," he gestured toward the illustrations, "and get right down to the results."

He led them to the first pedestal, which contained a modest Petri dish. "E. coli bacteria," Jurevicius explained almost reverently. "I should say, genetically engineered E. coli, which contain a human gene for producing insulin. It was the first biotech product, developed by Genentech in 1978. Before that, diabetics had to use insulin derived from the pancreases of slaughtered cows and pigs."

"Sounds *treyf*," Bruno commented.

"Actually, the Rabbis said it was kosher since it was injected, not eaten. But obviously the human protein works better." Jurevicius turned toward a pedestal supporting a bowl of rice. "The next example is a product of one of our competitors. Golden rice. It turns yellow when cooked. The color comes from beta-carotene. Any idea where the genes came from?"

Bruno and the Chief exchanged blank looks. "Carrots?"

Jurevicius smiled happily. "Daffodils, actually. The point is to efficiently supplement the amount of Vitamin A in the diets of malnourished people, chiefly in Asia, where they eat a lot of rice. Vitamin A deficiency is a very serious condition. It causes blindness and is implicated in the deaths of some five million children every year. Monsanto agreed to share the technology for golden rice, free of charge, for use in underdeveloped countries. But that's probably a devious plot on their part to gain control of the food supply, don't you agree?"

The question took them by surprise, which also seemed to please Jurevicius. "Am I boring you?" he asked. "No? That's good. Because it gets better." He gestured to a pedestal featuring an ordinary-looking tomato. "This is the Flavr-Savr tomato, designed to look good, taste good, and last longer on the shelf. Its critics complained it has a fish gene inserted. That can't be good: Fish rot and stink . . . don't they?"

"Sure," agreed the Chief.

"*Feh*," added Bruno.

"So why would you put a fish gene in a tomato?"

"No idea."

"Well, there was talk at the same time of trying to identify the gene that allows the Arctic flounder to survive in near-freezing temperatures. But that wasn't how they made the Flavr-Savr. Actually the scientists at Calgene merely inverted one of the tomato's own genes to slow down its aging process. No one knows how the fish gene story got started, whether it was a mistake or deliberate misrepresentation—it's useless to speculate. But it has spread like a mutant virus—if you'll pardon my hyperbole."

"Why would anyone worry or complain?"

"Because they're in the protest business. Their product is fear. To raise funds they have to scare people. When the fear starts to wear

off they come up with something new. Like the monarch butterfly."
He waved in the direction of another pedestal supporting the familiar
orange and black insect. "In a restricted environment, a scientist fed
butterflies the pollen of a biotech corn variety. The butterflies died,
proving the corn was toxic, right?"

"I'm not taking the bait on this one," snorted the Chief.

"Good man," Jurevicius commented. "*La dose fait le poison,* as we
say in French. Later studies did not support the original report, but the
scare persists. Protesters are everywhere. Street corners. High-priced
clothing boutiques. And we've had our share of run-ins here, I don't
have to remind Chief Black."

He nodded at the Chief, who had a slight grin of anticipation. "I
see the horse crap right over there," he chortled, pointing at a pedestal
supporting several large clumps of dried horse manure, complete with
projecting tufts of straw.

"It was brilliant, really. Entirely Dr. Fischer's creation. He altered
the gene for an enzyme in the horse's digestive system. This allowed us
to recapture unused nutrients in horse excrement by treating it with
a simple reagent. In other words, we could feed the animal the same
food over and over again. Not 100% of course. More like 65%, but still
a significant savings. Obviously, this could have been a boon to people
everywhere. It cuts down on the cost of owning animals. Reduces the
amount of land and water needed to raise the crops to feed them. And
the amount of pesticides and herbicides that farmers have to use . . ."

—"But remember, how all those chefs came over from France,"
Chief Black recalled. "Talk about a difficult, obnoxious bunch of people."

"I know all too well," said Jurevicius, "as I am French, myself."

The Chief reacted immediately. "I feel terrible for saying that. Let
me apologize. You have no accent . . ."

—"Now that you mention it, I can hear it, just a little bit," Bruno
observed.

". . . and I didn't mean to generalize. I had to arrest several of them
and they did nothing but complain about the food and accommoda-
tions. You'd think I was running a hotel."

"They wouldn't have liked that either," Jurevicius observed. "They are all pompous asses, without exception. I came here several years ago when my parent company in France became the largest investor in NewGarden." He stole a glance at his watch. "Come, I'd like to show you my contribution."

He led them through the greenhouses. Each room recreated a different environment: a rice paddy, a wheat field, a field of sunflowers. Finally they stopped in a large expanse planted with corn. Jurevicius grabbed an ear and husked it on the spot. The kernels were bright blue in color.

"This is our most successful product. We call it Scarecrow Corn. It is corn that's genetically modified to keep birds away. I'd prefer not to tell you where the gene came from that performs this trick. Let's just say it is not from a fish . . ."

"But is it edible for people?"

"Entirely harmless, but it doesn't taste very good. The idea is to plant the fields with, say, 15% Scarecrow Corn and the rest with our parent company's insect-resistant cultivar. That mixture is very effective in keeping both the birds and the bugs away. The resulting crop is intended as animal feed. The pigs don't seem to mind the taste, it's equally nutritious, and the violet color immediately identifies it, so it doesn't get mixed up with human food stocks."

"Very impressive."

Jurevicius led them to the next room. What they saw there caused them to gasp in astonishment. Flitting from tree to tree were crows. More than a dozen of them. All of them a brightly colored, iridescent blue.

"A harmless publicity stunt," explained Jurevicius. "We spliced a gene from the hyacinthine macaw into the DNA of crows and sent them to Seattle the winter we launched Scarecrow Corn. We thought having brightly colored birds stealing their garbage might cheer them up during the rainy season. This would send a message that good things are on the way. Of course we also rendered them sterile so they wouldn't permanently affect the corvine gene pool. Nevertheless, we sustained protests from the usual host of environmental groups."

"Polite, but nasty," said the Chief, recalling his arrests. "They kept complaining about the coffee."

Bruno didn't notice. The violet crows fascinated him. They were quite tame. One perched on his shoulder and stared at him. Bruno felt uncomfortable with the formidable beak so close to his eyes. He transferred the crow to his hand, but it immediately flew off to rejoin its buddies.

A moment later, they were back in the museum and Dr. Jurevicius was concluding his tour. "Here's the thought I'd like to leave you with." He pointed to an empty pedestal. "This represents all of the people who have ever been harmed by biotech gone awry. It's empty. Thirty years. No casualties."

As if on cue, Rhonda appeared and Jurevicius thanked them for their time. "I think you understand some of our concerns now and our need for security," he said. "Please let Dr. Fischer know as soon as Master Quentin decides about our offer."

"Quite a performance," Chief Black commented under his breath to Bruno, as Rhonda escorted them past the silent lobby guards.

"Never seen anything like it," Bruno agreed.

Just then Rhonda pulled up abruptly. "I *fowr*got to give you something." She ran back to her desk—as much as anyone can run in high heels—and picked up a slim package, which she handed to Bruno. "It's our annual repo*wr*t," she said, turning her head to catch his eye. Her jerky movements and the quizzical, almost beseeching, quality of her gaze reminded him of the bird's behavior in the aviary a few minutes before.

"I th*aw*ght you might find it interesting," Rhonda said.

As Bruno reached to take the package, he noticed with a start that her eyes were the same shade of violet as the crow's plumage. "Psychic overload," Bruno muttered to himself. He grabbed the envelope and hurried for the door.

CHAPTER 16

"WHO'S THE PSYCHIC HERE, YOU OR ME?"

Chief Black had just commented that Dr. Fischer seemed upset by something. "He used to be solid, steady. Every other time I saw him, nothing seemed to faze him."

"And today? What was different? Could you tell what he was thinking?"

It was the Chief's turn to be indignant. "That's your area. I just saw what I saw."

"Aha. The rational mind confesses its limitations."

"We use psychology all the time. I never said I was psychic. Did you manage to pick up anything?"

"Like you, I noticed his agitation. But his thoughts were in synch with what he was saying. He felt like an open book to me. He wasn't keeping anything back."

"Really?"

"Yeah. He's got a big chip on his shoulder. He works hard, he's idealistic and successful. But instead of getting credit, he feels people are blaming him instead. That whole devil thing really bothers him. I'll tell you, I can relate . . ."

"What do you mean?"

"Being psychic. It can be tough . . ."

"Don't tell me you're letting Peaches get to you."

"Peaches—*shmeaches*. It's more the everyday stuff. Regular people . . ."

"Women?"

"Hey, you're pretty slick with the psychology, Chief. Or was that a psychic observation? Speaking of slick, that Jurevicius can *hulyeh-hulyeh* with the best of 'em. I never knew there were already so many biotech products out there. Pretty bizarre stuff, too. Maybe they can figure out a way to turn off my psychic gene."

"Really? You'd want to do that? I think it's a gift."

"A gift with strings attached."

"And you don't think it's tampering with . . . you know . . . what you said in there?"

"Go ahead, Chief, you can say it. 'God's creation.' Don't be afraid."

"You'd let them try to fix your DNA. You're not against biotech?"

"Nah. I was just trying to get a rise out of Dr. Fischer. Which worked by the way. Did you notice?"

"I did," the Chief admitted. "But you said nothing useful came of it. Did you figure out what's going on between him and Master Quentin?"

"I think it's just what he said. He feels Quentin judges him . . . for not being quiet enough. Tampering with nature. Making money. Being in a business that employs armed guards. It goes way back. A long-standing feud. Now Quentin may need his help, but is acting too proud or stubborn to accept it graciously. Dr. Fischer feels vindicated, but it's a lousy situation with the school and the kids and the girl. He really feels bad about that girl."

The Chief perked up. "Really? Do you think he knew her?"

Bruno thought it over. "I don't think so. It was just her . . . face. That emptiness. And the fact that they found her in the meeting house. He was shook up. Horrified, really. Same way I felt about it. I just figured it was a normal response."

"But you actually saw her," the Chief persisted. "It's not likely he ever did, unless he deliberately went down to the morgue. Was he . . . I don't know how to ask this? Was he picturing her face or just thinking about it in a general way?"

"This kind of reading is pretty fuzzy. It's emotions. Not words. Not pictures."

"Is there any way you can tell if he actually saw her face?"

"I can try to do a remote viewing. But then I see what he's seeing and hear what he's hearing. But it's not possible to dredge up a memory, unless it happens to be in his consciousness while I'm connected with him."

"It's worth a try, I guess."

"I'll need a photograph of Dr. Fischer. Preferably a recent one where he's by himself."

"No problem. You already have one."

"If I do, I'm not aware of it."

"It's in your hand," the Chief indicated the annual report. "Those things always have photos of the execs. I guess your friend Rhonda must've known what she was doing. Anticipating your every need. She's cute. Maybe you should ask her out."

Bruno pursed his lips like a hamster. "No, noo, *nyo* way," he protested, trying to imitate her accent.

"Not nice," clucked the Chief.

"I like Rhonda," Bruno protested. "But she's not my type. Too high maintenance."

"She's just dressing up for work. Besides, with what we're paying you, you can afford to buy her a few trinkets," said the Chief.

"First you're psychic. Now you're a *shadkhan*, a matchmaker. How do you know she's available?"

"Because I'm Shotgun Buddy Black and something tells me the two of you are made for each other."

CHAPTER 17

"NO RECORD DR. FISCHER EVER VISITED THE MORGUE," Sergeant Harry Abraham reported to Chief Black.

The Chief mulled over the information.

"There's also this," Harry mumbled. He pushed a sheaf of printouts in the Chief's direction.

"What's all this?"

"Chatter from the student message boards."

Chief Black scanned the documents.

Sociology 40. Introduction to Deviant Behavior
Nathaniel Littlejohn
T,Th 2:00-3:20

A systematic examination of deviancy as a social construct. The course surveys the ways in which society uses normative ethics as a means of controlling behavior and also explores the concept of deviant groups and their role in revolutions. While some reading is required, the course emphasizes empirical research to familiarize students with a variety of deviant acts.

Then he started reading the first message in the pile:

Disregard the syllabus. This course is awesome. You actually learn useful stuff like: deviance as a weapon; identity theft; creating disinformation; covering your ass; manipulating the media; leveraging the legal system; and creating a sleeper cell. The only requirement is to commit a deviant act and write about it . . .

"Charming."

"I found out about it from the campus police," explained Harry. "Happens every spring and drives 'em crazy."

"What are they dealing with?"

"A lot of pranks, mostly. Soap bubbles in the fountains. Graffiti. Minor shoplifting. Now there's a lot of computer-based stuff. Hacking. Identity theft. Sometimes viruses. And then there's the occasional off-the-wall event that defies description . . ."

"Can't the university shut it down?"

"Academic freedom. The professor's kind of a cult figure. And the kids love having a course where they don't have to read anything. It's a tradition."

"Did you find out anything else on the message boards?"

"A lot of bragging. One-upmanship. The class has a nickname, Doggin' 'n' Dissin', and that's all we know right now," Harry concluded.

The Chief handed the folder back to Harry. "Maybe Bruno'll run into something when he's over there . . ."

In fact, at that very moment Bruno was buried in the Penn library, reading up on Quakerism and the origins of the university. It surprised him to learn that Benjamin Franklin was not a Quaker and that William Penn had no direct connection with the college. *So why did they call themselves the Quakers?*

Not far away, in another part of the campus, Alison knocked on the door of Professor Littlejohn's office.

"I'm very excited about the way my project is developing," she told him as she took a seat.

"That's good," said Littlejohn, studying the person sitting across the desk from him. The course was a large lecture, so he didn't ordinarily get to know many of the students. He'd never seen Alison before and she struck him as a typical undergrad. Face not formed yet. Baby fat, yet with a hard edge. Chewed fingernails. Atrocious posture. Ample breasts. Child's temperament in a woman's body fueled by adolescent rage. A bomb waiting to explode. He told himself to keep his distance, for the hundredth time. Then he heard himself saying, "It's always exciting when you step outside normative morality for the first time . . ."

That was all Alison needed. "I think it's immoral to obey unjust laws. Like Gandhi. He equated laws with superstition. People really have a duty to disobey. Just like you teach in the course."

Littlejohn tried to be modest, but he couldn't help beaming. "I can't take any credit. Students, people your age, are so idealistic and dedicated. It's the best time of life in many ways. One of the reasons I offer this course is to learn from you. All of that creativity is an inspiration."

"Well, I really put a lot of thought into it," she gushed. "My project has to do with the corporate manipulation and appropriation of the global food supply, which forces millions into poverty and submissiveness."

"Very impressive." Littlejohn drew a deep breath. Something told him this was going to be one of those projects. Every couple of years one cropped up and things could get really hairy. He reminded himself to be careful.

"Things started out well," Alison explained. "Then they took an unexpected turn. On the whole, I think it's really a good thing. But it turned out to be much, much bigger than I expected. Now, to really get the full impact, I need some help. *We have to get the word out.* It's so frustrating . . . !"

Littlejohn might have been confused by all these generalities if he had been listening more carefully, but he assumed he knew where she was headed. "It's very difficult to get work published these days. Even for faculty, it can be a challenge. Undergraduate work . . . I have to advise you not to get your expectations up. You have your whole career in front of you."

Alison tossed her head. "It's nothing like that. This isn't just research. It's something newsworthy. But it has to be handled just right, because I don't want to get mixed up with the police."

"I see." Littlejohn started to feel his blood pressure go up. Another naive kid, thinking she could change the world all by herself. It seemed they were always coming to him for validation. Lucky for them, he had plenty of experience: He knew how to let them down easy without squashing their ideals. "The police, huh? That sounds a little bit *complicated* for an undergraduate assignment." He smiled at Alison in a particular way when he said "complicated" to suggest that he recognized and appreciated her effort—in spite of what he was about to tell her.

Alison looked down at her fingers, which she was interweaving nervously in her lap. A good sign. Littlejohn continued, "Don't you remember the caveats on the project handout? I can give you another copy if you need one."

Alison's face started to turn red with frustration. Why wasn't Professor Littlejohn being more encouraging? "Like I told you, things escalated in a way that I didn't expect . . . I wasn't planning to do anything illegal. Except maybe trespassing. And a little bit of vandalism."

"Hold it right there," said Littlejohn. He stood up and started to pace the room. He needed to phrase this delicately. "It sounds to me like you've committed a *political* act. Am I right?"

Alison perked up a bit. "Yeah, that's it exactly. Technically illegal but morally justified: a political act."

The doorknob twisted open and one of Littlejohn's colleagues stuck her head in. Face framed with curly black hair, left long and natural, like the '60s. Bright red lipstick and tiny black-rimmed reading glasses pushed down on her nose. It was Nathalie Porthous, the resident expert in feminist theory—a celebrity in Alison's eyes.

"Still on for coffee tomorrow with Bill Conway, Nate?" said Dr. Porthous in a cheery, bell-like tone.

"Yes. The usual time and place." Littlejohn gave her a big thumbs-up; she mumbled a vague "Excuse me" in Alison's direction and withdrew.

Dr. Porthous' interruption allowed him to see the situation with Alison in a new perspective. He had to admit he was curious to find out what was going on. But it was so difficult to talk here, in his official capacity. "Where were we?" he wondered rhetorically. "Ah, yes. I was about to say it would be better if we could discuss this issue in a more neutral context."

"What do you mean?" Now it was Alison's turn to feel confused.

"It's very simple. Here at Penn, I'm your professor. And I have certain responsibilities."

She didn't like the sound of that. "I thought you'd want to . . ."

He cut her off. "I know. I know. You need to talk. I want to listen. I'd like to help you, but . . ."

"I don't get it. What are you saying?"

"It's not that simple."

Alison's look of derision made him hesitate. Then he plunged ahead anyway. "Look, you can't go around breaking every rule in sight. And you don't do it just for the fun of it." His voice sank to a whisper. "This isn't anarchy, it's about principle. Building on principle requires circumspection. And tact. Speaking freely in this office would be neither circumspect nor tactful." He resumed speaking at normal volume. "Are you beginning to understand?"

"I think so . . ."

"Good. The hypocrisy in this culture is absurd. That's why we have to do things in a roundabout way. In theory, our political views are protected speech. As a couple of concerned citizens, we have a right— or as you put it, a duty—to discuss the issues and act on our principles. We have a right to privacy."

"Exactly . . ."

"So if we're going to talk, we need to ensure we protect our right to privacy."

He wasn't actually winking while he said this, was he? "So, you're suggesting . . ."

Littlejohn did not reply. Instead, he wrote an address on a piece of paper and handed it to Alison.

"You want me to meet you at this address?" asked Alison, hesitating.

Littlejohn nodded affirmatively.

"Tonight?"

He nodded again as he half-ushered, half-prodded her out of his office.

CHAPTER 18

ALISON WAS ROYALLY IRRITATED as she walked across the campus. Was she the only competent person on the planet? If the police had been doing their job properly, they'd have connected the dots to the girl in the meeting house long ago. Then she could have written her paper, and received the credit that was her due. Was that too much to ask?

But things weren't going the way she expected. The police had hired that ridiculous psychic. No hope there. But at least he wasn't a threat. No, the newspaper really was her best option. P.C. Cromwell seemed like a serious person, though she had gotten seriously off track with all that mystical garbage. If she could set it up the right way, Alison could be like Deep Throat feeding Cromwell the information she needed to blow the whole rotten scandal wide open.

To do that, she needed Professor Littlejohn's help. She admired his ideas. Like many of her teachers, he saw events in terms of revolution. In class he was always speaking about the duty of the individual in an insane world and the need to speak truth to power.

So why was he being so evasive about talking to her? This business about context was a red flag. What difference did it make where they talked? Alison hated it when people referred to things off campus as "the real world." If the university wasn't real, then what was she doing wasting her time here? For all his talk, Littlejohn was acting like someone who was still part of the system. If it weren't for the fact that he was friends with Nathalie Porthous, she probably wouldn't trust him . . .

Alison was distracted from her reverie by an unexpected sight. A man was walking toward her on the pathway, gesticulating and talking to himself under his breath. There was something familiar about him. Was he one of her teachers? He was in the right age bracket. But he was dressed in dark business clothes. And his demeanor was definitely not professorial.

Alison edged to the other side of the pathway so she could watch him carefully without being too obvious as he approached. Then she realized why he looked familiar. She'd seen his photo in the paper. It was the psychic, Bruno X—speak of the devil. What was he doing on campus? Adrenaline shot through her system with the idea that he might be pursuing her. She steadied herself. She didn't want to make eye contact, but she also didn't want to attract attention by doing anything too obviously evasive. He had to be after her. Why else would he be here?

She summoned her courage to look at him directly as he passed. He hadn't noticed her. His mind was elsewhere. It might have been a complete coincidence that brought him to Penn. What a joke. Her confidence surged with every step.

When she got back to her dorm room it didn't even bother her to find Icky there. He was shooting up. It was almost a relief to not have to talk to him about Littlejohn and running into the psychic. She could tell he was too high to have a rational discussion and that left her free to mull things over. His excitement and incessant chatter seemed to fit her mood. It was like background music. It made her feel good, but she didn't really have to listen.

"Y'knowAlison,it'sreallycoolhereoncampus.Imetthisguyonth etrainwho'sreallyintoAfricanmusicandguesswhat,he'sstudyingit hereforcreditandeverything.Hesaystheteachersareactuallymusi-ciansandtheyteachtheclass.Mostlytheyjustjam.Lastweektheyhad-amasterdrummerfromAfricaastheguestlecturerandheworkeddirect-lywitheverybodyontheirdrumming.Icouldhandlethat.It'dbegreattoma

jorinsomethinglikethat.Myfatherisbuggingmetogetmyhighschoolde-
gree.MaybeIcoulddoitandmajorindrumming.OrinAfrica.Canyouma-
jorinAfrica?"

"Sure," said Alison. "Why not?"

"Myfather'sajerk," Icky continued, not really changing the subject—because it was always the subject. Alison had been through it so
many times, she knew exactly what he meant. Icky's father was a jerk.
Rude. Opinionated. Obsessed with money. Status. Not at all support-
ive. No wonder Icky was a speed freak.

"I'm meeting somebody and I have to take a shower," she said gently, starting to undress. "Want to take one with me?"

Icky lit a cigarette. The initial rush had worn off and smoking
helped him channel some of the nervous energy. "Nah. The girls in
this dorm aren't ready for the sight of the perfect male body."

"Right."

"Speaking of which, did I tell you?" he announced with an exag-
gerated wave of his hand. "DeKalb washed the school truck. And he
put on new tires, snow tires. Right after the snowstorm. Kind of stupid, don't you think? Weird, even, since it's so late in the season."

"No, you didn't tell me . . ." Alison replied. Her mind was elsewhere,
thinking ahead to the appointment with Littlejohn. She left the room
and came back about twenty minutes later, wrapped in a light blue bath-
sized terry cloth towel. She held another, smaller towel with a gaudy
pattern in her hand and was using it to chase some water out of her ear.

Icky watched, fascinated, as Alison prepared herself to go out. She
released the bath towel and tossed it over the back of a chair. Completely naked, she spread her feet to shoulder width, and bent over
quickly, her wet hair shooting a ribbon of water onto Icky's shirt.

"Hey, watch that," he protested, checking to make sure she hadn't
put out his cigarette.

Alison expertly twisted the patterned towel around her hair and
stood upright, fashioning it into a turban. With every movement, her
large breasts bounced and wobbled provocatively. Icky couldn't take
his eyes off them and Alison knew it. She picked up the bath towel and
began rubbing underneath her arms, taking special care to dry the
moisture that collected in the deep folds under each breast.

A similar performance graced each leg. Icky had to light another cigarette.

Now that she was dry, it was time for moisturizer. Alison chose a purple bottle from the top of her bureau. It was an herbal concoction, goat's milk with lavender, which was so volatile, it almost chased Icky from the room. Alison anointed herself with loving care. Then she took Icky's cigarette and shoved the moisturizer into his hand.

Icky knew the drill. Alison had a spreading lotus flower tattooed on her sacrum that was quite spectacular. In fact, the whole vista was quite spectacular when she turned her back to him and bent forward. Anyone but a meth addict would have been hardwired to respond. Poor Icky. All he could do was gather a handful of goo and rub it on Alison's back. As it warmed in contact with her skin, the moisturizer threw off vapors that combined the rank aroma of fermenting cheese and an oil refinery. Icky started hacking uncontrollably. He grabbed the blue towel to wipe his hands, then retrieved his cigarette, which was dangling from Alison's lower lip.

With a wry grin, Alison gave him a peck on the cheek as she slipped into a pair of skimpy, fawn-colored underpants and matching camisole. Icky got up to leave. "I need to check in with Julius, find out when my merchandise will be ready."

"Hang on a sec so you can walk out with me," said Alison. "I'm almost ready."

She unwound her turban and let it drop to the floor. She brushed her hair vigorously, four minutes by the clock. Then she slicked in a line of mousse to give it the right amount of attitude. Sensing Icky's impatience, she struggled valiantly to get into her jeans. She added a cashmere cardigan, leaving it unbuttoned to reveal a hint of the camisole, and plenty of cleavage.

Eyeliner. Mascara. Lipstick. Four studs in her left ear. Three in her right. A brushed silver lotus ring from India. Plenty of bangles. And she's ready to go. She threw her overcoat over her arm but didn't put it on, in spite of the cold.

"Hey you really look hot!" said Icky, a twinge of jealousy finally penetrating the penumbra of his high.

"I have to meet my professor." Alison sighed.

"Well, I'm glad to see you're so well prepared."

"Don't be silly." Alison laughed. "He must be, like, in his 50s or something. The other women call him Littlejohnson. I can handle him, no problem."

CHAPTER 19

AFTER AN HOUR IN THE LIBRARY, Bruno's head felt stuffed with useless information. The more he read, the more convinced he became that the Quaker connection at Penn was confined to sports. A dead end.

Bruno squinted in the bright sunlight. The courtyard was littered with relics from the past: a brushed aluminum peace sign, 15 feet in diameter; a similarly oversized replica of a broken button; and a bright red and turquoise sculpture of the letters "L," "O," "V" and "E" stacked up like building blocks. Calculated silliness, which everyone seemed to ignore.

He watched the students loafing on the green. Not a care in the world. He felt depressed. There's no worse feeling than a psychic whose intuition isn't working. He pulled out his map and headed for the athletic buildings. The old basketball palace, The Palestra, maybe it would hold some clue.

As he left the green, the people assumed a more sober, business-like manner. Crossing 34th Street, he saw the biotech building, an ultramodern facility named after one of the pharmaceutical giants. Interesting coincidence? He wondered if Dr. Jurevicius or Dr. Fischer might have some connection here?

The Palestra struck out, as did Franklin Field. The fighting Quakers were nothing after all.

Crossing South Street, he spotted a building that looked like a temple with a rectangular fountain in front. Gazing at the murky water, Bruno realized it'd be good to make a pit stop before getting on the train back to Jersey.

He entered the building and found himself facing a great hall with gigantic statues of Ramses II. He couldn't help but admire the scale and majesty of the art—in spite of its despicable origin. Ramses was the pharaoh who enslaved the Jews. He enslaved his own people too. Well, God punished him, didn't he? Bruno thought back to countless Seders and tried to remember the list of plagues. What were they? Locusts. Death of the firstborn. Boils. Night. That was four. Murrain—he only remembered that one because he could never remember what it was. Five to go. *I Love Lucy* reruns. Beef liver. Wife shopping at Bloomingdale's when there's a big sale at Macy's. Pants too tight. And of course, mother-in-law moves in—permanently.

Bruno approached Ramses defiantly. "*Mazel tov, alter kocker*—you old fart—you're still famous, but so what? You should've stayed in the smaller house, the one with all the stairs and no extra bedroom!"

Then he wandered into the next gallery, feeling rather pleased with himself. The feeling didn't last long. Thinking of mothers-in-law reminded him that he still needed to talk with his niece, Mimi. He wanted to see her, flesh and blood—and it could provide important leads. But her parents continued to put off Chief Black. Finding the victim had been traumatic enough. They couldn't expose Mimi to another interview. And that *shmuck*, Bill McRae, her father was carrying on about his character. Where did he get off feeling so superior? Who gave him the right to judge?

Bruno's indignation led to self-righteousness. Self-righteousness lapsed into sentimentality. And, inevitably, sentimentality devolved into self-pity: Why had this psychic stuff happened to him? He'd give anything to be free of it. It separated him from other people. His wife. His job. Look at him. Alone. Friendless. Trapped in a world that no one else could fathom or share.

Fortunately, this reverie was interrupted by a small, roundish figure in a uniform, with a walkie-talkie parroting amplified static from his belt.

"Huh?" said Bruno, not understanding what the man was saying to him.

"I get lonely here at night sometimes," the guard drawled in an accent that was a dead ringer for Peter Lorre's. "But I never get scared."

"Scared. Why should you get scared?" asked Bruno. He tried keeping his cheeks sucked in while he spoke to see if he could reproduce the guard's creepy manner of speaking. But he quickly abandoned the attempt. One Peter Lorre was enough.

The guard gestured toward the display cases. Bruno's self-absorption had been so complete, he hadn't noticed they were in the Gallery of Mummies. "A virtual necropolis," panted the guard, reading the sign on the wall. No less than half a dozen mummies, in various stages— wrapped, partially wrapped, unwrapped—were on display. Human mummies. Mummified animals. There were also coffins, canopic jars and other paraphernalia of the mummifier's art.

"Would you like me to show you around?" Peter Lorre leered. "I've heard the tour so many times, I can easily give it myself."

Before Bruno could protest, the guard launched into his explanation. "It takes 70 days to make a mummy. First you remove the internal organs. Except the heart," he gestured at Bruno's chest, ". . . and the brain." He touched Bruno's forehead. "Then you put the body in a bed of natron, which is a kind of salt that's only found in Egypt. Finally, you anoint the body with oil and spices."

"Sounds like making lox," Bruno joked. But the guard ignored him.

"The priests would pray and place golden amulets on the body. Then they'd begin wrapping the mummy in linen bandages."

"*Shmattes*," interrupted Bruno. "I'm expert in ancient Semitic languages and the technical term is *shmatte*."

Peter Lorre ignored him. "When that was done, they'd place him, or her, in a series of coffins. Why did they do all of this? Because the ancient Egyptians believed that a person was made up of four different elements. Each of these needed a place to reside after death. The Akh goes up to live with the gods. The Ka is the person's vital energy; that's what all this stuff is for, because the Ka needs to keep eating and drinking in the afterlife." Moving close to Bruno's face, Peter Lorre opened his eyes as wide as they could go. "I guess that's the scary part." He giggled. "Running into a hungry Ka at night. The Ba is a human-headed bird that goes flying around. And the Ren, of course, is the name that needs to be preserved and repeated."

Bruno went white. Hearing about the hungry Ka and the flying Ba had struck him with a new idea. "The name needs to be preserved and repeated." He smacked his fist into his open palm. "Of course. I'm such a *shmegegge*."

He ran out with the guard following him, yelling, "Hey wait, you haven't seen the mistake carved into the Pharaoh's throne. It's the world's oldest typo."

Bruno ran all the way to the station. He caught the train back to Jersey, just as the sun's rays turned bright orange in the polluted sky.

CHAPTER 20

THE ORANGE GLOW also highlighted Alison's hair mousse, making her look exotic beyond her years. Nate Littlejohn invited her into his living room and offered her a single-malt scotch. His apartment was ultra-modern, a bit museum-like with scientific apparati, phrenological heads, straitjackets, stuffed baboons and so forth displayed like art. The walls were painted in dark, masculine colors. *Typical bachelor pad*, thought Alison.

Littlejohn hadn't changed since their meeting earlier in the afternoon and Alison's splendor took him by surprise. "You look lovely tonight. I'm glad you decided to come. Here we can talk without artificial student-teacher roles getting in the way."

Alison smiled. She was determined to get what she wanted, and if Littlejohn was more comfortable talking in his apartment, so be it. "Thank you, Professor Littlejohn," she said. "I really need your help."

"Please, call me Nate," Littlejohn insisted, adding, "It sounds like you've done something that goes beyond the scope of the assignment?"

"Maybe I did." Alison feigned innocence for a moment, to get his guard down. Then she let him have it: "To tell the truth, though, I don't see what difference it makes, now that we've dropped our artificial student-teacher roles."

Littlejohn took a deep breath and started over. He decided to take the high road this time. "Alison, do you remember how Emerson went to visit Thoreau in prison? Emerson says to Thoreau, 'Why are you here?' And Thoreau answers, 'Why aren't you?'"

"Sure. *Civil Disobedience*. Thoreau's saying it's a responsibility. That's exactly my point."

"But Thoreau's in jail."

"So?"

"You said yourself, you're concerned about legal implications—that's why you want to talk to me."

"Yeah."

"But you have to realize, if you talk to me . . . about something illegal . . . that will definitely have implications for me . . . and my job. And I still don't have any idea what this is all about."

"I figured as the Deviant professor, you must be willing to take some risks. Aren't you a risk-taker, Nate?"

Littlejohn had to admit he liked this brazen tone and he responded in kind. "I guess I prefer Emerson to Thoreau. He spoke his mind, but he still had a comfortable place to live, a steady income and he didn't have to do any jail time. My philosophy is to corrupt from within."

That was all the encouragement she needed. "I was reading about women in the Third World; they grow most of the food on the planet, did you know that?"

"OK. I'm with you."

"Traditionally, they grew almost 200 varieties of plants. For thousands of years. Then these giant corporations come along and force them to just grow corn or something stupid like that. They patent crops and make people pay for their own seeds. They're stealing the world's biodiversity and starving people to death. I get so angry about it, I could scream."

Littlejohn nodded in encouragement.

"So I wanted to do something about it. Something deviant, like you talked about in class."

Littlejohn frowned but Alison ignored it.

"So my . . . friend and I, we . . . er . . . borrowed this truck and drove out to this . . . biotech . . . this awful company in my hometown, just across the river in Jersey that performs terrible genetic experiments. We wanted to sneak in and do something like liberate the lab rats and mice or at least throw rocks through the greenhouse windows."

"That's very daring," said Littlejohn. "But I don't remember reading anything about that in the paper. Usually they try to blow up these protests like they're a big deal and call them eco-terrorism."

"Well, you didn't read about it because it never happened."

"Ah."

"Like I told you, we ran into something we didn't expect."

"Yes. And . . ." He was getting impatient.

Alison sensed this was the moment of truth. She had to show him the goods or the deal was off. She moved closer and said in the most sincere voice she could manage, "I really need your help, Nate. Because what I witnessed there could make a big difference. It could bring down the company—definitely. But if we handle it right, we might be able to stop the entire industry in its tracks."

"Sounds unbelievable," Littlejohn said.

Alison reacted to his obvious lack of enthusiasm. "You aren't taking me seriously."

"I don't know what to say." Littlejohn faced her squarely and took a step closer. "You're making some large claims, but you haven't told me your basis for making them."

"This is important, Nate. I need to know if I can trust you." She looked him squarely in the eye.

"Alison, you can trust me." Littlejohn reached out and began kneading the muscles in her neck and shoulders. "I can see you're stressed. And I'm worried it may be affecting your judgment."

"Don't patronize me!" She wriggled free of his grasp. "What if I told you this was about murder, Nate? Would that be enough to earn your respect? Or would you sneer that I'm just another hysterical freshman?" She was pounding his shoulders as hard as she could, simultaneously, with both hands. "Because that's what they do over there at NewGarden Biosciences, Nate. They kill people. The question is, are you going to help me stop them?"

Littlejohn's mind was racing at top speed. This couldn't be happening: One of his students, involved in a murder while working to fulfill a course requirement. It'd be laughable if it weren't so horrible. It was time to take control of the situation. He caught both her hands so she would stop pounding his chest. "Alison, this is serious. If they really are killing people, why don't you report it to the police?"

Alison's frustration was uncontrollable. "This is supposed to be fucking deviant behavior! No matter how you cut it, calling the cops is not a revolutionary act . . . and . . ." she was starting to lose her composure, ". . . and I'm involved. It wouldn't be safe. I'm afraid of what might happen to me." She burst into bitter tears again, clearly suffering.

Littlejohn released her wrists and slid his hands up to her shoulders. "You did the right thing coming here, Alison," he said in his most soothing manner. "I can tell what you need most of all is to relax. Maybe a backrub would help you calm down."

Alison went numb. She had suspected it might come to this. But, one way or another, she still needed Littlejohn's help—even if it was just an introduction to Nathalie Porthous. She also thought of Thoreau . . .

The backrub was perfunctory at best, and Alison was soon naked except for the fawn-colored camisole. Littlejohn was only partially undressed as well. He discarded his khakis and outlandishly patterned boxer shorts. But his oxford shirt was pulled up partway, where it acted effectively as a straitjacket. Alison worked away on top of him, her breasts floating a few tantalizing inches from his mouth. She pressed on his shoulders like a wrestler while she ground down with all her weight and strength against his hips.

Just at the moment of climax, Alison pulled away.

"You little bitch!" Littlejohn snarled. "I'll be sure to send you my cleaning bill." Then he noticed the angry flush mounting from Alison's chest to her face, and he attempted a more tactful retreat. "You know, Alison, *this* is as deviant an act as anything my other students have ever performed. Why don't you write about it for your paper and forget about those other things?"

The callousness of the remark reignited Alison's fury. "Other things!" She grabbed his discarded boxers and tore them in half. "Maybe I should take you to the cleaners, you filthy . . ."

—"Alison, that just came out horribly wrong. I believe you. I really do."

She tried to hit him with all her strength. "Liar. Hypocrite. Asshole."

—"Alison, calm down. I'm on your side. I really am."

"I won't calm down. I won't calm down. I won't calm down," she raved in time with each attempt to beat him around the face and chest. "This isn't deviant. This is pathetic. It's routine. It's mainstream. I'm *not* going to write about this . . ." She gestured toward Littlejohn and the bed.

Finally Littlejohn capitulated. "OK, Alison. There's a journalist I know. I'll call her and see what I can do. Alison, please, you've got to trust me."

Alison stopped trying to beat him, though she still eyed him warily. She gathered up the careless pile of clothing from the bed and flounced toward the door, slamming it with every ounce of melodrama she possessed.

CHAPTER 21

AFTER ALISON LEFT, Littlejohn was surprised to notice that he kept thinking about the Sixers celebrating after the last time Philly won the NBA championship—back in '83. *Une belle souvenir.* Four straight against the Lakers. Julius Erving, Maurice Cheeks, Moses Malone, and Andrew Toney shaking bottles of cheap champagne and pouring the foam all over each other. That was the year he got tenure. A good time. One of his favorite memories. That, and taking over the Dean's office when he was an undergraduate at Columbia. *Those were the days, my friend.*

The memory gave him a hankering for real champagne. First he needed a shower: Six minutes under the hot water revived him. He dried himself, then padded into the kitchen, wearing a freshly laundered royal blue satin robe. Littlejohn always kept a bottle of Bollinger on ice and he opened it with flair. A practiced twist, a barely audible pop, nothing wasted. He sipped as he walked around his apartment.

Feeling clean and rejuvenated, Littlejohn got a jolt when he looked at his bed—the tangle of soiled sheets. This wouldn't do. He stripped the bed and plunged the sheets in the laundry hamper. Then he reconsidered and moved them to the trash.

Years of experience had taught him not to worry. But Alison did seem a bit worked up when she left. Was she a troublemaker? Probably. But so what? Plainly what had happened between them had been consensual. And after all, he was the professor of deviant behavior, what should people expect?

By now he'd nearly finished the bottle of Bollinger and was feeling quite "numinous." He put on some jazz, early Ornette Coleman and late Eric Dolphy, and, deeply contented, fell asleep.

Next morning, Littlejohn wasn't feeling nearly as chipper. He had a raging hangover and nothing seemed right. Littlejohn dropped his robe to the floor and waddled toward the bathroom. The combination of a hot shower and strong coffee should've done the trick. But it didn't.

They met in a coffee shop in Nathalie Porthous' neighborhood, just off Rittenhouse Square. An oasis, between the bustle of Center City and the intellectual frenzy on campus. Nathalie was already seated with Paul Conway, the litigation expert in the law school. He'd forged his reputation in the '60s and was still regarded as a keen wit and a feared legal opponent.

When Littlejohn entered, Nathalie held the floor. He could tell right away she was in good form. She had already launched into one of her famous rants about the sad state of intellectual life on campus. "Have you noticed how things have changed since we were students? We had a real sense of commitment, but also a sense of playfulness. Openness to discovery has been replaced with a kind of grim rectitude. I feel like students are putting notches in their belt for their different countercultural accomplishments: Be the first to OD on the latest designer drug. Get arrested at a protest. Smuggle Cuban cigars back from Paris. If I hear one more kid say they wish they had more black friends, or gay friends, I swear I'm gonna puke."

"I've noticed the same thing," said Conway. "But it's more like collecting *merit badges*. Give blood and live in a shantytown. Throw a brick through a store window. See the right bands in person—for the boys; sleep with the band members—for the girls . . ."

Littlejohn saw his opening and interrupted him. "I can never figure out the attraction of musicians when these women have the option of sleeping with their professors, which makes a lot more sense."

"You mean like that little grade grubber I saw in your office yesterday?" asked Porthous. She knew Conway and Littlejohn liked to test her sensibilities, and she relished the opportunity to respond in kind. "You should have seen the serious expression on Nate's face yesterday. I knew she was getting him excited."

Conway laughed. "Undergraduate pussy. It's our one professional perk."

Porthous glared. It never took Conway long to find her limit. "I've made my life's work studying how stupid and immature men can be." She looked right at Conway and shook her head in disgust. "Yet you guys always find a way to plumb new depths. You never grow up, do you?"

Conway was not about to be cowed so easily. He high-fived Littlejohn, laughing, "Nate Littlejohn: the Professor of Perversity."

Littlejohn high-fived the lawyer in return. "And Paul Conway? He's the Counsel of the Corrupt."

"The Dean of Depravity!"

"The Advocate of the Devil himself! But wait, we're forgetting about Nathalie." Both men stood and bowed in her direction.

"Our gracious queen . . ."

"Whom we honor and obey . . ."

"The ultimate arbiter . . ."

"Of the destiny of our tribe: *homo academicus* . . ."

"Femina aeterna cacademicus, materfamilias nostras. We grovel at your feet."

"Virilis perditoris maximama . . ."

"Enough!" shouted Porthous, playing along with the gag by raising both hands in a regal gesture. "I accept your obeisance and I command you to shut the fuck up."

When they all finally stopped laughing, she continued. "I was serious about what I was saying before. These students today, it's like I don't trust them. Sure, they say all the right stuff. But somehow the right spirit isn't there. I feel like, after all our hard work, they'll graduate and then just go out and get high-paying jobs and turn into their parents."

"I'm not so sure," said Littlejohn. "You know Alison, the student who came to see me, the one Nathalie called a tramp? Like you, I had her pegged as a grade grubber at first. But, after talking to her for a while, I think she may be doing something interesting."

"You really did get your ashes hauled, didn't you?" Porthous scoffed.

"What's so *interesting* about her?" Conway pretended to pout. "And why didn't you introduce me to her right away?"

Littlejohn ignored him. "Alison came to me because she really went over the top on her assignment for Deviant Behavior. She said she sneaked onto the grounds of a corporation over in Jersey that she was targeting for a deviant exercise. She wanted to destroy the greenhouses or let the lab animals go free."

"An eco-feminist," the lawyer commented. "That's good. They'll do or say anything."

"You're a bad boy, Conway!" Porthous laughed.

"Paul. Nathalie. This is serious. She said she had information about something going on over there that could get the company in trouble and, possibly, could be used to derail the biotech industry."

"A modest accomplishment," commented Porthous. "You know undergraduates. They always think the whole world's going to change, just because they show up on the scene. Just the other day, this kid comes up to me and says, 'My paper on the Minoan Phallosocracy is going to revolutionize gender theory in the ancient world.' I said to her, 'Did you ever try to get a grant all the time knowing all the men on the board are thinking I wouldn't give this black bitch a dime—unless of course I get to fuck her?' I said, 'Until you've had that experience, don't talk to me about revolutionizing anything. You got to pay your dues, sister.'"

"Way to go, Nathalie. Did you make her cry?"

"No." Porthous seemed surprised. "She thanked me. The women in my classes are tough."

"Nate, did she tell you exactly what she had on this corporation?" Conway asked.

"She said that they were killing people and it was up to her to stop them."

"Jesus. Do you think she meant it literally? I mean, of course corporations are rotten; that's a given. But I really doubt . . ."

—"I know. I know. But she said 'murder.' She said she was involved somehow. I assumed she meant she had witnessed something, because she said she feared reprisals."

"Doesn't make sense," said Conway. "Corporations do brutal stuff all the time—but murder on their own property? That doesn't fit the profile. I think she's just looking for attention. You don't think she'd be capable . . . ?"

—"Of violence? Alison? I don't think so."

"Really? You said she went there to destroy greenhouses. That's not exactly non-violent."

Littlejohn recalled Alison's attempts to bludgeon him and had to admit Conway could be right. But Conway's legal mind had already moved on to another possibility: "OK, let's give her the benefit of the doubt. She witnessed a murder. And she comes to you. Why you? Why not the police? Did you ask yourself that?"

"As a matter of fact, I asked her that, point blank."

"What did she say?"

"She said she's a revolutionary and she'd be damned if she would go to the police."

Conway and Porthous exchanged a knowing look, which they didn't bother to hide from Littlejohn.

"OK. Our little Rosa Luxemburg's got no stomach for the authorities. But why you? What does she expect you to do?"

"Use my contacts. Leak a story to the press. Talk to . . . people like you. Organize something. I don't know. We didn't get that deeply into specifics."

"But you did get that deeply into her pants, didn't you, Nate?" This was from Porthous, who clearly thought it was hilarious. Conway did too.

"What's wrong, Nate?" Porthous continued. "You feel guilty? Don't. I'm sure it was consensual."

"My guess is she planned it," Conway said.

"What do you mean?"

"Look, Nate. Most of the kids in your course put soapsuds in the

92

library fountain or parade around campus in drag. Harmless stuff. You warn them not to get carried away on the assignment sheet and most of them listen to you. Alison's a bit different, I think you're right about that. She's way more creative."

Littlejohn cradled his head in his hands as Conway continued speaking. "Think of the coup, if she not only screws the professor, literally, but also figuratively, by getting you to plant a bogus story in the paper."

"You really think . . . ?"

"It's the simplest explanation," said Porthous. "Everything fits."

"But I've already got a call in to a reporter."

"Just don't say anything about Alison or that biotech."

Littlejohn nodded thoughtfully. "I think you're right. People love to hear war stories about good old Doggin' 'n' Dissin' 401. It never fails to get the Mommies and Daddies riled up when they find out what they were getting for their money—4,500 bucks per class works out to $300 an hour—just to teach their kids to be litterbugs, shoplifters and generally perverse. The last time they ran this story, the paper received hate mail for weeks. Circulation soared. That was five or six years ago. The reporter will eat it up."

"Perfect," said Conway. "Sound kosher to you, Nathalie?" Both Littlejohn and Conway looked at their colleague expectantly. Nathalie Porthous definitely knew how to play her role. "All I have to say is, she better get an A-plus. She's making you guys jump around like trained monkeys and anyone who can do that deserves top marks."

"That went well," commented Littlejohn as he and Conway walked back to campus together.

"Yeah, Nathalie's smart and she has a great sense of humor."

"I owe you guys. Without you . . ."

—"Never mind, Nate. That's what friends are for. And, besides, I'm planning on sending you a bill."

Back in his office Littlejohn checked his watch. He still had a couple of hours before his meeting with P.C. Cromwell. He found he was still thinking about Alison. Hard to believe she had taken him in like that. She really seemed sincere. The way she spoke, the way she hit him and the tears. Planting a story in the *Pest* was a good idea, but it might not be enough. What if she did something crazy, like actually going to the biotech to concoct some phony evidence or something? If the security there didn't realize it was a prank, she could get hurt. Littlejohn woke up his laptop and quickly found the information he needed. The phone rang only once before he heard a woman answer, "*Nyew Gaw*den Biosciences. Can I help you?"

CHAPTER 22

DEVIANCE: A LEARNING EXPERIENCE
by P.C. Cromwell

PHILADELPHIA—It's after midnight. Cary Walters carefully approaches the Vagelos Laboratory on the campus here at Penn. He and two companions are dressed entirely in black. Walters uses a passkey he has appropriated from one of his professors. Once inside, he leads the group to the area where laboratory animals wait in cages for their turn to play their part in the steady march of scientific progress.

Walters and his cadre stealthily open the cages and transfer a dozen or so healthy white rats to the confines of a gunnysack . . .

Out of patience with the setup, Bruno scanned ahead to the meat of the article. Apparently the college kids waited until the next day and then dumped the live rats from the window of their dorm room onto the heads of passersby. They did this to fulfill a requirement for their course in Deviant Behavior.

Peaches was trying to spin it as a protest against animal testing, but the kids were quite emphatic.

"This is no protest," Walters affirms. "It's simply deviant. We need to learn to feel what social outcasts feel. It's about learning to empathize."

According to Peaches, other students fulfilled the course requirement by cross-dressing, abusing strangers with vulgar language and gestures, going to morning classes drunk, and refusing to pay their library fines. "Professor Nate Littlejohn is viewed as a sort of minor deity on campus," the article enthused,

> and while the campus police and administration generally find their workload increases every time Dr. Littlejohn's final paper is due, they bear it with good humor as a longstanding campus tradition.

"They're all *meshugge*," Bruno explained to Maggie. "They should learn to empathize with a good swift kick in the *tuchus*."

Maggie gave a low moan.

Bruno threw the article on top of a messy stack, which served as his work-in-progress file. He picked up the NewGarden Biosciences annual report, and thumbed through it until something caught his eye. A French company was the principal shareholder; that explained why Dr. Jurevicius, and also Dr. Fischer, might be a bit testy in his presence. "Alla sudden, everybody's a dahkta." Bruno snorted. "*Doctor* Littlejohn. *Doctor* Fischer. *Doctor* Jurevicius . . ."

He rummaged through the pile, and picked up his brand-new copy of *Kabbalah for the Complete Shmegegge* and the hair sample taken from the faceless girl. "It's funny that Peaches' article appears at the same time we're investigating this Deviant Behavior course. And Maggie, you know, you and I do not believe in coincidences."

Bruno sat in a comfortable chair and tried to reconstruct the chain of thought leading to the breakthrough he'd had that afternoon in the museum. He'd been staring down the Pharaoh, Ramses II. Then Peter Lorre interrupted him and told him how to make a mummy. All the careful washing and marinating and wrapping. To keep out the dust of centuries.

Bruno looked again at the plastic baggie with the hair sample. There was definitely some kind of sand or grit in there. Yellow-brown in color. Sort of loamy. He opened the baggie and again squeezed the hair between his thumb and forefinger. He concentrated. But nothing came into view.

It was time to try out the Kabbalah. He opened the book and turned to the chapter entitled "Visualization." Following the instructions, he thought of the Hebrew word for truth, *emet*, and visualized it spelled out in Hebrew characters. Aleph, Mem, Tav. He held the word in glowing letters steady in his field of vision, etching the characters in stone. Next, he wiped away the extraneous mental pictures surrounding the letters, substituting instead glowing white fire. The visualization held and Bruno's entire being was absorbed in it.

He came out of his trance sometime later and took Maggie for a walk. It was a quiet spring night in the Pines. Humid. Overcast. No stars to be seen. "Why did they bury her?" he asked. "Why bury her if they were going to leave her to be found in the meeting house?" He thought some more, then said with conviction, "Whoever planted the body was probably not the person who killed her."

CHAPTER 23

THE STATION WAS IN AN UPROAR, first thing the next morning, when Bruno arrived for his appointment with Chief Black. The next step, he felt, was to find a way to interview Mimi, whether her father liked it or not.

But the office was crowded with people he didn't recognize, milling around and talking excitedly. He'd never seen it like this before. Finally he caught the eye of Officer Randy Lewis, the force's high-speed apprehension specialist. Bruno pulled him aside and Randy filled him in: "A kid from the Friends school didn't turn up at home last night. We think it's a kidnapping."

"Is there a ransom note?" asked Bruno.

"Not that we know of."

Bruno made a face. "I need to speak to the Chief right away."

Bruno muscled his way to the Chief's office and peered through the glass. Inside were the child's parents, the mother crying hysterically: Gussie, little Gussie is her only kid. The father sat there, apparently a model of stoicism. More likely he was in shock. The Chief talked practically non-stop. He picked up the phone and, a minute later, Officer Michelle Coxe appeared. She tried to comfort Mrs. Parker. Bruno turned his head—this was a private moment, he shouldn't be watching.

Then he noticed he was standing next to none other than Peaches Cromwell. She was scribbling on her pad, practically salivating.

The Chief spotted Bruno and opened the door. Peaches quickly stepped in front and tried to barge in. The Chief restrained her with a stiff arm to the chest. Peaches opened her mouth in outrage, trying to imply she was being groped. The Chief threw her a look as if to say she was about to get far worse if she didn't back off.

Peaches backed off. The Chief beckoned to Bruno to come in.

As he stepped across the threshold, the energy level jagged up, as if there was a control knob and somebody turned up the lights and volume and the smells and the heat way past maximum.

The Chief didn't waste any time. "We can't hold you in reserve. I want to throw everything we've got at this one right away. I told the Parkers about you and they're willing to cooperate."

He handed Bruno Gussie Parker's class picture. A goofy-looking kid. His head seemed to be wider than it was tall. Spiky blond hair on top. Braces. Freckles. Gussie played guitar so he had calluses on the fingers of his left hand. One of them split open earlier in the week. Left pinkie. The poor mom explained it all to Bruno between sobs.

"What are you waiting for?" the Chief snarled. "Go do your psychic-Kabbalah-whatever thing."

"Is there anything else I can use?" Bruno stammered. No one wanted to get out of there more than he did. "Article of clothing, anything . . ."

"There's his briefcase. We found his briefcase. But it's evidence."

"That's exactly why I need it. I would need to touch it," Bruno said in practically a whisper.

"Go talk to Gary. See what you can work out. Now go."

On the way out, Bruno caught a look from the father, his first sign of life. Suddenly Mr. Parker was on his feet, shaking his fist in Bruno's face. He was screaming, "You find my boy. You bring him back for me."

Bruno backed away slowly, then turned quickly to get to work. He ran headlong into Peaches. She scowled.

All these looks, thought Bruno. Why was everyone angry? This was a time for compassion. Adrenaline was a funny thing. He had seen it countless times with Maggie. Somebody would see her and assume she was an attack dog. The adrenaline would flow from fear. She'd smell it and think they'd want to fight. Up would go her hackles, back would curl her lip. Fear and anger. Anger and fear.

That explained Mr. Parker. And probably the Chief as well. Mostly he's angry with the criminal; kidnapping, murder—both vicious crimes. And when it's a child involved, who wouldn't be angry? But there's also a certain amount of fear. Pressure about his job performance. From the parents. From the Mayor. What would the situation be like in the town now, with two children missing or dead? He and his staff would be working round the clock. And there'd be pressure from Peaches. What was her *shtick*? She wanted to be in the office. Wanted to hear what the parents were saying. Why? So she could reveal their emotional distress for everyone who reads the paper? What would drive anyone to behave that way? They teach 'em in journalism school to say things like, "The public has a right to know." Or talk about the First Amendment and the role of the Fourth Estate in a constitutional democracy. Big abstractions. How do you get from there to Peaches Cromwell? She was like a dog trained to attack the moment she sensed emotion: Fear or anger. Anger or fear. Maggie was lucky last time Peaches didn't bite her. Next time she'd probably bring a hamburger laced with poison or the old chloroformed hanky.

Enough about Peaches. She was a piece of work. Time to get busy and find that kid.

CHAPTER 24

BY ANY STANDARD, little Gussie Parker was Bruno's most successful out-
ing as a psychic detective. It was a textbook case of remote viewing—
or astral projection, as the more spiritually inclined like to call it—and
psychometrics.

First, he concentrated on the picture. That was a bit scary, because
he saw nothing. Normally, when remote viewing works properly, you
get to see and sometimes hear whatever the subject is seeing or hearing. It's like a remote-operated video camera, without wires or electricity—or confusing instructions translated literally from Japanese.
The fact that it wasn't working indicated Gussie was probably unconscious, as in asleep, Bruno hoped.

That left the briefcase. Gary dusted the whole thing for prints. Of
course the handle was full of them, so that was off limits. But there was
the area along the bottom, which had an accordion fold that was all
scuffed up and Gary said he could touch it there. Bruno wasn't hope-
ful. But it turned out that Gussie must've sometimes held the case
pushed right up under his armpit with a hand tucked under the bottom of the case for support. Maybe his arm was getting tired from
carrying it the other way?

Then the whole scene played out as clear as day.

Gussie was walking home from school with another kid. Talking about the teacher. Homework. The girls in the class. Underpants. Their arms would get tired and they'd heave their briefcases. That explained the marks.

The other kid's name was Don. He started teasing Gussie about his work at the racetrack. Shoveling horse poop a big theme.

"Yeah." Gussie got all puffed up. "I know which horses are going to win all the big races."

"That's 'cause your dad's a bookie, not 'cause you know anything about horses."

"Oh yeah? My dad is an accountant. He works for the track. He doesn't do anything illegal. Everything's on the level."

"You're lying!"

They tossed their briefcases at each other. Both missed.

Don came to his turning, and Gussie continued on alone. He was hungry. Thinking about Tastykake. Chocolate Krimpets. Then a car drove up.

There was nothing subtle about what happened next. No dialogue. No trickery.

A man hopped out. He was wearing an overcoat with a watch cap pulled down low on his brow. He grabbed Gussie, who tried to hit him with his briefcase. But he was too close. There was no leverage. The briefcase fell harmlessly to the sidewalk. The man forced Gussie into the backseat, where he hit him over the head with something and knocked him unconscious.

Then things got sketchy. Gussie's emotions were fading as he went out for the count. He tried to call for help and saw his mother's face. He thought he was saved. But she turned her back and stole away. Now there were two men, both wearing Halloween masks—big rubber *T. rex* heads with enormous yellow teeth. Gussie was terrified. They tied him up and threw him somewhere. It was hard to make out. Bruno was tiring. He broke contact with the briefcase and went looking for the Chief.

CHAPTER 25

PEACHES' ARTICLE WAS REASONABLY ACCURATE, FOR ONCE.
She described in intimate, heart-wrenching detail the scene at Logan Pond. Under the direction of the police, the county parks maintenance division was draining the water. It had taken some arm-twisting, but eventually Chief Black had convinced them there was compelling evidence that the remains of Gus Parker would be found there.

Bruno's psychic viewing of the crime scene had shown him that Gussie had been dumped, unconscious, in a body of water. Whether it was Logan Pond or the Atlantic Ocean, he didn't know. For cops and other hardboiled types who know about these things, it's a standing joke that 90 percent of the time a psychic will report that the body's near water. Then, if they find it buried in a crawl space, the psychic will say, "The basement always flooded when it rained," or "It was near the hot-water heater." Ninety percent of everything is near water, so Gary and Nancy and the rest of the force gave Bruno a well-deserved razzing when he burst in, out of breath, from examining the briefcase.

But after further concentrating on the scene, Bruno was able to identify an additional detail: "Something about fossils," he panted, struggling to bring the images into focus. "Big bones. Dinosaurs, I think. Yes, I think it's dinosaurs."

He came out of his trance and realized how ridiculous that must have sounded. But Chief Black and the others appeared to be mobilizing for action—men, dogs, the works. Gardenfield happens to be the site where the first complete fossil skeleton dinosaur had been discovered, more than a century earlier. It was in a marl pit, at the bottom of a ravine, densely wooded, and covered with underbrush. Chief Black organized a search party and invited Bruno to tag along.

As soon as he saw it, the site felt cold to him. It was at the end of a residential street, marked with a small park to commemorate the birthplace of modern paleontology. On a small table, children had placed toy plastic dinosaurs, several dozen of them, like pagan tributes to the creature that had given them so many hours of fun. And, though the ravine itself was heavily wooded, any number of houses overlooked its banks. The spot was hardly private; it just didn't feel right.

After about an hour the Chief wanted to give the dogs a shot. He'd been holding them in reserve to avoid trampling evidence. "The only tracks down there are deer and raccoon. No sign of digging, no sign of anything. Biff, let the dogs do their thing, but I think this site's a bust."

Michelle was perspiring from scrambling up the ivy-covered banks. She was out of breath and appeared to be irritated by something. She took off her hat, wiped her brow and announced, "I never believed this ravine was the actual dinosaur site. Back in the '80s, some kid who was doing a project for the Eagle Scouts said it was here, but I never bought it. They used to teach us in school that the fossils were found in Logan Pond."

The Chief shrugged. "The pond is just a couple blocks from here. What do you think, Bruno? Can't hurt to take a look."

"I want to see it," Bruno replied with conviction.

And, even before he saw the pond, as the Chief drove him and Michelle along the twists and turns of Lake Street, a peculiar tingling running up the insides of his arms told him they were on the right track.

Logan Pond is neither large nor deep. But it is muddy, with a weedy bottom and lots of debris and sediment that make it difficult to search.

Immediately, Biff wanted to run home to get his scuba gear, but the Chief insisted he groom and kennel the dogs properly.

"Pond's too murky," snapped the Chief, reaching for his radio. "We're going to have to drain it." Debbie patched him through to the Director of Camden County Parks.

The county's white trucks arrived quickly, but then things drew to a halt. A group of people—police and parks administrators—stood huddled in a compact group in the center of Lake Street, just below the sluice gates that allow the waters of Logan Pond to drain into the Cooper River. They were focused on a manhole cover, which provided access under the street to the antiquated valve that would open the sluice gates and allow the pond to drain. The parks administrator, a diminutive woman with curly brown hair, was explaining that no one could go down into the sewer system here without proper certification, due to fear of gas leaks.

A lengthy argument ensued, which the Chief finally resolved by calling someone he happened to know in Trenton who was willing to fax over the certification. Now he and the parks director—her name was Dora Goldstein—seemed to be getting along famously.

Two of the brawniest guys from the Parks Department couldn't budge the valve on their own. So the Chief asked Dora to ignore the fact that he was sending Biff down there to help out.

The machinery shrieked, and Biff emerged brushing the iron oxide from his hands. "Just like poppin' a cherry—takes a little spit, sweat, and elbow grease, but oh-so satisfying." The guys from the Parks Department grinned sheepishly—their boss was watching—and shuffled back to their truck.

Dora estimated it would take approximately 24 hours for the pond to drain. She and the chief assigned staff to supervise the site round the clock, and made a date to meet back there, first thing next morning for breakfast.

When they returned, the police had the area cordoned off, yet still there were numerous onlookers. Gussie's family. The team from the police. The crew from the Parks Department who were doing the actual draining. A paleontologist from the university–just in case. The ecology squad. And, of course, the media.

Peaches described the spring weather. The morning drizzle and the sun popping out around 10:30. The leaf shaped like a dinosaur's footprint. She noted the robins and the cardinals. Other birds with less conspicuous coloration, she declined to identify. As the pond level lowered imperceptibly, the various crews and teams and squads went about their work. The family chatted almost normally with the police and the maintenance crew.

Then, as the pond emptied, the atmosphere changed. The tension grew palpable. Mrs. Parker started biting a corner of her handkerchief.

Peaches noticed that, in her own case, her anxiety about the fate of little Gussie was intermixed with a strange notion: What if, instead of his body, another dinosaur skeleton emerged? She surmised that others, particularly the paleontologist, must be having similar thoughts.

Then at last, objects on the bottom began to break the surface. The rusted-out frame of an old Buick. A variety of footballs, cinderblocks, fishing tackle, pantyhose, and assorted trash.

Finally, there was Gussie. First there was the profile of his spine, like a whale breeching. He was lying face down. His spiky blond hair was smeared in muck; his exposed skin covered with leeches. His mother screamed and had to be led away. Mr. Parker had to be physically restrained. The paleontologist and ecologists were clearly uncomfortable with this level of emotion. The pond had been drained and examined; there were no important artifacts and the water level was enough to preserve the fish and other wildlife. They just wanted to leave.

The police did their job with professional efficiency. They photographed and labeled and bagged the rescued body. It was taken off in an ambulance without sirens or lights.

Within a few hours, the coroner confirmed Bruno's vision. Gussie had been knocked unconscious by a blow to the head and tossed into the pond, where he drowned. It looked like first-degree murder.

Peaches' article noted that Bruno's speed and accuracy in this case were uncanny. It wasn't clear that she meant this as a compliment. She quoted a few local residents who said it made them suspicious that he might have committed the crime himself. She neglected to say that this "public sentiment" was derived as follows.

Peaches: Does it make you suspicious that the psychic solved this crime so quickly?

Man or Woman in the Street: Not really.

Peaches: How else could he have known exactly where to look for that poor kid's body?

Man or Woman in the Street: I hadn't really thought about it. I figured he was just doing his job.

Peaches: But isn't it possible he did it himself and then just pretended to see it in a psychic vision?

Man or Woman in the Street: Sure. Anything's possible.

It took her about a dozen intercepts to get three people whose answers might be construed as yes. That's a consensus, and Peaches and the *Pest* were happy to run with it.

When word got out, all of Gardenfield went berserk.

CHAPTER 26

GARDENFIELD WAS LOCKED DOWN. When Alison came in on the train from Philly, she had to pass a security checkpoint before she could leave the station. At least the guards had been from the police force.

Throughout town, in "sensitive locations" such as schools, parks, and so on, there were "security deputies" wearing official DayGlo orange- or lime-colored vests. These were individuals recruited from the towns' contingent of school crossing guards, bicycle parking enforcers, and volunteer fire fighters. They'd been issued walkie-talkies and instructed to be suspicious, intuitive, alert, intrusive, and communicative. Debbie was going nuts.

Alison hurried into the Lenape King and she and Icky retreated to the basement.

"This is freakin' me out," said Icky. "All these vigilantes."

"Are they armed?" asked Alison.

"I don't know. I don't think so. Not most of them, anyway."

"Then it doesn't matter."

Icky couldn't believe it. Alison was so obsessed with that course and her professor, she couldn't see the danger. "Alison, can't you see how messed up this is getting? First, your teacher gets them to write about him in the *Pest* like he's some kind of hero."

"They made it sound like it's just harmless pranks," Alison fumed. "I wanted to throw up."

"He's covering himself so you can't come after him."

"He *thinks* he's covered. The pig. But I've got evidence."

"Alison," Icky pleaded. "Throw it away. Forget about it. Forget about him. I don't even care that you had sex with him. It doesn't matter. Drop the course. Walk away. We still have each other. I love you. I don't want to see you get hurt."

"Hurt? Who's going to hurt me?"

"This murder. Don't you see? This is the cover-up. They're trying to throw the police off the track or at least divert them while they plan their next move. These are dangerous people. Don't you get it?"

"I'm dangerous too," said Alison sullenly. "I want to bring those corporate assholes down. I thought Professor Littlejohn . . . I thought that was what he's all about. I thought that was the whole purpose of my education. To empower regular people like us. For him, it's just a pose. He used me. Now I'm going to use him . . ."

"Alison, what are you talking about? Are you crazy?"

"Icky. I'm not sure anymore. But I'm glad you love me. I love you too. But I need your help. So will you please shut up and just do what I tell you?"

CHAPTER 27

BRUNO FELT OK. But he wanted to be feeling much better. He was entitled. Finding Gussie's body had vindicated his abilities. He should have
been celebrating. Instead, he was under a cloud, thanks to Peaches'
rumor-mongering.

Usually the drive out to the Pines relaxed him. Less than 10 years
ago, Olga's Diner was a reliable landmark. Once you passed Olga's, you
wouldn't see so many strip malls and traffic would generally thin out.
Now you had to use more flexible, but less precise indicators. Bruno
found himself scanning the sky. As soon as he started seeing vultures
rather than crows as the primary scavengers, he knew he was out of
the suburbs and into . . . something else. You couldn't even call it the
country anymore. Marlton had grown up and, much as he hated to
admit it, the Pines was no longer the refuge it once was. He'd been
stuck in stop-and-go traffic for almost an hour and he was exhausted
and out of sorts by the time he got home.

Even Maggie's ecstatic welcome didn't cheer him up. She sat and
cocked an ear, which seemed to say, "Why sit around moping when
we could be playing ball?" The thought of a saliva-covered tennis ball
cheered him momentarily. Then he remembered the girl. They might

have found Gussie's body. But now they had two child murders and they needed to identify the perpetrator before anything else happened.

Bruno stretched out in his recliner. He picked up the NewGarden Biosciences annual report for the first time since he brought it home. Why had he been avoiding it? No answer. He thought about the receptionist. Why had she made it a point of giving it to him? She was beautiful in that decked-out professional sort of way. But the mask had come down for a moment when she'd called out to him. Her eyes seemed haunted. Were they really violet-colored or was she wearing contacts, using make up and choosing the right clothing for effect?

He looked at the annual report. It was printed on thick white stock with some sort of photo collage on the cover. Then he tried to open it. There were some tricky interlocking panels that puzzled him. He tried a couple of different approaches, then resorted to tearing the paper. Inside were the usual bar charts and several pages of text.

He flipped to the back and found what he was looking for. Executive headshots. Perfectly in focus and evenly lit with a warm, pleasant peach-colored light that formed a nice contrast with the potted plants in the background.

He started with Fischer. He looked him squarely in the eye and, after a few moments, succeeded in locking in. It was as if Fischer's eyes were a video camera and his ears a microphone. Bruno could see what he was seeing, both visual and in his mind's eye, and hear what he was hearing. He'd found Fischer at home, sitting in a well-appointed office. Leather chair, big wooden desk, silver writing instruments. *And he was thinking about angels. That's weird*, thought Bruno.

Now he turned to the Jurevicius photo. His eyes were steely. He hadn't really noticed that when they met in person. He concentrated and, again, locked in without difficulty. This time the connection seemed much narrower. He had no sense of where Jurevicius was physically. But all his attention was focused on a woman, lying in bed in what appeared to be a hospital room. The light was dim, and everything was a tone of white or light gray. White sheets and pillows, gray skin, white hair, light gray walls. She lay there sleeping, with a breathing tube and an IV drip from a bottle next to her bed. She appeared to be quite ill, though stable, not in danger of dying. There was a crucifix on the wall behind the bed, which gave the scene a foreign feel, probably French, given Jurevicius' background. And that was it. No movement. No change. Was Jurevicius staring at a photograph? Meditating? Or was there something wrong with the connection?

Bruno broke off and tried to look at more of the report. There were more paper folding problems that needed to be solved, this time involving Velcro fasteners and metal cleats. Eventually, he reached the prize. It was a formal legal document that he eyed with dread. Was he actually going to have to read all of it for clues?

He started scanning: Management's discussion and analysis of results. Ticker symbol—NGBS. Stock price—basically flat. Resistance to biotech in overseas markets. Fischer founded the company about a dozen years ago. Partial buyout by a French venture capital firm, LHOQ, a year later. LHOQ was a minority investor at first, but kept increasing its stake. That explained Jurevicius' role. But where did that leave Fischer?

It was hard to see how any of this mattered to the case. Bruno tossed the K-1 on the floor and tried to fold the rest of the report back into its original configuration. Without much luck. Finally, Maggie settled the issue by dropping her tennis ball in his lap. That was a sign. It really was time to stretch the old legs and get some fresh air.

Though it had been a warm day, it cooled quickly at night; the familiar smell of wood smoke clogged the air. It was overcast, with few stars visible and only a glimpse of a fragment of the moon from time to time.

Rural Tabernacle didn't have streetlights, but the neighborhood was filling in with homes on 5- to 10-acre lots. Some of them were those enormous 5,000-square-foot jobs. One of them had a copper turret and looked like a chateau. A few even had paddocks for horses.

Bruno couldn't wait for his washing machine to die so he could move it out to the front yard. There just wasn't the same sense of privacy or peace of mind that had brought him to the Pines in the first place. Along with the woodsmoke he felt the burden of people's thoughts, confusing background noise.

They turned the corner and headed back to the trailer. Maggie kept trying to run off and check out Carmine, but Bruno called her back. He needed company. Back inside he thought about the Chief chatting up Dora. It all seemed very natural. He didn't know anything about Buddy Black's personal life. Was he married? Single? Divorced? Other? Nah, not the Chief.

How come when Bruno ran into anyone it was a sociopath like Peaches?

He gave wide berth to the NGBS annual report and grabbed his copy of the *Complete Shmegegge* instead. He seemed to recall that there was a chapter on Golems in it. How to make them at home. Just what he needed. Companionship. Seeking long-term committed relationship with nice Jewish monster (female). No family hang-ups or strings attached. Uninhibited sexuality a must.

The chapter was prefaced with a number of warnings: CAUTION: FOR EXPERIENCED STUDENTS ONLY. DO NOT TRY THIS ALONE. Funny they'd put something dangerous and difficult in a *Complete Shmegegge* book. Golem making was supposed to be the most super-secret part of the Kabbalah. Well, Maggie'd be there to keep an eye on him. He trusted her judgment more than that of most people.

As usual, the section began with an annoying whimsical sidebar. It was headed, "The first biotechnologist?" and quoted a 1st-century Rabbi named Yehoshua ben Chananya, who said, "I can take squashes and pumpkins and, with the *Sefer Yetzirah*, make them into beautiful trees." Well, that was something. He'd have to remember to mention that to Dr. Jurevicius, or to Fischer, next time he saw them . . .

He read further and learned that the *Sefer Yetzirah*, or *Book of Creation*, was the oldest book of the Kabbalah. The basic idea was pretty simple. Since God created the universe, and everything else, by speaking words, and since words are made up of letters of the alphabet . . . Kabbalists can control the creative forces of the universe by manipulating the letters properly.

Then it started getting complicated. There were several different prescriptions for making Golems. And you could do it one way to create a male Golem and a different way for a female. That was good.

But then there were different instructions from different Rabbis. In Rabbi Abulafia's system, you had to sound out different letters in a special order, and also breathe and bob your head a certain way. This

113

allowed you to create each part of the Golem's body separately. But it took 35 hours of non-stop chanting to bring the entire being to life.

More accessible was the system of the Riva, where you had to recite a smaller number of paired sounds while moving in a circle. Bruno tried the sounds, "Uu-Yu; Aa-Ya; Ii-Yi; Ee-Ye; Oo-Yo; Bu-Yu; Ba-Ya; Bi-Yi; Be-Ye; Bo-Yo." That wasn't so bad. "Bo-Yo, Bo-Yo, Bo-Yo," he hummed. But that was just the chanting.

You also had to make a life-sized figure out of soil from a place that no one has ever dug and knead it with pure spring water right out of the ground . . . That might be a problem. He was pretty sure he could get by with Kabbalah Water, the brand they sold on the Kabbalah Co-op's website. But unless he could order the dirt online, too, he was probably out of luck. Where could you go in Jersey where no one had been before? Reading further, he saw that the practitioner also needed to wear special clothes and be spiritually and mentally purified. What was that supposed to mean?

To make matters worse, if you did it wrong—in other words, if your circle was going in the wrong direction—you could get trapped in the earth up to your waist and never get out, unless a Rabbi who knew how to do the Golem business correctly came along and got you out.

All of this for a cheap date? It'd be easier and cheaper to fly out to Vegas. You'd have to be a complete *shmegegge* to try making a Golem with instructions like these. He checked the acknowledgements to see if they'd outsourced parts of the writing to Japan or Korea. Then he let the book drop to the floor and shuffled off to bed.

CHAPTER 28

HE WOKE UP to the sound of someone banging on his door. The noise woke Maggie too, and she started to bark.

He looked through the peephole and saw a distorted angle on the Chief's face. He was leering idiotically and appeared to be staggering. Bruno opened the door.

"You just open the door like that, this time of night, out here in the Pines?"

"I figured if it was bad guys, they wouldn't bother knocking."

"What if it was something sinister? The Hookman or the Jersey Devil?"

"I'd have been out of luck."

The Chief pulled his arm out from behind his back and shoved the neck of a champagne bottle in Bruno's face. "The real stuff," he mumbled. "Not California. Definitely not New Jersey. This is French Champagne."

"What for?"

"We got to celebrate."

"Finding Gussie?"

"Yeah. You did a good job. Pretty amazing, you ask me." He popped the cork and poured the overflowing champagne into coffee mugs. He plopped himself into Bruno's recliner and they clinked glasses. "Success," sighed the Chief.

Bruno frowned. "We still haven't found the killers. We don't know the motive. One of the victims is still unidentified. The whole town's still at risk."

"Your glass is half empty," said the Chief. "I'm going to fill it up again." He poured a healthy slug into Bruno's mug. "Mine's half full, but I'm going to fill it up, too, just to be fair." He poured until the wine overflowed and then he stated, "My cup runneth over."

He looked at Bruno expectantly.

Bruno just sat there and patted Maggie nervously, until the Chief shot him another look, jutting his chin in Bruno's direction, until he capitulated and recited, "Surely goodness and mercy will follow me all the days of my life . . ."

"Attaboy. You really believe it, don't you? You're not just saying it?"

"Right." Bruno fidgeted, wondering where all this was leading.

"Good, 'cause I have total confidence that we're going to find a way through this. Or around it. Whatever it takes."

"Around what?"

The Chief went sober and deadly serious. "Mayor Dove just told me to terminate you, effective immediately."

The news blindsided Bruno. "He did what? Why?"

"The publicity . . ."

"You mean Peaches? That's nothing but innuendo. A cliché. *I'm the one who found the crime scene, so I must have done it.* What's my motive?"

"I dunno. Make yourself look good? The point is, the Mayor doesn't want to look bad. Ever. Even for a teeny-tiny moment. So he tries not to take risks."

"But he was the one who wanted you to hire me in the first place. At Peaches' urging. It doesn't make sense."

"I agree." The Chief raised his hand and let it fall in helpless frustration.

"And the killers are still on the loose."

"Don't remind me."

Bruno paced the floor. "I have to see my niece. If I can find out what she saw that day, it could be the key to the whole thing."

"Yeah, it could." The Chief yawned.

"What are you saying: You don't care? You're not interested?"

"No. I care and I am interested." The Chief straightened up and said in a low, sober voice, "I just can't help you anymore. Your niece's father, Bill McRae, works in my building. He's already told me that he doesn't want anyone to go anywhere near his daughter. And he said that applied to you in particular. He wanted to get a restraining order, but he can't since you haven't done anything or gone near her . . ."

"Yet."

"Right. You haven't gone near her *yet*. But since he does work in my building, and he has a . . . relationship . . . with the person I work for . . . he has a certain amount of influence. You see what I mean?" He spoke the word "influence" in such a peculiar way that Bruno had to ask him, "What exactly are you trying to say?"

"I'm glad you asked that. Otherwise I wasn't supposed to tell you. It's like this. They want me to put a tail on you."

"Marvelous."

"Yeah. It is kind of cool. It'll be like having police protection. I just wanted you to know. I thought it over carefully and chose Biff to keep you company. You'll like him more and more, once you get to know him. Really, he's pretty simple to figure out."

"I can't wait."

CHAPTER 29

GOING TO WORK always put Peaches on an emotional roller coaster: The *Pest*'s offices were right across the street from a Catholic high school; the sight of impressionable kids wearing uniforms, going in and out of a building with the words "Honor," "Faith," and "Loyalty" on the side, either made her blood boil or her heart sink. Sometimes both.

Raised Catholic, Peaches had attended the local public high school and then a famous Catholic liberal arts college in the Midwest. So she knew what she was talking about. Basically, it all boiled down to birth control. Peaches needed it; the Pope said she couldn't have it; ergo the Pope was a pig. In addition, she couldn't stand the girls' uniforms—white blouses and plaid skirts every day. End of story: the sight of a Catholic high school was scary and depressing.

Fortunately, the paper had planted a stand of large trees right in front of the entrance to the building. Ostensibly, this was to keep irate readers and other whackjobs from finding the building, or if they did find it, possibly driving a truck or an SUV into the entrance lobby. But Peaches liked to think—and she knew other reporters and editors who felt the same way—that the trees were planted to minimize the irritation of having to look too much at the words "Honor," "Faith," and "Loyalty" on the way to work.

In any case, her spirits always picked up as she passed through the grove of trees. And they got a big lift when she entered the building and was greeted by life-sized murals of heroically muscled printers and paperboys—getting the vital news to "the people." Peaches was a born journalist and by the time she reached her desk she was generally feeling everything was right with the world again.

Today, Peaches had been summoned to an emergency meeting of the editorial board. She'd been warned in advance that the paper had received an anonymous package containing what could potentially be evidence in a criminal matter. So she had dressed appropriately in a pair of Ralph Lauren jeans and a black cashmere pullover. She also took the precaution of bringing latex gloves and a respirator.

Waiting for her in the conference room were the *Pest*'s Publisher, Dan Snarrel, Executive Editor Moe "the Mule" Lubbock, and Managing Editor Jeanine Calisto. All were wearing rubber gloves and seemed to be focused, rather glumly, on a crumpled mailing container on the conference table.

As usual, Jeanine took charge. "Glad you're here, P.C. Now we can get started." She picked up the bag, gingerly, by the corners, adding, "I don't think you'll need the respirator. There doesn't appear to be any powder or anything like that."

Peaches left the respirator in place.

"The contents of the package include part of a garment that has been ripped or cut in half and a letter." Moe Lubbock spread a large sheet of plastic onto the center of the table, and Jeanine carefully shook the two items out onto it. She produced tweezers from somewhere and arranged the garment and the letter side by side.

"Wha's it all about; wha's the letter say?" Peaches demanded through her respirator. She didn't wait for an answer. She got up from her chair and leaned over the table and read the letter herself. It only took her a moment and she snorted in disdain. ". . . is nothing. Jus' a prank," as she fell back into her seat.

Then Dan Snarrel started as though he'd just woken from a nap. "Can you take off that damn mask and talk to me?" he shouted.

Peaches obeyed the publisher, though she took her time about removing the mask.

"This letter says there's evidence of a crime," roared the publisher. "How can you say it's nothing? Jeanine thinks I need to get the attorney in here, but I don't want to pay $250 an hour for his baloney unless I absolutely have to. So you need to explain this to me so I can understand it."

Snarrel was old, effectively deaf and habitually cranky, so Peaches didn't take him or his manner too seriously. "I think this is a just a college prank," she said, straightening her hair, which had come undone when she removed her respirator. "First of all it's anonymous so that tells you something right away. Then what does she say?" Her desire to make her point overcame her fear of exposure; Peaches approached the table without her mask so she could read the letter out loud.

"NATE LITTLEJOHN IS A HYPOCRITE AND A FAKE. STUDENTS IN DEVIANT BEHAVIOR ARE DOING SERIOUS AND IMPORTANT WORK. WE HAVE EVIDENCE THAT IMPLICATES CORPORATE *MALE* FACTORS IN RECENT CRIMES IN GARDENFIELD. LITTLEJOHN IS SUPPRESSING INFORMATION AND SEXUALLY ABUSING STUDENTS. YOU HAVE THE EVIDENCE IN YOUR HAND. PC CROMWELL SHOULD STOP COVERING LITTLEJOHN'S BUTT—OR IS HE FUCKING HER TOO?—AND WRITE THE TRUTH INSTEAD."

Peaches' voice dripped with derision as she read the signature, "A FRIEND." She pulled back from the table and added, "I'm glad to say I do *not* have the evidence in my hand. Read my lips: I did not have sex with Nate Littlejohn, not one single time. I hope that's perfectly clear."

"We appreciate your candor," said Jeanine, somewhat icily. "But I'm still not sure what to make of this . . ." She picked up the garment with the tweezers and turned it around in several directions to examine it. "It is stained, but who knows with what?"

"Looks like Karl Marx boxers covered with pecker tracks," the Mule observed sagely.

"Not funny, Moe," retorted Peaches, looking to Dan Snarrel for confirmation. The publisher appeared to be dozing—a good sign—so she continued. "The writer says this is evidence, but what does it prove? Even if the substance is . . . DNA, how did it get there?"

"It might not be Littlejohn's . . ." said Jeanine.

"That's easy enough to check," argued Moe. "But it should be on her clothing, not his. This only proves that she had access to his shorts . . ."

—"I don't think it's even a woman sending this," said Peaches. "Women don't think this way. We're not obsessed with body parts and emissions. That's how men think."

Moe tried to disagree. "She talks about 'malefactors,' and emphasizes the first four letters, MALE. It's like she's obsessed about being victimized."

"How insulting," said Peaches, raising her voice. "And predictable. Resorting to stereotypes and blaming the victim. I expected more from you, Moe, but you're just like all the others."

"So what do you think this is about?" quivered Moe, thoroughly whipped.

"I think this is from some guy in Littlejohn's class. He saw my article and that gave him the idea. I'm sure Littlejohn brags about what kind of boxers he wears; that'd be just like him. So the student got a pair online and then masturbated on them. A big joke. Ha-ha. If he can get us to publish the story, then he's committed a deviant act and received public credit for it. He'll be the star of his class and we'll be the laughingstock."

Jeanine and Moe were nodding in agreement, when Dan Snarrel came back to life. "What's it going to cost us?" he roared.

"What do you mean?" asked Jeanine. "How much is it going to cost, if we're wrong and we don't turn this over to the police?"

"There's no risk," said Peaches.

"There's always risk," Snarrel shot back.

"There's no connection between the stained shorts and the kids who were killed in Gardenfield. It's a logical fallacy. That's why I think it's a prank."

"She says it's proof she's telling the truth," Snarrel persisted. "If she's telling the truth about one thing, then she's got credibility for the larger accusation. It makes sense to me. How much does a DNA test cost?"

"I read that you can now get a person's entire genome sequenced for 10 grand," Peaches answered without hesitation.

Jeanine wanted to ask why they'd need the entire genome, but she wasn't sure and didn't want to sound like an idiot.

Moe had no such qualms. "You'd have to get Littlejohn to consent to provide a sample for matching. Either that, or P.C. would have to harvest some surreptitiously."

"Shut up, Moe. I can get you fired if you keep that up," Peaches snapped.

"On the other hand, if we turn this over to the police," Moe shot back, "we have a great story. Illicit sex. Recriminations. A new angle on the Quaker Killer. We could string it along for weeks. It'd sell papers."

"The advertisers might not like it," said Snarrel.

"That's true."

"And we'd have to get the damn lawyers involved, if we're treating it like evidence . . . how much did you say for the DNA test?"

"Ten thousand."

"That sound right to you Jeanine?"

"'Bout right, I guess. I can check on it."

"Let's not waste any more time on it. This is a college prank. An anonymous note with a foul enclosure. Toss the whole thing and get back to work."

CHAPTER 30

QUENTIN RICHARDS HADN'T FELT SO DEPRESSED since his time in the military. Now there had been two casualties associated with the school. Why was this happening? Who was behind it?

He walked out of his office on the ground floor of the main building, telling his secretary he was just stepping out for air. The school grounds were peaceful. It was nearing the end of the day. All of the children were inside, in their classrooms, awaiting dismissal.

Master Quentin walked around back toward the playground. Then he strode willfully into the cemetery where the lofty sycamores were just leafing out. In the children's butterfly garden, new blooms would soon be attracting a variety of insects—hungry for nectar, spreading pollen around. All was still and calm. He looked around from the back of the school, across the play field, toward the meeting house and back to where he stood in the cemetery. Everything was right. Everything in its place. Except for the presence of the security guards in their black commando sweaters and berets, he could have pretended that all was well, nothing out of the ordinary at Gardenfield Friends.

But there was no escaping the fact: the guards were there—Quentin himself had asked for them the day following Gussie's disappearance—and all was not well. He put his hand to his collar. Quentin realized he was feeling flushed and anxious. His skin was breaking out in sweat, and cold chills pulsed up and down his frame.

He mopped his face with a linen handkerchief and carefully replaced it in his back pocket. Then he walked quickly back to his office, clutching his suit jacket closed against the chill. He picked up the phone, and angrily punched the keys for the number he'd scrawled on his blotter.

"*Nyew gaw*den *buyo*-sci-ences. Can you hold please?"

Master Quentin held, dabbing at drops of sweat as he waited.

"How can I direct your *cawl*?"

"I need to speak with Dr. Fischer," replied Quentin, trying hard not to take it out on the receptionist.

"*Cyanni* tell him who's calling?"

"This is Quentin Richards from Gardenfield Friends School. He'll know what it's about."

"Hold please."

The sound of children exploding from the building after six hours of compression greeted his ear. They were shouting, cheering, raving. Not a care in the world, in spite of everything.

Suddenly he realized he was listening to Fischer's recorded voice. She'd dumped him into voice mail. OK. He'd talk to the machine. "Dr. Fischer, Quentin Richards here. I appreciate the use of your security people, but I have to say their uniforms are totally inappropriate for the school grounds. Can you please have them wear ordinary clothes while they're here? I . . ." He nearly added a more personal message, then thought better of it.

He stepped out onto the front porch to watch the children leave the schoolyard. Most were getting on the bus. They weren't letting kids walk home or ride bikes anymore, so that meant more parents had to pick up. The street was a hive of activity.

Alison and Icky walked by on the opposite side of Garden Avenue. They were holding hands. They released their grip long enough to wave to Master Quentin. He acknowledged them only with the slightest dip of his chin. He glanced nervously toward the commando from NewGarden, to see if he noticed. Some instinct told him that the less these people knew, the better. Now Alison and Icky were changing direction. They were crossing the street to approach the school. Frantic, Master Quentin ordered them away with a surreptitious shake of the head. It was definitely not the right time for a social call.

One of the last mothers to pick up her child that day was Judy Cohen. She was driving a Lexus hybrid SUV and was running late—mostly because of the baby. Mimi scrambled into the car without greeting her mother. She buckled herself into the seat next to her sister's rear-facing crashproof contraption and announced, "I'm hungry. Let's get Chinese food."

CHAPTER 31

BRUNO HADN'T FELT SO DEPRESSED since his marriage broke up. Watching Judy Cohen run her errands brought back a flood of memories. The good ones made him sad because they were gone forever. The first six years with Sharon—Judy's baby sister—had been OK, despite some of the obvious negatives, such as the unremitting hostility from his in-laws. He wasn't Jewish enough for Mr. and Mrs. Cohen. Judy saw him as a *shlimazl*. And her husband, Bill McRae, William R. McRae, Attorney at Law, always hated his guts, pure and simple. Why Sharon's parents tolerated McRae, who was not just a *goy*, but a dyed-in-the-wool *shaygetz*—a non-Jewish husband, and an arrogant *shmuck* to boot—while they were bothered by his weakness for ham and cheese sandwiches, was something Bruno never understood.

He'd always liked Mimi best. She was a mischievous kid who didn't take things too seriously. Bruno missed seeing her, and he'd never had a chance to meet the younger sister; in fact, he didn't even know what her name was.

But in order for that to happen, Bruno had to reach some kind of understanding with McRae. Thus he'd badgered the Chief to set up a meeting. Bruno realized it was the first time he'd actually come in through the front door of the Municipal Building, and the sinking feeling was unmistakable. The Chief had warned him he'd probably be wasting his time. "Ready to enter the lion's den?" he joked as he led Bruno down the hall to McRae's office.

McRae was sitting at his desk, aligning the edges of a stack of papers, when they entered. He had a stocky build with a barrel chest. Now in his mid-40s, McRae was mostly bald on top, yet he wore his gray-blond hair collar length, along with a mustache, a goatee, and a large gold earring that Mr. Clean would have been proud of. He looked more like a bouncer at a biker bar than an attorney, which is exactly what he intended.

McRae stood up when they entered. He greeted the Chief but only glared at Bruno. Without speaking, he set down the stack of papers he'd been studying and positioned it neatly in a precise location on his desk. Several quick strides brought McRae face to face with his visitors. He raised his right arm; Bruno couldn't tell if his ex-brother-in-law was going to put an arm around his shoulders or punch him in the nose.

McRae did neither. Instead he pointed a finger and shook it angrily. "Joey," said McRae as if he'd been having difficulty remembering Bruno's name. "Joey Kaplan. I thought I'd seen the last of you after Sharon dumped you. But here you are, in my office, going around with a ridiculous fake name, pretending to have psychic powers and bilking the taxpayers."

"I didn't bilk anybody, Bill. The Chief called me up and hired me to do a job. I just located that poor kid's body . . ."

"You sure did. You found it in record time. I wonder how you managed that? Just like always: setting up your tricks in advance to make yourself look good. Did you kill Gussie yourself, Joey, or did you just work with the people who did? How much are you going to charge us to cough up the name? Or are you going to murder somebody else so you can try to run up your bill?"

McRae's face was bright red. He was shouting, every muscle straining with tension, his lips within six inches of Bruno's face. Chief Black stepped between them. He tried to pull Bruno away, but the psychic held his ground. He sidestepped the Chief so he could look McRae in the eye. "I need to see Mimi," he said quietly. "I can solve this case, I just need a few minutes with her."

McRae exploded. "Who the fuck told you she was involved? That was supposed to be confidential. Was it you, Buddy? 'Cause if it was I'm going to kick your ass."

The Chief walked up to McRae and put his hands on his hips. "Go ahead, Bill. Take your best shot."

McRae seemed to deflate physically as he sized up the Chief's lanky strength. "I can sue you, Chief, and fine you. Nobody was supposed to give out her name."

"He was working on the case, Bill," the Chief said with a hint of menace. "He needed to know."

"Well that was a big mistake, and I won't tolerate any more indiscretions," hissed McRae, jabbing a finger past Chief Black in Bruno's direction. "You do not have my permission to go anywhere near my daughter. You're not working for the Borough anymore, so you have no business hanging around. If you go within 20 feet of my house or any member of my family, I'll have you locked up . . ."

"You can't say that, Bill," the Chief interjected. "We're not locking up Bruno."

"If he harasses my family . . ."

"He's not threatening anyone with physical harm. He's just requesting an interview. That's not a crime."

"I don't want him around my house. He's a suspect . . ."

"He is not a suspect. The newspaper does not get to decide who's a suspect and who isn't."

"The Mayor says he's a suspect."

"The Mayor is a politician. He's not the law in this town and neither are you. Now why don't you go collect some overdue property tax bills and leave us to solve this murder? You'd really be doing me a favor if you'd let Bruno talk to your daughter. I'd guarantee . . ."

"You'll do nothing of the kind. I guarantee that if I find him—Joey Kaplan—anywhere near my house or family, I will deal with it personally. I'll kick your ass like it's never been kicked before, Joey. I'll rip your face off. I'll break every bone in your body. I'll bury you, you dickless weasel."

"That sounds like a threat," said the Chief. "Maybe you're the one who needs a restraining order, Bill." And he reached for his radio to call for help. It took Gary and Michelle about 30 seconds to come upstairs. Chief Black told them to keep an eye on McRae until he calmed down. Then he hustled Bruno out of the office.

"You can't do this, Black," McRae ranted. "I'll have your badge. If anything happens to my daughter I'll hold you responsible. That man is playing you for a fool. If you won't lock him up, at least you better keep him under observation."

"Don't worry Bill. We're way ahead of you."

"I *am* worried, Buddy, which means you better worry too. You better make sure you keep tabs on this jerk. Cause if you don't, your ass is mine . . ."

McRae's threats melted into incoherence as the Chief led Bruno down the stairs to the police station. "Bill's a real asset to the town." He grinned. "When he litigates, he never loses. He either wins or gets tossed out for contempt. When he negotiates, we usually get sued. But we never lose."

"How satisfying." Bruno tried to match the Chief's jaunty tone without success.

"I'm serious now. Biff's going to be watching your every move to make sure you stay away from Mimi. So don't you even try." The Chief gave Bruno one of those direct looks that are supposed to confirm an agreement.

"I'll do my level best," replied Bruno, meeting his gaze head on.

"Make sure you do."

CHAPTER 32

AFTER AN HOUR OF TAILING BRUNO, Biff felt he was about to go out of his mind. Bruno had come up with a bike somewhere, which made him extremely difficult to follow. Biff couldn't keep up on foot and, when he used the prowl car, Bruno would duck into alleys or cut across parking lots to make it difficult for him.

Eventually, he called the Chief for advice. "Hey, Chief, can I impound his bicycle?"

"No. I've got a better idea. Why don't you come back here and borrow a bike from one of the meter maids?"

Biff had no choice but to assent. He didn't want anyone to see how shaky he was on a bicycle. As a body builder, he was in tip-top shape. But he was also muscle-bound and none too secure balancing a bike.

When Biff returned, he couldn't find Bruno. However, two of the red-headed speed freaks, Joe Kennedy and Sammy Pearl, were sitting on the low wall in front of the Presbyterian church, razzing him: "Biff, you ride like a pussy."

"Shut up, you hard-ons, or I'll bust you."

They laughed insanely, spurred on by Biff's obvious annoyance.

Finally, they calmed down enough for him to ask, "Have either of you seen the psychic?"

In response, they started wiggling their fingers like stage magicians casting spells, and making horror movie sound effects: "Whheee yuuuuuu zzzzpppp."

Biff let the bicycle crash to the ground. He set his jaw and approached the teenagers, his hand fondling his nightstick. They pretended to cower in fear, but they did in fact cough up the information he wanted, pointing up the street toward the Chinese restaurant.

Biff wondered how he hadn't noticed him before, but Bruno was standing on the sidewalk in plain sight, pretending to take a photograph. In fact, he was spying on Judy Cohen, with a pair of miniature binoculars.

"What's up?" asked Biff.

"Two egg drop, three wonton."

"That's funny."

"I know. Five soup, only four people."

Biff made a face. "I could arrest you for making a joke like that."

"You know, you're right," said Bruno segueing from Buddy Hackett to Jackie Mason. "I couldn't agree more. Ethnic jokes are degrading. But let's be honest about it . . ." switching on the fly to Milton Berle: "Do you remember the tornado that hit South Jersey?"

"What?"

"It caused $10 million worth of improvements."

"C'mon, Bruno," Biff protested. "This is a nice town. Lots of people want to live in a place like this."

"Yeah, it is nice here," Bruno agreed, pretending to muse over the glorious quality of life in Gardenfield. In fact, he was timing his transition back to Jackie Mason. "It's like a Jewish neighborhood. You can go wherever you please. Nobody's afraid of getting mugged by an accountant."

"That used to be true," Biff replied, "before all this trouble started . . ."

—"Trouble . . . ?" Bruno was teeing up the next one-liner, when an attractive young woman with a baby stroller approached them. "Yoo-wer Bruno X? The sy-kick? I've been reading about you in the pay-per!"

Bruno blushed. "You caught me red-handed." He looked at her carefully. The stroller was a sophisticated piece of machinery and the dog she was walking appeared to be a Maltese poodle, a bad sign. Bruno wondered if she was going to threaten him. Maybe she had a tire iron hidden under the baby's blanket to bash his head in. Or she might sic the Maltese on him. Many of that breed were known to be as vicious as they were neurotic.

Instead she extended her hand and gave his arm an affectionate squeeze. "I want to thank you *fwor* what *yoo-wer doo-in'* here. My husband would say the same thing if he were here. In fact, everybody we know is behind you. We think it's *harr-ible* what they've been saying about you in the *pay-per*. Just *ig-noowr* them and keep up the good work." Then she continued on her walk.

Bruno was staggered. He looked at Biff to see if he would confirm what had just happened. Biff must have read his thoughts. He howled with laughter. "You can't tell if she's kidding or not, can you?"

The joke was growing stale for Bruno. Better get back to the task at hand. He gave the binoculars to Biff and pointed to the restaurant. "Take a look at this. Can you tell me who those kids are?"

Biff trained the binoculars on the restaurant. "Judy Cohen and her daughters? They're the ones I'm supposed to keep you away from."

"Yeah, I recognized them. It's the other two love-birds I'm asking about."

"That's Alison Wales and her boyfriend, the Murphy kid. Everybody calls him Icky."

"They look pretty cute sitting there together all snuggled up." Alison had brought her iPod and she was sharing one of the earplugs with Icky. They were sitting together, listening to the same song, swaying slightly, arms around each other's waists. "It seems I see them everywhere I go. What's the story with them?"

"Alison's a college kid. She studies at Penn. She and Icky have been an item all through high school. He's not going to college though."

"What's he do?"

"He's one of our local scumball speedfreaks. We think he's trying to set up a meth lab along with those kids sitting on the wall."

"The red-headed ones?"

"The very same."

Just then Judy and Mimi emerged from the restaurant with two large bags of takeout.

"Aren't you going to follow them?" Biff grinned provocatively. He seemed bored, ready for some action.

"What's the point, Biff?" replied Bruno. "It's obvious they're about to go home. If I followed them, you'd follow me and grab me before I could talk to them. I know where they'll be, so I'm just going to have to ditch you before I go see them."

"I wouldn't advise that," Biff said.

"No, of course you wouldn't. I've been getting a lot of good advice today. All of it free."

"Not much of a day for you then."

"No," Bruno agreed. "And it isn't over. Not by a long shot."

CHAPTER 33

AFTER THE MUSIC ENDED, Icky and Alison were at cross-purposes. Icky wanted to smoke but was out of cigarettes. Alison wanted to get a copy of the paper to see if they were following up on the lead she'd provided.

They paid the bill and headed up Old Kings Road in search of news and nicotine. Alison scored first. She found a box selling the *Pest* and started riffling through it, looking for an exposé of sexual harassment at Penn.

Meanwhile, Icky was prattling excitedly about an apartment that he had rented with Sammy and Joe. It was cheap, discreet, and kind of a dump—not that any of them cared. As they approached the corner of Mechanic Street, Icky made a show of sniffing the air. There was an aromatherapy spa on the corner, and the place reeked of noxious essential oils and sinus-penetrating herbal concoctions. "It smells like a Superfund site." Icky was pleased with his clever choice. "Put down that paper for a sec so I can show you the secret entrance." Icky led Alison around the corner, where a door allowed entrance to the apartment in back. It was painted the same shade of white as the entire side of the building. Hardly secret, but certainly discreet. The only other feature was an old-fashioned fire escape with elaborate counterweights that provided emergency egress for the second- and third-story apartments. "We're movin' in our stuff and things'll be cookin' in a coupla days," Icky crowed.

Just then, one of the NewGarden security guards happened to be coming up Mechanic Street from the direction of the Friends School. He was still dressed in commando getup. The combination of the beret, several days' growth of beard, the commando sweater, and the visible sidearm gave him a startling and formidable aspect. Icky perked up when he saw him. He sniffed the air like a hound picking up a scent and told Alison excitedly, "Must be a foreign brand if I can smell it on top of this stench." And he rushed over to bum a cigarette.

Icky returned a moment later, inhaling with obvious pleasure. "Right again: Gauloises! I don't think that guy knows any English, but us tobacco connoisseurs speak the same language. He was so pleased that I like Gauloises, he gave me the rest of his pack." Icky held out the distinctive blue package with four or five cigarettes in it for Alison to see.

She had more pressing things on her mind. She'd already been through the *Pest* once, carefully, page by page. There was no coverage of her story. Now she was thrashing each sheet, her fury growing as she noticed what they were writing about instead: car crashes, the granting of liquor licenses, the weather and the heartbreaking tale of a family that couldn't buy a condo in Garden Township because they owned too many dogs. What did she need to do, connect all the dots, spell it out for them?

Furious, Alison wadded the whole paper into a ball and dropped it in the gutter where she started kicking it, swearing violently each time she struck it. Icky joined in and soon they were playing a form of soccer, punctuated by profanity and, eventually, laughter.

They sat on the curb in front of the barbershop to catch their breath. "Sonsabitches," moaned Alison, shaking her head.

Icky was lighting another Gauloises directly from the one he'd just finished smoking. "I keep telling you, let it go."

Alison shrugged. "Easy for you to say." She took the cigarette from Icky's lips and puffed distractedly. The harsh tobacco made her cough.

Icky tenderly took the cigarette from her so she wouldn't burn herself by accident. Finally the spasms died down enough for Alison to complete the thought that had just struck her: "If I were you, I'd stay away from those security guards. They give me the creeps."

CHAPTER 34

AFTER A BIT OF HAGGLING, Biff and Bruno came up with an agreement: drinks and a movie. Biff couldn't drink, of course, while he was working. The opposite was true for Bruno. After getting fired, screamed at and threatened by McRae—plus the stress of two murders to solve—he needed a cocktail or two.

They drove to the theater in separate cars; otherwise Biff couldn't credibly claim to be "tailing" Bruno. They headed out of town, caravan-style, toward the race track circle—which wasn't there anymore, it was just a maze of traffic lights and complicated turnarounds—and pulled into a huge parking lot directly across from the world-famous Berry Hill Shopping Mall. Fortunately the bar and the movie theater shared the same parking lot. So Bruno could imbibe as he pleased and then walk to the movie. That meant Biff wouldn't have to bust him for drunk driving.

Bruno only had the rough outlines of a plan worked out. He'd arranged for a friend to call McRae and tell him to stand by for an important service of process that would be arriving shortly. That would keep him stuck at the office for a while. Which meant that Bruno had to figure out a way to ditch Biff and make it back to Judy's house before McRae gave up and went home.

That part made sense. But Biff was a bulldog. Bruno really had no idea how he could get free of him: He would have to simply follow his instincts and hope an opportunity would come his way.

One thing in his favor was the fact that Biff had not yet seen *Flying Panda, Rolling Doughnut 3*. This was a Hollywood techno-thriller with Chinese actors, lavish special effects, and lots of fighting. Bruno felt sure Biff would find it totally engrossing. The story line featured a medieval Chinese sage who is given a cup of special tea that transports him to modern-day Los Angeles. He battles gangs, police, and corrupt business interests who are all trying to kill him—he doesn't know why. Only his incredible fighting skills and the friendship of big-breasted, ample-bottomed, dewy-eyed Latina heartthrob Katarina Martinez (Bruno wondered why the tabloids didn't call her K-Mart) enable him to defeat his assailants and reveal that the heirs of Confucius are actually the street people of L.A.

The bar was a gaudy place full of television sets tuned to different stations, faux Tiffany lamps, mirrors decorated with Bourbon Street themes, and other inducements to high-spirited fun. Fortunately, the drinks were "industrial strength." Bruno's martini filled a 16-ounce glass. He offered to buy one for Biff, but the gambit failed; Biff wasn't even tempted. He was busy studying the non-alcoholic drink menu, which featured concoctions containing ingredients like peanut butter, honey, peppermint extract, and whipped cream.

Bruno was amazed when Biff actually ordered one of them. *This was a good sign, wasn't it?* Bruno asked himself, feeling optimistic.

But the next thing he knew, the young cop was plying him with a list of questions and personal observations pertaining to all things psychic that he'd been storing up ever since Bruno had started working with the force.

"I think psychics are basically con artists," Biff confided.

"Me too."

"Do you really?"

"No. But I don't feel like arguing tonight."

Biff ignored this and launched into a discourse about what he'd observed about psychics from watching cable TV. While he was speaking, Bruno stole a surreptitious glance under the bar. He noted that the keys were attached to Biff's belt with some kind of heavy-duty hardware. Not much chance that he'd ever leave them lying on the bar when, or if, he happened to go to the bathroom. And they'd be impossible to pickpocket. He'd have to think of something else.

When Bruno started paying attention again, Biff was still debunking TV psychics. ". . . they just throw out these general statements that are cleverly chosen to produce predictable responses from most people. Isn't that how you do it, too?"

Bruno had to admire Biff's lack of tact. *Well, if he wants to get personal, let's get personal.* "Cold reading is kind of a skill in itself," Bruno responded. "It's like interrogating a suspect. Don't you get better results if you ask the right questions?"

"Yeah. But that's different."

"What's different about it?"

"We don't claim to have magic powers."

"Neither do I."

"People think you do . . ."

"I don't know where they got that idea. I'm certainly not responsible for anyone thinking that."

"But you take advantage of the perception. That makes you even more of a con than you already are."

"OK, OK." Bruno knew he needed to extricate himself from this conversation—right away. "Anyway, I don't do cold reading. I find clues that are the residue of people's emotions. You could think of them as emotional fingerprints or mental DNA. That's how I found Gussie. The record of his feelings was attached to his briefcase."

"That's amazing," said Biff. "Do you know who killed him?"

"Unfortunately, everything I saw was from Gussie's perspective. He didn't know what was happening or why. And he didn't get a clear look at the people that attacked him. My guess is they were professionals."

"Why do you say that?"

"It's hard to explain. The image of his attacker kept changing. At times it was an alien monster, a mobster, and even his mother. Sometimes there was one assailant. Sometimes two."

"Doesn't sound like any professional hit men I ever heard of."

"I think I was connecting to his fear. The killer must have been very non-descript. He, or they, did it without emotion. So Gussie's mind supplied the details."

"That part isn't really psychic, is it? It's more deductive."

"Intuitive, maybe? I don't know exactly how it works. But I do know that I can pick up clues that are too ephemeral for you guys to spot. But then we have to work together to anchor them to physical evidence."

"Wow. That's really cool. Why don't you try to get that reward from the Amazing Randi? One million bucks just for passing his test? No other psychic is willing to take him up on it. But you're the real thing."

Bruno sighed deeply. He hated answering questions like these. He really had to find a way to ditch Biff. Just to preserve his sanity. "It wouldn't work. I can't pick up anything when I'm in a hostile environment. I need subjects that cooperate. Or at least leave me alone. Speaking of which, why don't we get those movie tickets . . . ?"

He really needed to find a way to get to Judy's house and interview Mimi before McRae, that *shmuck*, figured out the service of process was fake and went home.

CHAPTER 35

CONNOISSEURS OF THE CINEMA in the South Jersey suburbs do not patron-ize the Loews 24-plex across from the Berry Hill Mall. They prefer the Ritz, in spite of its obscure location in Voorhees Township. Although the selection of movies is probably 80% identical in the two places, the ambience at the Ritz is not designed to attract mall rats, as it is at the 24-plex. The floors in the auditorium do not feel sticky from spilled soft drinks. And the lobby does not have a carnival atmosphere like the one at Loews with garish lighting, plenty of mirrors, action/adven-ture games lining the walls, and junk food. As it lacks the elements that teenagers find so appealing, it also lacks teenagers. Which has a certain appeal for serious moviegoers.

Bruno didn't realize this when they decided to catch the movie at the 24-plex. But as soon as he saw the lobby, he knew they'd come to the right place. Biff seemed to be in his natural element. His already formidable chest and shoulders seemed even more pumped up than usual, and his eyes darted greedily from shooting games to car chase games to intergalactic strategy and warfare games.

Biff waited in one line for popcorn. Bruno stood at the opposite end of the counter and purchased about a half-dozen giant-sized boxes of candy. Something made him choose two boxes of Milk Duds, one gigantic box of Almond Joy, and an equally large package of Dots. He quickly stuffed these into his pants and jacket pockets, before Biff could see what he was doing.

When the film finally started rolling, Biff seemed edgy and restless. The historical setup took a while. There was too much jawing and court etiquette, too many funny costumes. But when an unprincipled warlord sent his thugs to waylay the sage and his entourage, a gigantic battle ensued. Bruno could tell that Biff was studying each and every move. Even the impossible ones that were obviously generated by computer. Like when the sage jumped vertically 20 feet in the air and then started delivering a flurry of kicks and sword thrusts as he corkscrewed softly to the ground.

And this is a guy who thinks psychics are cons, thought Bruno to himself. He waited a bit, however, until the story reached present-day L.A. and the sage was going to have to take on an entire street gang single-handedly. "Gotta pee," he mumbled and got up to go as though it were the most normal thing in the world. Biff almost fell for it, but then recovered in time. He tore himself away from the movie and accompanied Bruno to the men's room.

They had the place to themselves, and Bruno took his time, talking to Biff about this and that while he performed at the urinal. Biff went as well, but didn't try to keep up his end of the conversation. Bruno thought that was a good sign.

When they found their places again, the street gang had been subjugated and, naturally, had decided to adopt the Chinese sage/martial artist as their leader. Then there was some confusing business about evil corporate types, who were deliberately selling faulty GFI outlets to orphanages in the Third World. Then the sage rescued K-Mart from a gangbang, but he had to fight her, too, before he could win her heart. They engaged in a dramatic confrontation, which, according to some critics, borrowed choreography from *Swan Lake*, substituting jabs and kicks for *relevés* and *entrechats*.

Bruno knew this was the moment. He uttered a low groan, "unnnhhhh," and punched Biff on the shoulder. "Sorry, man. When you gotta go . . ."

"You just went," Biff protested.

"C'mon," Bruno grabbed at his arm to hurry him along. "Gotta go *now.*"

In the bathroom, there was a small group of 13- to 15-year-olds, combing their hair, talking trash, and practicing their own karate moves. They were dressed in the latest rapper-approved fashion, but they were clearly harmless suburban kids.

Bruno hurried into one of the stalls and locked the door. The kids laughed that he'd come with his own armed guard. They also razzed Biff, who was not amused.

The psychic went to work. He started moaning and grunting like someone struggling to move his bowels. Then he made a noise like thunder as he dropped the entire package of Almond Joy into the toilet bowl.

"Diss-gusting!" cried one of the teenagers in a doo-rag and a green jersey with the name McCoy across the shoulders. His face wrinkled in pain, then broke out in a huge grin.

Inexplicably a stench filled the bathroom, as Bruno primed himself for the next bombing run. Was someone else in here, using another stall? Or was it a psychic artifact? Encouraged, Bruno revved up the sound effects for an even bigger strain. This time he emptied two giant boxes of Milk Duds into the bowl simultaneously. After the splashes, he moaned piteously. "I think it was the jalapeño poppers back there at the saloon."

The boys roared with laughter—even as their faces reflected total nausea. "You better go in there and help him, bro," they said to Biff, who couldn't believe his misfortune. He sensed that Katarina Martinez was about to get naked and here he was in the bathroom, keeping an eye on—what—a colleague with dysentery? What was he doing here?

Bruno started winding up for a new round of moans. Everybody knew what was coming. In fact, Bruno was getting the Dots ready for a strafing run. He muttered piteously, "*This* could take a while."

That did it for the kids. "Total gross-out, man. Let's go back and see what Emily and Natilda are doing. Even they ain't so disgusting as this is."

That left Biff standing there by his lonesome. He looked at Bruno's scrawny legs under the stall door with his pants pulled down around his ankles. Where was the psychic going to go in his condition? It was stupid to wait around. "Can I trust you?" he asked softly. "I think you need your privacy and I'd just as soon go back to the movie."

A handful of Dots splashed like machine gun fire peppering the surface of a placid lake. Bruno's moan had become a high-pitched sob. "I'll be OK. I'll be lucky if I'm not here all night."

"OK," said Biff, running for the door. "I'll look for you back in the theater."

It was all Bruno could do to force himself to wait a full minute, to make sure the coast was clear. Then he ran like hell. He figured he had about 45 minutes to get to Mimi's house and talk to her before Biff realized what had happened and called in the report.

CHAPTER 36

WHY WOULD A WOMAN like Judy Cohen stay married to an arrogant *shmuck* like Bill McRae? People act like this is some big mystery, but in fact it's pretty simple.

Judy was the eldest of three sisters, all overachievers, daughters of ambitious, education-endorsing, Depression-era Jews. As a Bryn Mawr grad, and a product of Jefferson Medical School, there was no question of her intelligence, her endurance, or her ability to make decisions under pressure.

So why settle for someone like McRae, when she could have had someone smarter, more sensitive, providing emotional support, a more compatible background, and a better income? In short, why didn't she marry a good Jewish boy, there were so many nice ones available?

The reason, to be perfectly blunt, is that Judy Cohen was even more arrogant than her husband, though possibly less of a fool. She needed a man with a thick hide; otherwise the poor jerk would be pulverized by her. No Jewish men from families who have been in America a generation or more have this quality any longer, though many have been destroyed in the vain attempt to prove that they do.

Judy had always liked Bruno. She found him amiable, eccentric. She enjoyed hearing about his misadventures—from a distance. She'd also thought he was a terrible match for her sister and never hesitated to say so. McRae had liked to think of himself as the virtuous defender of . . . what? He was too sophisticated to use terms like "morality" or "virtue." Instead he talked about what was "right," or "just," or when he was really inspired, "appropriate." He liked to brag that he "could have made four times as much working in a law firm," as if that made him a better person. Never mind that Judy's income more than made up the difference.

According to McRae's worldview, Bruno's behavior wasn't appropriate. He wasn't a proper husband. He didn't fit in with the family. He was a bad influence on the kids. He deserved it when Sharon cheated on him and divorced him. And if McRae had to break his skull to teach him a lesson, Bruno should thank him for the privilege.

Thankfully, Judy was a bit more rational. Once her baby sister was free of Bruno's lunatic influence, she knew there was nothing to worry about. It gave her a leg up on her sister to be on friendly terms with "the ex." She'd have welcomed Bruno's attention to the kids, as it would've given her another potential babysitter.

Her acceptance of Bruno further enraged Bill, and his anger gave her additional leverage over her husband. So Judy invited Bruno in for a glass of wine when he appeared, panting, at her door.

"Been a while," she noted laconically.

It was only then Bruno realized he hadn't planned what he would do or say once he made it to Judy's house. He couldn't just blurt out, "Where's Mimi? I need to interrogate her." On the other hand, every second counted.

As Judy rummaged through the fridge, looking for an open bottle of chardonnay, Bruno said the first thing that came into his head: "Judy, you look fabulous." And she really did. She was decked out in a smart, close-fitting wool dress, accessorized with a stunning gold brooch and matching earrings. Her dark eyes were expertly made up so there was no trace of wrinkles or signs of sleep deprivation in the young mother.

"Joey, you can't be serious. I'm up until all hours with the baby. It's even more exhausting than being on call. Fortunately I'm on extended maternity leave. Which is wonderful. I'm also using the time to catch up on some of my board work."

"Judy, I'm in trouble," Bruno said.

"Nothing surprising there. Actually, I've been reading about you in the paper. Quite a nasty little drama we have going on here in Gardenfield. I've been telling Bill we should move back to the Main Line; it actually seems safer."

"Judy, I need to see Mimi. It's urgent."

"I knew you'd ask that."

"So what's your answer? I hear she still upset, which is understandable, and I promise . . ."

"Is Bill still going around saying she has PTSD?" Judy scowled.

"Yeah. He's totally belligerent."

"He's just trying to protect his family, but I don't want us—and Mimi especially—to become objects of pity."

"So Mimi's all right? Is it OK to talk to her? I promise it'll be a nice little *mazel* for her and we'll all get *naches* from it."

"Since when do you speak Yiddish, Joey? I don't know. Bill . . ."

—"Bill's not here right now, and he won't be back for a while. Something came up at the office tonight . . ."

"How do you know that?" Judy started.

"I was downtown earlier, with the police . . ." Bruno fibbed, though the statement was literally true.

"Let me think about it. I'll show you the baby."

Bruno was chafing to see Mimi. He looked at his watch. He had maybe 10 minutes until the police showed up. Admiring the baby was the price of admission. Not much, really, under the circumstances. It was just that the clock was ticking.

Judy led him to the nursery, which was fully equipped, to say the least. The bedroom looked like a combination of the Mayo Clinic and FAO Schwarz.

The baby was sleeping soundly, but Judy picked her up. A tactical error in Bruno's opinion. He could have easily admired her in the crib. There wasn't much to see in any case. She was swaddled in a fleece sleeper and she had a nightcap. She was a healthy kid equipped with generic features—golden hair, round face, fat cheeks and upturned nose—that would modulate into individual attributes as time went by.

"Can I hold her?" Bruno whispered.

Judy handed him the sleeping child. She struggled to get comfortable in Bruno's arms, but didn't wake up. He guessed she weighed about 20 pounds. "How old is she?" he whispered.

"Forty-nine weeks," answered Judy, glowing with pride. Bruno wrestled with the math, then realized she was just shy of her first birthday. Why did parents have to be so precise?

"She's an angel," Bruno cooed. "Does she have a name?"

"Of course she has a name. Ernestine," said Judy proudly. "We named her after our favorite singer, Ernestine Anderson."

"Ernestine Cohen-McRae," sang Bruno, bouncing the child slightly in time with the refrain. "Sort of a mouthful." Bruno chuckled. "I'm gonna call you Ernie. Beautiful little Ernie. Ernie the Angel."

It's hard to get too upset when someone is calling your daughter a beautiful angel, but Judy tartly informed Bruno that no one was ever going to call her child "Ernie" and live to tell about it. It was Ernestine, plain and simple.

"Beautiful little Ernestine," Bruno acquiesced, handing the baby back to her mother, humming, *"Look out, baby, you might'a made your move too soon . . ."*

"Bill wanted a boy," Judy explained vaguely. "He still does. But it's not going to be Ernestine and I'm never getting pregnant again, so he'll just have to . . ." She noticed Bruno's expectant look and realized she didn't have to finish the thought. "I'll go get Mimi," said Judy. "She's downstairs watching TV."

A moment later, an excited eight-year-old in flannel pajamas decorated with Dalmatians wearing fire helmets bounded up the stairs and threw herself in Bruno's arms. She was followed by a lanky creature the size of a small giraffe, which turned out to be the Cohen-McRaes' Russian wolfhound.

Bruno was amazed to receive such a wonderful hug from his niece, whom he had not seen in more than three years. Was it the Hanukkah presents? Or just one of life's little mysteries? Nothing to do but enjoy it. For a minute or two. They were quickly running out of time.

"Mimi, it's so wonderful to see you." Bruno returned the hug. He had to be careful. His eyes were tearing up. "Did your mama tell you why I'm here? I wish it were more of a fun visit, but I have to talk to you about the day you found that girl in the meeting house."

"Oh that? That's no big deal. Ask me anything you want."

What a relief. Somebody was actually cooperating. He led Mimi to a soft leather armchair and knelt in front of her so he could take her hands in his upraised palms.

The wolfhound took advantage of this to come over and sniff Bruno's rear. Then he tried to lick his face. "What's your puppy's name, honey?"

Mimi giggled. "Trotsky."

"Ah, of course. If I were a dog psychic I would have known. Why'd you name him Trotsky?"

"Because the McRaes stick up for the underdog."

"What about the Cohens?"

"I dunno."

"Mimi, would you mind if we send Trotsky into exile? Just for a minute or two while we're trying to do this?"

Judy stepped forward. She still was holding Ernestine in her arms. "I'll lock him in the TV room," she offered. "But don't do anything till I get back. I need to watch every move you make."

"That's fine, Judy. I just need quiet."

He looked at Mimi in the big leather chair. She had dark hair like her mother's and eyes that were almost black. Her skin was olive-hued, but the excitement had brought a rosy glow to her lips and cheeks. There was no trace of McRae in Mimi's looks, which gave Bruno a sense of satisfaction.

Judy returned and Bruno again held Mimi's hands. He told her to close her eyes and try to remember exactly what she saw that morning in the meeting house. He closed his as well and tried to concentrate.

Nothing was coming, so he tried another approach. He told Mimi to fold her hands in her lap. He stood in front of her with his hands about a half inch from her temples. To Judy, it looked as though he was using her daughter's head as a crystal ball. Whether that was accurate or not, it worked. Incredibly well.

There was a loud zapping noise like lightning and contact was made. At that moment, Bruno had a clear view of the murdered girl, just as Mimi had seen her, disheveled and slumped over on the bench. The suddenness and clarity caused him to cry out. And Mimi cried out too; it didn't hurt, she reported later, it was just the surprise of something so totally unfamiliar.

Then, just as the noise of Bruno and Mimi's outburst subsided, there came a furious banging on Judy's front door.

"Must be that *furshlugginer* Biff," Bruno muttered with frustration. He could have used a few more minutes and he tried to reestablish contact with Mimi.

A moment later there was a heavy thud and the explosive sound of splintered wood. In burst McRae. He'd just broken down the door of his own house with a sledgehammer.

CHAPTER 37

NO ONE COULD HAVE PREDICTED the outcome of the epic battle between Joey Kaplan, aka Bruno X, Psychic Detective, and William "Mad Dog" McRae. Least of all Bruno himself.

In handicapping the contest, most would have given the advantage to McRae. He was bigger, stronger, meaner. And he was fighting on his home turf. But the reality of street fighting, bar fighting, domestic brawls and other disputes of the non-choreographed or cinematic variety is that they are so physically demanding that all parties—unless they happen to be trained fighters—are exhausted after the first minute. Physical exhaustion leads to mental fatigue, if not downright incapacity. Accidents start happening with increasing frequency, which means that if the bout lasts more than a minute or two, it's more likely to be decided by luck than skill.

In this case, McRae squandered his home court advantage, right off the bat, by breaking down the door of his own house. Why would anyone do such a thing? Didn't he have a key?

Of course he did. But it was in his briefcase, which he'd left in the office. It was all Biff's fault. Back at the 24-plex, Biff hadn't come to his senses until all the fighting was over. The sage was all over K-Mart, like tourists in Yosemite in August. Biff tried to elbow Bruno to see if he was diggin' it, too, and then he realized. Bruno had given him the slip.

Biff rushed out to his cruiser and radioed for help. They patched him through to the Chief, who told him to pick him up at the station. On his way to get the Chief, Biff ran into McRae, who asked him what was going on. Biff told him what happened and, before he could do anything about it, McRae hopped into Biff's Crown Vic and headed home at a recklessly high rate of speed. But without his keys.

The sight of Bruno's car in his driveway had thrown McRae into a rage, compounded by the realization that he'd left his keys at work. His immediate thought was to look for a weapon. The weapon that came to mind was a sledgehammer, which he knew was leaning against the wall of the garage.

In a matter of moments, McRae had smashed down the door and charged Bruno, screaming, "I told you to stay away from my daughter." This entrance certainly packed a lot of drama. What McRae didn't realize was that his adversary had just been watching *Flying Panda, Rolling Doughnut 3*, which had put him in a very martial-artsy frame of mind. Bruno could imagine himself waiting like a matador until the last instant, then elevating straight into the air, delivering vicious kicks in all directions. No one in their right mind would have thought it possible to actually execute those moves. But just the thought of it kept Bruno loose, which was a tactical advantage in a contest like this. If McRae actually connected with one of his roundhouse blows, it might enable Bruno to avoid serious injury.

By the time McRae burst in, his arm muscles were starting to feel the strain from swinging the heavy sledgehammer around above his head. He charged Bruno, screaming, "I'm gonna squash you like a bug!" As he swung, the head of the sledgehammer got tangled with the handmade chandelier that Judy had spotted in a boutique in Milan, shipped back to the U.S. at considerable expense, and then adapted for U.S. household current at even more expense. All that was destroyed in an instant; in addition, the blow was deflected from Bruno, who was trying to whirl away like a panda shimmying up a bamboo stalk. McRae lost control of the sledgehammer, which slipped out of his hand and flew into the living room, where it smashed the Steinway baby grand.

This delighted Mimi, who was sick of taking lessons, although the noise and destruction were obviously frightening. Judy was furious about the chandelier, apoplectic about the piano, which had been a gift from her parents, and boiling with fury over the front door.

Now she went looking for a weapon and she found the chardonnay bottle. The only problem was, she still had Ernie in her arms. Somehow she found a way to crack her husband over the head, while still sheltering the baby. This momentarily brought McRae to his senses. "I told you not to let him in here," he stated in an almost conversational tone.

"Shut up, you moron, look what you've done to the house. And all this noise is going to wake up the baby."

Judy's tone rekindled the rage in McRae. A wounded predator, the adrenalin was spurring him to attack. It might have been Judy, except Bruno made the first move. He was trying to sneak out the hole in the front door when McRae caught him and told him he was going to rip him apart with his bare hands.

Bruno imagined he could spin away from McRae with a magical pirouette. In fact, McRae's haymaker merely struck him in the forehead, instead of the chin where he'd aimed it.

The blow dazed Bruno and opened a gash that oozed blood. A dull pain filled Bruno's skull, struggling to get out. But apparently McRae was hurting even more than Bruno. He must have crushed a knuckle from the force of the blow. He was hopping in agony, bent over, holding his injured fist between his knees. "Mimi, get me some ice," he moaned.

"Don't bother," Judy countermanded the order. "Get a bucket of ice water to throw on these animals."

Realizing his movie magic wasn't working, Bruno tried to slither away. But McRae caught him and put him in a headlock. He fell over and they were both wriggling around on the tile floor of the foyer, amid the shards from the broken chandelier and sharp splinters from the door, trying to deliver and fend off a variety of body blows, sucker punches, knees to the groin, and other low blows.

Trotsky joined in, pouncing, growling—no doubt trying to figure out who the underdog was—and generally adding to the confusion. The baby finally woke up and was crying and Judy continued screaming, "Out of here! I want all of you out of here!"

Bruno had a lucid thought: Where was Biff? How long had it been since he'd left the 24-plex? Surely more than 45 minutes. Biff should have called the cops by now. Surely help was on its way.

But it wasn't. McRae improvised a move that enabled him to climb on top of Bruno and grip him firmly by the shirtfront. He commenced banging Bruno, head and shoulders, against the floor. Repeatedly. And all the while he was taunting, "How d'you like this, Joey? Let's see you do something psychic now."

Now Bruno was praying Biff would show up before it was too late. Poor stupid Biff whom he'd so cleverly left behind at the theater. Where was he now that he needed him to come and *biff* McRae's skull with his nightstick? Bruno tried to reach up and get his hands around McRae's neck to strangle him, but couldn't get any leverage.

Judy and Mimi were both screaming, the baby was crying, and Trotsky got so worked up he moved in and bit the nearest thing that was moving. It happened to be McRae's hand. McRae reacted violently. He whipped around to fend off this new threat, and somehow Bruno's pinky got caught up in his earring. McRae was moving so quickly he ripped the lobe of his ear in half. Distracted with pain, all McRae could think of was he needed to punish Trotsky immediately so the dog would get the proper message. This allowed Bruno to wriggle free.

That's when the police arrived. Bruno's prayers were answered. In fact, it was even better than he'd hoped, because it wasn't just Biff. Chief Black was there too. Biff waded into the fray without hesitation. He collared McRae and immobilized him in a wrestling hold. The Chief stood by Bruno, who was still lying on the floor.

"You get out of here, Black," screamed McRae. "This is a personal matter."

"Give us a break, McRae," said the Chief, smacking the palm of his hand with his nightstick. "You're disturbing the peace."

"This man invaded my home when I told him he wasn't welcome."

"That's not true," Bruno protested. "My sister-in-law invited me in. I needed to see my nieces."

"Is that right, Judy?" asked the Chief.

She nodded her head with a half-smirk that meant, "Well, I guess you could put it that way."

The Chief spoke slowly and calmly. "Biff, I think we should book Mr. McRae for breaking and entering. One of the neighbors called to complain and positively identified him as the one knocking down the door with a sledgehammer."

"Chief, can we really arrest a guy for breaking into his own house?"

"Sure we can. Cuff him."

McRae sputtered with fury. "Try it, Black, and I'll sue your ass."

"Now I'm scared," said the Chief, getting in his face.

Judy came to life. "Bill, look what you did to our house." Then louder, "Look what you did to the house." And even louder, pounding him on the chest, "*Shmucko*, look what you did to my house!!"

The Chief must have felt sorry for McRae. Or maybe he decided that leaving him here with Judy was the greater punishment. He made discreet gestures to Biff, indicating that he could take the handcuffs off, saying, "On second thought, there's a big mess here that needs to get cleaned up. Biff, why don't you watch Bill and make sure he doesn't get hurt. I'll take Bruno, er . . . Mr. X down to the station and deal with him myself."

Bruno shuffled over to Judy and tried to say goodbye. "Sorry, goodnight, thanks."

He gave Mimi a hug and a kiss. "You were very brave and what you did tonight was very important." He patted Trotsky, saying, "Thanks for watching my back, pal. I owe you."

Judy said, "If you ask me, you owe this entire family. And the best way to repay us is to never, ever, show your face here again."

CHAPTER 38

"DO YOU WANT TO GO TO THE EMERGENCY ROOM?"

Bruno had just come out of the washroom at the police station and was drying his face on a paper towel. "Nah. I'll be OK. Just cuts and bruises."

"You must be a pretty tough guy." The Chief seemed amused. "McRae has a busted knuckle, a torn ear and a couple of minor bites. Looks like he was fighting Mike Tyson."

"He's a real *shmuck*."

"Yeah, well I'm glad you're OK. That means you can start serving your sentence right away."

"My sentence?"

"Drunk and disorderly. You get 48 hours to sober up and think things over. Hopefully you'll mend your ways."

"But . . ."

"Biff saw you drinking. I saw you fighting."

"McRae attacked me. I was defending myself."

"Well, you weren't supposed to be at McRae's house. You promised me you wouldn't go. Then you ditched Biff."

"I didn't know breaking promises was a crime."

"It is when you break a promise to *me*. Consider yourself a political prisoner if it makes you feel better. Trust me, it's for your own good." The Chief ushered Bruno into a cell. It was a real cage, bars and everything. He confiscated his wallet, watch, keys; shut the door and locked it. "I'll get someone to pick up your car."

"So you're covering your ass. With Mayor Dove and McRae?"

"Don't forget Biff. You don't want to get on his wrong side."

"I see. But what about the investigation? I was right. Mimi was the key. I saw everything. The victim, the setting. Chief, she was wearing *clothes*. I need to get a reading from her clothes."

"Well, I'll see if I can round them up from evidence tomorrow."

"But Chief, why not now? This could be important."

"Could be . . . wait a sec. Here comes Biff now."

The Chief stepped out into the hallway to confer with Biff, who waited impatiently by the door to the Chief's office. Biff caught Bruno's eye and scowled.

"It appears McRae also has a fractured skull," the Chief announced brightly. "They've admitted him to the hospital overnight. Did you hit him over the head with a wine bottle?"

"No, that was Judy. I'm surprised that hurt him; it was only chardonnay."

"I gotta talk to Biff. Try to get some sleep. You look like you need it."

"But those clothes . . ."

"Maybe tomorrow. We'll see."

A few minutes later, Biff came out of the Chief's office. He was smiling. He walked over to Bruno's cell and put his hand between the bars. "No hard feelings?"

Bruno struggled to his feet. His head was killing him now and his entire body felt sore. "None on my part."

"Great," beamed Biff. "Chief explained the whole thing to me. I'm really impressed. Thanks." He jingled Bruno's car keys. "Now I'm going to go get your car and park it in back so it'll be ready for you when you get out . . ." Biff caught sight of his best friend on the force and hollered, "Yo, Randy, you pissant. Getcher sorry ass over here and help me with this." And he walked off whistling.

Another mystery, thought Bruno as he slumped back on his cot. The Chief really had a way with people. Forty-eight *furshlugginer* hours. Was this his idea of a joke?

Next morning, the Chief did manage to bring the clothes. He fumbled with the evidence tag as he filled out the chain-of-custody information.

Bruno was bleary. "How about a latte?" he begged. "Starbucks is just down the street."

"No can do."

Bruno pouted. "Anyway, what did you say to Biff?"

"I intimated to Biff that you might have hypnotized him, so it wasn't his fault. No demerits, no blame."

"That's it?"

"Well, I may have hinted that he'd get promoted sooner rather than later . . ."

"Great. I feel safer already."

The Chief didn't laugh. He stood there, looking at Bruno. Finally he spoke. "So, are you going to read these clothes?"

Bruno took the piles of clothes and did his best to get a reading from them. No luck. He tried several of his most reliable techniques, to no avail. In the middle of one his best efforts, the noon whistle shrieked from the firehouse and destroyed his concentration. Bruno's head sunk into his hands in disgust: "I don't think I can do this while I'm in jail."

The Chief took the clothes away.

McRae had just been released from the hospital and he came by to gloat. "You're where you belong."

"So are you, tough guy." Bruno didn't know what that meant, exactly. But it seemed to irritate McRae, which was all that mattered.

"I'm not finished with you. Not by a long shot. You'll get what's coming to you. And sooner than you think."

The Chief heard the ruckus and pushed McRae roughly out the door.

"*Kineahora, paskudnyak*," the psychic snarled at the departing figure. "Next time I see you, I'll be the *moyl* at your *bris*."

The Chief returned, rubbing his hands as though trying to wipe off the taint of touching McRae. "Whatever you said seemed to really get to him. What'd it mean?"

"*Kineahora* is protection against the evil eye. Whatever McRae wished on me, I sent it back to him—double. *Paskudnyak* is just what it sounds like: odious, contemptible. And the rest of it, well, I just promised to assist him with the long-overdue *mitzvah* of circumcision. But my knife's not gonna be very sharp or clean, and I'm not gonna use any anesthetic."

The Chief seemed to take it all in and ponder it seriously. When he finally spoke, they were back on their normal footing. "Chris from Tano's sends his regards. Says he's proud of you and wants to talk to you when you get out."

"Yeah, what about?"

"I don't know. But it must be important."

"What makes you say that?"

"He said he'd give you a free cheesesteak, with all the trimmings."

"This really is my lucky day," Bruno sighed. He stretched out painfully, wrapped his pillow around his head in an effort to block out the light, and tried to fall back to sleep.

CHAPTER 39

DRIVING HOME, traffic was thick again, as usual, until well past Olga's. Even though Bruno could see vultures circling overhead in the waning twilight, he was still stalled in a bumper-to-bumper nightmare. He had to admit it: Where he lived was no longer "remote." It wasn't even "rural" or "small town." Civilization had caught up to him, and would definitely overtake him in the next few years. Where could he go from here? *Not tonight*, he told himself. He was too tired to even think about it.

Chief Black had given Bruno a break, shaving several hours off his time in the slammer for good behavior. Even so, after spending two days cooped up in a small cell, his bruises were aching painfully. His neck was sore from McRae's pummeling. And between the sirens from the fire trucks and ambulances, the noon whistle, and all the banter and commotion in the police station, he'd barely gotten two consecutive hours of sleep. Yet the Chief actually had asked him to try reading the clothes again, as soon as he set him free.

It'd have to wait. Bruno told him he needed to go home, clean up, get some rest. He needed to feed and walk Maggie. Watch a little TV. Even the promise of a free cheesesteak didn't appeal on a night like

THE VIOLET CROW

this. He wanted to eat some home cooking. Soak in the hot tub. Go to bed.

As he pulled into his neighborhood, he reacted with surprise—for only the five thousandth time—at how affluent and well put together it looked. Only his trailer and, maybe, the Terranovas' house showed that the true Piney spirit was alive and well. After this case was over, he resolved to get some broken appliances to put out front. Maybe he could get a grant from some kind of historical society. The neighbors would love that.

But Bruno's good spirits vanished as soon as he pulled into his driveway.

The front door to the trailer was wide open. The upper hinge had pulled free, so the door sagged weakly. And where was Maggie? She normally came bounding up to greet him. Tonight, she was nowhere in sight.

Bruno got out of his car and left the door open so as not to make any noise. His heart pounded. He tiptoed up the front stairs. If an intruder was still inside he didn't know what he'd do. He needed a weapon. Unfortunately, his shotgun was inside, in the back bedroom.

Bruno peered cautiously around the doorjamb to reconnoiter. A moment's glance told him everything he needed to know. He emerged from his defensive crouch and strode into the middle of the room. The devastation was complete. It wasn't total—just the things he cared about. A cinder block nestled in the shattered remnants of his TV's picture tube. His mattress was slashed to ribbons and human feces defiled his leather recliner. All of his plates were smashed. Anti-Semitic slogans had been sprayed on the walls with DayGlo pink spray paint. And there was no sign of Maggie.

It must have been McRae. If someone had simply wanted to kill him, they would have been careful to leave the house in its usual condition so they could murder him easily when he walked, unwittingly, into the trap. This type of vandalism was an end in itself. It was the revenge of someone who drew the line at killing. *It must have been McRae.* Especially crapping in the chair; that was just his style. He hadn't been kidding about acting fast. But dognapping? Bruno wouldn't have expected that even a *putz* like his ex-brother-in-law would stoop so low.

He retrieved his shotgun and loaded it with buckshot. Then he tidied up the worst of the mess, just so he could move around. With an eerie sense of calm Bruno founding himself thinking how ironic it all was: *Now I have a dead TV set for the front porch.*

Just as he was about to step outside to search for Maggie, a gigantic pickup pulled up. Its throbbing diesel engine shook the whole property.

Was it McRae coming back to gloat? Bruno stepped outside and raised his weapon toward the driver's window.

"Doan shoot, Joe. It's me, Gil."

Bruno didn't lower the barrel, but he looked more closely toward the window of the truck. Gil Terranova slowly lowered his window so Bruno could see him.

"My place got trashed tonight and Maggie's missing. Did you see or hear anything?"

"That's why I'm here," said Gil. "We heard a commotion, then Maggie came running over to our place. She's hurt. Pretty bad, too. We've been tending to her and couldn't come over until now."

"Is she OK? Where is she?"

Gil paused before answering. "Yeah, I think she'll be all right. She's at our place, resting."

"What happened to her?"

"Whyn't you get in the truck and I'll take you back to my place so you can see for yourself."

Bruno climbed up into the passenger seat, holding the shotgun upright between his knees.

"You got that thing secured?" Gil asked Bruno. "I'd hate to go over a bump and have you blow a hole in the roof of my truck. Specially if it took a piece of somebody's scalp with it."

"Yeah, it's OK," said Bruno.

"Good. Hope we don't have to use that thing tonight. You say they busted up your home pretty good?"

"Yeah. They smashed the TV set, crapped on my recliner, broke all the dishes, slashed my mattress and dumped a couple of bags of ready-mix in my hot tub."

Gil whistled. "Somebody's mad at you. Think it's because of those murders you've been investigating?"

"You know about that?"

"Just what I read in the paper. Didn't realize you were a detective with a secret identity until we saw your picture."

Bruno shook his head in frustration. The *furshlugginer Pest*. He turned to Gil and explained, "Actually I think it was probably my brother-in-law."

Gil shot him a look that expressed his surprise. "Family stuff can get dicey, but . . ."

"But what? You think my family's over the top? No argument there. Besides, it was my *ex*-brother-in-law. I forgot to say 'ex.'"

"I hear ya," Gil muttered. "Here we are." He stopped in front of a '50s ranch-style home. Carmine was worked up because of what had happened to Maggie. He yipped and jumped up on Gil, who finally had to grab him by the collar and lead him to his kennel. Peering from the front door was a boy who appeared to be around three years old and a girl who had just started walking. Both had curly black hair and dark brown eyes that were spread wide with wonder. There had already been a lot of excitement, and now this late-night visitor seemed to promise more.

"That's Frankie and Olivia," Gil explained. "Kids, this is Mr. Kaplan—that's right isn't it, Joe? You want 'em to call you Kaplan, not Bruno X . . . ?"

Bruno nodded and Gil continued. ". . . Mr. Kaplan is our next-door neighbor. His dog is Maggie, the one we rescued tonight."

The kids' eyes bugged out even more, if possible. Just then Gil's wife, Angela, appeared. She was tall with wavy raven-black hair that fell down below her shoulders. She was rail thin, except for the bowling-ball-sized protrusion in her lower abdomen. Obviously number three was on its way. Angela was still wearing an apron and drying a serving dish. "I'm so sorry about Maggie, Mr. Kaplan."

"Call me Joe," said Bruno, feeling incredibly anxious because everyone was telling him how sorry they were. "I'd like to see Maggie right away . . ."

Gil lead him back to the TV room while Angela tried to get the kids to give him some privacy. When Bruno saw Maggie, he broke down and cried. She was sleeping on the couch and she struggled to raise her head and greet him when she detected his scent. Maggie appeared to be in good condition, except for her tail, which was bandaged about two inches above the base. The rest of it was missing. Her proud and beautiful tail. They'd amputated her tail.

Gil put his hand on Bruno's shoulder. "She lost a lot of blood. It was gushing when she showed up here. We slowed it down with a tight bandage, and I tried to put a clamp on it, but we couldn't completely stop the bleeding. Fortunately, I was able to get our vet on the phone and he ran right over. Never saw anything like it. You really think your brother-in-law'd do something like that?"

"I don't know. Maybe not. None of this makes sense . . ."

"Takes a pretty sick person, do something like this. Maybe Angela's family—you know, they're Sicilian . . ."

"Very funny, Gil," Angela protested. "They're from Sicily a long time ago. Really, Joe, my family's from North Jersey. Teaneck. My father was a realtor. My brother's a dentist. When they want to get rough with Gil, they tell him the Giants are better than the Eagles."

"And when they really want respect," Gil continued, "they tell me that even the Jets are better. North Jersey *stronzi* . . ."

The monologue achieved its intended purpose. Bruno had stopped crying, but Gil could see he was still upset. "Anyway, we're really sorry about Maggie." He shot a questioning look toward Angela, who nodded, yes, it was OK. "Do you need a place to stay tonight? You're welcome to stay here."

"Thanks. But I need to sleep at my place tonight."

"Do you think it's safe?"

Bruno shrugged. "I gotta go home."

Gil understood. "Why don't I drive you . . . ?"

". . . and take some of this bracciole," said Angela, moving toward the kitchen to prepare a dish, "so you don't have to cook."

"Yeah definitely take some," said Gil. "Angela's *bra-zhol* is delicious. It'll restore your strength. The vet left some painkillers for Maggie and I've got some Tylenol with codeine left over from my accident with the tractor last winter."

Bruno thanked him for all he'd done. As Gil drove him home, Bruno tried to rally himself with the thought that, at least, things couldn't get any worse. But they did. As the truck's headlights played across the porch, they illuminated a package that'd been left on the top step. It was long and fairly narrow, tied with a ribbon as though a florist had delivered a gift of a dozen roses. "Holy cow, Joe, what's that? I didn't see a delivery truck or nothin."

Bruno opened it, his hands trembling and a sick feeling spreading upward from his stomach. The ribbon came free. Inside, the box was lined with white satin and covered with tissue paper. When Bruno removed it he found Maggie's severed tail resting on a pillow. Next to it was a note. It read simply, "Your niece is next."

CHAPTER 40

THE COP FROM TABERNACLE was disgusted. Justifiably so. "You don't go barging into a crime scene and straighten things up. You oughta know better'n that."

"I thought it was my brother-in-law . . . ex-brother-in-law . . ." Bruno tried to explain.

"I doan' care if it was your mother!" shouted the cop.

". . . I just wanted to straighten up. It's my house, after all . . ." Bruno continued. "What would you have done if it happened at your place? Just left a pile of steaming crap on your favorite chair?"

—"That was evidence," the cop retorted. The Tabernacle police force so rarely had an authentic crime scene worth protecting, it was frustrating to lose one; at the same time, the officer was thoroughly pleased to have this opportunity to get in somebody's face about lousing things up. "You say you work with the police. You should have known better." And he turned his back on Bruno so he could mutter insults under his breath.

Bruno sat there and stewed until he heard the sound of Randy's buffed-up monster of a muscle car pulling into his driveway. This was Randy's pride and joy, and he used it from time to time when official

166

business required an unmarked car. He figured people would never expect a classic car, decked out in flat primer gray, belonged to the police. Randy's car was a 1969 Charger Daytona, built specifically for NASCAR competition. Though more than 35 years old, even the street model was more aerodynamic than many racing cars built decades later. Randy had it souped up with the fabled 426 Hemi, which produced at least 425 horsepower. It was an awesome machine for racing in the streets; using it for police business allowed Randy to open it up, from time to time, without having to worry about getting arrested for reckless driving.

Biff and Randy entered the trailer, hats in hand. The absence of banter showed they had heard the news and thought Bruno might be in a state of shock. Bruno immediately apologized for disturbing the crime scene. "I thought for sure it was McRae taking out his frustrations. Seeking revenge."

"He has a pretty good alibi for last night," said Randy. "He was with Mayor Dove, trying to get both you and the Chief locked up because of what he did at his own house . . ."

Randy caught the eye of the Tabernacle cop, who slunk off sullenly, handing him a business card on the way out.

Bruno didn't even notice. He sighed deeply. "I knew it wasn't him when I saw the note. Even McRae wouldn't threaten his own daughter."

"You never know," Biff said. "He bashed in his own front door. Maybe the note was a ruse to throw us off the track."

"He has an alibi," Randy said. "There's still plenty of evidence to collect here. We should still be able to get prints off of the note card and maybe the box. Plenty of DNA left on the recliner. And we can look outside for footprints, tire tracks and the weapon . . ."

He nodded to Biff, who had carefully picked up the flower box and was spiriting it out to the car without saying anything to Bruno.

"You try to get some sleep," Randy counseled.

Bruno nodded passively. The bed was trashed. Luckily he had a spare inflatable mattress. And drugs for pain and sleep. He and Maggie both took a dose. They curled up together on the mattress on the floor and slept through the night in a deep, dreamless state that was more like suspended animation than sleep.

Somehow, they woke up refreshed. Maybe it was the sunshine. The crisp morning chill, with a slight hint of mid-morning warmth. The signs of springtime all around.

Maggie was wagging her stump. Cautiously at first. Then with more of her normal gusto. Bruno checked the dressing. The vet had done a good job, but it was lucky Gil had known how to staunch the bleeding in the first place. Bruno resolved to find a way to repay him, or at least thank him properly, someday.

Now, with his mind starting to clear, Bruno had to wonder: Why were they threatening Mimi? Who knew about his relationship to her and her importance to the case? Was there a mole—or a rat?—on the Gardenfield police force?

With these questions percolating, Bruno sorted through all of the mail and other junk that had accumulated during the days he had been a guest of the Borough of Gardenfield. Bills. Junk. Newspaper supplements. And the newspaper itself. Nothing less appealing than a two-day-old *Pest*, Bruno reflected. Nevertheless, he flipped through quickly, scanning the local news. And there it was: the answer staring him right in the face.

Peaches had gotten word of the fight at McRae's. She'd called it "The Showdown at Casa McRae," adding a subtitle: "Psychic rumbles with City Attorney." So there it was in black and white, the information that McRae had been fighting to conceal about his family's involvement in the Quaker Killer/Ginnie Doe investigation. For such a smart guy, McRae seemed to have a knack for undermining his own interests.

But the real villain here was Peaches. She had tipped off the identity of a young girl and put her in a clear state of peril. Somebody needed to do something about her. She'd been giving him *tsuris*—pain and trouble—every step of the way. She'd accused him of colluding with Gussie's killer. She'd spoiled the secret of his dual identities and gotten him kicked off his best consulting gig. Now she'd almost gotten Maggie killed, as well as exposing innocent little Mimi to unwarranted risks.

It was time to act. Peaches had to be neutralized before she could do further damage. But how? Nothing sprang to mind right away, but he was sure he'd think of something in the next day or two. So he called Peaches and set up a lunch date for early the following week.

CHAPTER 41

"THIS IS PERSONAL NOW. You're really gonna let them have it, aren'tcha?" said Biff. He was trying to pump up Bruno, who had come to Gardenfield early the next day to read Ginnie Doe's clothing. "I mean, they were probably trying to kill you. Maybe they'd've done it, too, if we hadn't been keeping you here, safe and sound, in our jail. And, by the way, sorry about your dog."

Bruno wouldn't have felt any worse if Biff had punched him in the stomach. He hadn't considered the possibility that he may have been the intended target until now. "I'm no hero," he told Biff, quite truthfully. "Whatever I find out, you guys are going to have to do the heavy lifting. If I start taking things personally, it just makes it tougher to concentrate. I have to stay focused."

Nice speech, Bruno congratulated himself as he headed for the Chief's office. Truth of the matter was he was still back on his heels from the attack on Maggie. And even more troubled by the threat against Mimi. He'd already discussed this with the Chief on the phone. Obviously, there was no way to warn McRae to be vigilant without sending him into a homicidal rage. Bruno suggested putting McRae on medical leave and sending the whole family down to Puerto Rico to recuperate. The Chief agreed it was a good idea, but doubted anybody had the budget for it. "Best I can do is assign Biff to keep an eye on them," said the Chief.

The prospect did little to ease Bruno's mind about Mimi's safety. Once Maggie got better, maybe he'd be able to keep an eye on her himself.

The Chief was shuffling through a stack of reports when Bruno entered. "We got plenty of prints off the note card, but they don't match up with anything in the FBI database," the Chief announced. "And we didn't have any luck with the tire tracks. The soil out there is so sandy and there was so much traffic that night between Mr. Terranova's truck, the Tabernacle cop and your pathetic excuse for a car . . ."

"The Tabernacle cop destroyed evidence?" Bruno asked, brightening up.

"Yeah. The only really good cast we got turned out to be Randy's Daytona. We gave it to him as a souvenir."

The Chief held another report that he was not going to discuss with Bruno. The medical examiner had examined Maggie's tail and determined that the instrument used was certainly not a samurai blade—at least not one that had been sharpened properly. It had taken several strokes to sever the tail. Maggie must have suffered terribly. But the poor quality of the blade may have helped to save her life. Clean cuts bleed more readily; the crushed tissues may have slowed the bleeding enough to enable her to make it as far as the Terranovas' house.

Officer Nancy O'Keefe walked in holding the carefully folded pile of Ginnie Doe's clothing. "Say, Bruno, can you get a reading directly from Maggie?" she asked spontaneously.

This took the Chief by surprise. He hadn't thought of that. He looked questioningly at Bruno. So did Michelle. Bruno couldn't believe it. All these people staring at him. "Are you kidding? Do you think I'm some kind of freak?"

The Chief sensed he might be getting ready to go off on one of his tirades. He dismissed Michelle and tried to get the psychic to calm down. "OK. Never mind. She didn't know. Let's do something constructive." He sat Bruno in his chair and put the clothes in front of him on his desk. "Do you need anything else?"

Bruno didn't reply. He was already working his way into the stack of clothes. He unfolded everything and laid it out, like someone planning the day's wardrobe, on the Chief's desk. None of it matched particularly well. There was a rust-colored cardigan, a cobalt blue long-sleeved T-shirt and green pants. Next to that lay a red wool overcoat with a hood lined with fake fur. A pair of red rubber rain boots, but no socks . . . and there weren't any underclothes, either.

"Here's a clue," noted Nancy. "Either she was color-blind. Or her mother was."

Bruno ignored her. He placed his hands on each article of clothing in turn. His eyes turned inward. His lips trembled. He was obviously deep in concentration. The room was silent. Nobody dared breathe.

At length Bruno interrupted his trance. He asked the Chief to take notes. "I'm finding all of this very confusing. Just write down whatever I say. It may not make sense. But don't interrupt me. We'll try to sort it out later."

The Chief grabbed a notepad and Bruno re-entered his state of deep contemplation. He started with the cardigan. "This is strange," he whispered. "I see an argument. With a woman. A gray-haired woman. I'm not sure who she is. But this is not about the murder. They are arguing about . . . the sweater."

He moved on to the pants. They were green cotton corduroy. "She's climbing, climbing. Working her way higher and higher. Now she's frightened. She's scared. She's coming down. Uh-oh, one of the pockets is caught on a branch. It's tearing. She's frightened. She's scared."

Bruno put down the pants and moved to pick up the overcoat. At the same time Nancy reached for the pants; clearly, she wanted to check on the torn pocket. The Chief grabbed her wrist and gently forced it away. Nancy scowled, but obediently folded her hands and placed them on the table in front of her.

". . . she's in a car," Bruno continued. "With a man. A dark man. They're driving. Driving. She's cold. She needs the coat. She's scared. She lost it. She needs the coat. She's scared."

Nancy snickered. "Sorry. I can't help it," she whispered. "This girl sounds like an ordinary kid. Arguing with her mother about wearing a sweater. Tearing her pants while climbing a tree. And leaving her coat somewhere, probably the playground, and having to drive back with her father to get it."

Bruno was out of his trance, listening attentively. "She's right. I have no sense of connection between these clothes and the girl in the morgue. These clothes are attached to memories of a girl with a close-knit family. Where are they? Why haven't they been trying to find her? I don't believe Ginnie Doe was wearing these clothes when she was murdered."

"That would be consistent with your theory that someone other than the killer moved the body into the meeting house," observed the Chief. "Whoever moved the body also dressed her in these clothes. But why?"

"Obviously there was something about her clothes that would have helped identify her," Nancy suggested. "Alternatively, they could be secondhand."

"You mean, they belonged to some girl who's totally unconnected to the case?" mused the Chief. "She outgrew them; the family donated them to Goodwill and then Ginnie Doe got them? So Bruno's picking up on the emotions of the first girl and not the second?"

"Yeah. Something like that," agreed Nancy. "Maybe she was a homeless kid . . ."

"Other than the neck, the body was in good shape," the Chief reasoned. "She was well-nourished, had good teeth. Theoretically, homelessness can happen to anybody; maybe it was a recent thing for her."

Bruno had been following the interchange intently. Now he asked, out of the blue, "Were these clothes laundered before you stored them as evidence?"

"Of course not," growled the Chief. "They are evidence."

"They seem surprisingly clean," Bruno persisted. "I don't believe she was a homeless child, in the usual sense. I don't think she'd been living outdoors. Let me try again with the overcoat. Since she wasn't wearing it next to her skin, I figured I'd get a stronger response from her other clothes."

Bruno took the red wool jacket and hugged it to his breast. He shut his eyes and soon was back in his trance. Then his eyes shot open and he smiled broadly.

"What is it?" Nancy and the Chief demanded in unison.

"I recognized someone. The girl I just saw eating Chinese food with that kid with the funny name. The speed freak."

"Icky . . . ?"

"Yeah. This coat belonged to his girlfriend. I saw her trying it on and examining how she looked in the mirror; she hated it. She was sticking out her tongue and scowling. She was much younger. But there's no question. It was the same person."

"Alison Wales," said Nancy. "We have to find her and talk to her right away."

"She's easy to find," the Chief said. "We've been keeping an eye on Icky. Alison goes to school at Penn, but she comes here frequently to visit him. For all we know, she could be at the Lenape King with Icky right now . . ."

As the Chief finished speaking a tremendous explosion shook the entire building. Out in the main hallway, people were shouting and running for the exits. Police Chief Buddy Black recovered quickly. He picked up his phone and ordered the entire force to assemble. He wanted everyone in full riot gear in case the Borough of Gardenfield was under attack.

CHAPTER 42

BLACK SMOKE BILLOWED from a storefront in the heart of downtown—less than two blocks from the Municipal Building. A thin drizzle was falling and, already, the air was choked with fumes. From where Chief Black stood, just up the block and across the street from the firehouse, the alerts pierced his skull with their maddeningly insistent call to action.

Debbie's voice on the radio shook him by the lapels. Laced with static, her awful monotone blared, "The fire's at the corner of King's Road and Mechanic Street."

The meth lab? How could that be? Gary had told him the red-headed scum were still moving in. They could hardly have had time to get set up. How could they blow themselves up so soon? Never mind. Chief Black knew he needed to alert the firefighters about the hazards of the immediate situation. There were toxic chemicals to deal with. And if those weren't bad enough, often drug dealers booby-trapped their places with bombs rigged to go off when police or firefighters entered the premises. He doubted that Icky and his gang were that far gone. But it was protocol, and they'd have to take precautions just the same.

Here we go again, the Chief found himself thinking. One more accident, one more violent incident in a series that simply had too many coincidences to ignore. What if this fire were somehow connected to the other killings? Maybe it was a trap laid, not by meth cookers, but by whoever was behind the other murders? What if there were snipers? Armed commandos with grenades and automatic weapons? Should he call in a SWAT team? The National Guard?

Then he saw Bruno approaching from the back of the Municipal Building. Chief Black hated to say it, but trouble seemed to be following the psychic—and getting closer all the time. This was not what he needed right now.

He grabbed his radio and tried to contact the Fire Chief, Norm Cushing. As a matter of practice, the police and fire departments deliberately use different systems—to avoid interfering with each other's communications. This makes it maddeningly difficult to coordinate operations when necessary. After the terrorist attacks on New York and Washington, Chief Black and Chief Cushing had set up an emergency communications channel dedicated to this single function. Chief Black fumbled for his radio and finally found it on his belt. He called Chief Cushing and waited. No answer. He rang again. Nothing.

Now he noticed that Bruno was gesticulating wildly; the Chief figured he didn't need any psychic help just now. He turned his back to Bruno, and rang Chief Cushing again. Still no response. He was so frustrated, he was ready to stomp the radio under his boots.

Bruno tugged on his sleeve. "The Fire Department's setting up a command post across the street from the fire. It's right next to the Starbucks. Can I get you a latte or something?"

Stunned, Chief Black tossed the useless radio on the ground and took off running. The light rain was not enough to retard the fire, but sufficient to create a natural lid that bottled in the smoke and made it difficult to see. Half a block past Garden Avenue, he found Chief Cushing giving multiple orders simultaneously.

"Not now, Buddy," Chief Cushing barked. "The volunteers are still coming in and I have to get them positioned."

"They may need police protection," Chief Black barked back.

Chief Cushing grabbed his helmet in both hands and pulled it

175

off his head as though he wanted to slam-dunk it into the pavement. "What are you trying to tell me?" he roared.

"First of all, we think the apartment in back was being set up as a meth lab. So there may be hazardous chemicals."

"We can handle that."

"Yeah. I'm also worried about booby traps. We'll have to check for incendiary devices triggered to destroy evidence."

"I know the drill. That's standard procedure. I thought you were talking about something else."

"Listen, Norm, I don't have any solid evidence, but with all the crazy stuff that's been happening lately, I don't want anyone taking potshots at your guys."

Norm Cushing gave Buddy Black a long look, trying to assess whether he was starting to crack under pressure. Finally he replied, "I appreciate your concern, Buddy. But this fire's a screamer. We could lose half of downtown if we don't get busy."

Just then the police force arrived, armed to the teeth in riot gear.

Chief Cushing took in the situation. "OK, the cavalry's here. Can I go put out the fire now?"

CHAPTER 43

ALTHOUGH THE PLAQUE ON THE WALL indicated the site had been Gibbs' Tavern & Smithy in 1777, clearly the building dated from the early part of the 20th century. It was wood frame construction, with a brick facade facing Mechanic Street.

It wasn't clear if the fire had originated in the back of the aroma-therapy spa and spread up to the meth lab, or vice versa. In any case, when the fire hit the meth-making chemicals it exploded like a bomb, blowing gaping holes in the floor and ceiling. Now the fire was threatening to spread in all directions. Mechanic Street was a natural fire-break on the north; unfortunately it was an unusually narrow one-way street. To the rear were several more shops and a parking lot. The biggest threat was to the attached buildings on Old Kings Road. Immediately adjacent to the south was Sahadjian's Fine Oriental Carpets.

Chief Cushing wanted to get a team on the roof as soon as possible. He needed to create a vent for explosive gases and, if possible, carve out a strip ventilation trough to keep the fire from spreading to the rug shop. Those would be the tasks for the ladder company. The two engine companies would attack the flanks of the building. One would enter through the rug shop and hose down the walls on that side. The other would head up Mechanic Street and create a water curtain. Once they'd controlled the perimeter of the fire, they'd turn in on the building itself and drown the fire.

Simple to plan, difficult and dangerous to execute. The searing heat of the fire, toxic fumes from the chemicals, structural uncertainty of an older building and the X-factor, the danger of hostile activity, combined to make this an especially hazardous assignment.

The ladder company wheeled around the block, turned at the Friends School and came up Mechanic Street from the rear of the fire. Chief Black asked the two engine companies to park parallel, close together, on Old Kings Road. The trucks formed a defensive rampart, providing some protection for the firefighters.

Michelle and Harry were responsible for crowd control. They used wooden barricades to create a police line one block in every direction. Biff and Randy were armed with assault rifles and were stationed at each end of the two engines, keeping a lookout for snipers, assassins, terrorists, etc. Chief Black prayed that no poor fool would disobey the evacuation order and peek out from a second-story window. Biff would be all over him like a scalper on a corporate lawyer needing playoff tickets.

Officer Gary Malone was assigned to the hazmat team working with the ladder company. It would be his job to enter the meth lab and check for booby traps. Once he gave the all-clear, he would pull back to help with security while the firemen extinguished the blaze.

With the men deployed, the two Chiefs took control at the command station.

"Any people trapped inside?" asked Chief Black.

"Fortunately, the aromatherapy spa wasn't open yet. Seems their clientele has already achieved health, wealth, and wisdom without getting up early, so now they're free to pursue unwrinkled skin in the après-midi."

"That's lucky. What about the apartments?"

"Caught a break there, too. Seems that speed freaks are the only ones who can handle the stench of the aromatherapy oils, so that was the only apartment that was rented. All of those kids have families, right? So none of them actually lived there?"

"That's right," Chief Black confirmed. "But this was a new deal for them. We can't say for sure if any of them were in there or not. I'll get Debbie to call the families."

Bruno was watching from the sidewalk in front of the Starbucks. Chief Black noticed him when he finished talking to Chief Cushing. He pointed in the direction of the Pine Barrens, as if to say, "You still hanging around? Go home."

The psychic held his ground.

Chief Black realized he'd been coming down hard on Bruno all day. He stepped closer and said, "Look, whoever trashed your place may be somewhere in this crowd. I'm not saying you were the target here, but who the hell knows what's really going on? So get inside someplace and stay out of sight." Then he added an afterthought: "Check back in with me tomorrow. We need to talk."

Though he would have preferred to stay out on the street, Bruno ducked into the Starbucks as ordered. There, things were proceeding more or less as usual. The sound track was a jaunty Modern Jazz Quartet CD, with Milt Jackson on vibraphone and John Lewis on piano exchanging sophisticated riffs. The music seemed very out of place. Bruno felt worse than out of place. He felt useless, guilty, and somehow responsible for the whole mess. He watched Gary suiting up in a brown fireman's jacket with DayGlo yellow stripes. He would be one of the first in. He was capable—nimbly climbing up the fire escape— unselfish and heroic.

In fact, Gary was numb with fear. An adrenaline junkie, he actually relished the challenge of working undercover with drug dealers and mobsters. But he was in his element there.

Here, they wanted him to climb up a rickety old fire escape and enter a building engulfed in flames. *Any sensible person would run the other way*, he told himself. "But me? No. I'm goin' to go right in. Why? Because I'm the black man. Every time they's a tough job to do, who's gotta do it? The black man!"

Gary knew full well that every member of the Gardenfield Fire Department was white. They all had other jobs, many of them cushy white-collar jobs, but they all volunteered to drop everything and fight fires whenever they were needed. They were brave men and he respected them. He just needed to steel himself to face a truly danger-ous and terrifying situation, and talking trash to himself was how he did it. "Worst thing is, they're making me wear this ugly raincoat with a bulletproof vest underneath. How'm I supposed to climb up these old steps dressed like that? And once I get inside, I gotta go looking for—what: refrigerator door triggers for an incendiary bomb? Honest, I was just looking for a cold beer. DVD players packed with plastic explosives? I had my heart set on watching *Die Hard* again. Who else'd be fool enough to do something like this? The black man."

From Bruno's perspective, the men of Ladder Company No. 1 seemed to have superhuman agility and courage. They scaled the lad-der as though it were a toy and began attacking the roof with axes and chain saws. Almost instantly, gases rushed up through the vent, flared up and died back just as quickly. Somehow the firemen managed to dodge the blast of flame. And then the men from the engine company came up, aiming water from their pressure hoses at the blaze.

When it was over, Gary would claim he'd had the time of his life. He'd talk about how hard it was to see anything. How sections of the floor were gone, so you'd have to pray you weren't stepping into a hole. How burning sections of the ceiling and walls came crashing down around him. Gary was supposed to work through an official check-list of known meth lab booby traps. First was electronically controlled detonators. No worries there. They'd shut down the power right off the bat. *Check.* Number two, light bulbs filled with gasoline. Wouldn't be a problem either: If there had been any, they surely would have exploded by now. *Check-check.*

No man or bear traps by the front door; no boards with nails driven through under the window that allowed access to the fire escape.

Rattlesnakes did not seem likely to present a problem. Those were on the list as a tribute to the ingenuity of cookers in rural areas of states like Florida and Arkansas. No attack dogs either.

Trip wires were a trickier problem. Gary had to crack open cabinet doors and closets—gently, gently—then visually inspect, if possible. In cases where visual inspection was not possible—like when there was so much smoke you could barely see—then he could risk inserting a blade, using extreme caution. According to the manual, this technique was "not recommended, for emergencies only." But in Gary's experience, whenever you were poking around for bombs to defuse in a meth lab, it was always an emergency. Who were they kidding? You just had to get good with the blade and hope to God it never encountered resistance.

Gary worked his way around the kitchen, testing as many cabinets as the fire would allow. The blaze raging next to the sink suggested that was where the chemicals had been stored. No sign of a tank, though. Was that a good sign? Yes, if it meant they hadn't stolen any anhydrous ammonia yet. No, if it meant the tank was someplace else.

He retreated to the living room. It was empty of furniture and did not have any closets. All clear. Gary let out a sigh and headed for the bedroom. *Just a few more minutes*, he told himself. With any luck he'd be out of this hellhole and back on the street in time for lunch.

Unfortunately the bedroom door was either wedged shut or locked from the inside. No way he was going to break it open. He could sense the heat in there; forcing this door would be asking for all kinds of trouble. They'd need to go in through the roof—and fast.

It was time to go. Gary placed a backwards-check next to number six and got his black ass moving out as fast as he could.

As he downed his third latte, Bruno saw nothing but chaos. He was in limbo looking out at perdition. Hoses snaked everywhere. The water curtain cascaded toward the street, while the smoke just got thicker and thicker. Not many people were gawking at the barricades. The news that there were hazardous chemical vapors kept all but the most curious and foolhardy souls at bay.

Besides, they could watch it at home on TV. There were multiple crews filming the blaze from a safe distance with telephoto lenses. One diminutive reporter, dressed in a Barbour jacket, Timberline construction boots, and a Maine lobsterman rain hat was right in the thick of things. Who'd let her in? She seemed to be interrupting firemen while they were working and asking them for comments. It could only be Peaches. She had a respirator in one hand, tape recorder in the other, worrying the crowd like a hungry jackal on the fringes of a savannah barbecue.

The Starbucks crew was pouring free beverages and sending them outside to anyone who needed them. Bruno was tired of feeling useless, so he volunteered to pass out coffee. As he moved from group to group, he kept overhearing snatches of conversation:

"These guys are real heroes. They got day jobs, for Chrissakes."

"See that man over there with the droopy mustache? That's Farouz what's-his-face, the owner of the rug shop. He looks like someone who just sold his entire inventory at retail."

"The cops didn't find any booby traps; now they can put out the fire."

"I hear it's a Nazi lab, which is way worse than Red P."

"Everything bad that could happen has already happened."

Miraculously, the fire company contained the fire with minimal damage—most of it from water sprayed at the building next door. All of the firemen and police were present and accounted for. Two were suffering from dehydration and heat exhaustion, but nothing serious. With the fire out, the Chiefs were giving interviews to the press. "No, we haven't determined what caused the blaze." "Yes, there will be a complete investigation." "No, we do not have any tentative conclusions. The investigation will take a while." "Yes, it was a meth lab." "Yes, of course we are surprised it blew up . . ." On and on.

The police and firemen waited for the camera crews and reporters to leave. Then Chief Cushing sent two firemen back inside. Five minutes later they reappeared, carrying what was, unmistakably, a body bag. They loaded it into an emergency vehicle, which pulled away on the long, slow ride to Dr. Cronkite's lab in Pennsauken.

CHAPTER 44

"FATAL EXPLOSION STUNS GARDENFIELD
"We're all terrorized now
"by P.C. Cromwell

"GARDENFIELD, NJ—Yesterday was our September 11. There was no dramatic attack from the sky. But the acrid smoke, the shell-shocked faces were the same. The Fire Department performed heroically, but couldn't protect us from the reality of death. I guess we should feel lucky only one person is dead or missing—not thousands. But that's a question of scale, not substance.

"What is the substance? That's the question I was asking myself as I left the scene. The embers still glowed and my face was smeared with soot because I got too close. What does it all mean?

"This is the answer I came up with as I drove home. It's not comforting. It's not flattering. But it's the truth.

"Yesterday was the tipping point. We had already experienced the unknown girl—'Ginnie Doe'—found dead in the Quaker meeting house.

"Then came little Gussie Parker, found in the pond. First bludgeoned, then drowned. But yesterday was the day that changed us forever. It was our Pearl Harbor, our Inchon, our Tet. The lesson couldn't be clearer . . ."

"We have to take the offensive, right?" said Biff. "We coulda won in Korea and Vietnam if we'd taken the offensive the way we did in World War II." All of the cops were assembled in the situation room while Chief Black read Peaches' article aloud.

"Wrong. You're not going to believe this . . ." the Chief resumed reading.

"The lesson couldn't be clearer. We've already tried to meet violence with violence. We've taken the 'law enforcement' approach. We've locked down our town, trying to keep the troublemakers out. We've turned ourselves into vigilantes.

"I can't walk the streets with my video camera without getting a funny look from passersby. In our local library, the librarians tell me they are uncomfortable because the police asked them to report anything suspicious.

"Our charming, historical town has been transformed into an Orwellian nightmare.

"And whom do we have to blame? Mayor Dove? He had the right idea, authorizing a variety of approaches. Chief Black? He tried his best, but came up empty and, in some cases, contributed to a heightened level of violence . . ."

Several voices rose in protest: "What's that supposed to mean? What a bunch a B.S.!" But the Chief silenced them. "We're just getting to the good part.

"But it's not all the Chief's fault. I think we also have to blame ourselves.

"For too long Gardenfield has been an island of complacency in the midst of a world that has far more grit and substance than we do. We're just across the bridge from Philadelphia and all its corruption. We're just up the road from Camden, crime capital of the U.S. two years running. Prosperity and privilege can't exist in a vacuum. It's the new law of social thermodynamics.

"Who do we think we are?

"Why should we be different?

"Let's tell the vigilantes to take off their sashes and go home.

"Let's let meter maids be meter maids again.

"The war on terror has come to Gardenfield. We're just going to have to live with it."

The room was silent as the Chief finished reading. Finally someone hazarded a mystified, "That's it?"

The Chief nodded.

"She's out of her mind."

"Is she trying to start a panic?"

"Whose side is she on?"

"What a loser! No way we're going to let some creep take our town away from us."

"That's it exactly," said the Chief. "I want to ask everybody, here in front of the entire force, do any of you think we're defeated? That we can't do this job? That we can't restore peace and safety to Gardenfield, like it was before?"

"Hell no!" they roared in unison.

Bruno felt a glow work its way up his spine. Though the language might have been a bit *purple*, the feeling was most definitely genuine. It was an inspiring moment.

Even the Chief seemed a bit choked up. "Thanks." He smiled. "That's what I hoped you'd say. Now if any of you run into Ms. Cromwell, make sure to be polite and treat her with respect. We don't want to give her any more ammunition."

"I'm having lunch with her tomorrow," Bruno announced to a chorus of boos, hisses, and pointedly rude suggestions.

Before he could explain that he was meeting Peaches as part of "a proactive public relations strategy," the phone rang. It was a call from the medical examiner's office. Dr. Cronkite was reporting that the dental records confirmed the identity of the body found charred beyond recognition in the fire.

"Everybody here had some kind of connection with him, for better or worse," the Chief said. "The man killed in the fire was Newton Ichabod Murphy III, better known to all of us as Icky."

CHAPTER 45

AFTER THE MEETING, the Chief invited Bruno to join him in his office.

"What do you make of all this?" asked the psychic.

"I think it's connected. We now have three deaths. All of them senseless attacks on innocent young people." He wrote a list: "GINNIE DOE—GUSSIE PARKER—ICKY," adding, "Icky wasn't exactly innocent. But . . . you know what I mean. They had no reason to kill him."

Bruno nodded. "Plus Maggie. You don't get more innocent than a dog."

"Right." The Chief added Maggie's name to the list, with the designation "K-9" in parenthesis. "And don't forget the threat against your niece." He wrote "MIMI C-MCRAE" in brackets, continuing, "None of this fits the profile of a serial killer. There's no sexual component. No pattern of physical abuse."

"So where does that leave us?"

"My hunch is that the first murder is the key," said the Chief, circling Ginnie Doe's name on the board. "The rest of it's all an attempt to distract us or cover up the first one." He crossed out the other four names on the list. "That's the one thing that is consistent, by the way, with serial killers. The first crime is the most significant, in terms of M.O." The Chief circled Ginnie's name yet again.

"Why's that?"

"The killer reads what they're reporting in the press. He knows what we're looking for and deliberately alters the pattern to confuse us."

"That's why I wanted to talk to Peaches!" Bruno punched his right palm with his left fist, making a loud smacking noise. "Remind her that bad guys read the paper too."

"Hopeless cause, in my book. I'd stay away if I were you."

"I'm thinking we could feed her some information, you know, strategically. Throw her off the track. Use it to our advantage."

"Like what?"

"I don't know. I'm trying to think of something. Maybe tell her Mayor Dove's wife's a suspect. Something like that."

"Don't. It could get us all fired. Speaking of which, did I ever formally re-hire you after the Mayor made me fire you?"

"I can't remember. You did let me out of jail early, but I can't remember if I'm officially working for you or not."

"Well now it's official. But you have to keep a low profile."

"Tell me about it." Bruno rubbed his battered forehead ruefully.

"Alison Wales is our best lead," the Chief continued. He erased the list of names and wrote Alison's instead in huge letters. "Ginnie Doe was wearing Alison's clothes when Mimi found her. Remember, we were talking about that just before the building blew up? That's the thread we need to pick up now."

"You don't think she was in the building?"

"We only found one body."

"I heard there wasn't much left of Icky."

"Until we have evidence otherwise, Alison lives. She is our number-one person of interest." The Chief circled Alison's name several times, then capped and put away the marker for emphasis.

Bruno sensed the meeting was coming to a close. "Too bad Peaches is so unreliable . . ." He yawned and stretched. "With the right publicity, we could have the whole county looking for her."

"That'd just ensure the bad guys would be looking for her too. I was hoping you could find her more discreetly."

"Sure, I just need a recent photograph."

"Good. We'll see what we can come up with. It's nice to have you back. But remember, your job right now is to make sure we're the first ones to find Alison Wales."

CHAPTER 46

"THIS INK IS RED," SCOWLED FISCHER. He had a pained look on his face. The CEO was meeting with Jurevicius and NewGarden's Investor Relations Director, Joli Nathan, to plan for the annual meeting that was now only three weeks away. He had just seen the printer's dummy for the new annual report for the first time.

"It's not really red. It's orange," Joli insisted, her face turning a definite shade of red due to the stress of the argument, which had been going on for some time now. An experienced professional in her late 30s, she had been at NewGarden for four years and felt a bit proprietary about the annual report. She was willing to acknowledge the CEO's expertise in matters of science, and his authority when it came to business. But he had no formal training in design; that was her specialty and he ought to listen to her, she felt.

"Orange, my ass!" fumed Fischer. "Do you think I don't know the difference between red and orange? Is there anybody who doesn't know? It's not a matter of opinion."

Joli was starting to hyperventilate. "The graphic designer says it's orange," she panted.

"You mean that gangly freak with the weird glasses and hair goop?"

Offended, she supplied the name: "That's Ted. Ted Manson. He did our report last year too."

"The origami Rubik's Cube that nobody could figure out how to put back together?"

"It won all kinds of design awards."

"The board hated it. And they're going to hate this one too. You never use red ink in a financial report. It has extremely negative connotations: You know, red ink. Losing money. Bad business. In the red. Bleeding red ink. Everybody knows this. I can't believe we're using red on the cover of this report!"

Jurevicius finally entered the conversation. "It's a moot point, Manny. The report is already printed. It'd cost us, how much . . . ?" He looked at Joli and she supplied the missing number: $25,000.

"It'd cost us 25,000 bucks to pull it now," Jurevicius resumed. "Maybe 30,000. And we'd miss our mailing deadline. That'd put us out of compliance, unless we postpone the meeting, which we simply cannot do."

Joli looked at Jurevicius with gratitude, though she wondered why he'd waited so long to come to her rescue.

"How did this happen?" Fischer grimaced.

"I approved it, Manny," Jurevicius replied tersely. "Maybe it's because I'm European; our semiotics are . . . different than yours. We are not afraid to use red. It is a bold color. It has a wide range of associations besides losing money."

"Such as?"

"Everything from Bauhaus to Louis Quatorze. The Duke of Wellington's jacket and the fabulous reds of Burgundy . . ."

"Don't forget Stalin's Red Army and the color of blood," Fischer interrupted angrily.

"Manny, Manny. That's a cheap shot. Nobody really notices these things. Nobody really cares. They'll look at the financials, not the cover."

"And those aren't great, either," Fischer continued. "I wanted to take a lower profile in this report. Yet you've splashed my picture all over the place. My face takes up an entire page."

"You're the founder, Manny. You're the CEO."

Fischer turned beet red. "Serge, you know damn well you and your investors are calling the shots and you have been for the last . . ."

"Manny, do we have to do this in front of Joli?" Jurevicius asked in a coldly formal tone. Joli glanced over to see if he wanted her to leave, but a discreet signal from Jurevicius told her to stay.

"I don't care who hears," said Fischer. He was screaming now at full volume. "It should be public information. I may be the CEO, but your group's running the show here. You should take accountability for the results. Look at the Letter to Shareholders. Nothing about medical research. Not a damn thing. It's all about Ag. But I've made a commitment . . ."

—"Ag pays the bills. As you well know."

"Well when I speak at the meeting I'm talking about medical . . ."

—"It's irrelevant and it confuses the shareholders . . ."

"Dammit, I made a commitment!"

". . . and upsets our institutional investors."

"Serge, I promised."

Jurevicius eyed him coldly. "Things have changed since then. My backers won't permit it. End of story." He turned to Joli, indicating that all of Fischer's issues had been addressed—and dismissed. "You should know that there may be protesters again. Security will be in place if needed, so you can focus all your attention on the meeting."

She nodded. His confidence was contagious. Everything would be handled.

Jurevicius regarded the brooding Fischer and smiled broadly. "Cheer up, Manny. You'll be happy to know my backers have authorized French champagne. A special bottling with our logo etched in the glass. And there'll be other surprises, too. It should be a memorable meeting."

CHAPTER 47

ALISON'S PARENTS LIVED IN A RESTORED VICTORIAN on Washington Avenue. Rebecca Wales invited Chief Black and Bruno into a room she called the parlor, which was furnished with overstuffed chairs, Oriental rugs, ornate lamps with poufy shades, and other Victorian-style bric-a-brac.

Her physical resemblance to Alison was striking. Rebecca's jet-black hair had turned white but she wore it in a loose ponytail that hung halfway down her back. She was plump, but her face was unlined and she had a steady, confident gaze.

"I'm so proud of Alison," she announced, her voice quivering slightly, looking up at the grandfather clock. "She's her own person. Passionate. Determined. She marches to the beat of her own drummer."

"Er, Mrs. Wales." The Chief was growing impatient. "Do you know where she might be right now?"

"Heavens no. I'm not that kind of parent. I never intrude. Herbert, my husband, teaches over at the university. His office is right around the corner from her dormitory. But he never, never pries. How she lives her life is her business. We're so proud of her."

"You know, Mrs. Wales, her boyfriend . . ."

"Yes of course I know about Icky. The poor boy."

"Alison could have easily been with him when the fire started. We assume she's alive because of the absence of evidence otherwise . . . It would be nice to confirm it with positive evidence. We would like to speak with her. Have you spoken with her?"

"No. Not for a week or so. No, I haven't."

"You're not worried about her?"

"Of course I'm upset by the situation. What kind of mother, what kind of person wouldn't be? But I know Alison's fine. She wouldn't get caught in a fire like that. It's not in her character. You see, she's not into drugs. She always left the room when that kind of thing was happening. She's very committed to her studies and other causes. She loved Icky, but they are very different in many ways. Their relationship didn't stop her from going away to college."

"So you have no idea where she is right now?"

"I assume she's at school, where she's supposed to be. It's not unusual for her to spend days on end in the library and for me not to be able to get a hold of her in her dorm room."

"You read my mind. We haven't had any luck tracking her down at school. What about your husband? When is he due home this evening?"

"Perhaps not until late. He's involved in a very demanding project. Interdisciplinary research with tremendous potential . . ."

The Chief had to interrupt her again. "Please, Mrs. Wales. If you don't mind, it would help us tremendously if you could provide a good, recent photograph of Alison."

She scurried off and they could hear the sound of her rummaging through drawers. Finally she returned with a framed photograph that she handed to the Chief. "I thought I had something more recent, but you couldn't really see her in any of those. This is a very good photo, however, and it's my favorite. It's from her performance in *The Miracle Worker* in the school play, junior year. Please take good care of it. I'll need it back when you're done with it."

"We'll take a scan of it and send it back right away," the Chief promised. "And Mrs. Wales?" He caught her eye to make sure she was paying attention. "Be sure to call us if you hear anything."

They remained silent until they were back in the police car. Then Chief Black sighed and shook his head. "Denial."

"What?"

"Denial," the Chief repeated. "It's one of the stages of grieving."

"I've heard of that, but I can never remember what they are."

"Denial. Anger. Bargaining. Depression. Acceptance. We're trained to go through this process every time when dealing with the families of victims."

"Really? It goes that way every time?"

"Hard to say. Take Mrs. Wales. Far as I can tell, she's in a permanent state of denial. It's not just Icky. Or Alison. She's in denial about everything. The world. People. Reality. Evil. Whatever you want to call it, she's not aware of it. That's why her face is so pure and unlined."

Bruno thought about it for a while. "You know those stages? I just realized those are just like my bar mitzvah, except backwards."

The Chief stared at Bruno, wondering if Rebecca Wales' goofiness might be contagious. "When we were sending out the invitations," Bruno continued, "my parents were fighting about whether or not we should invite my Uncle Dave and his family. Everyone hated them, but my father felt we better invite them anyway. He said he was worried about what his mother would have said, if she had still been alive and found out he didn't invite his own brother to his son's bar mitzvah.

"None of that made any difference to my mother, but he convinced her by saying, 'We should go ahead and invite them; they probably won't come, they live so far away.' But he was wrong. We invited them and they came, all the way from Schenectady. So that was *acceptance*."

Bruno was picking up momentum. "Naturally, we were all *depressed*. That's when the *bargaining* started. My mother figured we could put them at a table in the corner, where they wouldn't bother anyone. My father had to relent, since he'd been wrong about them coming in the first place. But when they saw where we'd put them, they made a big stink. Everybody was *angry*. They left early and took all the cold cuts. Even before the rest of the guests had finished eating.

"My parents are still fighting about it to this day. My father says it's my mother's fault. She *denies* it. She says it's all his fault. He *denies* it."

The Chief shook his head. Maybe everyone was on crank. Maybe the whole town had inhaled it via the fumes from the explosion. "That's amazing," he commented. "Your family sounds really messed up. Or did you just make all that up? I hope you did."

"It's mostly true, I guess," Bruno replied. "I never really thought of us as messed up before, but now that you mention it . . ." He lapsed into a visible pout and then, suddenly, brightened: "I wonder if Dora's family is like that?"

"What does Dora have to do with anything?"

"Dora Goldstein? Has to be Jewish. Have you asked her?"

"No."

"You better find out right away. Have you ever dated a Jewish woman before?"

"No. And Dora's been busy. The EPA's threatening to sue her for draining the pond. They're giving her 30 days to restore the habitat, which is no big deal, but then there's the paperwork."

"No way she's a *shiksa*. I need to explain a few things to you as soon as possible . . . "

—"No time for that right now," the Chief said. He handed Bruno the photograph that Rebecca Wales had supplied. "Whoever we're up against is smart, resourceful, and ruthless. We need to focus, and you need to be at the top of your game."

The Chief put the cruiser in gear, and Bruno began a careful study of the picture. "They've been one step ahead of us the entire time," the Chief continued. "I think that bomb was meant for Alison. Somehow she escaped. Hopefully she's still OK. We have to find her right away. What do you think? Can you get anything from this picture?"

Bruno frowned. "She has her eyes closed. I guess if you're playing Helen Keller, you might do it with your eyes closed. I can accept that. But for her mother to say it's her favorite picture—that's just ridiculous. Pathetic, really. I need something straightforward where she's looking right into the camera."

"I was afraid of that." The Chief turned the Crown Vic up the hill onto Tavistock Lane. "Maybe we'll have better luck at Icky's. Besides, I'm curious to talk to Dr. Murphy."

CHAPTER 48

ICKY'S FATHER COULD NOT HAVE BEEN LESS LIKE HIS SON. Dr. Murphy was dark-haired, tall, and energetic—without the use of drugs. Bald on top, he wore his hair close-cropped and cultivated a moustache, with reading glasses low on his nose and a polka dot bow tie.

He was clearly angry. In fact, Dr. Murphy had been angry ever since Icky had shown a lack of interest and aptitude for sports at the age of eight; a fair amount of his rage was directed toward Chief Black, who had been the coach who cut Icky from his first Little League baseball team. He didn't bother to try to hide his hostility as he answered the front door. "Fantastic. You're here with that charlatan. I can assure you I've been answering questions all morning. I'm in no mood to be pestered with nonsense."

"Wouldn't dream of bothering you at a time like this if it weren't important," said Chief Black.

"I need to get back to my patients. At least I can help them. Some of them even listen to me."

"Icky had a wild streak," the Chief remarked sympathetically.

"Yes, he did. He got that from me. But he didn't get my sense of direction. Instead he got his mother's preference for living in the

197

moment. A bad combination. But it all would have come right if he hadn't got tangled up with that slut."

"Excuse me?"

"The Wales girl. She's the one who got him started, mixed up with the wrong sort of people. Her parents provided no supervision. When they were 15, they'd go to her house and do whatever they wanted."

Chief and Bruno exchanged embarrassed glances. "Actually, the reason we're here is to ask if you might have a recent photograph that we could borrow . . . ?"

Dr. Murphy didn't let him finish. "Of Newton? Why would you want that?"

"Actually of Alison. We're trying to locate her. Guys often keep a photo of their girlfriends, you know."

"Not in this house, you wouldn't find something like that. He was always at that job of his at the Lenape. I imagine he might have kept some things there."

"Thanks for the suggestion. That'll be our next stop." The Chief turned to leave.

He pulled up short when he heard Bruno speaking for the first time. "Dr. Murphy. You're taking this hard. Is there anything I can do for you?"

Icky's father looked at Bruno as though he were an alien asking if he wanted his brain removed. "I am fine, thank you," he replied through tightly pursed lips. "I lost my son about a dozen years ago and have been moving on since then. I am simply irritated by all the red tape and your inability to establish a safe environment in this town. Now please leave me alone and don't intrude on my personal affairs again."

CHAPTER 49

GARY ROUNDED UP MEMBERS of the Red-Headed League and brought them in for interrogation. Kennedy was a hard case: heavily muscled, with a rough complexion. His hair was clay-colored and he looked at the world through narrow slits. He didn't seem concerned that he could be brought up on a variety of charges. "I don't know how any of that stuff got in there," he lied—brazenly. "Probably it was left there by the previous tenants."

"And why were you renting an apartment that none of you actually lived in?" Gary asked.

"We needed a place to get away from our families. We were talking about starting a band or something."

"So you won't mind if we test your skin and clothing for chemical residues?"

"That won't tell you anything," Kennedy sneered. "That stuff goes all over the place."

"Not if you never opened any of the bottles, it wouldn't."

"If the previous tenants were cooking, it'd be all over the apartment. I'm going to sue the landlord for not warning us."

Klinger was a head case. He had close-cropped carrot-colored hair, thimble-sized inserts in his ears, and a full array of other piercings and tattoos. His skin was broken out with terrible running sores and his breath could steal your appetite for weeks. Did he even realize exactly what had happened to Icky? It was hard to tell. Maudlin one minute, convulsed with insane laughter the next, then racked with coughs, he was barely worth interviewing. He did tell a long and rambling story about driving around with Icky in "farm country." Apparently they were looking for unattended fertilizer tanks, but didn't find any. In Klinger's case, ineptitude was a blessing that helped to keep him from killing himself for the time being. Icky hadn't been quite so lucky.

Finally, there was Sammy Pearl. Standing only about five feet, six inches tall, he had shiny, copper-colored hair and was reasonably coherent and cooperative. Pearl was genuinely shaken by the loss of Icky and clearly felt something approaching remorse when he stated, "That coulda been me in there." He provided valuable information about contacts in Philly. But he claimed that the group didn't have it together to start cooking, so the fire could not have started as a lab accident.

"What about Alison?" Gary asked. "Was she hanging out with Icky in the apartment?"

"No way. She was, y'know, going to college; she didn't want to have anything to do with speed freaks. I haven't seen much of her since high school."

Hearing Gary's report, the Chief sighed. There'd be nothing conclusive until they confirmed the cause of the blaze. "Time to visit the Lenape King." He rolled his eyes. "Are you ready to walk back in time?"

"No more dinosaurs, I hope," said Bruno, hurrying to keep up with the Chief as he left the Municipal Building.

"Just a little stroll along Ye Olde King's Highway," replied the Chief. He pointed to the canopy above them. "Just think, some of these trees were planted during the reign of George III."

Bruno surveyed the spreading branches of the sycamores and oaks. Did they have anything they could tell him? If he touched the bark, could he sense the emotions of people who had passed beneath them? The Hessian troops or the Continental Army? The spirit of Washington? The wit of Franklin? The fury of the mob? The vision of liberty? It had never occurred to him to try this. He suspected it would all be too remote, abstract.

The Lenape was well maintained with its mustard-colored clapboards and black shutters. It didn't look like a 250-year-old building, as it fit right in with the rest of downtown. Only the plaque by the door indicated its status as a historic landmark.

The Chief rapped firmly on the wooden door, which opened slowly. "May we come in?"

The man who answered stood half hidden in the interior as the door swung open. "My, there are a lot of you," he murmured.

Bruno looked around in surprise. Had other cops decided to come along at the last minute? Maybe some passersby had sensed a tour was about to start and decided to tag along. No, it was just the two of them . . .

"Well, come in," said the man at last.

Once inside, the Chief introduced him to Scott Spurrier, curator of the Lenape King Historic Monument. Bruno recognized the type immediately. He was tall, but not athletic. Weak vision. Thinning blond hair worn long, with a sort of Prince Valiant cut. Wrong side of middle age. Dressed in matching corduroy trousers and camel hair sweater vest—identical in spirit, if not in detail, to the way his mother dressed him in the sixth grade. No doubt about it. Mr. Spurrier was a *shmendrick*. Classic example. If he opened the refrigerator door, a bottle of ketchup would fall out and break. If he tried to wipe up the ketchup, he'd get a splinter in his hand from the wooden floor. If he tried to take out the splinter, he'd find a way to poke himself in the eye with the tweezers. If he went to the hospital for his eye, he'd contract a drug-resistant staph infection.

"Look . . ." whispered the Chief, grabbing him by the elbow. Bruno emerged from his reverie to realize he was standing in a poorly lit hallway. The inn's rooms were marked off with velvet ropes. Tables were set with period utensils to show how people ate and drank two and half centuries ago. No detail was overlooked, including mugs filled with papier-mâché beer and mucusy-looking oysters on the half shell.

"Looks like he swiped DNA specimens from Dr. Cronkite's lab."

The Chief chortled. Then he resumed his professional demeanor and asked Mr. Spurrier, "You heard what happened to Icky?"

"Can't say I'm surprised," the curator replied petulantly. "He was a walking disaster, an accident waiting to happen."

"You seem almost relieved," Chief Black observed.

"I won't mince words with you, Chief Black. I am glad he won't be coming back here," said Mr. Spurrier. He paused for breath, then continued with moderate heat. "You forced me to give him a job here, but I was never happy about having him around. He didn't have the education, the training. This wasn't his vocation."

"Yes. You were born to take care of the Lenape, weren't you?" The Chief grinned. Talking to Mr. Spurrier clearly put him in a good mood.

"What he and his girlfriend did to Dolley Madison's bed was no joke. We had to have the team from Rutgers set up a special project to restore it. That should never have happened. We have such limited resources."

"Where did they hang out when they weren't banging away on Dolley's bed?"

"I don't know. I was never sure." Mr. Spurrier looked uncomfortable.

"Could it have been the cellar?"

"No! The cellar is off limits. He wasn't permitted down there."

"Could he have gone down there anyway?"

"Certainly not. It's potentially dangerous. The foundations may not be safe. There could be gas leaks. I only go down there when I absolutely have to."

"When was the last time you absolutely had to?"

"A fuse blew."

"When was that?"

"Last month."

"And you replaced it. Did you notice anything? Any signs Icky was down there?"

"None that I noticed."

"Where is the fuse box?"

"At the bottom of the stairs."

"So you replaced the fuse but didn't look around?"

Mr. Spurrier indicated that he had not looked around. Bruno was beaming but trying not to show it. This was true *shmendrick* behavior; Mr. S's *shtick* was letter-perfect. Now if only he'd be so kind as to trip and fall down the basement stairs . . .

"Mind if we look around?" The Chief's deep voice intruded into Bruno's thoughts.

"I can't permit it. This is an historic building. This is where New Jersey threw off its shackles and signed the documents that renounced our status as a colony and declared our independence from England. The team at Rutgers insists . . ."

—"I'm afraid *I'm* going to have to insist," the Chief broke in, his good humor starting to wear off. "This is a murder investigation. Icky may have been a pain in the ass, but he died last night. We have to look around."

"Can you come back later, after visiting hours? I'm just one person here, I can't do everything at once."

The Chief ignored the objection. Instead, he strode nimbly to the front door and locked it. "I can guarantee there won't be too many tourists trying to visit today. With the exploding meth lab, I don't think many people are going to want to risk their health just to brush up on their colonial history."

CHAPTER 50

HEADING DOWN THE STEEP, NARROW STAIRCASE Bruno felt the weight of all the recent events pressing in on him. He could hear his heart thudding inside his chest. The nameless girl. Gussie. Maggie. Mimi. Icky. He was still a kid, really. Alison too. Maybe Biff was right. Maybe it was time to start taking things personally. Like it or not, he was in harm's way. He'd been selected. He was a target, a combatant.

It wasn't about emotion interfering with his psychic ability or mental state. Or power corrupting. He had no selfish purpose here. It was self-defense. If he waited for the killer to make his move, he'd likely be dead. It was as simple as that.

Bruno heard the Chief's voice ahead of him, "Remember this is a crime scene. Keep your eyes open and your hands in your pockets."

The basement of the Lenape King was, in fact, a series of brick-lined chambers. Each room was on a different level. Some required several steps to get in or out of. Others were separated by a sill of two or three inches. The mortar between the bricks was drying out, leaving piles of gritty gray powder everywhere.

They wandered around from one dank chamber to the next. The basement was poorly lit and it seemed like they might be walking in circles. Finally they stumbled into a room that was full of furniture. It was Icky's boudoir, containing all the items he'd brought in to make himself comfortable during the long hours when he was supposed to be the inn's night watchman. There was his filthy mattress covered with deplorable sheets. The cheap wooden bureau topped with a reading light and an overflowing ashtray. A Shop-Vac—they heard Mr. Spurrier murmuring, "I wondered where that had gone . . ."—and assorted piles of clothing, both male and female.

The Chief pulled on latex gloves. He was picking items up with tweezers and dropping them into Ziploc baggies, measuring, drawing diagrams, and taking notes feverishly.

Bruno was overwhelmed. Memories from his school days were starting to come back to him. "This used to be part of the Underground Railroad, didn't it?" he asked Mr. Spurrier.

"That's nothing but myth or legend," the curator explained with a long-suffering sigh. "Of course there was a lot going on throughout this area. The Quakers were quite active in the abolition movement. However, there are no documented efforts to help runaway slaves escape through Gardenfield. The center of activity was Philadelphia; they moved slaves north along the Delaware, crossing the river at Burlington. Or else through Lawnside. All of this has been thoroughly documented by experts in the field. The curious thing is that the legends about this place persist, despite all the evidence. I can't understand it."

"Look at this," the Chief called out gleefully. He had secured a cigarette butt with the tweezers and was holding it up like a trophy-sized fish for the world to see. "Gauloises. Pretty sophisticated taste for teenagers." He bagged it and moved to the next item, which provoked an excited, "Bless my soul, look at this. Bruno, quick, put your gloves on."

As Bruno struggled into the latex gloves, the Chief asked Mr. Spurrier, "Was this place used as a dungeon?"

The curator stepped back and rolled his eyes. "Another myth. The basement was a storage area for beer kegs. There were locked iron gates on some of these rooms to prevent the help from stealing."

"I see. And what did they use those iron rings for?"

"It's possible that prisoners were kept here, at times, during the

Revolutionary War. However, we believe those rings were used as a sort of pulley system for lifting heavy items: beer kegs, food stuffs, and such."

"Hmm? You mean to tie down the ends of the rope, or to give the men doing the hoisting some leverage? That makes sense. But then where are the actual pulleys? Wouldn't there be some evidence of them in the ceiling near the center of the room?"

He handed around Polaroids that depicted Icky or Alison chained to metal rings that were bolted into the wall. Neither was wearing a stitch of clothing.

"That little bastard," hissed Mr. Spurrier. "If he weren't dead, I'd fire him!"

"Quite the love nest," mused the Chief. "I can see it now: a new legend in the making for the Lenape King. If you handle this right, Mr. Spurrier, you'll have more visitors than you ever dreamed of . . ."

Bruno left the Chief and Mr. Spurrier mulling over the possibilities. He had to see the room with the iron rings. A few minutes later, he reemerged, panting and flushed with excitement. "Come quick! I found something!" The Chief and Mr. Spurrier dropped everything and followed him. "You're not going to believe this," the psychic promised.

And he was right.

Bruno seemed to have developed a keen sense of direction down in the Lenape's basement. He led them unerringly to the very last chamber, which was the one with the iron rings. Actually, now there was only a single ring attached to the wall. The other had pulled free and was lying on top of a pile of crumpled bricks. Next to the pile was a ragged hole, about two and a half feet in diameter. "Feel the breeze?" Bruno shouted, waving his hand in front of the opening.

The Chief moved forward with his flashlight at the ready. "It's a tunnel. I can only see about 30 yards back, but it's a tunnel, alright."

Mr. Spurrier bounded forward and tried to restrain him. "You can't go in there. This is an historic artifact, an important archeological site. We have to wait . . ."

The Chief gently extricated himself from his grasp. "This doesn't exist," he reminded Mr. Spurrier. "Remember, all of the experts have determined the Underground Railroad passed Gardenfield by. Besides, it's already been compromised; Alison and Icky have already been through it, who knows how many times? That means it's my responsibility to check out what they've been up to."

With that he disappeared into the hole, and Bruno followed. Chief Black felt twinges of guilt as he moved through the tunnel. It was only about four feet tall, with roots protruding from every direction, so he had to walk with care, bent over with his head out in front of his knees. The flooring was packed earth, and he could see traces of footprints moving through in both directions. He tried to stay to the right in order to leave as many intact as possible. But there was no question that recent use had probably destroyed historical evidence. That was too bad. He knew exactly how he would have felt if archeologists had interfered with his crime scene. It was just a case of competing and mutually exclusive interests. Lives were at stake.

Spurrier would just have to deal with it. And, the Chief consoled himself, the tunnel's support beams appeared to bear carved inscriptions. If this proved to be 150-year-old graffiti from escaping slaves, Mr. Spurrier and his experts would have an incredible find on their hands. In fact, it would attract so much attention, it'd probably be best not to say anything about it until the investigation concluded.

Finally Chief Black reached the end of the tunnel. He guessed it must have extended a couple of hundred yards. Right above him was a trap door. He opened it cautiously and found himself staring out at the back of a row of benches. He was in the Friends meeting house. The trap door was hidden in the floorboards of the first landing of the stairs that led up to the loft.

"Now we know how Ginnie Doe found her way into the meeting house without breaking in or leaving any trace," Chief Black reported when he had returned to the basement of the tavern. He was talking on his radio but staring directly at Bruno as he announced, "And, we know who brought her there. We're still looking for Alison Wales, except now she's not a witness. Now she's our number-one suspect."

CHAPTER 51

BRUNO FOUND IT DIFFICULT TO CONCENTRATE. He couldn't believe Alison was a suspect. The Chief said he was simply doing it by the book.

"No way," Bruno protested. "We've known for a long time that the meeting house was not the murder scene. Now we know *how* the body got there. It's an important fact, but it shouldn't change our assessment of Alison's role."

"Not true," Chief Black retorted. "It adds a critical element of pre-meditation. We know that Alison had the means to transport a body into the meeting house in secret."

"What about Icky? It could've been Icky. He also knew about the tunnel."

The Chief frowned. "Coupla things. First, Icky's life centered around drugs. There's nothing about Ginnie Doe's death to indicate it was drug-related."

"But Icky's death *is* related to the others. Do you think Alison started the fire? If she was mad at Icky, there are easier ways to break up."

The Chief held his ground. "Alison had quite a temper. Gary used to watch her kicking Icky's butt up and down Old Kings Road some-times when she caught him cheating."

"That's different than blowing up a building . . ."

"I know. I agree, it doesn't seem plausible that Alison is directly responsible for Gussie and Icky. But—I've said this before—everything starts with Ginnie Doe. It kicked off some kind of chain reaction, and Alison was involved right from the beginning. She knew about the tunnel. Ginnie was also wearing Alison's old clothes when Mimi found her. Alison had to take the trouble to get them from her parents' house. Everything we have points to her."

Bruno was silent. His instincts told him the Chief was wrong. But there was no point arguing. He'd have to find evidence.

"Do you think you can read that Polaroid?"

"Sure." Bruno shrugged, trying to sound equivocal. "It's recent. Her eyes are open and she's looking right at the camera. Shouldn't be a problem." He didn't tell the Chief that certain aspects of the photo were incredibly distracting. How could he ignore a tasty *knish* like Alison? No question, this was going to be a difficult assignment. "With any luck," he drawled, "we may even be able to find where she's hiding out, assuming she's still alive of course."

Back home, Bruno felt conflicted. He was using his normal technique, focusing on the subject's eyes in order to merge with her perceptions. But this time, a mysterious, still, small voice was whispering in ear, "You shouldn't do this. This is pornography."

Whose voice was it?

"It's beneath you," the voice continued to nag him. "Why are you lying in bed?"

Well, he was tired, for one thing . . .

"You don't need this *nafka*, this whore. The Kabbalah contains the mystic union of male and female. Kabbalah provides everything you need."

Bruno sat up. He focused intently on her eyes. Soon he could see her. Alison was working on a laptop. Like him, she was sitting up in bed. He tried to pick up details of the apartment, but it was difficult because she was focused on the computer screen. She was in a room. It definitely wasn't her dorm room at Penn. The bedspread was too floral and there appeared to be a doily on the bureau. Somebody's guest room? But it could be anywhere.

Now he looked more closely at the computer. She was writing something. It was difficult to make sense of it. There was so much jargon, liberally sprinkled with what appeared to be ancient Greek, based on the two words he recognized, *phallus* and *gynos*. Ah, she must doing her homework. Good girl.

Suddenly, the lights went out. Had he lost the connection? No. He sensed that she was still there, but just lying low. Had she sensed his presence? He'd never heard of anyone being able to do that, but there was a first time for everything. No. She didn't seem to be hiding. He didn't sense any resistance. Then he realized, she had shut her eyes. The paper must have been boring her too. She was trying to take a nap. Relax. Get inspired. Would he be able to see her dreams? That might be interesting. But wait. Someone was coming. A male form emerging from the shadows. It was Icky. Was he still alive? Had the fire been a set up? It couldn't be: The dental records showed it was Icky . . .

Then it struck him. *Shmuck-o!* This was all a fantasy. She was imagining herself having sex with Icky. Yuck. He was stuck inside her head, feeling everything she felt while that nasty *night-of-the-living-chazerai* crawled all over her. Was he an evil spirit? A *dybbuk*? On the one hand, the physical sensations were quite enjoyable; Alison was an experienced hand at giving herself pleasure. But the mental image of this thin, hairy, alabaster-bottomed, pustulent teenager with raging hormones, pawing and salivating, almost made him burst into tears.

Then the phone rang and hauled him back to safety. It was the Chief, impatient to know the results of his distant imaging work. Bruno somehow managed to pull himself together and affect a breezy tone. "I was just about to call you," he reported. "Alison's alive and well. And I think she's still somewhere in the area."

"What makes you say that?"

Bruno explained he had caught her in the act of doing her homework. The room itself provided no clues as to her location. But they could assume she must have some way of submitting her work.

"So all we have to do is interview her teachers to find out how they're receiving her assignments . . . Nice job. Thanks."

Before they rang off, the Chief asked if he was really planning to meet Peaches for lunch tomorrow. "Nothing good can come of it," he warned.

"I know that's what you think. But she's an intelligent person. I think if I can just get her to consider our perspective . . ."

"Forget it. That won't work."

"You've told me that. So I have a backup plan."

"Yeah?"

"Yeah. Appeal to her self-interest."

"Uh-oh. What do you have that Peaches wants?"

"Many things, foremost of which is a scoop."

"Oh no you don't," the Chief hollered. "I forbid you to tell her about the tunnel. This is a critical piece of information that the bad guys don't know we have in our possession. But we have to figure out how to use it to our advantage. Tell it to Peaches and the game's over."

"Maybe I could just sort of dangle it . . . without actually telling her what it is."

The Chief groaned audibly. "Don't even think about it. You're out of your league in this kind of thing. I'm begging you. Cancel the appointment. Call in sick. Shoot yourself in the foot. Do whatever you have to do. Just don't meet Peaches for lunch tomorrow."

"No can do. I'm feeling lucky."

The Chief groaned again. He sounded like he was passing a kidney stone. "What's that word you always say? It sounds like 'King of Prussia?'"

"Kineahora?"

"Yeah. That's the one. *Kineahora.* And keep checking in on Alison, every few hours or so. I want to know right away if you find out anything."

CHAPTER 52

PEACHES WANTED TO MEET BRUNO at one of the trendy new places on Garden Avenue in Killingswood. Peaches liked the ambience, but wouldn't be caught dead in any of the numerous Italian joints. The concept restaurant, formerly known as La Vache Folle, was much more to her liking.

It was a "slow food" kind of place that emphasized the use of local ingredients. The chef, Jacob Creutzfeldt, had brought his culinary skills to South Jersey all the way from Vienna. Many considered him a certified genius. Chef Creutzfeldt focused on beef (or veal). He would buy a single animal that he selected himself, and then create a menu featuring every cut of meat and internal organ. Nothing was wasted and it was all delicious. There were melt-in-your-mouth tenderloins and juicy rib eyes—to be sure. But he also prepared spicy tripes, delicately seasoned sweetbreads, brains, and the house specialty—kidneys in red wine sauce.

Despite rave reviews from Peaches and her colleagues at the *Pest*, the restaurant was losing money at an alarming rate. In response, Chef Creutzfeldt nimbly migrated to a surf-and-turf concept, changing the name to La Vache Folle et Le Poisson Nu. More mainstream cuts of meat and the addition of seafood certainly broadened its appeal. "If you liked La Vache Folle, you'll love La Vache Folle et Le Poisson Nu," crowed the *Pest*. Privately, though, Peaches said she missed the tripe.

Bruno was in reasonably good humor as he sat down to claim the table for their 12:15 reservation. Peaches had told him to "bring an appetite," so he'd eaten only a minimal breakfast. In fact, he was quite hungry and could have happily munched on a piece of bread. Unfortunately, the wait staff studiously ignored him, even though there was only one other couple in the restaurant.

Perhaps if he picked up the menu someone would notice? Inside the handsome blue leather cover was a handwritten document that explained the Walt Whitman theme inspiring many of the chef's preparations. Reading further, Bruno learned that the poet and his family were entombed in a cemetery on Garden Avenue, just a few blocks away in Camden. This had inspired Chef Creutzfeldt to create a series of dishes with ingredients mentioned in the poem. In addition, he'd been inspired to invent a new way to grill meat—the signature Singe-the-Body-Electric preparation, which had earned widespread acclaim.

"I prefer charcoal briquettes moistened with unleaded gasoline," Bruno reflected, "but who knows? Maybe this guy knows what he's doing."

He put down the menu and finally managed to catch a waiter's eye. He requested bread but, much to his surprise, the waiter refused to bring it. "We serve the bread after you order your food. Do you have a bottle of wine you'd like me to open? I can do that right away."

Out of luck. Bruno'd forgotten that Killingswood was dry, too. All he could do was sit and wait for Peaches. He thought about how uncomfortable the chairs were. This reminded him of his advertising days. Every meeting was *mano-a-mano* competition. Who called whom? Who chose the restaurant? The ordering protocol? Did you dare order for the other person? Eat more, drink more than they did? Who shows up first? Who grabs the check? Sure, he could go ahead and order something, even just a salad. But if he did that, he'd lose any leverage he might have had. Might as well take the Chief's advice and not even meet Peaches in the first place.

Then it struck him. Did Peaches call ahead and instruct the

waiters not to serve him any food until she arrived? Let him drink all he wanted, but nothing to eat . . . She said she was a regular here. He wouldn't put it past her. He had to stay focused. The goal was to locate Alison, without alerting her—or the real murderer—that they were looking for her. To do that, they needed Peaches to understand how people were using the information she was printing. Surely once she understood the impact, she'd be eager to cooperate.

When Peaches finally made her entrance, a crowd of waiters swarmed around her, taking her jacket and her hat; producing bread, mineral water. Addressing her every need. "She thinks she'll have me groveling before we even say hello," Bruno fumed. "Well she's in for a big surprise."

As usual, Peaches looked fabulous. Her hair was pulled back in a bun, rather severely, which only set off her white skin, ferociously dark eyes, and scarlet lips. It took several moments for Bruno to realize she was dressed in riding attire. Her off-white blouse had a frilly front, framed by the leather trim of her short, oatmeal tweed jacket. The trousers were skin-tight fawn-colored riding breeches with reinforced thighs.

Very erotic, those reinforcements, Bruno couldn't help thinking.

The outfit was completed by black lace-up riding boots and matching leather chaps. Bruno was busy checking her boots for manure—there wasn't any—and he noticed that she was carrying a riding crop, which she did not surrender to the wait staff. The only discordant element in this Victorian dominatrix getup was a twist of red yarn tied around her left wrist.

"Isn't this fantastic?" she greeted him warmly. "Have you ordered? No? Come on, I'll get Jacob to explain the menu . . ."

Peaches grabbed Bruno by the arm and led him to the kitchen. They burst through the swinging doors to find Chef Creutzfeldt and his sous-chef inspecting the catch of the day. They appeared to be arguing about something and Bruno could have sworn he heard snatches that sounded like *"feh!"* and then *"farbissiner,"* followed by something indistinguishable and then *"feygele."* Was Chef Creutzfeldt criticizing his sous-chef's selection of fish and calling him a "stubborn fairy?"

Or was he just misunderstanding German spoken with an Austrian accent?

Peaches was still holding Bruno's arm and she gave it a warm little squeeze as she trilled, "*Bonjour*, Jacob."

"*Bonjour*, mad'm'selle," Chef Creutzfeldt replied somewhat thickly. Bruno was getting the impression that she pulled this stunt every time she came here, and the Chef did not particularly appreciate it. Nevertheless, he was willing to play along for his best customer. "Ve got in der shad roe because ve knew you vas comink." He displayed the glistening strand of eggs for Peaches to inspect. Was it this that had provoked the Chef's derisive "*feh*"? If so, Peaches didn't notice anything wrong with it. "That looks *wonderful*," she chirped.

The chef explained that the choices for soup were either snapper (*Do not call the tortoise unworthy because she is not something else*) or Brooklyn Ferry Chowder. The main course was grilled fish or meat, using the Chef's signature Singe-the-Body-Electric technique, or the other house specialty, Mullica Tawny Stew, featuring a selection of the freshest catch from the nearby Mullica River.

During the recitation, Peaches squeezed her eyes tightly shut and breathed deeply with obvious pleasure. When she gave Bruno's bicep another squeeze, he decided to respond in kind. He freed his arm from Peaches' grasp and tried to slip it around her waist. She tolerated this only for a moment or two. She stepped forward out of his grasp and was about to ask a question but Chef Creutzfeldt cut her off: "Da choice for salad is Leaves of Wheat Grass mit Thousand Island Dressing." He was all business and clearly wanted to get back to work. "Da meal concludes vit Open Road Dessert Loafe, coffee, tea. Bill vill take your order, enjoy da meal." He gestured grandly toward the dining room and turned his back on his guests.

Peaches opted for the Grilled Delaware River Shad Roe. She urged Bruno to do the same but, with the memory of the overheard "*feh!*" still lingering, he decided he'd rather take a chance on something else. The menu listed Carpe et Brochet Farcie avec Crudités with the description "*local pondfish*" in parentheses. That sounded safe enough, so he ordered it.

Now they could get down to business. Peaches seemed to be in a good mood. Bruno felt confident that his strategy would work. And her opening remark seemed to confirm it. "You really look beat up," Peaches commented sympathetically. "I didn't realize . . ."

"It's a dangerous occupation," the psychic replied with what he thought was appropriate modesty.

Peaches frowned. "You just need a thick skin."

"True. True." Bruno was trying to keep his tone light and agreeable. "But you don't need such a thick skin," he added, "if they don't hit you in the first place."

"What's that supposed to mean?" she retorted.

"If the bad guys don't know what we're up to, if they don't know where to find us . . ."

"Bad guys," Peaches scoffed. "I can't believe you said that. It's like, they're the bad guys. What does that make you . . . the good guys?"

"Of course it does," Bruno stumbled on. "They're out there murdering people, we're trying to stop them . . ."

"That's so simplistic! It's completely normative, and so typical . . . In reality, things are much more complicated than that."

Bruno couldn't figure it out. Things had started out so well, but in less than two minutes the whole tenor of the conversation had changed. "OK. Forget I called them bad guys. I'll use a neutral term like 'murder suspects.' Does that work for you?"

Peaches looked noncommittal.

"Persons of interest?"

She stared at the saltshaker and drummed her fingers rhythmically.

"Let me spell it out," Bruno said, his voice rising with frustration. "Can I talk to you off the record?"

"Off the record doesn't work for me. It's a waste of my time."

That did it. Trying to be nice to Peaches was getting him nowhere. "On the record gets people hurt," Bruno spat back. "Let's review the facts, one by one, shall we? First, you write that I'm working on the case . . . then Gussie gets killed."

"So you think I'm working with the murderer?"

"No. Here's my point: I made up that stuff about the Quaker connection on the spur of the moment. You wrote about it and the next thing that happens is a kid from the Quaker school gets killed. What if the murderer read your article, saw we were up a blind alley, and decided to do something to keep us going in the wrong direction?"

"That's just a hypothesis," she pouted. "You're still just making things up."

Bruno ignored her. "Then, you write about my fight with McRae and the next day—the very next day—my dog gets mutilated and they're threatening my niece."

"Your niece? What are you talking about? I don't even know who your niece is."

"McRae is my ex-brother-in-law; his daughter is still my niece. She's the one that found Ginnie Doe's body. The police refused to release her name, but they—the bad guys—figured it out because *you* had to write about the fight. Why else would the psychic detective be mixing it up with McRae? Now they're threatening *her*. She's eight years old."

Peaches turned beet-colored. "You can't say that's because of what I wrote. That's ridiculous. How insulting."

"How else could they have found out?"

"Any number of possibilities. Maybe one of the cops is an informer. Or they picked it up off the radio with a scanner. Maybe they're tailing you. It's so unfair of you to accuse me. I'm just doing my job."

"Oh come off it. Why does the public need to know that I had a fight with my ex-brother-in-law? He's a jerk who's always had it in for me. So we had a fight. It's just family gossip. Where's the news value in that?"

Peaches reply was clinically perfect. "He's the city attorney. As a public servant, he needs to know how to behave himself in public. If he doesn't, then the public needs to be aware he may not be qualified for his job."

"But he was in his home! I can't believe I'm defending this *shmuck*, but doesn't he have a right to privacy in his own home?"

"Not if he breaks the law."

For a fleeting moment they almost connected. To Bruno, Peaches seemed like a journalistic automaton. He was getting desperate. What if he took a chance and told her about Alison? The tender moment he'd observed when she shared her iPod with Icky. Just before they blew him up. Now Alison, too, was in danger. Maybe that would penetrate her professional armor?

Instead, he heard himself asking, "But . . . but . . . couldn't you do it . . . out of friendship?"

The look on Peaches' face was one of total outrage. It was as if he had suggested they perform an obscene act right there on the white tablecloth.

"What kind of friend have you ever been to me?" she spat. "The very first time we met you were making fun of me in front of Buddy Black with all that stuff about the Catskills. OK, I'm not Jewish. I never went there. So why is it so funny that I don't know Yiddish or unfunny comedy routines from the '60s?"

Unfunny? At that moment, the light went on for Bruno: *Peaches had no sense of humor.* No wonder she was impossible. He decided a new strategy was in order. "I see you're wearing red yarn on your wrist . . ."

But before Peaches could respond, the waiter appeared with their dishes: "Delaware shad roe pour ma'moi'zel et le pondfish pour le m'zieur."

The presentation was truly a surprise. At a time when people were accustomed to tiny portions on pretentiously large plates, it was a revelation to be served a meal of Whitman-esque proportions, with food literally spilling over the edges of the plates. Peaches' dish consisted of the entire egg sack that they'd seen in the kitchen. It was seared on the outside and raw within. Wrapped around it were thick slabs of bacon and next to the fish rose a small mountain of scrambled eggs.

Peaches was in heaven. She tucked into the food with a ravenous appetite, from time to time grunting with approval. "This is exceptionally good! Do you want to try some?"

Bruno shook his head. On his plate were three pieces of something that looked like the inside of a bratwurst, each about the size of . . . a turd. There was also a gob of horseradish, several hard-boiled eggs, slices of cooked carrots and celery in a delicate gelatin, and a sprig of parsley for decoration.

Bruno started to remark that it looked like a seder plate, then remembered Peaches' sensitivity to Jewish references. Better be nice. "I couldn't help noticing the red yarn . . ." he resumed.

"I got it from that Kabbalah place in L.A." She showed her wrist as if to display a diamond bracelet. "It's incredible. They have an 800 number. I spoke with a Rabbi and he said he'd prepare this just for me."

"Really? How'd he do that?"

"I don't know exactly. The yarn comes from Israel. From the tomb of Rachel the Matriarch . . . "

"Hmpf," Bruno grunted, trying not to say anything critical. "I thought you said you weren't, er, familiar with Jewish traditions."

"C'mon, Bruno. You know yourself you were making fun of me. This is different." For a moment Peaches appeared to let down her guard as she smiled at him. "I have to admit it's ironic. After I interviewed you, I did that research and I found myself getting interested in Kabbalah. So I called them up—and it really wasn't anything like the things you were talking about. They were really nice. They said you don't have to be Jewish: Anyone can benefit, and they had a sensible attitude about the whole Magdalena-Tiffany-Pupik-celebrity thing, I thought."

Bruno reached across the table to touch the red string. "It's funny. Do you know what this means in my world? It's for warding off the evil eye. Grandmothers in the *shtetl* used to hide a small piece out of sight, pinned to their underwear . . ."

Peaches pulled her wrist away. "I believe in coming prepared. I brought this, too." She flourished her riding crop and flashed a shark-like row of teeth. "So you see, I'm like a Jewish grandmother and a Protestant bitch from the burbs, both at the same time. Even though I'm actually Catholic—not a practicing one, of course. Now eat your lunch." She pointed at his plate with the tip of her crop: "You haven't touched a thing. Don't you like it?"

Automatically, Bruno began eating. After a few bites, he realized he had a nagging sense of déjà vu. He took another small bite, paying close attention this time. "Interesting," he commented, munching on a carrot.

"Faint praise," said Peaches. "I love this place. In fact, Jacob, the Chef, is one of my dearest friends."

"I could see that," Bruno lied. He was preoccupied with the food. He was weak with hunger, and the bite of fish had piqued his appetite. Yet there was something funny here and he was starting to feel suspicious. He took a bigger bite this time, chasing it with a large helping of horseradish.

That did it. Now he knew. He could see the whole picture. This was the genuine article: Manischewitz gefilte fish. Not "brochet farcie," or "pondfish" or whatever they called it on the menu.

He took another large piece and put it on his fork with the rest of the horseradish. "This is so good, you really have to try it," he cooed at Peaches.

"Oh no," she demurred. "I really couldn't. I've had so much to eat already."

"Really, I insist." He waved the fork closer to her face. "There's an incredible similarity to something my mother used to serve."

"Oh I doubt it. Jacob is a genius. And totally original."

"So why don't you try it? I bet Rachel the Matriarch would've liked it . . ."

"Bruno, please! Stop! What are you getting at? Please take your fork out of my face, right now!"

"You were setting me up, weren't you?" Bruno's voice was low and menacing. "You had your friend put together a seder plate to see if I would recognize it—didn't you? You were going to write that I went out to lunch with you, ate a huge plate of gefilte fish from a jar and didn't even know it wasn't some fancy preparation your friend made up. Local-*shmocal*. You wanted to get even by making me look like some moron who's happy to pay $35 for a few lousy bites of Manischewitz. That's really low."

"What are you saying? You're insane."

"This meeting is over!" he snapped and stalked toward the door.

Peaches' anger reduced her to tears. "You horrible man," she snarled. "I hate you!"

And with good reason. Not only did she miss out on dessert, but Bruno's abrupt departure meant she was stuck with the check.

CHAPTER 53

LOUSY LUCK, THOUGHT BRUNO, as he drove back toward Gardenfield a few minutes later. *There were a few moments there when she and I were starting to hit it off.* He'd have to admit the Chief was right. And then there was the red string. "I can't believe it's authentic; I'm sure it was acrylic, not wool."

Just then Bruno realized how hungry he was. That reminded him. He'd forgotten that Chris, the guy at Tano's, wanted to see him. What better way to turn his day around than with a cheesesteak? It seemed like a lifetime had passed already since the morning he got out of jail. He hoped Chris would still be there since the lunch rush was probably over.

He needn't have worried. "Hey, Bruno, where you been, you loser?" shouted Chris as he walked in the door. This was more like it: an island of sanity in a demented universe.

"Hey, Chris, make it the usual, with everything on it."

Instantly he could smell the onions frying on the grill. "I been waiting for you to come by," Chris called out over the roar of his exhaust fan. "You know those security guards that are all over town?"

"Sure. How could you miss them?"

"Right. Well. They keep coming by for lunch. You ever talk to any of them? No? Well, take it from me, they don't spikka-de English too good. And they're not Italian, because I told them to *va . . . a . . . fare . . . in . . . culo,* y'know, real slow and distinct, but they just smiled. Anyway, I think my steaks remind 'em of their home cooking."

"Makes sense."

"Yeah, I asked one of them for a patch for my collection. Since they work in security and all, they must have a shoulder patch. But I couldn't get through to him. I thought maybe you could explain it."

"Why me? I don't speak French," said Bruno. Knowing the parent company for NewGarden Biosciences was French, he assumed the security detail was probably French-speaking.

"Hmm," mused Chris. "I wondered if they might be Israeli or something. They kept making this sound like they were clearing their throats. You know, *cha-kha-rissa.*" He made a series of horrible gagging noises deep in his throat. "So I figured it was Hebrew or something."

Bruno laughed. "That's not Hebrew. It sounds like they were saying *harissa* with a Middle Eastern pronunciation. Harissa's hot sauce. Your steaks must remind them of couscous, which they usually eat with harissa. So that's French, not Hebrew."

"How am I going to get them to give me one of their patches, then, if you don't speak French?"

Bruno thought for a moment. "You could try Peaches. You know her? P.C. Cromwell. I've heard her speak French and I can tell you, her accent is almost perfect."

"That lady who works for the *Pest*?" said Chris. "She speaks French?" He served Bruno his cheesesteak, adding, "She doesn't come in here too often, but I know her. She's a piece a work."

CHAPTER 54

THE DISCOVERY OF THE UNDERGROUND PASSAGE at the Lenape King generated much excitement, as it seemed to promise a speedy conclusion. In fact, it was a brick wall. Everything pointed to Alison. But they needed to find her and, in spite of Bruno's regular monitoring, there were no solid leads to indicate where she was hiding.

Chief Black dispatched Michelle and Nancy to the Penn campus. Most of the faculty showed appropriate concern and were quite helpful. Each explained in turn that Alison had written to say she could not attend classes due to health reasons. But she was keeping up with the reading, downloading the lecture notes, and mailing in her homework.

The one exception was Professor Littlejohn in the Sociology Department. He actually had a lawyer sitting in on the interview with him. Instead of answering questions, he made a speech. Obviously, he was trying to evade the issue. Why? Did he know something? Or was he just another pompous blowhard? Nancy and Michelle ducked out at the first opportunity.

Then they caught a break. One of the professors, an odd, old duffer named John Barker, admitted that he remembered receiving the envelopes, but hadn't opened them. "They must be here somewhere," he muttered as he riffled through a stack of papers piled on a credenza. "I teach a course in physics for non-majors," Professor Barker explained. "We used to call it Physics for Poets but the students didn't like the look of it on their transcripts. Said they wanted something more robust. So now we call it Postmodern Physics: The Flow of Energy in the Cosmos and on Earth. In fact, it's the same course I've been teaching for 30 years. Physics is physics."

He moved to another pile and continued rummaging. "I assign the papers, but I can't bear to read them. They're utterly idiotic." His face brightened as he moved aside a stack of journals, "Ah, I think I've found them." Michelle moved closer. She pulled out her latex gloves and evidence bags.

"Yes, here they are. Alison's are the ones in manila envelopes. She's quite attractive. I was sorry when she stopped coming to class . . ."

"Excuse me, professor," said Michelle, gently moving him aside. She carefully extricated the tan envelopes while Nancy held open the bags to receive them. "You have been extremely helpful," said Michelle, "and we are grateful."

She turned to go, but Professor Barker detained her. He was blushing. "I'm a bit embarrassed about not reading the papers and I wanted to explain . . ."

"It's not necessary, Professor," said Nancy gently. "You're doing your job the best way you know how. If the kids do some of the reading, learn a little about physics, you're way ahead of the game."

"Yes, but . . ."

"Professor, I understand." She fixed him with her steady green-eyed gaze.

Professor Barker struggled to maintain some of his dignity, but Nancy pressed the advantage: "Professor Barker? There's one more thing . . ."

"Yes. What is it?"

"You wouldn't mind if we took your fingerprints, would you?"

The Professor rolled his eyes toward the unfeeling cosmos. Why was he putting up with this, he asked himself, when he could be casting dry flies to rising rainbows? It really was time to retire.

CHAPTER 55

ICKY'S FUNERAL WAS A NOTABLE AFFAIR—sort of like Woodstock, without the mud. Of course, everyone was dressed in black. Black T-shirts. Black leather. And a sprinkling of traditional black suits and dresses, worn by the minister, the Murphys, and their friends.

The day was exceptionally hot. The mourners were sweating profusely, which, somehow, substituted for tears. It was a graveside ceremony; people brought blankets to sit on, hampers stuffed with good things to eat and drink, and other goodies such as Icky himself might have enjoyed.

Jay Miller, Icky's friend since kindergarten, got things rolling with a Hendrix-inspired version of "Taps" played on solo electric guitar.

Then a young woman gave a soulful rendition of "Amazing Grace," a cappella.

This was followed by "Amazing Grace" on the bagpipes. The inexperienced piper had trouble managing his breath, so the music came out in a herky-jerky, barely recognizable fashion, and some of the mourners started hooting.

Next, a bluegrass combo started in on an interminable version of "Will the Circle Be Unbroken?" on fiddle, banjo, and washboard. By now the crowd had moved beyond restive; they were downright hostile.

This was the moment when Icky's father decided to take control of things. "Why don't you all go home, you freeloading degenerates?"

Icky's friends had learned to ignore Dr. Murphy long ago and they responded with obscenities and threats. Someone threw a half-eaten cheeseburger at him. As Dr. Murphy retreated, the band segued into a bluegrass version of "Danny Boy." The mob roared its approval and tried to sing along.

Standing in the back, Chief Black whispered to Bruno, "If this gets any worse, somebody's going to have to call the cops."

Bruno was sulking. There was no sign of Alison. He hadn't wanted to drive in from Tabernacle, but the Chief had convinced him she might show up.

"Could that be her over there?" the Chief indicated the direction with a nod of his head. "The woman in the gypsy costume?"

Bruno squinted. The sweat was getting in his eyes and this was about the half-dozenth time the Chief had thought he'd spotted her. "That's no gypsy," Bruno explained. "It's Alison's mother, impersonating Janis Joplin."

Now it was Joe Kennedy's turn to give a personal remembrance of his friend. He couched his remarks in terms of a drug deal, praising Icky's character because he "paid his dues" and "gave good weight."

Dr. Murphy razzed him repeatedly as an "insipid lout," a "characterless reprobate," and a "drug-crazed Neanderthal," until finally Mrs. Murphy managed to pull him off to the side, where the two argued with some intensity.

Some of Icky's high school teachers said they regretted the fact that he had dropped out because he never fulfilled his potential. This produced a round of snickers from the recent graduates.

Finally, Mr. Joyce, the Unitarian Minister, got up to deliver his eulogy. He announced that he'd taken his inspiration from the plaque on the side of the building where Newton (Icky) had spent his last conscious moments. It seems that back in 1777, one Jonas Cattell had performed a heroic feat, not far from the spot of the tragic fire. Young Jonas had escaped the captivity of His Majesty's minions and run a distance of 10 miles to alert the commander at Fort Mercer that the Hessians were coming; the attack would come by land, not by the river, and he must turn his guns around. By this effort, Jonas Cattell enabled a revolutionary American army of only 300 to defeat a force of 1,600 mercenaries.

Why did he mention this? Icky could not have run 10 blocks, Mr. Joyce conceded, let alone 10 miles . . .

—"Yeah, but he could do 10 lines faster than anyone," a voice interrupted, much to the mourners' delight.

Mr. Joyce gracefully acknowledged the witticism before continuing, ". . . and certainly, he was no soldier. Yet like Jonas Cattell, Icky was 18 years old. And he was also fighting long odds."

"I know his middle name was Ichabod," Mr. Joyce continued, his voice resonating as he neared his conclusion. "But I like to think of him as Icarus. He was the fair-haired boy who flew too close to the sun. He singed his wings and fell to his death: senseless, tragic, and premature. *But what a glorious figure he cut while soaring so high!*"

Somehow these words silenced the hecklers. They knew it was utter nonsense, but at the same time, it was the right thing to say about Icky. It was exactly what they would have wanted said about themselves, if they had come to ruin due to their own stupidity.

As the crowd dispersed, Bruno and the Chief walked off together, scanning the crowd for Alison in disguise. No luck. She'd skipped the funeral.

The Chief quickly brought Bruno up to date. The manila envelopes Alison was using to send in her homework had all been postmarked "Gardenfield." The only identifiable prints were those of Alison and Professor Barker. Chief Black had the force pulling extra shifts so they could stake out the post office and keep an eye on as many mail boxes as possible. He also had Harry researching the possibility of putting different types of ultraviolet powder in some mailboxes to try to narrow down where the envelopes were being mailed from.

CHAPTER 56

FOR THE NEXT WEEK, Bruno stayed out in Tabernacle, tending to Maggie, going for long walks, watching the vultures circle, and trying to repair some of the damage to his trailer. He also checked in on Alison once or twice a day. She was invariably inside, in the same room where he saw her before, doing homework or indulging in sex fantasies. She seemed to Bruno omnivorous and insatiable. At first she seemed content to recall her greatest hits with Icky. Then she branched out to other men, famous actors, rock stars, and even a horse. Unbelievable. Eventually Bruno realized he was eavesdropping on her dreams.

Unfortunately there were never any details that could indicate where she was staying.

Finally, Chief Black interrupted this peaceful interlude. He called to say it was time to interview Rebecca Wales again.

Alison's mother retained her sunny optimism. They were sitting out on the screened porch, sipping lemonade as a series of cats came in and out at will. "Alison will be fine," Mrs. Wales insisted. "I assume she's laying low until you discover the real killer. Isn't that what anybody would do? I know it's what I would do. And of course I wouldn't tell my mother where I was. Alison would have to know that you'd come here to ask me and she wouldn't want to put me in an awkward position where I'd have to lie."

"That's very considerate of her, Mrs. Wales," the Chief said politely. "But we'd really be in a better position to help protect her if we knew her whereabouts and could ask her some questions."

Mrs. Wales gave them a big moony smile and stroked the nearest cat.

"Who were her friends in Gardenfield?" the Chief persisted. "Where could she be staying?"

"I really don't know." Mrs. Wales sighed. "I suppose if it's something devious it might involve some friend of Icky's." She thought about the funeral and shivered. "Of course, I'm not nearly as judgmental as Dr. Murphy."

"Of course not." The Chief decided to try another tack. "You know the key to this case may be what we've been calling the Quaker connection. You're a Quaker, aren't you? Why do you think Alison would bring a body to the meeting house?"

"I really don't think that was Alison. That sounds much more like something Icky would do. You know they both attended Gardenfield Friends in elementary school. I think they met in third grade. Teacher Mildred's class. She lives in a retirement home, now. Over by the mall. Which reminds me. Have you heard the news about Master Quentin?"

No, they hadn't.

"He had another relapse of his old illness. It's something he picked up at the time of the Vietnam War. He and Dr. Fischer used to have such big disagreements back then. They wanted to read Dr. Fischer out of meeting . . ."

"Read him out of meeting? What does that mean?"

Mrs. Wales frowned. "It's a Quakerism. It just means 'kick him out.' Give him the old boot. We Quakers aren't always that gentle, you know."

"Why would they kick someone out of meeting?"

"There are all sorts of reasons. Usually it's for not participating, either by showing up to meeting or making a financial contribution. But with Manny Fischer it was different, because he was doing that research and, you understand, Quakers believe something like biotech is tampering with the order of things—it's not peaceful, if you see what I mean. When word got around that Fischer's work involved messing around with the genetic code . . . a lot of people got upset."

"So that's when they—what do you call it—read him out of meeting?"

"There was a lot of discussion. But they never did read him out."

"No? What happened?"

Mrs. Wales sighed. She seemed to have run out of energy. "I don't know. Maybe he wrote a big check or something. I don't think Master Quentin was too happy about it."

"When did all of this happen?"

"Whenever Fischer launched his company here. I can't remember what year that was."

"So it couldn't have been anything Alison was involved in?"

"Of course not, are you crazy? I was signing her up for pre-school, for goodness' sake. I remember talking to Master Quentin about the school and wondering whether the rumors about him and Fischer were true. How could Alison be mixed up in anything when she was four years old?" Mrs. Wales broke down. She was sobbing violently. "You're trying to blame my Alison for everything. But she didn't kill anybody. She couldn't. She's a gentle, loving girl."

CHAPTER 57

FIRST THING BRUNO DID WHEN HE GOT HOME was to check in on Alison. She was banging Prince Harry.

Next, he picked up the phone to call Dr. Fischer. Chief Black wanted to find out more about the connection between Fischer and Quentin and, because he was busy with some kind of training, he asked Bruno to take the lead on the Fischer angle.

Bruno said he'd be happy to do it. However, he was terribly let down when a different receptionist answered the phone. "Dr. Fischer will be extremely *hawd* to reach during the run-up to *owr* annual meeting," she cawed. But her accent could not compare to Rhonda's delicious nasalizations. "Try *cawlin'* back after May 26. Or would you like to speak with Dr. Jurevicius?"

"This is a personal call for Dr. Fischer. Tell him Bruno X, Psychic Detective, wants to speak with him."

He didn't expect to hear back, but at noon the next day Bruno received a call. It was Dr. Fischer, inviting him for a drink at his home around five that evening.

Why not the office, Bruno wondered? Was this a set up? Dr. Fischer lived in Garden Acres, the most exclusive—and most remote—neighborhood in Gardenfield. Was he luring the detective out to this lonely area in order to dispatch him?

Bruno drove over early to avoid any chance of getting stuck in rush-hour traffic. As always, Garden Acres felt a bit like a theme park or a museum. Every house sat back from the street on a comfortable five-acre lot and there were never any people visible. Each house had a different architectural style. As you drove down the lane, it was like an encounter with a different culture—the Tudor mansion, the Russian dacha, the Swiss chalet, and the mid-century modernist glass-and-concrete bunker.

Dr. Fischer lived in the Spanish eclectic hacienda with stucco walls and red tile roof. Bruno drove up the circular drive and parked under the ornate portico that protected the main entrance. Fischer came to the door, dressed in jeans and a worn oxford cloth shirt. He seemed agitated. His rumpled gray hair was out of place. Bruno looked around. Instead of the arrases, suits of armor, and blunderbusses he'd expected, the home was simply decorated with an interesting collection of contemporary landscape paintings.

Fischer was drinking a gin and tonic and he offered to make one for Bruno.

The psychic tried to decline. "Thanks, but I'm really here on business."

"I invited you for a drink and conversation. I thought I made that clear on the phone." Fischer mixed a drink and handed it to Bruno. "I genuinely want to help your investigation in any way I can. But I see it as a personal matter. So I prefer to discuss it at home instead of the office. And I'd appreciate your discretion, as much as possible." He lifted his glass and proposed a toast: "*Lchaim.*"

Bruno winced. Fischer sure was laying it on thick. "*Lchaim,*" he echoed, touching glasses.

Fischer led him into his study. It was a comfortable room, lined with bookshelves holding, primarily, medical texts and journals. Bruno looked around and chose to sit on the leather recliner. It looked like it might keep him from falling on his face—in case the cocktail was spiked.

"I'll come straight to the point," said Bruno, leaning forward to propel his question with greater impact. "Do you know Alison Wales?"

"Who?"

"She's a college student. Comes from a local Quaker family. In fact I was just speaking with her mother yesterday. Rebecca Wales."

"Never heard of them. The name sounds familiar but I don't know them personally."

"We think Alison may be mixed up somehow in the nameless girl's death. It's possible she transported the body to the meeting house."

"That's terrible."

"Yes it is. Personally, I don't see Alison as a murderer. But why the meeting house?"

"Why are you asking me? I told you I don't know her."

"You are a prominent member of the meeting . . ."

"Hardly." Dr. Fischer rose from his chair and paced back and forth behind his desk. "I think I'm catching on to your line of reasoning. This Rebecca Wales must have told you some of the old gossip that people used to say about me."

"She told me that they wanted to read you out of meeting."

"Right." Dr. Fischer grimaced. "When they found out what NewGarden does, they started labeling me as another *Dok-tor Frankenshteen* . . ." He said it with a German accent, holding his arms stretched out in front of him à la Boris Karloff. "And they brought out, point for point, all of the standard misconceptions about biotechnology. I think there must be a manual out there that all of them read."

Bruno took a sip of his drink. Fischer seemed in the mood to talk. Bruno wanted to encourage him. "Dr. Jurevicius explained all the counter-arguments when we met in your office. He was very convincing . . ."

Fischer nodded in acknowledgement. "I suppose Mrs. Wales must also have said something about my relationship with Quentin Richards?"

"As a matter of fact, she did." Bruno raised his glass, as though toasting Fischer's mind-reading abilities.

Fischer barely noticed. He had the bit in his teeth and was off to the races. "I met Quentin during the Vietnam War. We served together in Fort Detrick. That's in Maryland. Nice town, Frederick. Ever been there?"

"No."

"You like soft-shell crabs?"

"Sure. Doesn't everybody?"

"Then you'd like Frederick. And you know what goes on at Fort Detrick?"

"Enlighten me."

"USAMRIID," said Fischer, pronouncing the word as if it were deadly. "The acronym stands for U.S. Army Medical Research Institute of Infectious Diseases. It is our main facility for biological and chemical weapons research. Fort Detrick has the world's most sophisticated containment facility, which makes it the ideal spot for the U.S. military to do most of its testing."

"But . . ."

"You were about to say that the United States gave up producing bio and chemical weapons a long time ago?"

"Right. I thought . . ."

"You thought we discontinued our offensive weapons programs in 1969? You are most definitely right about that."

Bruno nodded. He was annoyed at Fischer's interruptions and his habit of putting words in his mouth. He was about to take another sip, but all of this talk about biological weapons renewed his suspicions. Didn't the drink have a strange chalky undertaste?

". . . but we continued our *defensive* weapons programs," Fischer droned on. "You see, you can't test your *defensive* capabilities without having some *offensive* weapons to put them up against. And where were we going to get the *offensive* compounds needed for the tests? Buy 'em on the black market?"

Fischer sat down again. He was pleased with his joke, and that seemed to relax him. "Things were different when Quentin and I were there in the early '70s," he recalled. "The Fort was transitioning out of weapons production, but that was happening at a different part of the facility. We were involved with a program that continued a line of experimentation that had been going on since World War II. You see, after Pearl Harbor, there was a great need to learn more about fighting in the tropics: What kind of rations should you send up with pilots who might get shot down over the Pacific? Was it or was it not a good idea to drink seawater if you were stuck on a raft and that was your only option? These and a thousand other things you wouldn't normally think of."

Fischer retrieved the bottles. Bruno assumed he was preparing to refresh his drink.

"A critical issue was malaria." Fisher held up the bottle of tonic water for Bruno's inspection. "Quinine was the most effective remedy, and the Japanese controlled access to its principal sources. Thus, the U.S. military had to conduct extensive experiments on how to protect the troops from malaria. These experiments required human subjects and, believe it or not, people actually volunteered. They allowed themselves to be bitten by malaria-carrying anopheles mosquitoes. Now that takes courage, does it not?"

"Who were these volunteers? Did they really know what they were getting into?"

"Yes, they knew. Some of them were conscientious objectors, wanting to prove they weren't cowards. Others were prisoners, hoping they'd get time off for helping out. It wasn't like what happened in the 1950s, with MK-ULTRA and the radiation experiments. In those days, they'd even experiment on each other. Turn your back and they might put a huge dose of mescaline in your drink." Fischer winked. "By the way, you look like you need your drink freshened up."

Bruno shivered and tried to pull his glass away. Nevertheless, Fischer refilled it. "They would have loved to experiment on you, back in the '50s." Fischer chuckled. "With your psychic powers. They'd want to examine your brain to see if they could understand how it works. But, I digress. Where was I?"

"Malaria experiments."

"Correct. During World War II, two medical breakthroughs enabled us to save countless lives. Penicillin and DDT. Sounds funny, doesn't it? DDT is very effective against mosquitoes. It enabled us, first, to protect our soldiers in the tropics, and then to virtually eradicate malaria in the U.S."

"But it is so carcinogenic," Bruno protested.

Fischer shrugged. "Drinking coffee is 50 times more so. Drinking one of these per day," he held up his gin and tonic, "carries more than 2,000 times the cancer risk of DDT. You choose your poisons. Where was I?"

"DDT."

"Right. They banned it. 1972. Nixon created the EPA and what's the first thing they do—ban DDT? Don't get me wrong. I remember walking by Logan Pond 25 or 30 years ago and seeing soapsuds blow across the surface like tumbleweeds. You could choke from the exhaust of unleaded gas. And people would throw cigarette butts and beer cans out of their car windows and not think twice about it. Things have clearly changed for the better. But malaria still kills millions of people around the world each year—and it's preventable. That bothers me." Fischer looked at Bruno. "Can I get you another drink?"

"Do you have any . . . bottled water?"

"Always the quick wit." Fischer toasted Bruno and took another drink. "I'm sorry this is taking so long, but the story won't make sense without the background: In the '70s, one of the larger programs at Detrick was Operation Whitecoat. They had a whole contingent of Seventh-day Adventists who agreed to be subjects in experiments for a variety of infectious diseases. I was working in a parallel program. Since I'm a Quaker, they put me in charge of an experiment using Quaker volunteers. We were targeting malaria.

"Basically, we had to resume where they'd left off back in 1945, and that's where I met Quentin. He was a quiet man. One of the few black Quakers, despite the Friends' longtime opposition to slavery and their championing of civil rights. Well, we don't sing in church, what can I say?"

"Amen." Bruno raised his glass, but didn't drink.

"Quentin was a volunteer subject in my program," Fischer continued. "I infected him with malaria. And the treatment I administered . . . did not work. He developed a fairly serious case, though he did recover for the most part. He still has relapses. And he experienced a loss of hearing that may get much worse as he gets older. Unfortunately, a man he met at Detrick, who later became his close friend, Bennett DeKalb, was much more seriously affected. The disease permanently weakened his heart and lungs. His capacity for work—and other things—has been seriously limited. As you may know, Quentin employs him at the school, but doesn't expect too much from him in the way of duties."

He sighed deeply. "Quentin knew the risk he was taking in volunteering for the malaria program. DeKalb did too. Neither of them ever blamed me. But I blame myself. I swore to them that I would devote my life to medical research, curing infectious diseases, as a way to discharge my debt to them.

"Once I got out of the army, I did a post-doctorate at Stanford and that led an to opportunity to do breakthrough work in recombinant DNA at Genentech. Several jobs later and a lot of hard work, I founded my own company. We were doing monoclonal antibodies. The bottom dropped out in the early '90s. No one saw that the big breakthroughs were just around the corner. Funding dried up. We needed a new business strategy.

"That's when I met Serge. He and his backers were interested in making an investment in the U.S. Their expertise was agriculture, ours was medicine; we saw that as an opportunity, not an obstacle. We went public, changed the name to NewGarden Biosciences. That got local attention. For some reason, agricultural biotechnology gets the public stirred up, but medical biotechnology does not. People at our local Friends Meeting were disturbed. They accused me of tampering with God's creation. And they did threaten to read me out."

"What'd you do?"

"I increased my financial stewardship. Quentin was skeptical. I said, 'I'm like the Free Quakers during the Revolutionary War. I'm a pacifist but I don't mind fighting for a good cause.'" He sighed again and grinned weakly. He seemed pleased with himself, with his confession. "So that's my scandalous past. Honestly, I have no idea what this Wales girl is up to. College kids think corporations, and biotechs in particular, are the devil incarnate. In fact, we're just trying to feed more people and keep them healthy."

"So, according to you, there's nothing sinister going on at New-Garden?"

Fischer looked stunned. "You don't believe me? I'm telling the truth. We're a serious research facility and a business."

"What about Dr. Jurevicius?"

"He's a brilliant scientist. We've had a successful business collaboration for more than a decade."

"You two get along great, see eye-to-eye on everything."

Fischer frowned, thinking about the argument over the annual report. He wanted to be careful how he talked about this. "Of course we have professional disagreements. Over business strategy, for example. We compete for resources, but that's just budgeting. Nothing relevant to your case . . ."

"You want more money for malaria, he wants to focus on seeds?"

"Yes, that's basically it."

"But the deal hasn't worked out as well as you expected?"

Fischer again was startled. "What makes you say that?"

"That angel you were thinking about," said Bruno. He looked intently at Fischer, who wore a horrified expression.

"You . . . ?"

—"Yes, I really do know about that." Bruno savored the opportunity to interrupt Fischer and finish his thoughts for him. "Don't ask me how I do it, I really can't explain it. Anyway, I was puzzled by that angel. Just now it hit me. It's not a Jacob's-ladder angel, or a cute little cherub. The kind of angel you're thinking about is the one who gives you money without taking control of the company. Angel investors. You'd like to bail out of NewGarden, get rid of those French directors, and start over—wouldn't you?"

Fischer recovered his composure almost instantly. "I won't deny I was thinking that. But that's all it was, a passing reflection. As CEO, considering different ways to increase shareholder value is my chief responsibility."

Bruno was amused at Fischer's transition into business platitudes. "I guess the social part of the evening is over. My advice to you, Manny, is to relax. If I were in your shoes, I'd want to get out from under those snooty Europeans too. Get out on your own. Kick up your heels a bit. Nobody looking over your shoulder. You really should do it."

"I appreciate the advice," Fischer replied, leading him to the door. "Now I have a bit of advice for you: Go see Quentin Richards. Tell him what I've told you and see if he corroborates my story. Maybe he knows of some other scandal I'm not aware of. But I'm not the hypocritical murdering Quaker you seem to be looking for."

CHAPTER 58

QUENTIN DID CORROBORATE FISCHER'S STORY, in a sense. The next morning, Bruno found him in the hospital, too weak to talk. He'd had a relapse of malaria.

It was a shock to see Quentin lying there, weak and disheveled. Whenever Bruno had encountered him before, he'd been well put together in his formal black suit and hair combed neatly back. Now he looked so different. Quentin was much smaller physically than Bruno had realized. Between his wild hair and all of the tubes and electronic gizmos, Quentin had the look of a madman under intense sedation.

It was too bad. Bruno would have loved to ask Quentin questions about Fischer. A sense of unease, if not actual suspicion, lingered after the previous night's meeting. Fischer's apparent nervousness, compulsive drinking, and evasiveness made Bruno wonder what he might be holding back. He seemed like a man under a great deal of pressure. No doubt he was. It was no picnic running a public company these days. But what if something else was going on? Quentin's perspective would have been helpful. On the way out, the nurse informed him that Quentin had relapses every few years. They lasted about a month, but Quentin might be well enough to talk in a week or two.

Back at home, Bruno delved more deeply into the Kabbalah. Leaving behind the cheerful confines of *Kabbalah for the Complete Shmegegge*, he had made some sense of the ancient numerology in the *Sefer Yetzirah,* the *Book of Creation.* He'd dabbled in the kaleidoscopic delights of the *Zohar,* a candidate for the most eccentric book ever written. Now he was trying to fathom the mysteries of the Lurianic Kabbalah, which essentially taught about the flow of energy in the cosmos prior to Genesis. He had to admit, he was most intrigued by the terminology: the *Ein Sof,* or infinite nothingness; the *tzimtzum,* a cataclysmic cosmic contraction of the infinite; and Adam Kadmon, the primordial man who appeared in the wake of *tzimtzum.* He wondered if the physicists knew about any of this: the great searing light that had shattered the *vessels,* leaving divine *sparks* as part of every living being. How this cataclysm had shaken the foundations of the entire universe, causing the different realms of creation to sink down one level below their proper places—like your plumber's pants when he's trying to figure out what's causing the leak under your sink.

All of this talk of 10 *sefirot,* four worlds, five levels of the soul, and how they interact was starting to leave him dazed. Bruno found his thoughts drifting to the long, dark tunnel under the Lenape King and how he felt when he saw the sparks of light as he approached the meeting house. He could feel the fear of the runaways and the anticipation of freedom; their tentative joy at the thought of finally being able to live with their loved ones in a place where no one could tear them apart.

That led to ruminations on his own ancestors, wanderers in the desert, who later wept in Babylon for the destruction of the Temple and the loss of home and freedom. Exiles across the centuries. Living in ghettos with actual walls of stone, within the greater, figurative ghetto—the Pale of Settlement. No wonder so many Jews had jumped at the chance to come to America. These immigrants started fresh in the New World and could barely tell you where they had come from. Russia, Poland, Romania, Ukraine? Political boundaries were always shifting: You lived in your town or village with other Jews; it almost didn't matter who was in charge.

Bruno knew only that his great-grandparents had come from Eastern Europe. They migrated to Jewish neighborhoods in New York and Philadelphia and followed the classic occupations: butcher, tailor, silversmith, scholar.

His grandparents were born in America and he knew them. English-speaking, with some Yiddish, they were raised within the Jewish work ethic and its corollary, the paranoiac penny-pinching that seemed justified by the Great Depression.

His parents recoiled at the rancid breath of the *shtetl*, which still lingered about their elders. They fled the cities for the more gracious suburbs. High-quality education propelled them far beyond the traditional trades. They advanced to the highest rungs, buoyed along by a rising stock market and a decades-long housing boom. With the Depression and the war behind them, life was fun. And they enjoyed it. Why not? They'd paid their dues.

Then came Joey Kaplan and his cohort. Born into affluence and freedom, they quickly grew bored. They despised the beautiful suburban towns, with their neat gardens that their parents had sought out or created. *"What's not to like?"* It was as different from the ghetto or shtetl as you could get. "Shame on you. How can you be bored? Remember, you have to work hard: *Nobody owes you a living."*

Joey's generation. They ran back to the city. Sought out the ghetto and mimicked its mores—sex, drugs, music—at the same time as they succeeded beyond their ancestors' wildest dreams. They decried gentrification—it lacked authenticity—yet they wanted to live in style and comfort. Successful capitalists by day; cynical revolutionaries by night. Who did they think was buying the warehouse lofts and the condo conversions: Kansas farmers? Texas trailer trash? Their *parents*?

It was different than assimilation because you could consciously decide which elements of a culture to adopt. Your name's Ben Glass. You're from Newton, Massachusetts. You work at Citibank and drive a $70,000 German import. But you decorate your loft with bamboo and lacquer and watch anime on your plasma TV: so you're practically a Zen master.

It was like genetically engineered culture. Start with your basic Jewish chromosome; splice in a kente cloth gene here, a chopsticks gene there. What have you got? A *meshugge*.

This was Bruno's curse. It seemed to work for most people, but he just couldn't handle the contradictions. The splicing was a failure. The grafts didn't take. At the same time, the culture of his grandparents— or even his parents—wasn't really accessible to him. He couldn't speak Yiddish or Hebrew, except for a word here or there. His version of Jewish culture was Alan Sherman parodies and, "Did you know the Three Stooges were Jewish? Yes, even Curly. And from Philadelphia, too!" Where else could that lead but to ad agencies in New York? Looked at this way, his problems as a psychic weren't all that significant. Even without them, he wouldn't have fit in anyway.

Same with the Kabbalah. It was part of his culture, yet he had to approach it as an outsider. He picked up his book and continued reading where he'd left off. Apparently, God was willing to clean up most of the mess left by the broken vessels, but he required human help. As a Kabbalist, Bruno would be expected to "struggle with and overcome not only the historic exile of the Jewish people but also the mystic exile of the *Shekhinah.*" The *Shekhinah*, of course, was the Divine Presence, generally represented as a female.

Bruno saw that he'd also be responsible for performing enough good deeds to liberate the sparks and raise the universe back to its proper level.

He put down the book. He wouldn't mind getting next to the *Shekhinah.* She sounded hot. But the rest of the job description seemed like a lot of heavy lifting and he doubted the boss would have much of a sense of humor. Maybe being a psychic detective wasn't so bad after all.

CHAPTER 59

"MAGGIE, LEAVE ME ALONE." Bruno was trying to hide under the covers to prevent her from licking his face. It was well past 10 a.m. and she needed to go out. He sat up and had to laugh at the funny way she was wagging her stump. The wound had healed nicely. He missed her beautiful tail, but only when he thought about it.

The phone rang and Bruno knew it had to be the Chief. He let it ring. He pulled himself out of bed and opened the front door for Maggie. She bolted outside as the answering machine clicked on. The Chief barked, "Get out of bed and come over here right away. Something big has come up."

Less than an hour later, Harry showed Bruno a printout from an online bulletin board he'd found, called Doggin'n'Dissin'. There was a long thread entitled: "No Good Bull Shit (NGBS)." The initial post was dated about a month previously and it read as follows: *Calling all deviants: Our time has come. NGBS meeting 5/26. Buy a share and be there 10 sharp, with bells on. All will be revealed.* It was signed, Cavedweller.

There were enthusiastic comments posted by Ratrapper, Forger, Vandal, Psycho, Moondog, and St. Fightin Girl, saying they were spreading the word far and wide among the different activist groups, from anarchists to the Save the Zebras Coalition.

In the ensuing weeks, posts had filtered in from across the region, pledging solidarity. "Look at all of this," said Harry. There were pages and pages of pithy comments along the lines of "Right on, bro," "Be there or be square," "Got my bricks all packed," and "*Ça roule!*"

Then came a long post from someone with the handle "BigJohn." It was a manifesto-sized screed, written in all caps. The message was addressed to ALL PAST PRESENT AND FUTURE DEVIANTS. The substance was that it was time to put their training to work. WITH PROPER ORGANIZATION WE CAN MAKE SEATTLE WTO LOOK LIKE SHRINERS PARADE. And it concluded with the exhortation, GREAT CREDIT WILL BE YOURS. DRESS APPROPRIATELY. THE WHOLE WORLD'S WATCHING.

Bruno whistled softly. "Have you alerted Fischer and Jurevicius about this?"

"Yeah. Chief'll brief you about that in a minute," Harry replied, rapidly shuffling through the replies. "There's one more thing I want to show you. Look down here." He gestured to some lines highlighted in yellow. St. Fightin Girl had weighed in, "No fair. Littlejohnson musclin' in on CD's gig. Somebody tell him to stop shouting . . ." And Cavedweller had messaged back, "'scool. More the merrier."

"It's Alison! You found her!" Bruno was so excited, he shook Harry by the shoulders. "Way to go, man. Now you can locate her, right, since she went online?"

"Not exactly," Harry said. "All of these posts were logged on from public access computers, in the libraries no doubt. And our trail ends there."

Chief Black joined them. "We just showed Alison's picture to librarians in Gardenfield, Maplewood, and Berry Hill. What an ornery bunch they are. I can never understand why they think it's in the public interest to make it harder to solve violent crimes. Anyway, we got a hit in Berry Hill. Somebody remembered seeing Alison, but that's it. It's a big place—probably why she chose it instead of Gardenfield. No one saw her come. No one saw her go. She wasn't with anyone. And they said we'd have to get a special warrant to see what else she looked at on the computer. Even if we got a court order, they said they'd fight us all the way to the Supreme Court."

"So what are we going to do?" asked Bruno.

"I guess we're just going to have to show up in force at NewGarden's annual meeting. We'll coordinate with Maplewood's county, state, and local municipalities to manage the protests. And I've been talking to the folks at NewGarden. I explained the situation with Alison and I assured them that we'd try to arrest her with minimal disruption to their meeting."

Bruno looked troubled. "Did you discuss this with Dr. Fischer?"

"No. Dr. Jurevicius. Why do you ask?"

"I'm curious how he reacted to the news about the protests . . ."

"Funny you should mention it. I was kind of surprised by that. I expected him to be upset or angry . . ."

"He wasn't? What did he say?"

"He seemed almost amused . . . or maybe grimly determined. It was hard to tell over the phone."

"Really? Do you remember his exact words?"

"I think he said, 'Bring it on,' or something like that."

CHAPTER 60

THE CHIEF DIDN'T WANT BRUNO TO COME ALONG. He said the security situation outside the NewGarden shareholder meeting would mainly involve routine police work. There'd probably be drunks and dopers to arrest. There might be tear gas.

Bruno was stunned. "Chief, this is the moment we've been working toward. We know Alison's going to be there. She'll probably be in disguise. Trust me, you're going to need me. I promise I won't get in the way."

The Chief relented, but began to regret the decision almost immediately. Bruno was nervous and talking incessantly. "Why did Jurevicius say what he did? 'Bring 'em on.' That's so stupid. It's just a bunch of college kids. What can they do? Can't he just refuse to let them in?"

"Not if they're shareholders."

"But if they're noisy and disruptive. Can't he refuse to admit them?"

"They'll probably behave themselves when they present their tickets. And NewGarden will not admit anyone wearing a costume or disguise."

"But we know they're conspiring to disrupt the meeting. We have it in writing. Can't we do something to stop it?"

"I talked to Jurevicius about that. He said he was confident their security could handle anything that happens inside, as long as we can keep things orderly outside the perimeter."

The suspense was starting to get to Bruno. He asked, "Chief, what do you really think is going to happen?"

"We'll identify Alison as soon as we can and detain her in a way that causes minimal disruption."

"Will there be a confrontation?"

The Chief sighed. "My guess is that she'll stand up and make some kind of speech about biotech and the environment—if she gets the opportunity."

"And if that happens, what will Jurevicius do? Did you ask him that?"

"Bruno, this is a routine situation. He said that security will handle it in the usual way . . ."

Bruno started to panic, but the Chief didn't let him.

"Which simply means that guards will escort her from the building. Politely but firmly. You've seen it happen on TV a hundred times. It's not a big deal."

With that, he turned onto Marter Avenue, the treeless boulevard that led to the entrance to NewGarden Biosciences. The police were well prepared for a demonstration. They had set up barriers to keep the protestors out of the street and allow shareholders to approach the gates unmolested. There, security examined each car, ensuring it contained shareholders with proper credentials before allowing it to proceed.

Behind the barricades was a scene that took even Bruno and the Chief by surprise. Obviously, they knew that Alison and her friends would come to protest. But they weren't expecting the kind of crowd that jammed the sidewalks along the entire length of Marter Avenue.

The "Deviants" who, of course, were Nate Littlejohn's students, were well represented. They came dressed as court jesters, Che Guevara, Arab terrorists, and Bozo the Clown. Bozo had a brightly colored poster that read, "Biotech is for bozos."

The Deviants' call to arms had spread far and wide, with gratifying results. The crowd was much larger than anyone had expected and the various contingents were both geographically and ideologically diverse.

There were organic farmers from across the U.S., angry and sullen, with signs that read, "Keep your seeds out of my field," and "An ill wind blows no good."

There were environmentalist contingents including Greenpeace, the Sierra Club, PETA and Earth First bearing a variety of slogans. Some were relevant or almost relevant, such as "Save the Crows," or "Why do the only Eagles in Philadelphia wear helmets and weigh 250 pounds?" Others seemed to have been recycled from other campaigns: "Save the Whales" and "I'm for the Spotted Owl."

There was a lone religious fanatic, dressed in early Christian garb and bearing a large cross with a sign that read, "God Bless South Jersey."

Nathalie Porthous led a group of feminists who had created replicas of dead or dying crows. Their signs read, "First crows, then women. Protect your rights." Littlejohn joined her and they tried to invent a chant especially for the occasion. "One, two, three, four/We don't want your filthy . . ." What? They argued back and forth: Floor? Poor? More? Nathalie almost eviscerated Nate on the spot when he suggested "whore." Finally, they agreed on "One, two, three, four/No GMOs at the local store . . ." But they had a hard time getting anyone to chant with them. There were so many other things to do and see.

The anti-war groups were there, armed with American flags, lighter fluid, and matches. The anti-WTO cadres were also showing their flag, a blue field with the Whole Earth in the center.

More down-to-earth were several local chapters of the Teamsters union. Their placards read, "Ron DiAngelis for Governor."

Gravitating to the unions was a contingent of farmers who had flown to New Jersey all the way from France. They'd rented tractors and seemed to be looking for windows to smash. Their signs exhibited the European genius for ideograms—a drawing of a Big Mac, an equals sign, and a dog squatting to poop.

Drawn inevitably to the French was the Slow Food contingent, led by Jacob Creutzfeldt. He'd brought along a sow named Tammy, specially raised on an organic farm in Woodbury. Tammy was slated to follow Walt Whitman as the featured attraction at La Vache Folle et Le Poisson Nu. Creutzfeldt was flying in chefs from Hawaii to help him create a new classic luau recipe using only South Jersey ingredients. He was serving a local wine—a rough approximation of zinfandel—as the suggested pairing for pit-roasted pork.

Then there were the hemp aficionados, slyly asserting that they were interested in all the myriad uses of hemp—except smoking it.

On the outskirts, anarchists in ninja outfits mingled with Jedi knights while the American Friends Service Committee argued the sanctity of creation with a group of Gaians holding "Love Your Mother" placards.

Meanwhile, the Prius Pride of South Jersey, consisting of more than a dozen late-model hybrid vehicles, scootered up and down Marter Avenue in perfect formation. They performed precision figure eights, while honking their horns and waving to promote energy efficiency.

"This does remind me of a Shriners' parade," Chief Black observed, gesturing toward the Pride.

Then he noticed a commotion across from where they were standing. The crowd seemed to be heaving back and forth. "That's a street fight," said the Chief matter-of-factly. "Let's take a closer look."

They crossed the street and asked Che Guevara what was happening. He explained that one of the French farmers had seen Bozo the Clown and gone berserk. Apparently he'd mistaken Bozo for McDonalds' world-famous emissary. He had tried to attack the poor clown, despite his comrades' attempts to restrain him. In fact, if Bruno or the Chief had understood French, they would have heard someone shouting, "C'est pas Ron-ald," over and over.

Fortunately for Bozo, the Teamsters stepped in. Politically, they weren't sure which side to take; but their natural instincts asserted themselves and they began to pummel the Frenchmen. The Chief was pleased to see that Biff was on top of it immediately. "Watch this," he said to Bruno. "Crowd control, just the way I taught him. He's going to let the union thugs and farmers work off a little bit of excess energy—and then arrest them. Easy, entertaining, and safe."

The college kids all rallied around Bozo. They helped the clown up, offered water, and tried to rearrange the oversized pants and tiny vest.

"Seems like the VIP of the group," commented the Chief. "Think it's Cavedweller?"

"Full make-up." Bruno squinted. "Could be anybody. An excellent disguise." He scanned the crowd. "I don't see anyone else that's fully covered like that—except the Palestinian terrorists and those ninjas. But I'm guessing those are computer geeks and anarchists. So let's focus on Bozo."

"Agreed."

Just as they started to make their move, the security gate opened and a pair of black limousines pulled into the road. Driving side by side, they swept away the Priuses and everything else in their path. A few minutes later, they returned with something extraordinary following behind them. It was a full-sized parade float bearing a 20-foot-high sculpted figure of a violet crow. On each corner stood security guards, dressed in commando outfits, with wireless headsets and visible sidearms.

An unmistakable voice emerged from the head of the crow: "*The meeting is abowt to begin. Ownly ticket holders will be al-loud to enter the premises. Anywon wearing a costume will be thoroughly searched.*"

The commandos produced wicker baskets and began tossing handfuls of what looked like purple corn into the crowd. The protestors didn't know what to think. To some, the military garb suggested explosives or maybe tear gas . . . Others thought it was NewGarden's product—actual Scarecrow Corn—and who knew what that might do to humans? With a collective shriek of "Run! GMOs!" the stampede started. Within minutes, the crowd had scattered like chaff before the wind. All that was left was a pile of placards and a scattering of violet-hued candy.

CHAPTER 61

CHIEF BLACK AND BRUNO STOOD at the back of the auditorium and watched as people filed in. The majority of regular shareholders had come in earlier. They were in their places, enjoying French champagne served in special flutes monogrammed with the NGBS logo. On stage, a tuxe-doed pianist played Debussy's "Images" on a Bösendorfer grand piano.

It took a while for the protestors to filter in. They had remained out on the street until the float pulled up and then had to discard their costumes or submit to a search. The Chief pointed out to Bruno that the ushers seemed to be leading them to a specific area in the front of the auditorium, right behind the VIP section where they put the board of directors and the other big shots.

"I'd have put them in a locked room with armed guards and a video feed," snapped Bruno.

"This isn't really that different," explained the Chief. "They've got them all in one place where it's easy to keep an eye on them."

They watched anxiously, waiting for Alison to appear. It didn't take long. After all those hours of interviewing, online searching and psychic surveillance, she simply walked into the room. Completely anti-climactic. Yet there she was. She'd jettisoned the cumbersome Bozo outfit and tried to remove the clown makeup with only partial success. She'd dyed her hair blond and cut it short. But it was still, quite obviously, Alison—dressed simply in jeans and a black cardigan.

"She looks great," commented Bruno. "I think she's lost weight."

"Must be all that exercise she was getting while she was hiding out."

"That was a tacky thing to say." Bruno glared reprovingly at the Chief; then he got distracted by a disturbance in the crowd. It seemed that Alison's friends were jockeying to sit close to her—but two interlopers were trying to butt in.

The Chief checked it out through his binoculars. It was Littlejohn and Porthous.

"What's going on?" Bruno asked impatiently.

"They're arguing. There's pushing and shoving."

"What do you think it's all about?"

"Hard to say. I'm guessing the man may be what's-his-name—Littlejohnson. The woman's got big hair, like an afro, so she's probably a professor too. It looks like Alison's friends want to be there right with her for the big event, or maybe they're trying to protect her."

"From what?"

"Exactly my point." The Chief kept narrating like a sportscaster. "The ushers are moving in. They're breaking it up. They've placed Littlejohn and Big Hair in the seats directly in front of Alison. Now she's arguing with the man. He keeps trying to grab her arm and she keeps pulling away." He turned to Bruno. "I wonder if we should get her out of there. Go in and grab her right now?"

"Let me see." Bruno grabbed the binoculars. But just then the pianist took his bow, the lights dimmed, and the room went quiet.

When the lights came back up, Emmanuel Fischer was standing alone in front of the curtain. He thanked the audience for coming and welcomed them to the Garden State. Then he tried to launch into the main part of his speech. "For 15 years, our mission has been to transform our world into a new garden, through the promise of biotechnology . . ."

That was as far as he got when he was interrupted by a chorus of jeers and hisses. Littlejohn and Porthous were standing up and trying to get the other protestors to shout down the speaker.

Fischer studied them with contempt. Obviously he wasn't prepared for such juvenile behavior, which is normally confined to college campuses. Fischer stood uncomfortably while the disruption continued.

People in the audience grew restive. A few hollered, "Let him speak." Littlejohn and Porthous exhorted the students to join them, but most refused to join in. Their eyes were glued on Alison, who sat solid and silent.

A voice came on the loudspeaker. "*Anywon* disrupting the meeting will be removed from the *awditworium.*"

Littlejohn and Porthous stopped hissing and jeering. They cast hostile looks at the students and tried to disappear into their seats.

Dr. Fischer resumed speaking. "For some reason, I felt compelled to invite a couple of my in-laws," he ad-libbed. "They're too shy to tell me how they really feel about me." The audience exploded with laughter and applause.

The curtain opened behind Fischer, and he continued his presentation. On the stage were the glass-covered exhibits, which Bruno recognized from the company museum. In fact, Fischer was giving the exact same speech on the promise of biotechnology that Jurevicius had delivered on Bruno's first visit to the company. Fischer roved from exhibit to exhibit, while a video camera followed him and projected enlarged images on the screen behind him.

As Fischer concluded, Chief Black looked at his watch and called Biff on his radio. "Tell everybody to stay in position outside. It's a bit dicey in here. We may need to move fast."

Fischer introduced Dr. Jurevicius, who seemed to have twice the energy as his predecessor. He moved briskly around the stage while he talked about the company's financials. Since all of the revenue came from agriculture, that was his focus. He mentioned medical research briefly, noting, "The burn rate is still manageable for the time being."

Then he stepped to the front of the stage and shielded his eyes from the glare. "Some of our newest shareholders are students in the Sociology Department at the University of Pennsylvania," he announced genially. "Can we give them all a warm NewGarden welcome?" The spotlights panned across the section where Alison was sitting. Most of the audience applauded politely, with a few ironic jeers and whistles mixed in.

"Judging from the signs I saw on the way in . . ." The crowded interrupted Jurevicius with a lively chorus of boos.

The Chief took advantage of the noise to send another quick radio message. Bruno couldn't hear what he said, but there was a look of urgency in his eye.

Jurevicius quieted the crowd with an upraised palm. "Now, please. Let's show our friends we welcome debate as an exchange based on *facts.*"

There was a hearty round of applause for "facts."

"The fact is, Scarecrow Corn does not kill crows. It merely makes the corn unpalatable to them, without changing the taste or nutritional qualities for humans and animals."

More applause.

"Now I'd like to show you a little movie we've made to illustrate how our technology works. It's a remix of a couple of classic tales. I hope you enjoy it."

The film started out as a homage to Hitchcock. Filmed in lurid Technicolor, it played off the promotional newsreel for *The Birds.* Instead of repeating, "*The Birds* is coming," the NewGarden version said, "The birds are going" over and over. And of course it didn't show crows attacking schoolchildren. It showed crows dive-bombing cornfields, then pulling up at the last second, shaking their beaks with disgust.

Then the film segued into the famous hangover scene in *Dumbo,* where the crows sing, "When I see an elephant fly." The corporate version was called "I Doan Like Dat Scarecrow Corn" and it had new words dubbed in. It started out with the crows half-talking/half-singing among themselves:

I like corn on the cob.
I like corn dogs, too.
I even like corn chowder.

Then they break into rollicking, full-fledged harmony:

You can hang me from the highest treeee
If y'ever see me eatin' dat Scarecrow Corn.

The audience was laughing and cheering wildly while Jurevicius came prancing back onto the stage. "Isn't that a hoot?" he yelled, stirring the crowd to further excesses.

The university contingent sat dumbfounded. No one showed *Dumbo* in public anymore. It was beyond offensive; it was taboo. Was this a shareholder meeting or a KKK rally? Some of the more suggestible even worried they might not get out of there alive.

Then things got even spookier. At Jurevicius' signal the light dimmed. Next, the audience saw the image of a giant crow floating four feet above the stage in ultraviolet light. Jurevicius, decked out in an ultraviolet suit, hopped nimbly up onto the float and stood at the feet of the giant crow—to the audience's continuous applause. At last the noise died down and he bowed his head in thanks. "We'd like to end the meeting with a brief Q&A. We have time for about a half-dozen questions."

Bruno felt his heart beating rapidly. Why? What did he think was going to happen? If Alison had something to say, she was going to say it now. He looked over at the Chief. He could see his jaw working. He must be feeling the tension, too. The Chief held his radio close to his mouth. Bruno heard him say, "This is it. Get ready."

But the first questioner was a money manager. An usher presented him with a microphone and he asked a lengthy question about the quality of earnings. Jurevicius provided a detailed answer with references to the supply chain and overseas demand.

The next question was from an individual investor. She wanted to know when the company was going to start paying a dividend. Jurevicius hit that one out of the park. NGBS was a growth company. When it reached a cap size of say, $10 billion, which implied a share price growth of 1,000%, then he'd start paying a dividend.

The audience went giddy. The applause started to hurt Bruno's ears.

Jurevicius fielded a few more questions from money managers. Bruno looked at the Chief. He gestured frantically to Bruno, "Let's move. Now." They stayed low and started creeping down the center aisle.

Then Jurevicius scanned the audience. "I'll take one final question from one of our friends at the U of P. But please, no politics. This is a business meeting."

Several hands were raised. Then it struck Bruno. He was searching for Alison. What if the microphone were rigged with a detonator or something? He looked at the Chief. He was down in his crouch, walking crablike as quickly as he could. Then it happened. The ushers had found Alison. They were handing her the mike.

Bruno felt frozen in place as Alison lifted it to her mouth and started to speak.

"Where is Dr. Fischer?" her voice boomed.

"You don't have to shout, my dear, your voice is amplified," said Jurevicius.

"Where's Dr. Fischer?" Alison repeated.

"He's right here, backstage, of course. What is your question?"

Bruno thought Jurevicius looked momentarily confused. He looked around as though trying to catch someone's eye. Was he summoning Fischer?

"I'm asking," said Alison, her voice rising in volume along with her emotions, "because I came here today to accuse you, you and Dr. Fischer . . ."

Jurevicius frantically gestured with his hand cutting across his throat.

". . . of murder. I saw the whole thing . . ."

The lights went out and they cut power to Alison's mike. Above the crowd noise you could hear her shouting, "I saw the whole thing . . . and I found Ginnie Doe's body on your property!"

Then there was a flash of light and a loud noise. It seemed as if the violet crow was exploding. People started screaming, "Someone's been shot."

Then they stormed the exits.

"We have to help her," Bruno screamed, trying to push his way against the crowd.

The Chief grabbed Bruno and pulled him back. "You'll never get to her that way." He used the crowd's momentum to carry them to the nearest exit. Fortunately, the door opened easily and they were hurled safely out onto the NewGarden loading dock.

CHAPTER 62

THE PARKING LOT WAS CHAOS. People were screaming. People were injured. People were crying.

The Chief spoke quickly but calmly on his radio. He was summoning more help. He put out a call for all available emergency medical response units. And he called the State Patrol to put them on alert.

"Why isn't their security coming out to help?" he radioed Michelle.

"Don't know, sir. Probably busy dealing with the situation inside."

The Chief turned to Bruno. "What are you doing?" he shouted. The psychic had been lurching from student to student, trying to find out what had happened. The responses were incoherent. The Chief pulled him away and led him to Randy. "I want you two to stay together. Keep a low profile, and if you see Jurevicius or Fischer, let Randy know right away."

They got into Randy's Charger and pulled into a spot in the parking lot where they wouldn't look too conspicuous.

They waited for what seemed an impossibly long time. The line of cars trying to clear the parking lot had almost dissipated. Medical vehicles were arriving with sirens blaring and their crews were rushing around treating the victims. Then the radio crackled to life. It was the

Chief. "I'm inside the building. Security is non-existent; they seem to have melted away. One of the professors got shot; it's sort of serious, but not life-threatening. Fischer's having a nervous breakdown. No sign of Jurevicius."

"What about Alison?" shouted Bruno.

"No sign of her either," the Chief reported. "I guess she escaped."

Bruno knew he should not be taking this as good news. Nevertheless, he felt elated. Alison wasn't killed or injured. She was safe.

A few minutes later, a red 5-series BMW whipped out of the garage and headed out of the parking lot. Serge Jurevicius was at the wheel and he appeared to be alone.

"That's him," said Bruno, hopping into the passenger's seat.

"What are you doing?" asked Randy.

"It's *simcha* time. Let's party."

Randy stared at Bruno with a mixture of dismay and disbelief. He had come to the NGBS circus in undercover attire, jeans, and a leather jacket—the right look for someone driving a '68 Charger. After facing combat in the first Gulf War, with live ammunition spraying at him from hostiles with automatic weapons, he was not prone to getting too worked up over matters of lesser urgency. He saw Bruno as a civilian, nothing more, nothing less. Bruno's lack of training concerned him. However, the Chief had ordered them to stay together.

He grunted, "Fine," and dropped the Charger into gear. "Don't touch this unless things get really crazy." He placed a small revolver on the console. "It's my backup. Smith and Wesson 340PD."

"You just point and shoot, right?"

"Very funny. It's got .357 loads, five of them. Use two hands or it could break your wrist."

Jurevicius drove furiously out of the gate. He took the turn onto Marter Avenue with tires squealing, then slowed to a moderate pace when he saw no one in hot pursuit. He didn't seem to notice Randy, who was following at a prudent distance. Slowly, they wended their way through downtown Maplewood and the endless succession of traffic lights in Berry Hill.

Bruno had nothing to do and, after the excitement of the meeting, a peculiar sort of manic boredom started to set in. His face twisted into a snarl as he assumed a crazed Edgar G. Robinson voice: "Coppers ain't gonna get me! Not me. Yahahahaha?"

Then he switched to a different character, a big, dumb lug, who replied, "Yeah boss."

Randy stole a quizzical look at Bruno, who was grinning idiotically. "*Dow. Dow. Dow. Dow.* Dey shot the *door* off, but dey ain't gonna get me! Yeah, boss."

Randy shook his head. Guys had funny ways of preparing themselves for battle, but this was pathetic. He tried to ignore it, but Bruno wouldn't let him.

"*Ganefs,*" he pronounced, putting down his imaginary gun and resuming his own voice. "The story appeared in the premier issue of *Mad Magazine.* October 1952."

"OK."

"'*Ganefs*' means 'thieves'—not that they ever bothered to translate, or even tell you it was Yiddish. The *ganefs* are the boss and his assistant, Bumble. They're trying to get away, but the coppers keep shooting their car apart, a piece at a time. The boss keeps yelling, 'Nyaah, coppers. You'll never get me.' And Bumble keeps saying, 'Yeah, boss.'"

"I think I get it."

"You do?"

Randy thought for a moment. "Hold on a second." They were on Old Kings Road in Gardenfield, right in front of the Municipal Building. He called to report his position. They were stuck at the light at Garden Avenue, about four cars behind Jurevicius. Then he said, "I think we're the coppers. So we don't want the bad guys to get away."

Bruno had to admit he had a good point. Jurevicius turned down the old Lenape trail. The light turned yellow, but Randy was able to nip through. The way Jurevicius was driving, he didn't seem to notice he was being tailed.

—"We're leaving Gardenfield," Randy radioed to the dispatcher. "Heading south into Barrington." He turned to Bruno: "Does the boss have a name?"

That took Bruno by surprise. He thought Randy was ready to change the subject. Before he could answer, Randy stomped on the brake and swore, "Hot damn."

They had just passed the White Horse Pike and Jurevicius had pulled over at a gas station. Randy eased off the brake and kept driving.

"What do we do?"

"Pull over and hope for the best." Randy drove ahead two more blocks and pulled into an empty parking lot. It was a Korean restaurant that didn't open until 5. Randy warned Bruno not to turn around. Instead he slumped down and used the side mirror to keep an eye on their quarry. Jurevicius gassed up his car, and even took the time to clean his windshield. He handed the attendant his credit card and waited.

Randy whistled. "Either this guy's innocent or else he's cold as ice. Look at him standing there like he's got all the time in the world."

"Something's funny," said Bruno.

"What?"

"His license plate. It reads SBGN."

"You're looking at it backwards," Randy scoffed. "NGBS is the company's stock symbol."

"Yeah. But when I first started working on the case, I dreamed about SBGN. Now I know what it means."

"Too bad you didn't figure that out two months ago . . ."

Bruno could tell Randy was starting to get antsy. He resolved not to say anything for a while, but then he noticed something else. "His car is shaking, isn't it?"

"I see what you mean." Randy looked closer. "It could be a rough idle. That car doesn't look like much, but I have to admit it's got some muscle to it."

"But the engine's shut off, isn't it? Don't you have to shut it off before you fill up?"

"I don't know. Crooks don't always follow the rules," said Randy. "Get down, don't let him see you, he's pulling out." Moments later Randy eased into traffic about a half-dozen cars back. The next intersection was the Black Horse Pike. Jurevicius turned left and Randy followed him.

"This will take him to Atlantic City," said Bruno. "Why would he go down the shore?"

"Maybe he's feeling lucky . . ."

"Or he's looking for a small, out-of-the-way airport. Do they have one in Atlantic City?"

Randy shook his head. "I dunno. I think they keep an eye on who comes in and goes out of ACNJ. Maybe Jurevicius has contacts at one of the casinos who can help him disappear." He called on the radio: "Heading south on 168. Repeat that, 168, the Black Horse Pike. We're heading to Atlantic City for an afternoon of fun and entertainment. Still on his tail. No sign of evasive action. Over."

The Chief came on the radio. "Change of plans. Repeat. Change of plans. We believe Jurevicius has kidnapped Alison Wales. We don't know if she's dead or alive, injured or healthy. It's time to reel him in. Confirm."

"Got it, Chief. Will proceed to apprehend suspect. Over and out." He turned to Bruno. "Here, open your window and put this on the roof." He handed Bruno a detachable red roof light.

At that moment Jurevicius started to accelerate. They were right at the junction with 42, the north-south freeway that led to the Atlantic City Expressway. Randy floored the Charger and Bruno felt like he'd left his stomach back in Gardenfield.

"Make sure you're buckled *tight*," Randy howled, "'cause I promise you've never seen driving like this."

CHAPTER 63

BRUNO THOUGHT HIS FACE WAS PEELING OFF and his eyeballs might pop out of his head. He was afraid to look at the speedometer. Finally he managed to ask Randy out of the corner of his mouth, "How fast?"

Randy chuckled. "You mean how fast are we going? About 120. But don't worry, this baby has a lot more left in her." He stole a look at Bruno, who was plastered in his seat, and tried to reassure him. "Everything's OK, you're in good hands. Look on the bright side. We'll get where we're going twice as fast. And we don't have to worry about speeding tickets."

The Atlantic City Expressway is the best route when you're in a hurry to get to the shore. Built in the '60s, it bypasses the old local roads with their endless delays: traffic lights, traffic circles, fruit stands, towns, taverns, and the like. A straight shot, the Expressway offers from two to four lanes of generally excellent, flat pavement, supported by tolls collected at booths along the way and at the relatively infrequent off-ramps.

No wonder Randy liked his chances. Other than a drag strip, you couldn't hope to find a straighter road. Raw speed was the Charger's advantage over the BMW, whose strength was maneuverability. Jurevicius might try to make a dash for an off-ramp, but the approach would be difficult at these speeds. If the BMW slowed, Randy would be on top of him in moments and would nudge him into the ditch. So what was Jurevicius' exit strategy?

Randy grabbed the radio. "We're on the Expressway, heading toward AC. We need road blocks at all toll plazas."

"Roger. When will you be there?"

"We're doing 120 to 125 . . ."

Bruno heard shuffling paper on the other end. "It's about 25 miles, you should be there in twelve and a half minutes."

"Can the State pull it together that fast?"

"Dunno. I'll call you back."

The scenery screamed by. Deciduous trees, not pines. Lots of weeds and bare patches of sand in the median strips. Jurevicius was weaving in and out of traffic whenever the opportunity came up. He used slow-moving vehicles as obstacles, trying to force Randy into a mistake.

The dispatcher called back. "The State Patrol will do their best. The personnel at the toll plaza have vehicles at their disposal. But there are seven bays at Egg Harbor and only four cars in the vicinity."

"Are you telling me they can't seal it off?" Randy shouted.

"Calm down, OK? They're doing their best. Backup plan is to block-ade the next plaza, which comes up right after you cross the Parkway. That only has four bays and they can get the cars there, guaranteed."

"OK," said Randy. "How far is that?"

"The Atlantic City Plaza is about seven miles past Egg Harbor. Less than 15 minutes from your current position."

"Roger. Out." He turned to Bruno and said, "Get ready. That first toll plaza is going to be on top of us before you know it. If the state cops succeed in blockading it, we're going to have a little situation to deal with."

"I'm listening."

"There are three probable scenarios. One, the fugitive surrenders; two, he stops and attempts to flee on foot; or three, he attempts some sort of evasive maneuver in his vehicle. All are potentially dangerous. So I want you to have your weapon ready and stand by to do what I tell you."

"In scenario three, what kind of evasive maneuver could he pull? Just try to blow through one of those parked cars?"

Randy squeezed the wheel more tightly. "That works in the movies, but it'd be suicide at these speeds. No one in their right mind would try it."

"What if his car is specially—whatdya call it—armored or reinforced?"

"If he gets through, we'll nip in right behind him and keep following him till we catch him. But nobody has an armored car like that. At least not one that can handle these speeds."

Now it was Randy's turn to look tense. Traffic was slowing as they approached the toll plaza. Jurevicius tried every trick he could think of, darting from lane to lane, and then sprinting ahead whenever there was a clearing.

The buses were the biggest obstacles. Long and lumbering, they were generally transporting loads of gamblers to the casinos. In many cases the party had already started. People were delighted to see an actual police pursuit. They'd smile and wave, form their hands into the shape of a gun and pretend to shoot. Someone even flashed a real weapon.

Randy eased back to a safe distance as they approached the plaza. He had Jurevicius in his sights and there was no point crowding him.

"Can you tell if it's barricaded?" he yelled with 200 yards to go.

"I'm not sure. There are too many other cars."

Now there were 150 yards to go. Randy had throttled down to 50. The road was becoming congested as drivers chose their lanes. "The two inside lanes are definitely bottled up by big vans," Bruno reported.

With 100 yards left, the BMW sprinted out to the right. The far lane was still open, protected only by an orange cone. The toll collector was waving cars away, which effectively cleared a path for Jurevicius. He floored it and took the toll plaza at 100 miles per hour and was still accelerating. Randy did the same, but Jurevicius had a head start. Also Randy's angle was more extreme. The Charger clipped a corner of the tollbooth on the way through. They had a clear view of Jurevicius pulling away from them in the four-lane final straightaway built over the marshes leading to Atlantic City.

"What does he think he's doing?" Randy shouted. Veins protruded on his neck and forehead. He floored the Charger and they shot ahead like a rocket. For the first time, Randy was pushing the engine right up to the red line, and the results were spectacular. They gained on the BMW as though it were standing still.

"Remember, the next toll plaza's in seven miles," Bruno managed to mutter through gritted teeth.

"Right. This race will be over in three minutes or less. Dr. Jurevicius will find he's moving much slower in a six-by-nine cell."

The signs announced the exits for the Garden State Parkway, north and south, in one mile. Randy could have pulled into the BMW's slipstream, but he chose to hold off, as the road appeared to be clear of other vehicles just ahead. In front of them, a tour bus lumbered along in lane two. Jurevicius was poised to pass in lane three—with Randy and Bruno close behind.

Then, without warning, another car swerved in front of them. It was a dark green Subaru Forester with Washington plates, loaded with luggage and bicycles on top. They must have been stuck behind the bus and decided to pass it, moving into Randy's lane without looking. Randy hit the brakes and managed to swerve in the nick of time. He swore, flashed his lights, and ground his siren. But the Subaru was oblivious. They weren't even trying to pass the bus.

"Goddamn cruise-control nitwits!" Randy screamed. "We're losing Jurevicius." Bruno looked over and saw teenagers in the backseat with mocking faces; they were flipping him the peace sign. Infuriated, he raised Randy's .357 and started to roll down his window.

"No time for that," shouted Randy. He jerked the wheel to the left, which spun the Charger around the Subaru, and then accelerated, driving the engine as hard as it could go. "Do you see him? Do you see him?" he screamed as they pulled even with the bus.

"Yeah," said Bruno, deflated. "I see him." Jurevicius had used the bus to cover his exit from the Expressway. He was winding down the off-ramp at a leisurely pace, onto the Garden State Parkway heading north.

There was no way Randy could recover in time. The race was over.

CHAPTER 64

RANDY WAS A SORE LOSER. He always expected to win and had never developed the skills needed to accept defeat with grace or humor. He sulked all the way to Atlantic City.

By contrast, Bruno approached life as a 50-50 proposition at best. When things didn't work out, he took it for granted that someone, if not everyone, would blame *him*. As a result, he felt deeply guilty—and totally blameless—at the same time. This fundamental inner schism rendered him temporarily incapable of speech, which Randy interpreted as sulking. He figured Bruno was trying to lay the blame on *him* for letting Jurevicius escape.

In fact, both men had wanted to continue the pursuit. After Jurevicius exited, Randy cut across three lanes of traffic and screeched to a halt on the shoulder. Bruno was terrified he'd attempt a U-turn; fortunately a solid concrete divider made that impossible. Instead, Randy slammed the Charger into reverse and drove along the shoulder at speeds approaching 40 miles per hour. Somehow they arrived at the off-ramp without incident.

Then Randy radioed the Chief to explain the situation.

"Break off pursuit," came the reply.

"What?" Randy exploded. "I can catch him. He's headed north on the Parkway."

"You lost him," said the Chief. "The State Patrol can handle it from here."

"I've come this far, no way I'm quittin' . . ." Randy sputtered.

"I understand. Here's the situation. We picked up some of the NewGarden security guards. You wouldn't believe the weapons they're carrying. State-of-the-art military-grade stuff. Late-model Russian Veresk submachine guns and high-powered Heckler and Koch sniper rifles. If Jurevicius has a couple guys like that with him, they could hold off a small army."

"He's by himself," Randy protested.

"Randy, listen to me. You're traveling with a civilian. Bruno has no training; we can't put him in harm's way. You guys are done for the day. Go have a drink or something. You did the best you could."

Randy practically destroyed his radio, slamming it down on the center console. Bruno wished he could just disappear. Somehow, the natural flow of traffic led them to the parking garage of Caesar's Palace. From there they were drawn like stumbling zombies into the casino's garish lobby, which combined reproductions of friezes from the Parthenon, mosaics from the Roman Forum, statues from St. Peter's in the Vatican, and Baroque *trompe l'oeil* paintings. Finally, the sight of a 30-foot statue of Caesar Augustus, holding an American flag, broke the spell.

"If I'd known that Jurevicius was going to get away," scowled Randy, "I'd have let you go ahead and shoot those people in the Subaru."

"My mother drives the same way," Bruno agreed sadly. "And what do they think they're going to do with mountain bikes in New Jersey?"

They drifted upstairs to one of the lounges that had slot machines built directly into the bar. They nursed a couple of beers, while Bruno fed a steady diet of quarters into the machine in front of him.

"So what happened at the end of your story?" asked Randy.

"What story?"

"The 'Yeah, boss' one."

"Oh, *Ganefs*," Bruno said listlessly. "Let's see, Melvin—that's the boss—kills Bumble so he doesn't have to share the loot. He makes it to his secret desert island hideaway and he's cackling with glee. But then he opens the package and, guess what? It's a stink bomb."

Randy didn't crack a smile. "Bumble's fault, I take it?"

"Yeah, he mixed up the packages . . . "

Bruno had had enough. "What do you say we get out of here? Go for a walk on the boardwalk or something."

"Sure," Randy agreed.

Bruno put one last quarter in the slot, but it was another bust.

"You didn't win at all, did you?" Randy observed. "I'd have thought a psychic would have more control over winning and losing here."

"Sometimes it works, sometimes it doesn't."

"Same with me," Randy sniffed.

Out on the boardwalk, the sun was shining and the sea breezes were invigorating. They wandered aimlessly. Bruno excused himself. He walked to the water's edge and studied the surf, hoping Randy would pull himself together by the time he came back. No such luck.

"Hey, look," Randy called out with fake enthusiasm. "There's a psychic, Madame Celeste. Let's go see what she has to say."

"No way," Bruno protested. "I'm not going in there. Look at that potted plant. Look at the pink vase . . ." Obviously, Randy was trying to humiliate him. But after several minutes of arguing, Bruno decided to humor him, hoping it might help the venom work its way through Randy's system.

Madame Celeste was a woman in her 50s, with dark eyes and dyed black hair piled up on top of her head. Her place was not much larger than a closet. Celeste was talking on a cell phone when they walked in; apparently she was trying to convince her daughter into going grocery shopping for her.

Randy pressed a $20 bill into her hand and told her to read Bruno's fortune. He was acting drunk, even though he'd had only one beer.

"Why not you, sailor boy?" she leered. "Don't you want to know your future?"

"He's the interesting one. I'm just a dumb cop."

"I can see that." She turned to Bruno: "You don't mind if he listens in? This could get personal."

"I'm resigned to my fate."

He sat down and Madame Celeste took his right hand in both of hers. She examined the back side, noting the shape of his cuticles, then turned it over, tracing the lines with her index finger.

"This is some hand you've got." She looked first at Bruno, then at Randy, then back at Bruno again. "Let me do the cards." She reached for a tarot deck; Bruno cut the cards before she could even ask him and watched while she laid out a basic pattern. "Can you read it?"

Bruno shook his head in the negative. "I can't see my own future."

Madame Celeste sighed deeply. "I have to tell you, sweetheart, you better be ready to accept all kinds of good things coming your way. I see long life, good health, and a fabulous love life along with great wealth. You got the whole package, baby."

Randy couldn't believe it. "You can't be serious?"

Madame Celeste ignored him. She shook Bruno's hand and stroked it invitingly. "It's a pleasure to meet you. Today is your lucky day."

"What a bunch of baloney," Randy exploded when they were back on the boardwalk. "Admit it."

"I wasn't the one who wanted to go in there," Bruno retorted. "Without question, today is one of the worst days of my life. But I have to say I feel better after talking to her. That's the kind of reading you need to give if you want repeat business."

Randy didn't comment. As they wandered down the boardwalk, each casino or eating establishment was blaring music at high volume—a premonition of what to expect inside. Jungle drumming, country and western, Puerto Rican salsa bombarded them in turn. Finally Bruno caught sight of a friendly-looking restaurant, with its windows wide open so they could sit inside and still enjoy the ocean air. "Let's grab some lunch before we head back," he suggested. "I'm buying."

The restaurant was a Greek taverna called Penelope. Randy and Bruno grabbed stools at the counter looking out over the boardwalk and the beach. Behind them on a giant screen, Shakira wiggled her *pupik* while they munched on souvlaki sandwiches.

By the time lunch was finished, their temperaments were restored to something approaching normal. Bruno felt comfortable enough to ask Randy for a favor: Would he mind driving him back through the Pines? That way he'd get home at least an hour earlier. He'd worry about his car later.

Randy said it was no problem. He'd had enough of the Expressway to last him quite a while. The back roads would be a relief.

They headed up Route 9, following the contours of Absecon Bay, home to marsh grass, thousands of gulls and egrets, and the occasional billboard. After about 10 miles, Route 9 dumped them onto the Garden State Parkway, which is the only road that crosses the Mullica River. The bridge spans a considerable length, perhaps a quarter or a half-mile, as the river broadens into an estuary. Bruno marveled at how empty it was, as if Atlantic City never existed. From the bridge, his view was unimpeded across the bay to the barrier islands beyond it.

Then he saw something that made him stop. His heart was pounding so hard he wasn't sure he could see straight. On the other side of the bridge was a rutted lane leading to what appeared to be an abandoned building. Next to it was a red speck that could only be Jurevicius' car.

CHAPTER 65

BRUNO WAS ALL FOR STORMING THE HOUSE "without mercy or regret." But Randy pointed out they needed to weigh certain strategic and tactical considerations before acting.

"You want to sit here talking while who-knows-what goes on in there?"

Randy coolly picked up his radio. He described their position and requested backup: "Make sure you alert the Coast Guard. We control the only road out of here, but they may have a boat."

He turned back to Bruno. "Right now, we don't know how many men Jurevicius has with him. If he has even a couple that are armed like his other security people, then we have a serious situation on our hands." Randy pulled out his weapon and checked the clip. "However, if we wait for backup, the odds shift dramatically in our favor."

"That's fine, but these people are murderers. Alison may still be alive, and if we act now we'd have the element of surprise."

"Let me show you something," said Randy. "Be quiet, keep low, and don't shut the car door." They had parked in a turnaround just off the main highway. It was, in fact, the beginning of the dirt road they'd seen from the bridge. "This line of trees along the water blocks our line of sight to the house. There are only two places we can go to get a good look. One is the bridge and the other is standing right next to the house. In both cases there's no cover. The basic principle—if we can see them, they can see us—applies. To mount an effective assault, we need a plan. To develop a plan, we need surveillance. But we can't do surveillance without being seen."

"But . . ."

"I know what you're going to say. I feel the same way; I'm ready to fight, right now. But we have to be smart about it."

"We can't just sit around and wait . . ."

"That's what I'm trying to explain, if you'd just shut up. We do have an option, but it's risky. We have to engage them in a delaying maneuver."

"Uh-oh." Bruno was starting to see where this was leading.

"We'll try to get them to negotiate, keep them talking and stall for time. The more time they spend with us, the less time they have to prepare their escape."

"But what if they just shoot us . . ."

"Yeah, that'd be a bummer. I told you this was risky. But in the past they've only attacked children . . . and your dog. And they seem to do it surreptitiously. When confronted by armed men, face to face, in broad daylight, I like our odds."

"You do? You just said they have superior firepower . . ." Bruno felt himself trembling. The fear was mounting and he couldn't control it.

"You've got a better weapon—up here." Randy patted Bruno on the head, then let his hand rest on the psychic's shoulder, trying to impart some of his courage through physical contact. "All you have to do is talk. It doesn't even matter what you say. Just get them talking. I'll cover you, and if shooting starts duck behind the car and pray the cavalry gets here in time. Whatdya say? It's your call."

"My call?"

"Yeah, your call. You're the civilian. The Chief doesn't want you involved in this stuff. But I can't stop you if you want to do it." He stepped back and looked Bruno in the eye. "Whatdya say?"

"Yeah, boss."

CHAPTER 66

THE CLEARING HAD A NAME: DELANO LANDING. It was the point where the Mullica River began breaking up into various side channels, separated by small islands covered with marsh grass. It was a beautiful spot for bird-watching or fishing for striped bass in early spring. A painter would have been thrilled with the subtle shadings of green and yellow, contrasting with the white sands and the lead-gray waters of the bay.

It was also a good spot for a shootout. The clearing was flat and open for 100 yards in every direction. A lonely spot, with no other buildings in sight, Hamilton and Burr could have used it for their duel—pistols at 15 paces—if they hadn't been typical New Yorkers, insisting on staying close to the city.

The house was built right at the water's edge. It was an old wood frame structure with boarded-up windows. No Trespassing and No Littering signs were plastered across the exterior. At some point, a second story had been added. This was an awkward-looking addition, with only a few functioning windows. Behind the house was a yard enclosed by a galvanized metal fence about seven feet high. It appeared to contain various vehicles, old trucks, dredging equipment.

When Jurevicius arrived he must have been in too much of a hurry to bother unlocking the gate. He'd parked the BMW about 25 yards from the house, front facing the water.

Randy didn't like the idea of putting Bruno in harm's way, but he couldn't think of an alternative. They needed one person to talk and the other to shoot. The choice of roles was obvious; he just hoped Bruno would be able to keep his nerve. Ten minutes, even five, might make all the difference.

However, he couldn't send Bruno marching across the clearing. What if they did have a sniper? Apparently, Bruno was thinking along the same lines. He stammered, "What if she's . . . still in the trunk?"

"Meaning we wouldn't have to engage the hostiles if we can find Alison and bring her to safety."

"Exactly."

Randy studied the BMW through his binoculars. "It's not bouncing up and down like before. But that could mean she's saving her strength."

"Or got bored and fell asleep."

The plan was for Randy to drive right up to Jurevicius' car, wait while Bruno forced open the trunk, and then drive back, ideally, with two healthy passengers. Randy did not like the fact that both of them would be exposed to gunfire from the house for a substantial period of time. However, the house's windows were all oriented toward the water; if somebody wanted to shoot at them, they'd need to expose themselves, too. And, if Alison wasn't there, which Randy thought— but did not tell Bruno—was the likely scenario, at least Bruno would be properly positioned to execute Plan B, which was the stalling tactic with Jurevicius.

In addition to his own police duty pistol and the revolver he'd lent Bruno, Randy had a Remington pump action patrol rifle and a brand-new 870P Max police shotgun. Good weapons, but certainly no match for the firepower the Chief said they'd found on the NGBS commandos. Too bad there was no Kevlar body armor: Gardenfield just wasn't that kind of town.

Randy started the Charger as gently as possible. Muscle cars aren't known for being quiet, but there was a chance the water and wind would cover the sound of their approach. They had to act fast. Randy floored the Charger for the dash across the clearing. He made an oblique approach on the far side of the BMW, then hit the brakes so the Charger went into a controlled skid. It spun around 270 degrees and stopped dead. Randy had his revolver in his left hand, ready to return fire if any came from the house.

All quiet so far.

Bruno sprang from the car and attacked the BMW's trunk with the crowbar. He was having difficulty finding the seam. The bar kept slipping. Randy cursed. "Don't worry about the paint job," he hissed at Bruno. "Ram it in there."

Using more force, Bruno found an edge and leaned on the pry bar with all his weight. The trunk popped open with a shriek of tearing metal. It was empty. "No sign of blood," he called, crouching behind the BMW for cover.

"Good luck, pal," said Randy, who handed him the shotgun and roared out of the clearing.

The dust settled and all was strangely silent. Had Jurevicius left already? From this vantage point, Bruno could see that there was a dock, which acted as a front porch for the house. He crawled to the front of the car. A fast-looking boat was moored there. What was Jurevicius up to? It was time to engage.

"Jurevicius," he cried. His voice sounded weak and feeble in the vast space of the clearing. He tried again. There was a churning in the pit of his stomach, and his second attempt was more pathetic than the first.

Bruno looked behind him. Randy was crouching behind the Charger's fender. When he saw Bruno looking at him, he jumped up and started shaking his fist: "Bash the roof in, break the windshield, shoot the doors off."

This is insane, Bruno reflected. He thought of the people Jurevicius had killed and those he might still be harming. Alison was in there; and Bruno's own life was in danger—whether he acted or not. Randy's life was on the line too. Now Bruno's strength came surging back. He liked the heft of the crowbar; he couldn't wait to use it. He walked to the front end and started smashing things. The headlights, one after another. Then the windshield. "Jurevicius," he croaked. "Look what

I'm doing to your car." He took the sharpened end of the crowbar and raked it across the hood, producing a horrible metallic screech.

The door to the house flew open, but Bruno didn't dive for cover. Randy shouted for him to get behind the car. Bruno didn't hear him. He was focused on Jurevicius. The doctor stepped out of the house. He'd traded his business suit for some sort of waterproof boating outfit, and he was pulling something behind him. "Sorry to keep you waiting, but your friend wasn't dressed for the occasion." With that, he jerked a chain he was holding in his left hand. Alison stumbled out behind him, screaming and cursing. Her hands were cuffed behind her back; the chain was attached to a metal dog-training collar that was fastened tightly around her neck. It was the kind of collar designed to control the strongest, most stubborn dogs, using a ring of sharpened metal spikes pointed inward. Alison was squirming and trying to kick Jurevicius, who brought her up with another tug on the collar. She howled with pain. Bruno instinctively started forward but was driven back as the ground in front of him came alive with a hail of bullets.

"Put your weapon down gently," Jurevicius hissed, brandishing one of those nasty Russian submachine guns. Bruno had no choice but to comply. Jurevicius forced Alison to her knees, snarling, "Be silent or I'll blow your brains out."

Now he stood behind her, the chain in one hand, the barrel of his weapon within inches of Alison's temple. He shouted in Randy's direction, "Put down your gun and come out in the open or I will shoot her."

Randy laid down his rifle. He positioned himself half hidden behind the Charger's front fender, but Jurevicius didn't seem to care. From his position, Randy could see that Bruno still had the backup revolver shoved into his belt above the small of his back. "Don't try anything," Randy prayed inwardly. "Just say something. Talk to him. Distract him."

That was exactly what Bruno wanted to do. But he couldn't think of anything to say. Jurevicius relieved him of the burden. "Put your hands on top of your head where I can see them. Interlace your fingers." He turned toward Randy. "You do the same."

Bruno focused on Alison. He could see her chest heaving. She seemed on the verge of a panic attack. Other than the lacerations on her neck, though, she appeared to be unhurt. "Alison," he called out. "You're going to be OK. Others are coming. Just hang in there."

Jurevicius tightened his grip. He forced the muzzle of his weapon deep into her rib cage and growled at her to be still.

"Why is this happening to me?" she sobbed.

Bruno winced. "Don't hurt the girl. She has nothing to do with this. Let her go."

"You are a fool," Jurevicius snapped. "*She* has everything to do with this. Her practical joke will end up depriving me of everything I've worked to build for the last 15 years. Now I will have to leave my nice job and my comfortable home, and start over someplace else."

"Spare us the self-pity," Bruno answered with genuine indignation. "You're the one who's been running around killing people. Don't try to say that Alison made you do it."

"But in truth, she did," Jurevicius said. He lifted his weapon away from Alison and pointed it at Bruno. "I don't need to be lectured by you. And if you don't put your hands back on top of your head, I *will* shoot you."

Bruno had actually forgotten he was being held at gunpoint. He'd been gesturing with his hands as he spoke. Now he replaced them as Jurevicius directed.

"That's better," said the Frenchman. "Neither you, nor anyone else, understands what happened that night. The girl . . . it's no use talking about it. You are in no position to judge. It was nobody's business, and if she . . ." he again prodded Alison with the weapon ". . . had not been trespassing, none of this would have had to happen. She had many warnings, but still she pursued me. Fortunately, you and your friends were too obtuse to understand."

Bruno stole a glance at Randy. He had moved to a better position by the car and Jurevicius hadn't noticed. With his good hand, Randy was signing like a bird's beak flapping. He wanted Bruno to keep talking.

"Obtuse? What do you mean, obtuse?"

"Do I have to explain everything?" Jurevicius' expression betrayed a mixture of anger and amusement. "She moved the body to the meeting house hoping to direct your attention to Dr. Fischer who, she assumed, was responsible for everything at NGBS. Fortunately the police didn't get it, but it was too close for comfort, especially when you started spouting off in the paper about the Quaker connection. We killed the boy to keep you focused on the school and the meeting house, rather than on us. I was rather hoping you'd arrest Master Quentin, but you disappointed me."

"No one in their right mind would suspect Master Quentin. He's a pacifist," Bruno objected.

"Obtuse." Jurevicius shrugged. "Just like I said. Your imagination is limited—unlike your young friend here." He tightened his grip on Alison's chain. "She is persistent, rather than intelligent, but she uses her imagination. I'll give her credit for that. If she had only heeded our warnings and stayed away from our meeting today, this might not have been necessary . . ."

Bruno struggled to think of a reply. "So this is about revenge?"

Jurevicius wound the chain one more turn around his fist. "No, you fool. This is about *hostages*."

Just then a shot rang out. Bruno heard Randy falling heavily and a loud "Damn." Instinctively, Bruno moved in that direction, but a burst of live ammo kept him glued to the spot. A commando rushed to Jurevicius' side and whispered urgently. The doctor nodded and sent the man away.

"I've just been told that your friends are on their way." His manner was so nonchalant, he could have been simply confirming that he wanted an egg salad sandwich and a pickle, no chips, for lunch. "As a result, you now have a man down." "Just a flesh wound," Jurevicius mocked. "Nothing serious, but it focused your attention. I have no doubt my boat can outrun even the Coast Guard. Yes, I know they too are coming. But it would be simpler not to have to worry about them. So I want your friend to radio his superiors. Tell them that we overpowered you and escaped by car. Tell them we're headed for New York."

"Why should we do that?" Bruno asked. It was an inane thing to say—and he knew it.

Poor Alison paid the price. Jurevicius gave the chain a vicious yank.

It practically choked her, in addition to the painful injuries inflicted by the spikes. She fell forward at his feet, gagging and writhing in agony.

"You are my hostages," Jurevicius explained. "If you want to live, you will do as I tell you."

"I'll do it," shouted Randy. He struggled to his feet. He was clutching his left forearm with his right hand, trying to staunch the bleeding. Somehow he managed to pick up his radio, and Bruno heard him make the call. By now the adrenaline was wearing off. Jurevicius was torturing Alison to death before his eyes. Randy his trusty sidekick was injured. And worst of all, he could no longer count on backup arriving in time, if at all. There was no point in stalling anymore. He had to do something, right away. But what? How about a Golem? If ever he needed a supernatural helper, now was the time. He could have laughed at the absurdity of it. How could anything as horrible as this actually be happening? He felt a wave of cold passing through his body from head to toe, as his last hopes died away.

The commando reappeared and urged Jurevicius to hurry. The Frenchman seemed to be mulling over some decision.

"You have nothing to gain by killing us," Bruno pleaded. "We did what you asked us. Now let us go."

Jurevicius frowned. He didn't reply.

A bad sign. Bruno shut his eyes and let the words come without thinking about what he was saying. "Be a *mensch* for once—a human being. That woman in the hospital bed. The one you think about all the time. She must love you very much. What will she say when you tell her about all the people you've been killing?"

Jurevicius glared at Bruno. "What do you know about that? You're just guessing . . ."

Bruno could tell he'd hit a nerve and tried to press his advantage. "I observed you many times, but you didn't know it. She is always in your thoughts." He described the hospital room in detail and watched closely as astonishment registered on the Frenchman's face.

"She's your wife, isn't she, Serge? You had an accident and though she survived, you still feel like you've lost everything. This whole thing is about her, isn't it? But why? Why'd you kill the girl? I still don't get it . . ."

A picture was forming before Bruno's eyes, but he couldn't bring it into focus. The more he struggled to catch hold of it, the slipperier it became. Finally, he blurted out. "Ginnie Doe must have been your daughter. You killed your own daughter!"

Jurevicius roared with anguish. "No! Not my daughter, you babbling idiot, *she was my wife!*"

Jurevicius forgot he was holding a gun. He wanted to destroy Bruno with his bare hands. He lunged forward, forgetting about Alison as well. The chain brought him up short. It tripped him and sent him sprawling onto the sand. Alison began shrieking woefully. Bruno rushed to her side. Her neck was bruised and bleeding. He fumbled with the collar, trying to remove it so he could treat the wounds.

From the corner of his eye, he saw three commandos rush out of the building. They picked up Jurevicius, who was struggling to free himself from the chain. He pulled a gun from his waistband. Bruno did the same.

Then something unexpected happened. The commandos pinned Jurevicius' arms behind him and took his gun away.

Bruno stared in astonishment. *Why are they protecting us?*

Then he heard it. Over his right shoulder came the unmistakable sound of chopper blades slicing the air. He stole a glance over his shoulder. They were approaching rapidly. It looked like they were going to arrive just in time.

A shot rang out. He felt Alison's body shake with violent spasms in his arms. One of the commandos had raised his weapon and, rather casually, shot her in the thigh. The wound was spurting blood. Bruno dropped the revolver and pulled off his jacket. He shouted to Randy, "Make sure the helicopter lands here! She needs help!" Then he forgot everything except the need to stop the flow of blood.

A roar coming from the water forced his attention back to Jurevicius. The commandos had retreated to the boat, dragging Jurevicius with them. Suddenly, they cut back on the throttle. Bruno saw Jurevicius staring at him. The Frenchman reached into his pocket.

Bruno reacted instinctively. He pulled himself on top of Alison's prone figure and braced himself for a final round of gunfire. Instead, he saw Jurevicius pull out a small blue package. Apparently, there was only one Gauloises left. Jurevicius lit it and tossed the empty package contemptuously in Bruno's direction. The boat throttled up with a roar that carried Jurevicius and his men at top speed into the open water.

CHAPTER 67

TWO DAYS LATER, Chief Black and Bruno met to make the rounds at Berry Hill Hospital.

At Bruno's insistence, they visited Alison first. As a result of their shared ordeal, a bond of friendship had grown between the student and the psychic; Bruno wanted to be at her side, providing what comfort he could.

The bullet had missed the femoral artery, sparing Alison's life. However, it had done significant damage to other blood vessels, muscles, and nerves, so the wound was serious and painful. In addition, she had ugly puncture wounds and deep bruises on her neck and throat, which made it difficult to speak. Her voice was hoarse and breathy, and she tired easily. Nevertheless, Chief Black insisted on hearing the story in her own words.

Alison kept it short and sweet: "I got Icky to drive with me out to NewGarden that night. We were just going to break some greenhouse windows and leave it at that. But the security was tougher than we expected. We had to lay low and figure out how their inspection rounds worked. While we were waiting, we smoked some hash and fooled around a bit to stay warm . . ."

Bruno bridled at the reference but didn't say anything.

Alison squeezed his hand and continued. "Then something happened. We heard doors slamming. A group of men marched a girl into the parking lot. It was Ginnie Doe. They made her stand in the middle of a blue tarp, which they had spread out on the ground. She seemed oblivious, not scared or anything. I think she was drugged. Someone stepped up behind her and wrung her neck with his bare hands."

Alison voice started to fail. She asked for water.

"Could you see who did it?" asked the Chief. Bruno had never seen him look this intense.

Alison shook her head. She said it was one of the security people; they were all dressed the same; she didn't get a clear look at anyone's face.

For a long while, she and Icky were too petrified to do anything. They watched as the men wrapped the body in the tarp and drove it down to a grove of trees on a far corner of the property. Alison and Icky waited for the men to disperse. Then they escaped.

Over the next day or two, she had time to think it over. Icky was trying to say they'd imagined the whole thing: they were on drugs, after all. Alison insisted it was real. The incident had clearly been planned and executed by men who were following orders. The fact that it happened at NewGarden suggested the leaders of the company were responsible.

"I told Icky he was being ridiculous: You don't hallucinate from a little bit of hash. And I felt sorry for the girl, being buried that way. That was when it occurred to me that I had been given the opportunity to transform this tragedy into something useful. I could make it into a political act, like we'd been talking about in Doggin' 'n' Dissin', and other classes too. Instead of just smashing a few windows, what if I could *get* the CEO of this awful company? Bring him down. Lock him up. Treat him the way he deserves."

Alison remembered hearing her parents talk about Emmanuel Fischer and how he was causing trouble at Friends Meeting. They'd never accused him of anything like murder, but she'd seen it happen with her own eyes. She and Icky had stumbled upon the underground tunnel just about a month earlier. All of the pieces were in place. She felt like a perfect plan had been presented to her on a silver platter.

"In theory it was perfect," Alison continued. "But take it from me, digging up a grave is kinda weird. I brought along some of my old clothes—Mom never gets rid of anything. We washed Ginnie's body and dressed her at the Lenape and then wrapped her in plastic as we carried her through the tunnel. It didn't take long, she was so small and light. We wanted her to look decent when people found her. We didn't want the little kids to have nightmares."

Chief Black frowned, but didn't interrupt. Bruno helped Alison take a drink of water so she could continue.

"We expected everybody to get the connection right away, but they didn't. That was so frustrating. I tried to get Professor Littlejohn to help me. It was his course that got me started, after all. But he just screwed me over . . ."

"Literally," Bruno added angrily. Alison had shut her eyes. She was struggling to keep her composure in the midst of these memories.

"Is that what you were arguing about at the shareholder meeting?" asked the Chief.

Alison snapped back to life, fully indignant. "I couldn't believe it. Here he'd been avoiding me all this time. But as soon as I start organizing against NGBS, he tries to take over.

"By that time, I didn't even care that much. I just wanted to get Fischer. That's all I was thinking about. At that point I didn't even know about Jurevicius—what a psycho! I wanted to speak the truth. I had to expose them. I was doing it, not just for Ginnie Doe, but for Icky and Gussie and everybody else as well."

Alison had to pause for breath. Her chest was heaving and she was having trouble speaking. Bruno held her hand; he raised the cup to her lips so she could sip more water.

"I guess Bruno didn't tell you," the Chief explained in a low voice. "It was Littlejohn who got shot when the lights went out. They had hidden a sniper inside that giant crow . . ."

Alison looked incredulous. "He was sitting directly in front of me . . . Oh my gosh. Is he dead?"

"No. He survived. The bullet smashed his jaw. He's in rough shape and they say he may never speak, intelligibly, again. His room is just down the hall. You can visit if you want."

Alison thought it over for a moment, then stated without emotion: "He got what he deserved."

Chief Black rose to leave. "There's one last question that I have to ask." His voice was stern and serious. "When you saw the girl get murdered, why didn't you come to me right away? By law, that's what you were required to do. Think of all the trouble, all the deaths and injuries you might have prevented."

Alison lowered her head. Her breathing was labored. Hints of tears showed in her eyes. "My whole thought process was out of whack. The drugs, my friends, my education, everything . . . I just couldn't believe I could trust you guys. I thought you were the enemy."

"And now?"

She gulped painfully. "I know I made some serious mistakes . . ."

Bruno rushed to the foot of her bed. "Things are definitely going to be different from now on," he announced, pulling aside the sheet and pointing to the little toe on her right foot. There was a tiny pinprick of blood. "See that?" he cried triumphantly. "Few people know this, but that's a sure sign a *dybbuk* was there. These *dybbuks* are demons or evil spirits that possess people. And when you chase them out, you can tell because there's a small spot of blood on the little toe of the right foot." He gestured toward Alison's toe. "See. There it is, in exactly the right place!"

Just then a nurse bustled in, angry and officious. "Is he ranting on about her toe again?" She frowned and pulled the sheet up to cover Alison's legs. "That mark is from a tiny fragment of the bullet. The doctor says he's absolutely certain of it, without any doubt. Now all of you have to leave immediately. Look at this poor girl, she's all worn out."

CHAPTER 68

THEY TIPTOED PAST LITTLEJOHN'S ROOM, taking care not to look in, as if even making eye contact would have been venomous. Quentin's room was in a different wing of the hospital. When they entered, Dr. Fischer was there and the two men were chatting warmly.

"Two for the price of one," commented the Chief. "Dr. Fischer, we were planning to come visit you next."

"They released me this morning. Apparently I did not have a stroke—or post-traumatic stress disorder. Though I have to admit, the sound of gunfire in our building did give me quite a start."

"Glad you're feeling better," Chief Black said to Fischer. "Mind sticking around so we can ask you a few questions? In fact, it's probably OK to interview you two together. Either of you gentlemen have any objections?"

"Certainly not." Quentin was in a cheerful mood. "Manny has been telling me about new treatments for malaria and other infectious diseases. I had no idea the kinds of things they can do these days."

Bruno and the Chief exchanged surprised looks. They were not prepared for such a love-fest between these two. Too bad they had to interrupt them now, but there were lingering questions that demanded answers.

"We just came from Alison's room," explained the Chief. "She's in pretty rough shape, but the doctors say she's going to be all right."

"Oh dear," sighed Quentin. "I hope she's not going to have too much trouble, legally."

"It's up to the DA," said the Chief. "I just had a conversation with her. I think she's starting to understand the seriousness of what she did. She expressed remorse. All of that speaks in her favor."

"I'm glad to hear it. I feel responsible as well. She and Icky both attended Gardenfield Friends School. I knew them when they were children and I feel a bit proprietary . . . about all of my former students. I could see that they were struggling and I wanted to help them out." He sighed deeply. "You know how hostile and uncommunicative young people can be. Instead of confronting them and demanding to know what was going on, I thought providing refuge, a chance to think things over, removed from the fray, would offer the greatest benefit. After Newton had that terrible accident . . ."

"Accident, *shmaccident*," Bruno interjected. "Icky was murdered."

"Yes, exactly," Quentin agreed. "After *Icky* was *murdered* I didn't know what to think. It seemed Alison had gotten mixed up in something terrible, and she was in over her head. I sent her to live at Bennett DeKalb's place out in Burlington. It's so peaceful there. He has an extra room . . ."

—"And he could send mail for her from Gardenfield without looking suspicious," said the Chief.

"I know nothing about that," Quentin stated defensively. Then he sighed. "I am extremely upset that Alison saw fit to use the meeting house in such an inappropriate way." He nodded toward Chief Black: "Please, make sure she's punished a little bit for that, just not too much."

The Chief frowned. "It's out of my hands . . ."

—Bruno was more sanguine. "If she has a good lawyer, she could get off with community service and a suspended sentence. Or how about this: Quentin could make her write, 'I will not put dead bodies in the meeting house,' a thousand times with a leaky fountain pen. What do you think, Chief?"

Chief Black studiously ignored him.

Now it was Fischer's turn. "I have a confession as well," he announced. "I wasn't completely frank when Bruno visited me the other day. You probably want to hear what I know about Jurevicius . . ."

Bruno was about to offer a rejoinder. But the Chief cut him off. "I'd appreciate that," he said.

"Serge was a difficult person, *always*," recalled Fischer. "I've known him more than 15 years. But you come to expect and tolerate that kind of behavior in business—and in medicine. There's so much competition. Brilliant people have big egos. And Serge Jurevicius is a brilliant researcher . . ."

—"You can skip straight to the bad news," Chief Black growled.

"Of course." Fischer was clearly nervous. "When you visited me," he looked at Bruno apologetically, "the subject of Maria, that's Serge's wife, didn't come up. If it had, I would have told you how dramatically Serge's personality changed after her accident. This was understandable, to some extent. She was struck by an automobile near Place de l'Étoile and left largely incapacitated. Caring for her put quite a burden on him. But it also seemed to affect his attitude toward the business. He became very aggressive in getting his own way. His directors had the controlling stake, so there was little I could do. At least the emphasis on agriculture made sense, from a business perspective. I could rationalize that. But the investment in that grandiose building and the security force did not."

"What can you tell us about the security detail?"

"Not much. They came from France. They were like his private army. They'd come with him, one or two at a time, every time he came back from Europe. And each time he'd return, his nerves were rubbed raw. He was insulting, angry, violent. I guess it was from seeing his wife . . ."

Bruno spoke up. "Just before he escaped, I asked him if the first victim, the unknown girl, was his daughter. The way he was abusing Alison made me think of that, I guess. Jurevicius became enraged and said something strange. *He said the girl was his wife.* Does that mean anything to you?"

Dr. Fischer looked disturbed. "What an odd thing to say, even for Serge. That girl was only 9 or 10 years old, wasn't she?"

"That's right. Dr. Cronkite thinks she was 10."

Dr. Fischer wrote something on a scrap of paper and handed it to the Chief. "You should probably talk to Rhonda, our receptionist. Here's her address and phone number. "I didn't mention it before," he reddened perceptibly, "because I thought Serge's personal life was none of anyone's business. But the fact is, he was in a relationship with Rhonda since right after his wife's accident. She was his mistress."

CHAPTER 69

MATTERHORN ROAD IS A CUL-DE-SAC in one of Berry Hill's more exclusive developments. Most of the houses are large and well built and, thanks to 15 years of growth, the yards look reasonably well established.

Rhonda Vick answered the door immediately when the Chief rang the bell. "What took you so *law*ng to get here?" Her voice resonated deeply in the marble-floored, high-ceilinged foyer. Rhonda was still dressed for business at eight o'clock in the evening. She wore one of her fitted wool suits and was fully made up with every hair in place. Again, Bruno marveled at the pure violet hue of her eyes, possibly the most beautiful he had ever seen.

Rhonda led them to the plush-carpeted living room and, without prompting, began telling her story.

"He terrorized me *fwor* years," she stated, almost clinically. "Most people think he's so intelligent and urbane, but the man I knew was a *mwon*-ster. I think he was insane, I really do."

"Can you be a little more specific?" the Chief urged. "Tell us exactly what happened."

"He never laid a finger *awn* me," Rhonda explained. "That was part of it. I always had to look perfect. I was the first person anybody met *owhr* talked to at the company. He used to say I was his public face. And he put me up here." She looked around at the walls. "Pretty nice, huh?"

"So you're saying he bribed you with nice things? With luxury and comfort?"

Rhonda crossed her legs and lit a cigarette. "There was no com-*fawght*. He threatened to kill me every day. And I could tell he meant it." She took a puff. *"Why didn't you come sooner?"*

"What do you mean?" asked Chief Black. "How should we have known to come talk to you?"

"I gave him a copy of the annual re*powrt*." She pointed at Bruno.

"And what were we supposed to conclude from that?"

"That you should come *tawk* to me. He's supposed to be a psychic. I thought he'd know and try to read my mind. I've been *cawn*centrating *awn* what I needed to tell you all this time."

"And what do you need to tell us?" the Chief persisted.

Rhonda became even more agitated. She was bouncing like a bird on its perch, her hand oscillating back and forth in front of her face. "This is so *hawrd*. I've been repressing this for so long. Even though he's gone, I'm still so afraid."

Bruno sat next to her. He put an arm around her shoulders. "Would you like me to read your mind now? I can establish a psychic link, so you don't have to say anything out loud."

Rhonda nodded yes. Her face betrayed extreme anguish and extreme relief.

Bruno took a seat across from her. He held out both hands, palm up. Without having to be told, Rhonda took both of his hands in hers. She closed her eyes and sat with her back extremely straight. Bruno whispered to the Chief to dim the lights.

They sat that way, in silence, for at least 10 minutes. The Chief was growing more and more impatient by the second. "Her thoughts are jumping from subject to subject," Bruno explained. "I can't get a fix on anything. You'll just have to hang on."

After another five minutes he spoke again. His voice was different. He seemed to have Rhonda's accent. "Serge and I met right after his wife's accident. We were both taking a *yow*ga class and he came up and *tawked* to me afterwards. He was very sweet. He told me about his wife right away. He spoke as if she didn't exist any*mwor*. He said he cared about me. One thing led to another. Soon we were lovers. He got me my *jawb* at *NyewGaw*den. And we moved into this house together."

Bruno started crying; he could barely speak. "Then . . . he asked me . . . if I wanted to have a baby. I was so happy."

The Chief couldn't believe his eyes or ears. Knowing Bruno the way he did, hearing this story from his lips made him want to laugh out loud. At the same time, the emotion was so deep, so real, he could not possibly have laughed; it was so astonishing, so strange, all he could do was listen.

"I was *sooo* happy," Bruno continued. "Then Serge said he didn't mean it in the usual way. He'd been developing this special technique. I knew genetics was his specialty. I thought maybe he wanted to have twins. *Owhr* to make sure it was a boy. *Owhr* that the boy would have his nose *owhr* his IQ *owhr* something. But that wasn't it at all."

Bruno was breathing hard. The Chief glanced from Rhonda, who looked strangely calm, back to Bruno, who was panting as if from extreme physical exertion. "He wanted me to have someone else's baby. I was going to be the surrogate mother. But it wasn't even the *nawr*mal kind of surrogate. He said he'd perfected a way to grow a cell from his wife. He needed one of my eggs; he'd replace the nucleus with his wife's DNA, and then implant it in my uterus. He was cloning his wife, and I was just the host."

With that, Bruno collapsed onto the carpet; Rhonda slowly came out of her trance. She seemed much more relaxed. "Did you hear the story? The whole thing?" she whispered. Then she noticed Bruno. "What happened to him?"

"I think he just gave birth," said the Chief, helping Bruno to sit up. "Do you have any whisky? That should bring him around."

It took several minutes for Bruno to recover. "Did I just dream that or did it really happen?"

"It happened," said Rhonda, lighting another cigarette. "Serge made me quit my *jawb*," she explained, then inhaled deeply. "I was like a prisoner, taking care of the baby. We never re*powrt*ed her: Serge was her *dawk*ter; I was her teacher. No one knew she existed."

"But why did he want to kill her, his own . . . whatever she was?"

Rhonda looked at him coolly. She exhaled smoke and explained. "He wanted his wife back, just like she was be*fowr*. He loved little Maria intensely at first. But then as she grew older, he discovered she was having problems similar to those of other clones. Like that sheep, *Dwolly*. Maria's DNA was old, so even though it didn't show yet physically, she was already like an old person. Serge went mad. It didn't happen overnight, but gradually. Every time he came back from France, he'd *tawk* about needing to have her 'put down.' Those were the exact words he used: 'put down.' He *thowt* of her like an animal, not a person. *Fwortunately*, he'd always lose his nerve and nothing ever happened. Until his last trip; he came back *totally deranged*. I didn't even know him anymore. There was nothing left of the man I once loved. I knew it was the end. At that point, I didn't even know how I felt about her. I loved her as my sweet child, but hated her as my rival. One evening about three months ago, Serge went back to work. It was the middle of the night, and I knew it was over. How I hate that man. Now I'm free."

Her pure violet gaze bore directly into the Chief and Bruno. "This is the first time I've been free in 15 years. Do you know how that feels?"

CHAPTER 70

ABOUT TWO WEEKS LATER, Chief Black drove Bruno down to Atlantic City on official business. Bruno insisted on going back to Caesar's. He said he wanted to get his money back. In fact, they were sitting at the same seats, in the same lounge, where he and Randy had rested after the big chase with Jurevicius. They were sipping beer, feeding the slots and chatting comfortably. Every time they started to run low on quarters, one of them would win, and they'd start over again.

"How's Dora?"

"I don't know," said the Chief. "She works all the time. I don't really get to see that much of her. How's Alison?"

"Better every day."

"You fell in love the moment you saw the pornographic Polaroids of her in the dungeon. Don't deny it. You're an incurable romantic."

Bruno grinned sheepishly.

"Ready for your performance review?" asked the Chief, pulling out his notebook.

"Do we really have to do this? I'm not an employee after all."

"I told you this was official business," the Chief said. "I have to do things by the book. The manual says I need to evaluate your work by objective criteria, so we need to review the entire case, point by point. Question number one. 'What verifiable positive results did the psychic produce?'"

Bruno rolled his eyes. "Can I look at my notes? So many things happened. I can't remember all of them."

"Sure. Go ahead."

Bruno removed a tattered sheet of paper from his jacket pocket and started to read. "Let's see. The Quaker connection and SBGN. Those came to me in a dream. As it turned out, the dream was uncannily accurate, but I didn't know how to interpret it at the time. Alison was at Penn, and SBGN came from the score of the game. I used the basic Hebrew technique of translating numbers into letters."

"But that didn't get us anywhere because it came out backwards, right?"

"Yeah. I stupidly forget that you read Hebrew from right to left. I didn't figure it out until I saw Jurevicius' license plate in the rearview mirror. Speaking of which, it was good to see everyone again today. Biff, Gary, Michelle, Harry, Nancy. I was really glad to see that Randy's arm is healing."

"He's a tough guy," said the Chief. "You earned his respect, the way you faced Jurevicius . . ."

"We got lucky. The choppers showed up just in the nick of time." Bruno flushed. "Anyway, let's just stick to the psychic stuff, OK?"

"Sure, what's next?"

"Gussie Parker. I found him using psychometry."

"Right." The Chief wrote down "psychometry."

"And don't forget, that's where you met Dora. So you owe me for that, too."

"We'll see. If things keep on the way they are right now, you'll be owing me. What's next?"

Bruno consulted his list. "Remote viewing of Fischer."

"Check."

"Remote viewing of Jurevicius."

"Check. That's where you saw his wife, right, but didn't figure out who she was until later."

"Yeah," Bruno admitted. "You're right. You have to understand that I can only see what the subject is thinking. If Jurevicius had been thinking, *There's my sick wife who I'm cloning*, then we'd have solved the whole case right then and there. Unfortunately, that's not how it works."

"Right. Anything else?" He scanned his notes. "Let's see, remote viewing and ongoing surveillance of Alison Wales . . ."

—"OK, OK," grinned Bruno. "Let's move on to the discovery of the Underground Railroad tunnel, although I have to admit that was just luck."

"It was an important find, anyway," the Chief noted. "I'll put it down as a value-added service."

"Fine."

"By the way," said Chief Black, "did you hear about what's-his-name? Mr. Shmendrick—the curator at the Lenape King? He's famous."

"No kidding? That's great. He deserved a break."

"He's miserable now."

"Really? Why?"

"Remember how he was always complaining that he didn't have help there?" explained the Chief. "Now he's got a huge staff, but that means he's always busy doing administrative work. There's nothing hands-on and he hates it."

"Poor guy. I like him."

"Me too." The Chief was scribbling more notes. "Lucky for you, I like administrative work. What's next? How about finding Jurevicius parked by the Mullica River? Was that luck or skill?"

Bruno had to think about that one. "The boardwalk psychic, Madame Celeste, said it was my lucky day. But nothing about that afternoon seemed that lucky at the time. Looking back, I guess I'd say it was more like *destiny*."

"Hmmm." The Chief frowned. "There's no category for 'destiny' in our personnel database. Do you mind if I call it 'value added' too?"

"Go ahead." Bruno yawned and stretched. "I guess that's it." He started to get up.

"No way," said the Chief. "You're not getting out of here without explaining what happened between you and the receptionist. You should have a TV show called *Channeling Rhonda*."

"Very funny." Bruno tried to look away. "I was hoping you wouldn't ask me about that. I'd never had an experience like that before. I didn't even know I could do it."

"What was it, like a mind meld or something?"

"Yeah, I guess so. It was incredibly intimate. I felt like I was breaking into somebody's house at night and rummaging through all their possessions . . ."

"Go on," urged the Chief. "What is it?" He could see that Bruno was hung up on something. The psychic wanted to speak, but couldn't find the words.

"I couldn't see *everything*," he said at last. "The whole story about Ginnie Doe, or Maria, was laid out like a suit of clothes on a bed, waiting for you to put them on. But there were other places . . ."

The Chief waited patiently. Bruno collected himself and started again. "I said it was like being in somebody's house . . . Anyway, there were other doors in there that I couldn't open. There was a lot of fear connected with them. I don't know if it was coming from her . . . or from me."

The Chief remained silent, waiting for Bruno's emotions to settle. "Maybe that's normal. To have private places that you guard even in your most unguarded moments."

"Maybe. Like I said, I never did anything like that before."

"What about what you did with McRae's daughter? Wasn't that sort of the same thing?"

"Mimi? No way. Not at all. With Mimi, I was just seeing the general outlines of what she remembered. With Rhonda, I was mirroring every detail of what she thought and felt."

"Mimi was the big breakthrough, wasn't she? Good thing you didn't pay too much attention to Bill McRae."

Bruno grinned sheepishly and rubbed his forehead, still tender from that encounter. "Is that it? Are we done?"

"Not quite. I have to talk to you about the way you handled Peaches. That was not so hot, to put it mildly."

"What could I do?" Bruno protested. "She had her own agenda. Everything she wrote was tipping off Jurevicius to our next moves. We had to stop her."

"I told you to steer clear," the Chief insisted. "You wouldn't listen." Bruno hung his head. "Don't get down. It's constructive criticism." The Chief jostled his shoulder. "Just look at it this way. Public relations is not your job. Let somebody else do it. End of story." The Chief paused for emphasis. "Bruno, anybody asks for a psychic, I'm recommending you. You did a great job. Thanks."

"Thanks, Chief. I appreciate that." They shook hands.

"Speaking of Peaches, I brought something I figured you'd like to see." The Chief tossed a recent issue of the *Pest* onto the bar. "It has her final article on the case."

Bruno scanned it rapidly. "She credits Littlejohn for saving Alison's life. Unbelievable. He says even if he can't speak, it won't stop him from teaching. He'll just use American Sign Language, '*which everyone ought to learn anyway*.' Great idea." Bruno read further. "Hey, what's this about the Feds looking into the case? What's that about?"

"Does that seem strange to you?" replied the Chief, his voice rich with irony. "I guess because Jurevicius is French, it's being treated as some kind of international incident. National security concerns. It was supposed to be classified information, but somehow Peaches got wind and printed it anyway."

"Unbelievable!" Bruno put down the paper. "I wish 'em luck. Maybe they can track down Jurevicius and extradite him."

"That'll be a miracle, if he's back in France. They're more likely to name a street after him than send him back here for trial."

Bruno's attention was drifting. He couldn't help recalling his final exchange with Jurevicius as the cigarette boat roared across the bay and disappeared.

"But look at this, Bruno." The Chief was shuffling the pages of the *Pest* until he found the place where Peaches' article continued. "This is the part I wanted you to see," he said excitedly. "Read it out loud."

"For me, the part of this case that's most *extraordinary*," Bruno read, imitating Peaches' overeducated drawl, "is the spiritual aspect that permeates it from beginning to end. Maria Jurevicius, aka Ginnie Doe, was found in the Quaker meeting house; the Kabbalah was partly responsible for solving the case. What do these two disparate traditions have in common? Light. In Kabbalah, light is everywhere and everything. Divine sparks inhabit every living being. Is this so different than the Quaker's inner light? I think not. There are no coincidences. Everything happens for a reason."

They were both laughing uncontrollably by the time Bruno finished the recitation. "I never realized, Jews and Quakers . . . are exactly the same. Chief, why'd you do this to me? I can't control myself. I think I'm gonna *plotz*."

But the Chief showed no mercy. "I'm catchin' on to this Jewish *shtick*," he announced with considerable pride. "I made something up especially for you."

Bruno sensed that this was an important moment. "Let's hear it, Buddy. Show me what you got."

Chief Black warmed to the task. "I think you'll like it because it's about Peaches . . ."

—"Skip the prologue. If you got something to say, say it."

"Right," said the Chief. He was a little bit nervous. "There's a lot of women you could say . . ." and he put on a voice that was a pretty good imitation of Bruno's, "'with a *tuchus* like that, who needs brains?'" He paused for effect. "But Peaches is different. With her it's: 'With a brain like that, who needs a *tuchus*?'"

Bruno looked at him in astonishment. "Chief, that's incredible."

"You really think so?"

"Yeah, I love it. There's just one problem."

"Uh-oh. What's that?"

"Generally, people don't makes up new jokes. They either buy them, or steal them from somebody else."

"But . . . I sort of stole this. You see . . ."

—"Chief! I'm sorry. It's a rule . . . carved in stone."

"But where do new jokes come from, then?"

"Chief, really. A man your age ought to know . . ." Bruno stood up and assumed a theatrical pose. "This mystery was only revealed one day *when I was at the seashore*," he quoted. "That's from the Zohar and, as you can see, we *are* down the shore."

"Yes, we are."

Bruno continued his exegesis. "Elijah came and asked me, 'Rabbi, do you know the meaning of *Who created these*'?"

"Who created these?" The Chief repeated, somewhat perplexed.

"By that, Elijah clearly means, 'Who created these *jokes*?'" Bruno opined. "Don't you agree?"

"Makes sense."

"I answered"—and don't forget, I'm speaking as the Rabbi here—"I answered, 'There are the heavens and their array, the work of the blessed Holy One. Human beings should contemplate them and bless Him.'"

"So you're saying jokes come from God?"

"Yup. The funny ones, anyway."

The Chief thought it over. "Let's try something different," he suggested, standing and beckoning for Bruno to follow. "There's an area where they still have 'vintage' slots, actual one-armed bandits where real money comes out if you win."

"Sounds good to me. I don't get these computer games anyway . . ."

They fought the crowds milling about between the gaming tables and the machines, the televisions, bars and restaurants, the boutiques, and all the other distractions. Eventually, the Chief stopped in front of a slot machine decorated with a trio of Egyptian sphinxes. "Think this is a winner?" he asked.

"Sure. Why don't you play it?"

The Chief put the coin in the slot and pulled the handle. Wheels spun, flashing brightly colored fruits, brass bells, and black bars. Then a red light on top of the machine began throbbing. Mechanical bells rang and sirens sounded wildly. Finally, a cascade of dollar coins spewed out. The silver flowed and flowed, dazzling and brilliant, overflowing his lap and spilling onto the floor.

He and Bruno fell onto their knees and scooped up coins by the handful; they stuffed them into their pockets and tossed them into the air, laughing and carrying on like children.

Afterword

First, I want to acknowledge some deliberate geographical distortions and anachronisms in *The Violet Crow* that could upset a few people who are familiar with South Jersey—but won't matter much to anyone else. There is a town called Haddonfield and it is remarkably similar to Gardenfield. It has a school like the one I've called Gardenfield Friends with a meeting house in easy walking distance. I attended that school from kindergarten through sixth grade, including Meeting for Worship every Wednesday morning from third grade on.

"Why didn't you just call it Haddonfield?" my friend Jim Lyons once asked.

The answer is that I needed to take some liberties to make my story work. The tunnel and the biotech complex are a couple of examples. Also, there are some features of the region that don't exist anymore, but I couldn't let go of them: the racetrack and Tano's Deli come to mind. So I called the town Gardenfield—just to remind hometown readers that I am taking license to alter reality throughout *The Violet Crow*.

I haven't lived in South Jersey in decades, but the region's unique character shaped my outlook and I still follow the sports teams and

AFTERWORD

the local news, albeit at a distance. I regret some of my antics as a teenager, so I tried to portray the Gardenfield police as positively as possible—a belated "sorry about that" and "thank you."

While I'm apologizing, I might as well get this off my chest—Rhonda's South Jersey accent. Elmore Leonard's seventh rule of writing is to use regional dialect sparingly. I probably should have followed his advice. However, I broke all his other commandments, so it seemed a shame to leave out number seven. I love hearing all of the regional accents of the U.S. and trying to identify where the speakers come from. I get especially excited when I hear the distinctive, clipped "o" sound from the mid-Atlantic states. Here on the West Coast, when I tell people where I grew up, they often reply, "Oh, you're from Joisey." And I say, "No, that's a Brooklyn accent; in South Jersey we say "aw," not "oi." *Mea culpa*.

Attending Haddonfield Friends had a lasting impact on me—and also on many of my classmates. We still meet for occasional reunions of our sixth-grade class, lo, these many years later. The ritual of silent worship strikes a deep, resonant chord.

We also had the example of headmaster Reed Landis. As I began thinking about *The Violet Crow*, I recalled an incident in fourth or fifth grade when one of our teachers told us that Master Reed was out sick for a while due to a recurrence of malaria, which he'd contracted as a conscientious objector during World War II. None of my classmates remembered that but, thanks to Reed's cousin, Sarah Johnson, I was able to locate him in Arizona and speak with him on the phone. He talked freely about his experiences as a CO, which, in the book, I assigned to Master Quentin and described as accurately as possible— with the exception of placing those events in the Vietnam War era rather than during World War II.

Unfortunately, Master Reed passed away a few years after I spoke with him. I'm honored to be able to tell his story in *The Violet Crow*. At a time when what he experienced would be widely viewed as torture, it's remarkable how *conscientious* Reed Landis and his fellow Quaker COs were in their approach to non-violent protest.

You would probably not be reading *The Violet Crow* without the vision and intelligence of Adam Bellow and David Bernstein, who

304

founded Liberty Island and rescued my work from oblivion. When they posed the old question from *A Tale of Two Cities*, "I hope you care to be recalled to life," I said, "What! Are you kidding me?" They've earned my eternal gratitude.

Friends and advisers who also helped by reading, commenting, and improving the story include Hallie Gay Walden-Bagley, Charlie Barnett, Gary Carr, Don Chew, Dan Grossman, Ian Lamberton, Don Lippincott, Pat McCarthy, Don McQuinn, Jay Merwin, Manette Moses, Jan Murphy, Francoise Perriot, Thomas Perry, Giuliana Sheldon, Elena Vega and Janice Willett.